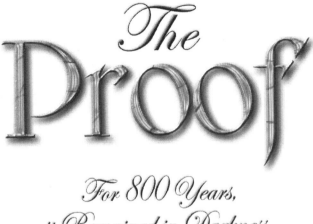

# The Proof

*For 800 Years,*
*it Remained in Darkness...*
*Until Now.*

## Cheryl Colwell

INSPIRED FICTION BOOKS

ISBN: 978-0-9892371-3-0

**The Proof**

PUBLISHED BY INSPIRED FICTION BOOKS
www.inspiredfictionbooks.com

ISBN 978-0-9892371-3-0
Printed in the United States of America

The Proof is a work of fiction. Though some actual towns, cities, and locations may be mentioned, they are used in a fictitious manner and the events and occurrences were invented in the mind and imagination of the author. Any similarities of characters or names used within to any person past, present, or future is coincidental.

Category: Fiction/Suspense

In gratitude to all who make my life rich beyond imagination:

My God. My family. My friends.

Bless you all.

# CAST OF CHARACTERS

Present Day Characters:
Gabe (Gabriel) Dolcini: eldest grandson of Conte Louis Dolcini
Conte Louis Dolcini: Gabe's grandfather in Siena
Contessa Christina Dolcini: deceased wife of Louis Dolcini
Livia Ambrogi: art history student from Italy
Ralph Witte: Conte Louis Dolcini's grandson
Geneva Dolcini: deceased daughter of Conte Dolcini, mother of Ralph
    Witte
Kendrick Witte: deceased father of Ralph Witte
Marcella: Louis Dolcini's sister-in-law
Rinaldo Paravati: Conte Dolcini's butler/driver

Medieval Characters: Fiction
Secundus Cerilius: Italian shepherd
Antonio Louis Dolcini: Louis's ancestor and Templar knight
Helena Dolcini: Antonio Dolcini's wife
Russo and Gavino Dolcini: Antonio Dolcini's sons
Haydn, Oberon and Rafer: King Barbarossa's crusaders
Reverendissimo Lorenzo Casselli: Abbot at the Abbey of Saint John,
    Palombara, Argentella, Italy

Medieval Characters: Non-Fiction
Saint Bernard: Cistercian Abbot from France, 1090 - 1153
Galgano Guidotti: knight, saint, 1148 - 1181
Alexander III: Pope from 1159 - 1181
Armand: Grand Master of Knights Templar, 1178–1247
King Frederick Barbarossa, Holy Roman Emperor, 1122-1190
Gaius Cassius Longinus: Roman centurion at Golgotha
Jacques de Molay: Grand Master of Knights Templars, 1244 - 1314
Innocent III: Antipope from 1179 - 1180
King Baldwin of Jerusalem, 1161 - 1185
Saladin: Leader of Saracen army, 1137 - 1193

# Chapter 1

Sequoia National Park, California

"Coward!" Gabe's father shouted. He threw Gabe to safety across the waterfall and went back for Angelica.

Stifling a cry, Gabe struggled against the wind. He grabbed a tree and pulled his trembling body up. Bark dug into his small palms. He glanced up the mountain at his sister. *Angelica feared nothing.*

"Get. Down. Here!" Their father's fury intensified with the storm. With his neck craned upward, he shouted at her to move faster.

Eyes wide with excitement and black hair whipping around her beaming face, she leapt gracefully to another large boulder. But this time, her worn tennis shoes slid off the wet rock. Her mouth opened in surprise as she pitched headfirst down the steep terrain.

Anguish contorted their father's face as he watched, helpless.

Inhaling the driving rain, Gabe coughed while straining to see her. *There!* She clung to a root on the steep bank, her thin arms and face gashed by sharp rocks. Her shoes thrashed against the muddy slope in an effort to get a grip.

Their father charged toward her, fighting the mud and debris. He extended a strong hand to grasp her struggling arm. He almost made it.

Angelica's terrified eyes met Gabe's for a brief moment before the mudslide hit her. In an instant, she was gone. Guilt seized him. He had only meant to slow her down.

##

1

Santa Barbara, California, Twenty-six years later

Fingernails biting into his palms, Gabriel Dolcini awoke from "The Memory," as his therapist called it. He kicked back damp sheets and rolled out of bed. Pressure in his chest failed to produce new tears. Just guilt. *Twenty-six years of it.*

He pushed his shaking body up and headed for the shower. After a five-year absence, he had hoped the dreams had surrendered their hold on him. He had finally dared to believe Dr. Carver's therapy would yield permanent results. *So much for faith.*

After downing the last of his coffee, Gabe raced downstairs to his car. He fumed as he pumped the gas pedal. Of course, this would be the morning his car would act up. "Come on, Baby," he coaxed, giving the old Audi more gas. His exasperation mounted and was just about to explode when the engine finally started.

His phone buzzed and he glanced at the bank's text message. "Urgent. Please call." Gabe tossed the phone on the seat. *First the dream, then the bank.* He couldn't miss another payment.

He shoved the car in gear and maneuvered out of the drive. Freedom taunted him. The ice-blue roadster, so full of promise, chugged down the road. The same road as yesterday. And the day before. Sludge cleared, and his engine roared with increasing power. A gust of wind whipped a curling strand of his black hair in front of his face. He swatted it back. *I need a plan.*

Breaking through the canyon, a wide expanse of ocean opened below him and the road narrowed. Treacherous cliffs threatened just feet away from his tires. He focused on the center line, wind whipping the moisture from his upper lip. Relief hit when the road gentled and U.C. Santa Barbara sprawled before him. He wiped his hands on his slacks.

Traffic thickened to a crawl and a news story caught his attention. "A police officer is in intensive care after a high-speed chase ended in a crash early this morning. An art thief escaped after stealing six Jannell Parone paintings from The Leaf, an exclusive West Hollywood gallery."

"No way." Jaw clenching, Gabe whipped into the faculty parking lot and screeched to a stop. He had studied with Jannell. Her abstracts sold for upward of a hundred thousand dollars.

The story continued, "Investigators were questioned about a distinctive feather found at the scene, insinuating that the Kestral, a flamboyant international art thief, was responsible for yet another spectacular heist. Caught on video, the thief appeared as an athletic, dark-haired woman."

"*Fesso*—stupid!" His father's favorite Italian expletive slipped easily from his lips. He punched off the radio and grabbed his keys, craving instant, harsh justice for the Kestral. Rushing toward the building, he glanced at his watch, then yanked the door open.

Down the hall stood the head of the art department, Howard Sutton, master of underhanded intimidation. A pretty student hung on Howard's words. Gabe frowned. *Risky business.* The girl looked over and smiled as he approached.

Howard followed her eyes and turned. "Hey Dolcini, that's some pickpocket, huh?"

Gabe nodded.

Howard ignored the girl and stepped in stride as they hastened to their classrooms. "Darla is managing The Leaf now. It took her months to acquire Jannell's paintings for the exhibit."

Gabe paused. "How do you know that?"

"We've been out for drinks." He watched for Gabe's reaction with amusement playing on his lips.

Heat advanced to Gabe's cheeks. Uninvited images of Darla shot through his memory. Cappuccinos. Art walks. Their last conversation. His jaw tensed.

Howard glanced sideways with a smirk. "Thought you were over her."

"Ancient history."

A smug grin widened Howard's face. "The Kestral must have quite a collection by now. There's some concern over the insurance coverage." His eyebrows rose. "I'll bet Darla's sweating it out—could go badly for her." He turned toward his classroom.

Gabe shook his head. "Not my problem." Yet the news disturbed him. Darla. Her quick wit had caused him to laugh more in their six months together than in all the previous years of his life. Pressure burned behind his eyes. She had used him for his contacts, then left. Called him a small fish in a smaller pond. Not true. He might be stuck teaching for now, but he had grand plans.

He set his briefcase down on his desk, his shoulders relaxing as the creative energy in the room worked its magic. Many students were already at work on their canvases. Judy, especially, reminded him how it felt when he had first discovered oils.

She gave him a quick glance. "Hi, Professor." Taller than he, with large brown eyes and ebony skin, she had developed a keen eye for composition. Finishing her task, she turned and smiled. "Thank you."

He grinned. "For what?"

"I got my scholarship!"

"You're welcome, but you did the work. I just helped open the door." He scanned the room. Creativity blossomed in this light, open space. In a corner, a student pulled back her straight, dark hair and bunched it into a ponytail—as his sister used to do. An ache tightened his chest. He raked his fingers through his hair. What was up today? He made a mental note to call his therapist, Dr. Carver, for an appointment before he took another nosedive. He was thirty-six. How long would this go on?

"Professor Dolcini?" A student waved a hand in front of his face. "Hellooo."

Gabe jerked his attention to his student. "What, Stuart?"

"I need help."

Chagrined, Gabe grabbed a brush and went to his easel at the front of the class. *This* he could do. With quick flourishes, he demonstrated the technique assigned for the week. Students gathered close and watched in silence. Gabe lost himself in the composition and when he finished, spontaneous applause broke out. The lavish praise caused his ears to burn. Head bent, he cleaned off his brush. "Okay. Back to work."

At the end of class, he dropped into his chair and watched the groups of friends walk out. If only he had someone to advise him. He leaned his head back into his laced fingers.

*You have a grandfather.*

"Yeah, a rich lunatic," Gabe mumbled. He dismissed the thought, heeding decades of warnings his father had issued against the man.

## ##

After classes, he drove away from the university, tapping his fingers in time to a bluesy song, the pungent scents of saltwater and eucalyptus mingling in the air. Brilliant sunlight shimmered off the Pacific Ocean, and a breeze played with his hair. Buying a convertible had definitely been a good idea—the old Audi was a sweet model, its weak spots hidden from view.

He escaped down the freeway that flowed through the heart of the city. With a million things to do before the upcoming celebration, he needed to focus and calculate his stops.

Friday afternoon's traffic required him to circle twice before parking at the bank. Inside, angst gripped his gut. When his educational loans threatened to overwhelm him, his mother insisted he consolidate them and use the house as collateral. Now, her home was at risk. This extension only bought a five-week reprieve.

His grandfather's invitation lay in a drawer at home. The man was wealthy. *No.* It was useless to count on others.

Gabe pushed back his hair. *Just a little longer.* His career had plodded slower than planned. All he needed was the recognition that would put a premium price on his paintings. *You and thirty million other artists.* The shaking pen in Gabe's hand mimicked his rollicking insides.

"Is there a problem, Mr. Dolcini?" The loan officer flashed the smile of an unfeeling shark.

"No." Gabe scribbled his name and left the bank with clammy hands. He downshifted and sped away. He'd had to invest in his career—painting was the only pursuit in which he excelled.

Preoccupied, he almost missed the dry cleaner. "*Fesso*—stupid! If you're gonna drive, drive."

Inside, Carlotta, the owner's wife, turned white. Her husband,

Salvador, came out from the back. "Mr. Dolcini, we are happy to pay for a new jacket."

Gabe blanched. Two week's salary had gone for this one splurge. It gave him confidence when dealing with his sophisticated clientele.

Salvador attempted to hold his head high, but a difficult swallow gave him away. "It got caught in the machinery."

Gabe's jaw dropped. He stared at the butchered garment. There was no time to have another made before the award ceremony tomorrow. Blood pounded against his temples.

Salvador gave up and let his head droop, and opened his cash register. "How much do I owe you?"

Gabe glanced around the small mom and. It wouldn't do to break him, but Gabe would not humiliate him with a paltry sum either.

"Two hundred dollars."

Salvador looked surprised and nodded with relief. Reaching into the drawer, he counted out five twenties, eight tens, and three fives. After digging some more, he added five ones. Gabe held his breath, hoping he wouldn't have to take change. Beads of sweat trickled down the man's forehead. "We appreciate your business. Please accept our apology."

"Accidents happen." Gabe tried for a smile. Stuffing the money in his pocket, he headed for his car, taking his frustration on the road. Where could he get a decent jacket in a day? For two hundred dollars?

His last stop was to pick up Sonia from work. His mother had attached herself to the seventeen-year-old, newly emancipated orphan. One look at the girl's brilliant smile and dark hair and Gabe had immediately understood why. *Angelica would have grown into just such a beauty.*

He entered the restaurant and checked his watch. Sonia passed plates of hamburgers to three college athletes. One flirt held onto her wrist. She laughed, attempting to pull her hand away.

Behind her, one of four jealous high school girls hurled an insult for all to hear. "I wonder what border she crawled over."

Sonia turned and blanched. Gabe was certain she didn't have a mean-spirited retort in her vocabulary. She yanked her hand free from the jock and fled.

Gabe was about to let the little beasties have it, but an idea occurred to him. He found Sonia crying in the kitchen. "Ignore the playground antics." He wiped her tear with his thumb. "Go put on a pretty face and meet me out front."

Waiting in his convertible, Gabe turned up the stereo. The obnoxious girls came out and loitered nearby, attempting to get his attention. He recognized Howard's daughter. *It figures*. When he spotted Sonia coming out the front door, he sauntered to her, taking her hand and kissing her on the cheek.

She whispered, "What are you doing?"

"Just play along." He opened the driver's car door and said in a loud voice, "Thanks for letting me borrow your car."

The girls were stunned to silence as Sonia started the Audi and drifted past them with a cool smile playing on her lips. After turning the corner, Sonia broke into laughter and pulled over to let Gabe drive. "That was fabulous."

Downshifting, he turned up the mountain. "I deal with their mothers in the art world. It must be in the water." He hated to admit that he needed these people. Everything he held dear—his career, his reputation, and his mother's home—rested in their capricious hands.

# THE PROOF

# Chapter 2

Rome, Italy

Abbot Porta sat in his cubicle, far from the pomp and power associated with Rome. He rubbed his clammy hands together. It was all too extraordinary. He now possessed the key—the power to escape the mundane, barren existence of a mere abbot. Pungent odors and depressingly dim overhead lights conspired to drive him mad.

He flung his wrist across the chessboard. The pieces clattered against the stone floor and echoed down the hall, mimicking the rest of the underlings that scurried about. He scoffed. After centuries of fruitless searching by the *Soci*, the "Associates," *he* had been the one to locate the prize. Now, they were the pawns and he the bishop. Soon, they would understand that. He dialed his superior.

A male secretary answered his call. *"Buon giorno."*

*"Buon giorno*, this is Abbot Porta. I need to speak to His Excellency at once." Porta stood and paced the length of his office as he listened to the powerful man barking orders on the other end of the call. Porta calmed his ecstasy, ready to deliver the astounding news.

An annoying draft permeated the crumbling walls of the abbey, chilling his neck and ankles. He shivered. Summer would soon give way to winter. With the missives he had discovered, he savored his likely advancement, following the *Primo Consul's* footsteps from a *Tribunus* to become a *Prefect*.

From there, his contributions would assure the votes he needed to rule as one of the two *Consuls* within the *Soci*—as soon as there is a vacancy. He smiled. Perhaps he would even rise above the man on the other end of the line and become the *Primo Consul.*

At last, the *Primo Consul's* voice boomed through the tiny speaker. "Porta, what is so urgent that you demand my time?"

Waiting for effect, Porta said, "I have uncovered the thread that will lead us to the "object" you instructed us to seek." He was careful. Someone was always listening.

"And where did you find this *thread?*"

"I was invited to the Abbey of St. John in Argentella, where I examined the old vaults used to house documents from the previous abbots."

Impatience and disappointment resounded through the speaker. "Those vaults were emptied ages ago."

"*Si.* After inspecting a suspicious area, however, I discovered a hidden niche."

"What did you find?"

Porta smiled at the instant jump in the *Primo Consul's* interest. "Letters. A detailed account of an attempt to prevent the "object" from traveling to Seborga."

"Seborga?"

"*Si.*"

"So you believe it rests there?"

"Possibly." Porta proceeded with caution. It would not due to overstate his hopes and later disappoint this powerful man.

"Send me the letters by courier, and then send someone to investigate." The line went dead.

Porta exhaled his disappointment. Not a word of appreciation. He dialed the number of a particular member of the *Soci.* One skilled in building trust.

# Chapter 3

Santa Barbara, California

In less than an hour, Gabe's talent would be validated on a national level. After receiving the nomination for the coveted award earlier this year, photographs of Gabe's work had appeared on the front of California's most prestigious art magazines, along with lavish praise from respected critics. He smiled.

Inside sources had already sent their congratulations. In their opinion, the only serious contender did not measure up to Gabe's quality. The proof waited in a simple silver plaque.

It was payback time for the immense effort Gabe had expended. After his doctorate, he'd advanced through a prominent art academy—working two jobs while doing it. He wanted the best, but the best had cost. A pang of guilt hit. Unfortunately, his actions had put others at risk. His mother's wealth consisted of her home.

He grimaced, thinking of the thousands of dollars he'd paid pompous masters to learn their guarded techniques, enduring oblique jabs from the wealthy dilettantes playing at being artists. One incident still burned. After unveiling his finished painting to one of his instructors, the man fell silent, then accused him of copying another master's work. The piece was uniquely Gabe's and the professor knew it, but it robbed the moment of its joy.

Gabe shook away the dark thoughts. He'd obtained what he needed from them. After tonight, the path to national recognition spanned out before him. The voice of doubt could find a new victim.

Striding toward the ocean front hotel, he found his imagination piqued by its elegant style. What other grand events had it hosted during the years of its existence? He inhaled the pleasant sea breeze that infused the Santa Barbara coast with a magic it alone could conjure.

Glancing down, he frowned at the sleeves of his jacket, an inch too short. Howard would be the first to notice the ready-made replacement. Gabe inhaled deeply. The scent of jasmine helped clear his mind and dispel the residual disappointment. He stood tall, grasped the stainless steel handle of the massive hotel door, and entered the capricious world of art, critics, and glory.

Cut glass prisms, arranged in free-form chandeliers, dangled their brilliance from strategic points across the ceiling, their reflections glancing off the polished marble floors.

"Gabriel, dear," Viola Hudson cooed when she spotted him. A wealthy heiress, she flaunted her advantage. Her glamorous heels clacked on the shining surface as she rushed to him and whispered, "Let me be the first to congratulate you." She laid her hands on his shoulders and gave him a kiss-kiss on each cheek.

It felt phony when these bejeweled women mimicked that European custom. He took her hands in his, distancing her with a polite smile. She might have helped him with her connections, but he wouldn't be made out to be one of her pet artists. He had worked hard to arrive at this pinnacle.

Assuming her trademark of self-importance, she spoke in a staged whisper, loud enough to be heard across the room. "They checked all my security this morning. After that devastating theft in Hollywood, who knows where the Kestral will strike next? My extensive collection is not a secret, and you would be wise to keep your work under lock and key as well. After tonight, your values are certain to skyrocket." Words poured nonstop from her lips and ran together like a recording on fast forward.

He put her on mute while his eyes swept over her shoulder. Planted in imaginative containers of marble and steel, an assortment of fringed palm trees partitioned the guests and clustered them into intimate spaces. In every corner, Gabe observed serious art devotees in animated discussions.

Tonight he was the star, but this crowd frequently proved fickle. As soon as they *discovered* another promising artist, they would stampede to be the first to claim the new sensation. A queasy feeling grabbed his stomach. That would not happen to him. He knew in his soul that his work was extraordinary. The stamp of just how extraordinary was up to the gatekeepers.

His breath caught unexpectedly. A young woman stood across the room, engaged in serious conversation with an art critic. A shoulder-length tress of her black hair lay tucked behind one ear, allowing the rest of the glossy strands to fall around her striking features. Ebony lashes and charcoal grey eyes made make-up a useless commodity—except for the transparent gloss applied to her ample lips. His gaze stayed locked on those lips.

She turned, watched him with Viola for a moment, and frowned. Twisting back, her hair flipped sharply, sending a dismissive signal.

*Fascinating.* Gabe stepped away from Viola and raked a stray curl off his forehead. "I have to see a client," he said, in answer to the frown tugging at her mouth. Avoiding most of the guests who tried to get his attention, he spoke with others while maneuvering in the direction where he had last seen the woman.

Two of his young female students ambushed him, halting his progress. He steeled himself for the charge. Cherie, a gorgeous California blond, did nothing to veil her flirtatious glances in the classroom. Jenn, on the other hand, gloried in death-defying risks. He was not sure which girl unnerved him more.

Jenn said, "I drove into town Sunday night and saw you on the climbing wall."

Gabe's head jerked backward. Who else had witnessed his feeble late-night endeavor?

She continued, "If you want, I can show you some awesome climbs that hang you out over the ocean, then go vertical, straight up the cliff."

Her enthusiasm mounted. "There's one spot where you can get almost horizontal. If an extra big wave breaks on the rocks below, the water can reach high enough to spray you. It's so cool."

*Was she kidding?* The image of crashing water below him made his head reel. In his latest attempt to conquer his fear of heights, he had regressed instead of moving forward. Jenn went on to describe, in considerable detail, a leap she had made—just catching her hold before she would have fallen into the waves below.

His palms grew clammy and his throat constricted. A waiter passed and Gabe snatched a glass of champagne and gulped it down. He mumbled a polite excuse and left, ignoring their pouting faces.

Though he knew its origin, no amount of logic tamed the dragon of fear that could reduce him to a pile of ashes. Angry at his lack of control, he drifted through the room, reciting calming words in his mind while letting the air conditioning cool his face.

Slowing, his eyes picked out the dark beauty again. She stood next to an easel, studying *Pacifica*, one of his smaller, but highly praised paintings. His heart smiled. Though aware of the feminine glances directed his way, Gabe could count on one hand the few women who had ever appealed to him. Since Darla, this woman was the first. The strength of his attraction surprised him. Something about the serious way she considered the canvas pleased him. His shoulders relaxed and he eased forward.

She bent closer to the painting and a half smile lit her gorgeous Italian face. Stepping back, her attention flicked around the room. She started when she caught Gabe watching her. Their eyes connected, linking them for a heart-stopping moment. Confusion betrayed her attempt at disinterest. Lifting her glass to her lips, she turned and walked away.

Now, thoroughly enchanted, his mind raced. He needed an introduction. Another art collector stepped over to congratulate him. Distracted, Gabe thanked him, but glanced in the direction the woman had gone and spotted her listening to Howard Sutton. Gabe strode toward him, taking a chance on the man's good manners in public.

"The man of the hour," Howard said, "ready to make his fortune and leave our humble life of academia. Right Dolcini?"

Gabe forced a thin smile. "Perhaps." He reached out to shake hands.

Howard ran his eyes over Gabe's jacket, prompting a cocky smile. Gabe held his breath, but Howard let it go. He shook Gabe's hand and introduced the circle of guests. Just beyond the group, the exotic woman leaned against a cream-colored column like a Roman empress in her palace. Shining from the ceiling, a spotlight danced over the crimson highlights in her hair.

Howard's eyes followed. "Oh," he smiled. "And may I introduce Livia Ambrogi." He took a step and raised her hand to his lips. "She's visiting us from Florence, where she has completed her degree in the history of Italian art and language. Livia, may I introduce an art *teacher* in my department, Gabriel Dolcini."

Gabe ignored Howard's intended slight. He stepped toward her and searched for another connection with her smoky eyes. Her fragrance—a mix of lavender and something exquisitely foreign—permeated his senses as he waited for her to extend her hand. Instead, she nodded and granted him the faintest of a polite smile.

His lips tightened. He gave her a curt nod and turned back to catch Howard's smirk from the corner of his eye. Fighting frustration, Gabe smiled and answered questions about his work from the small cluster. He risked a glance in Livia's direction, but she had moved away.

Across the room, he spotted one of the other finalists. Thomas Neilsen, a politically connected, wealthy art guru from Denmark, owned an expansive estate atop a hill overlooking San Francisco Bay. Neilsen glanced at him. Gabe nodded, but the artist turned his back. His prerogative. Though the art world proved highly competitive, Gabe attempted to keep his ego out of the equation. He grinned. *Attempted.*

Loud voices interrupted his musings. In the hallway toward the rear of the stage, Viola argued with two of tonight's judges and a third man Gabe did not recognize. Her mouth uttered obscured, yet vicious-sounding words while she shook her fists at them. After four years of watching her drama, Gabe shrugged with indifference.

Disappointed at Livia Ambrogi's disinterest, Gabe continued to circle around the room and greet guests. By the time he stepped forward with the other recipients, he had eased back into his sweet spot. Elevated on a small stage in this Five-Star hotel, he waited through the many lesser awards for the announcement.

A smile pasted on her lips, Viola stepped to him and spoke into the microphone. "Having mastered the masters, Gabriel Dolcini's oil paintings have surpassed his predecessors—in our humble opinion," she added, causing an enthusiastic round of applause throughout the large room. "With an unusual depth of color and subtly stylized design as his signature, his work is easily recognized by the best of critics—and we love him."

He glanced over at the magnificent painting that had moved him into this echelon. His finest yet. In fact, he had felt infused with inspiration while painting it, more than on any other canvas. The subject was common enough—an Italian beauty reclined on a velvet sofa, an open letter lying in her lap. Flowers fell from her fingers and hung in midair, never to reach the intricately woven carpet waiting below them. The woman's face held intense sadness, with grey eyes gazing to some distant place that Gabe could never go. He had named it, *Il Viso*, "The Face."

Other images and symbols had floated into his imagination while he had worked. He painted them with equal obscurity—a fact that caused a great sensation in the art world. Layers of obliquely identifiable impressions entwined between foreground and background, as in dreams and waking. The paint flew off his brushes, and he had completed the large canvas in less than a month. It felt as if a gift had settled upon him and poured through to the canvas.

A break in Viola's voice brought his wandering thoughts back to the celebration. "It is my honor to announce Gabriel Dolcini as the *second* place award winner in the American Oil Painters Excellence Award."

The crowd gasped. Murmurs of disbelief filled the room.

Viola gave him a kiss-kiss on his cheeks, avoiding his eyes while she handed him a ribbon.

His face thought to smile and nod and did what anyone should do when winning something. Underneath his impassive expression, a claw gripped his heart in an effort to rip it from his chest. Faces in the crowd watched him and he blanched under the hot lights. An exultant smirk from Howard drove the message home: they were not going to let him in. Gabe glanced at the judges standing next to him, their lips tight with disdain.

Had he been mistaken about the quality of his work? *No*. His supporters looked just as shocked as he felt. He knew his value. Had studied his competition. What was left? Was the competition fixed? He watched through a dark tunnel as Viola presented the first place award to Thomas Neilsen. The man's proud chin lifted. The crowd applauded, but the night's sparkle had flatlined. Many, heads shaking, turned to leave.

Following Viola's presentation, city officials and high-ranking members of the artistic community stepped forward to congratulate the winner. Gabe stepped off the stage as soon as he could. People he knew nodded to him as he made his escape through the crowd and past the expansive windows. Outside, the setting sun painted the clouds in golden tones to reflect what should have been his highest accomplishment. He chanced a quick glance around, then ducked out, glad that Livia Ambrogi had left the room.

## 

Gabe sat in his car on Monday morning. He had parked in the far corner of the faculty parking lot in case his resolve failed. How could he face his colleagues? But it would not be any easier tomorrow. He closed his eyes and took a slow breath, in and out, then stopped thinking and opened the door.

Entering the building, he looked straight ahead and focused on getting to his classroom. He shut out the awkward expressions as he contended with the gauntlet of the, "I'm so sorry," comments and, worse, the congratulations from his peers in the long hallway. Relieved, Gabe realized Howard's duties must have detained him elsewhere.

He stepped into his classroom and shut the door behind him, cringing at his smug attitude over the last week. His students immediately surrounded him, expressing their outrage. Their loyalty and courage to speak what others would not, eased his bad temper and helped to soothe his wounded spirit.

"You were robbed," Judy ranted.

He *was* cheated. But it was over. "Enough," Gabe hushed their angry outbursts. "All judges maintain their own criteria. Sometimes it doesn't fall in our favor. So, back to work."

They drifted back to their canvases, but Judy stayed near his desk. "I won't be a part of this. I'll paint what I want and thumb my nose at whoever thinks they have the right to judge it." Her eyes watered and she swiped at an angry tear before it trickled down her silky black cheek.

Gabe took her hand in his. "It's okay, really. Just a disappointment." No one could possibly know how deep this cut. The world was cruel, ripping small, relentless gashes in tender hearts and tentative hopes. Judy walked to her canvas, but did not pick up her brush.

He stared through the window at nothing. Second place did not count for anything in the art world. Or in life. Even after Angelica died, their father made certain Gabe knew he would never move into first place. It became unbearable to be the single focus of the man's loathing. Gabe blinked away the past and darted his eyes from student to student. Every one of them had a story. He needed to buck up.

## 

After three days, the sting of disappointment failed to lessen. With the summer term ending soon, and nothing to look forward to, Gabe dreaded the boredom headed his way. He hadn't touched his current painting since losing the award.

Even his students seemed frustrated with their projects this afternoon. He frowned at his waning willingness to help. One of them dawdled with his paintbrush. Gabe grabbed it and smashed it into a dab of red paint on the student's palette. "If you're gonna paint, paint."

The startled student jerked awake. "Yes, Sir." He took the brush back and created bold strokes that instantly improved his composition.

"Good." Gabe grimaced at his outburst and patted the young man on the shoulder. He walked to his desk when his cell phone vibrated. "Hello."

There was a hesitant pause on the other end. "Uh, Gabe, Carl here." Carl was the Dean of Faculty at the university.

"Hi Carl, how are you?" He hoped it was not another obligatory congratulations call.

"I'm fine, but something disturbing has come to my attention. I need you to come in today and answer some questions before this goes any further."

The tension in Carl's voice, mixed with the foreboding message, pinned Gabe to the spot. "May I ask what this is about?"

"Yes. A complaint has just been filed against you for misconduct involving a minor. Sonia Sanchez."

Gabe turned away from his students, his hand clenching the back of his chair. He whispered, "Don't believe a word of it, Carl. Sonia has lived with my mother since she was emancipated by the state."

"Do you live there also?"

Heat blasted through him. "No. And it wouldn't matter if I did. I don't get involved with children. You of all people should know that."

Carl would not yield. "It's my job to investigate complaints regarding faculty. Come in, and I'll take your statement."

Furious, Gabe resisted slamming his phone on the desk and stuffed it into his pocket instead. Who would make a complaint like this? His jaw clenched. Howard. It would not be the first time he pulled a stunt against a fellow professor, and it would be just like his daughter to embellish what happened at the restaurant.

An hour later, Gabe paced in Carl's office while the Dean explained. "Apparently, someone saw you kiss Sonia in front of the restaurant where she works and drive away with her."

Gabe raked his hair off his forehead and clarified the situation. He studied Carl's unyielding face and shook his head. *So much for good deeds.*

"I've asked Miss Sanchez to come in this afternoon. I'm sure you realize this could have serious consequences. I'll be in touch." He hesitated. "And Gabe, you should know this was why you lost the award."

"WHAT?" Gabe could not believe he heard right.

"The judges couldn't risk the bad press if their winner became embroiled in a sexual misconduct controversy."

"How dare they!" Gabe seethed. "No one asked me. No one said a word."

"Apparently they were made aware of it just before the presentation. You would have been disqualified altogether except for Viola Hudson's rage. She convinced them that second place never makes headlines. And she threatened some kind of lawsuit if they were wrong."

Too many thoughts bombarded Gabe's confused mind to find coherent words to speak.

"Until we get to the bottom of this, I have to suspend you. There are only a few days left in the summer term. I'll get a substitute."

Gabe stormed out, livid. And scared. This injustice would not be easily reversed.

Arriving home, he threw open the door and watched it bounce off the wall. He closed his eyes, shaking his head at his outburst. Throwing a tantrum was not going to fix his career, his finances, or this attack on his character.

He slammed into his office chair and opened the drawer to throw in his keys. His grandfather's letter lay on top of an art brochure. Rubbing his forehead, Gabe sighed in resignation. The only option left was to respond to his grandfather's invitation to show his work in Italy—unless he wanted to stand on the sidewalk and hawk his paintings to passing tourists.

It had been two months since he had received the correspondence. He had never replied. Would the old man still want him? He pulled out the letter and dialed the phone number, almost hoping there would be no answer.

Someone answered the call on the second ring. "Dolcini residence."

##

Two weeks later, Gabe felt resolute when he stepped into his mother's house to face her fury. After the awards debacle, desperation had swamped him, but now he had a direction. His grandfather's eagerness for his visit provided the one bright spot in Gabe's dismal prospects. The timing proved uncanny.

He leaned against the kitchen counter in the house where he grew up. It was a muggy Saturday morning, and the eastern light shone dimly through a streaked aluminum-framed window. He caught a glimpse of the ocean down the hillside, too far away to see its tide ebbing and flowing.

Under the window, outdated turquoise tiles did their best to be cheerful in a house with a history of bitterness and loss. Studying his mother's face, he traced the ravages of sadness that tugged her features downward. Deep frown lines obliterated the sweet dimples that once graced her cheeks. Year after year, his father's venom had poisoned her. Gabe felt thankful death had taken the brute first.

Spoken in her native Italian, his mother's protective warning made him smile. "Do not do this, Gabriel."

He waited for her to finish her tirade while he sipped coffee from an old cracked cup. His father had smashed it in one of his fits. Gabe wondered why she had glued it back together after retrieving the broken pieces from the scarred wooden floor. *Why keep a reminder?* He had never understood the complexity of his parents' relationship. Now he didn't need to.

"We have nothing to do with Conte Dolcini," she continued. "Your grandfather is a lunatic, trouble. He marked your grandmother for death by his fascination with tales of lost treasure—without any regard of how he attracts crazies to our family." She ended on a shrill note, "He is not safe."

Gabe set the mug down. He took her hands and leaned to kiss her on the forehead. Her four-foot, ten-inch frame stood a foot below him. She had always made him feel taller than he was. Around his father, he had always felt he was trying to break the forty-eight-inch mark.

"Mama, this is the next step in my career. Conte Dolcini knows the best families in Siena, and they are anxious to meet me and see my work.

It's perfect timing for him to invite me."

"You speak Italian like an Americano. You will embarrass yourself."

He laughed. Her attempt to dissuade him was futile. "True, I understand better than I speak, but I managed just fine the last time I traveled in Italy." Besides, he had no choice but to go. Though there had been considerable interest in his work after the award presentation, his agent had only managed to sell two paintings.

So far, his mother was not aware of the impending threat to her home. He turned away as the accusations in his mind screamed, *Fesso. And selfish.* That's what his father would say about him. And he was right.

Gabe sucked in a quick breath and let it out. So far, no publicity had surfaced regarding the false accusation. That was all he needed—to scare off the important collectors he had met before the ceremony. He hoped they still planned to contact him, but his ever-present inner critic relentlessly spewed its noxious toxins. *People never come through.* His constant schoolmaster since childhood, it reminded him not to stand on the shifting sand of trust.

He squared his shoulders. He had done the work. Now all he needed was someone to open the door. He gave his mother a peck on the cheek. "In three weeks, I will be in Italy." His voice was silky while he worked to calm her, keeping his own doubts at bay.

Worry wrinkled her face. "Please listen. There are reasons we never allowed you to meet this man."

He glanced toward the ocean's vague horizon. Even when he had visited Siena for his studies a decade ago, he had obeyed his father's vehement demands and made excuses to turn down his grandfather's frequent invitations. Now, however, the time was right. Louis Dolcini's letter lay folded in his desk drawer at home. His grandfather, a count no less, wanted to help his career. *At least someone wanted to.*

Though no resolution had been reached regarding the charges against him, the administrators at the university seemed glad to distance themselves. When Gabe requested leave for the fall term, they agreed that he should go. *Without pay.* The plane ticket to Siena used the last of his available credit on his card. *This had to work.*

# Chapter 4

Rome, Italy

Abbot Porta barely contained his exhilaration as he reported to the *Primo Consul*. "I sent one of our associates to Seborga. He overheard the prayers of the priest, Tito, at the orphanage near the Church of San Bernardo. Tito prayed for a man named Dolcini and the swift return of Saint Bernardo's *great secret*."

"Did this Tito say what it was?"

"No, he was very guarded when my associate inquired about it."

"Hmm. What action have you taken?"

"None since my associate returned. I wanted to know your orders first." If Porta had learned anything about dealing with the *Primo Consul*, it was never to make a move without his knowledge.

"Then use any means to get the information."

Porta immediately made a second call, and within the hour, his contact arrived.

"Ah, Niccolo, come in."

"You have an order for me?" Niccolo's deep voice matched his massive strength. He was the perfect emissary to retrieve the information.

"*Si*. I want you to take Arturo with you to Seborga. There is an insignificant priest there with a vital secret. Get it out of him."

Niccolo nodded and left.

After the door closed, Porta sprang to his feet and paced rapidly. He was so close. Too many intriguing scenarios raced through his mind. This was no day for ordinary work. Instead, he headed for his favorite restaurant to celebrate his certain advancement.

##

A jarring touchdown threw Gabe back in his seat. It rattled his nerves and the loose objects around him as the Air France flight from Los Angeles landed in Paris. An unshakeable apprehension gripped him after he deplaned from the crowded coach section and headed for customs.

He arched his back to stretch out the kinks while waiting in line. The official glanced at him, then stopped what he was doing and took another long look. When Gabe stepped to the front of the line, the man took Gabe's passport and compared it against a piece of paper poorly concealed by the stainless steel countertop. He gave Gabe a stiff nod and handed back his passport.

Gabe followed the official's eyes as they darted past him to a solemn man who leaned against a far wall. A thin, David Niven mustache accented a wiry frame. Although the man's attention focused in another direction, the hair on Gabe's forearms rose, as it did whenever someone was watching him. He shook it off and hurried to board the plane for the last leg of his journey to Florence.

##

After the eighteen-hour trip from California, Gabe felt relieved to see his name on a placard held high by a stocky chauffeur in a tailored black jacket. Below the man's black cap, straight brown hair revealed a precision cut.

"*Buon giorno*. I am Rinaldo Paravati, Conte Dolcini's chauffeur." Gabe enjoyed the sound of his ancestral language, but it had been awhile since he had immersed himself in it. Rinaldo had to repeat a few of the words until Gabe nodded that he understood.

Rinaldo's strong hands clenched Gabe's scuffed silver and black designer bags. He led the way through the small terminal on the edge of

Florence, threading them through the huge crowd that filled every corner. All the faces looked expectantly in one direction as they jockeyed for closer positions.

"What are they looking at?" Gabe asked.

The butler's face remained impassive. "The Vicar General of Rome, Cardinal Vincenzo Bergesio, will arrive soon on his way to America as a peacemaker."

Gabe chuckled. "Are we at war?"

Rinaldo did not share his mirth. "*Sì*, the worst kind—religious. The Cardinal is hoping to bring a common sense agreement between a contingent of churches and the American Religious Cultural Center."

"What's that?" Before Rinaldo could answer, two enthusiastic men shoved Gabe to one side as they rushed toward the arriving limo. He recovered his balance and asked, "Why is he so popular?"

A smirk twisted Rinaldo's thin lips. "As Vicar General, he is the second most powerful man in Rome. And he exudes a personal charisma that makes him well respected."

They reached a sleek black limousine, and Rinaldo opened the door. Gabe slid into the cloud-soft leather seat and they drove to Siena, the city that held the Dolcini ancestral home.

For years, he had heard comments about the Palazzo Dolcini and had secretly dreamed of visiting it. Now it was time. His father had done everything possible to break the ties—married a woman from a competing Sienese neighborhood, moved his family to the United States, and refused to have anything to do with the Conte. Gabe thought it was time to put an end to a lot of unnecessary drama.

A little over an hour later, Rinaldo opened the limo door and led Gabe to the entrance. Stepping across the wooden threshold into the foyer of the magnificent residence, Gabe realized that nothing had prepared him for the opulence that greeted him. He felt as though he had traveled back in time—the same way he had felt when entering the *duomo* in Siena years ago. The palazzo beckoned, luring him to explore within its grand walls.

High gilded ceilings, frescoed in luxurious hues, pulled his eyes upward. Scanning across the stuccoed walls that displayed centuries-old oil paintings, his breath caught. He stepped nearer. It couldn't be. At first glance, it appeared that his grandfather had Anotello da Messina's *Salting Madonna* hanging above an ornate chest—but that piece was hanging in the National Gallery in London! "The lost *Madonna with Child*?" he whispered reverently.

"My collection impresses you, *sì*?"

The melodic voice of his grandfather, the Conte Louis Dolcini, rang in Gabe's ears for the first time. Gabe turned and was pleased to see a vibrant, silver-haired gentleman, sporting a distinguished white beard and mustache. Years past, Louis Dolcini probably stood at Gabe's height, but now Gabe looked down an inch into warm eyes and a trembling smile.

"Gabriel Russo Dolcini. I have dreamed of this meeting for thirty-four years—my grandson, in my home." He reached for Gabe's hands and kissed him on each cheek.

This was the real deal. When tears came to his grandfather's eyes, Gabe blinked back the moisture stinging his as well.

Louis cleared his throat, his emotion transparent, "Come." He favored one leg as he escorted Gabe into the huge library filled with plush Windsor blue and gold sofas and chairs. The faint aroma of expensive cigars conjured up scenes from an historical novel. More magnificent oil paintings filled the walls. One in particular, of a humble dwelling atop a verdant hill, had been executed so brilliantly that instant envy and appreciation ran through Gabe's veins. This was heaven.

Louis motioned for him to sit by the fireplace in one of two high-backed chairs. The rich leather accentuated the ornately carved wood of the arms and legs. Wine glasses and a porcelain plate filled with *prosciutto*, *pecorino* cheese, and green olives sat on the intricate *pietre dure*, a stone-painted table that stood between them. After a few moments, Rinaldo appeared in a black vest, now serving as the butler, and poured the wine.

Louis raised his glass. "I bottled this Brunello from my vineyard in Montalcino the year you were born. I swore I would drink it with you when you were old enough." He smiled, partially concealing a pained grimace. "It waited in my cellar perhaps longer than I planned, but let us taste it and see what we think."

Gabe swirled the red liquid in the crystal glass. He could detect the bouquet long before he tilted the glass to breathe in the aroma. He smiled at his grandfather as they tasted the wine together. Year thirty-four proved to be a magic number for the celebratory bottle. Though smooth as silk, the liquid burst with flavor in his mouth.

"*Magnifico*," his grandfather whispered. He gazed at Gabe. "It was worth the wait."

## ##

Two days later, Gabe met Louis as he was descending the stairs to the grand foyer. "Where are we going today?"

"To introduce you to some of your family. Though quite distant as relatives go, Marcus is my best friend. I consider him a brother."

Gabe loved the warmth that pervaded Louis' voice whenever he spoke of friends and family. His own excitement grew more with each passing day. Life was rich here, and not just the money. If he could conjure up the perfect character for a grandfather, Louis fit the image.

"What are you grinning about?" Louis asked.

"Just happy." Gabe reached an arm around Louis' shoulder and hugged him.

"Let us be off," his grandfather said. His eyes misted again—a frequent happening since Gabe had arrived.

Entering the Chianti region, Gabe marveled at the vineyards that stretched over every hill and valley. Soon, a road sign announced the town of Radda. Rinaldo slowed to accommodate the massive number of shopping tourists. Gabe grinned as he studied the varied architecture of the mansions set close to the tree-lined streets. Charm exuded from every building and iron fence. They turned into the driveway of a once impressive home, ancient compared to its neighbors. Struggling vines and grass seemed at home with fallen roof tiles and the stone balustrades lying on their sides. Piles of stones sat abandoned next to a new section of house that gaped open through a partially framed wall.

Louis studied the signs of decay and sighed. He glanced at Gabe.

"Marcus was in a severe auto accident some years ago. His wife died, and he was left in a wheelchair with four young daughters to care for. He tells me all is well and will not accept my help. But look at this, Gabriel." He pointed and shook his head.

After tapping the knocker on the eight-foot metal-clad door, Gabe heard a female voice inside call out, "They are here." Then a charming Italian girl pulled the door open. Louis introduced her as *Signorina* Gemma. She blushed at Gabe and extended a graceful hand.

"*Buon giorno*," he greeted and shook it.

"*Buon giorno*, Louis," a hearty welcome greeted from the next room. "Please come in." Gemma escorted them to a library with a wooden floor and wide window. Though impressive, it wasn't a quarter the size of Louis' massive library at the palazzo.

With great import, Louis said, "Marcus, may I introduce my grandson and heir, Gabriel Russo Dolcini."

Gabe did a double take. That was the first time his grandfather had mentioned his inheritance.

Marcus reached out and gave Gabe a hearty shake with a strong hand. "You are the very image of Louis when he was younger. Welcome to my home."

They sat down, and Louis wasted no time. "You are a stubborn man, Marcus. When will you let me help with this restoration?"

The remark made Gabe uncomfortable, but Marcus seemed to take no offense. Instead, he shook his head. "We are managing, my friend. But let us talk about your grandson, here, *eh?*"

That was all the encouragement Louis needed to expound upon Gabe's many attributes. Gabe blushed at the praise, but it fed his soul. "My grandfather is a bit partial, I think."

Marcus studied him. "I think not."

Before Gabe had time to evaluate his comment, Gemma brought in a tray of espresso and biscotti. Again, she blushed as she sat it down in front of Gabe and left the men to talk.

Marcus nodded his head toward the door through which she had disappeared. "I worry about her. Her only purpose is taking care of me.

How will she meet a husband if she does nothing more than buy groceries and clean this old villa?"

Louis patted him on the back. "She is only nineteen, and beautiful. I do not think you have to worry about *that* one." Their eyes met in a knowing way that made Gabe wonder about the others. Louis took a sip of his coffee. "*Scuzi*, I need to speak to Gemma." He disappeared through the door to the kitchen.

"Do your other daughters live nearby?" Gabe asked.

Marcus smiled. "They all live here, although I rarely see them. I suppose they take after me, relentless in their business interests around the country. At least that is how I used to be." Marcus' body slumped unconsciously in his wheelchair. "We have owned land and companies for centuries. Each needs leadership, but my health tethers me to this chair. My eldest daughter has taken the burden upon herself and is especially driven beyond what is good for her."

Louis stepped back through the door and sat down again, his face stern. "Gemma tells me you are not participating in the harvest festivities this year. This is not good for the community or for you." "If I choose to stay in my home and not attend community functions, that is my choice. And you can tell Gemma to quit spreading my business around town."

Louis grinned at Marcus' agitation. "She only told me, and she has your best interest in mind."

For over an hour, Gabe witnessed the ongoing controversies the two men obviously enjoyed rehashing. They argued about the harvest and local politics until Gabe eventually stifled a yawn.

"I believe we have not been fair to your grandson, Louis." Marcus changed the subject and turned to Gabe. "You are an artist. Perhaps you would like to see the plans I created for the renovation here, *eh*?" Gabe nodded and Marcus directed him to a large table next to the window that faced the street. "My daughter says work should start in a month or so."

Gabe examined the plans. "Are you an architect?"

"Not anymore. That is, I work for myself now." His lips tightened with a hint of bitterness.

"These are amazing ideas," Gabe said. He realized that the stones piled in the front yard would cover a new portico that wrapped around the front of the villa. The portico supported a second story patio that would provide a view across the street and overlook the vineyards and mountains beyond. "If I ever need a designer, I will call on you."

Marcus sat taller in his wheelchair. "That would be my pleasure."

It was obvious to Gabe that Marcus had been a powerful force before his accident. The man's inner strength defied his disability. Handsome and confident, it would have been out of character for this man to ask for help prior to his injury. But what about now? He obviously needed Louis' help.

Louis cleared his throat. "These are good plans, my friend." He patted Marcus' shoulder with his left hand. "We must leave now. I will see you on Saturday evening, *eh?*"

Marcus shrugged his shoulders. "We will see."

Louis shook Marcus' hand in both of his. "*Ciao.*"

Outside, Rinaldo sprang out of the waiting limo and opened the door for them. Gabe turned back and imagined the renovation plans from the outside. "This will be impressive when it's finished."

Louis eased in and frowned. "Those plans are ten years old. Marcus and his wife worked on them together until she died." As they drove, Louis' attention drifted to the passing grapevines and he grew quiet. When they were almost home, he rolled down the center window and spoke to Rinaldo. "After you return me to the palazzo, escort Gabriel downtown. I wanted to have him fitted for his tuxedo today, but my body refuses to cooperate." Rinaldo nodded.

"Sir, that's not necessary," Gabe argued.

"Certainly not necessary, but very enjoyable for me to give, *eh?*" A wide smile broke across his face, creating a dimple in his cheek. Gabe grinned back, aware of his matching indentation, and basked in the connection.

# Chapter 5

Siena, Italy

Only three days had passed, yet Gabe's mind reeled. His grandfather had filled him with many stories about the family treasures housed in the 1,000-year-old structure.

Lingering after breakfast in the rectangular, windowless dining room, Louis now pressed for the details about Gabe's late father, his family, and his life. Gabe fingered the crystal water glass that remained on the table. Translucent alabaster chandeliers provided soft illumination for a hard subject.

"And what about Angelica? What is your sister doing?"

Gabe glanced up in surprise. Surely, his father had notified him of her death. But no, Gabe could see the anticipation in his eyes. "I'm sorry, sir, Angelica has passed from us also."

Louis sank back in the tall chair, his strong hands gripping the claws carved on the walnut arms. His face held such pain that Gabe trained his attention on the red and gold pattern of the carpet underfoot. He dreaded what would come next.

"How did she die?"

A simple question, but the answer held so much torment. "It was an accident. She was lost in a mudslide while we were hiking in the mountains."

"How old was my granddaughter?"

"Twelve."

An anguished gasp escaped the old man. "So long ago, but no one told me. Am I that much of a monster that my own son would stab my heart this way? Gabriel, am I?" His breathing accelerated and his hand pressed against his chest.

Gabe called for Rinaldo and rose to get help, but Louis motioned for him to sit. His grandfather waited for an answer. Meeting the old man's anxious eyes, he said, "No, you are not a monster. This was a monstrous thing to be done to you." Gabe's own resentment seeped into his words. His father had been heartless, except where Angelica had been concerned.

Rinaldo appeared from his quarters opposite the kitchen, took one look at his employer, and reached for his medication from the sideboard.

When Louis had calmed down, he said, "I need to go to my room." Rinaldo and Gabe helped the distressed man to his suite and helped him lie down on a black and tan upholstered chaise next to his bed.

Gabe left and pulled the door closed, wishing he could lock out the fear that hid in the shadows of his mind. Craving the growing bond with his grandfather had made him vulnerable. He had been close to revealing his darkest secret. But with truth came consequences. Shaken, he escaped to the ballroom where all the preparations to honor him were taking place.

Empty crates that had contained his paintings lay in neat stacks. As soon as he had accepted the invitation, Conte Dolcini had notified Serena Romano, a popular art dealer, to make it happen. And it was happening.

Strain tugged at Serena's face. She carried a metal clipboard and ordered her crew to transform the ballroom of the Palazzo Dolcini into a grand salon to exhibit Gabe's work. Thin and wiry, with her face pulled tight at the hand of a surgeon, she looked anything but serene. A string of emotionally charged Italian streamed out of her mouth, causing alarm in the eyes of the young men who were not moving fast enough after lunch. They had only four more days to finish the details.

When she explained the significance of the night to Gabe, her self-importance seemed to cause her head to rise to new heights. "Members of the old guard are anxious to see the Dolcini collections again. Their children have only heard tales about the palazzo. They are thrilled to be included on the guest list to see you, the famous American painter." She flashed a wily smile. "Your Italian heritage only heightens the excitement."

She was less forthcoming with other information, but Gabe was able to pull a few facts together. Although his grandfather carried on a vast array of business responsibilities, the Palazzo Dolcini had not opened its doors for an event in four decades, not since its mistress, Contessa Dolcini was murdered. Not since Gabe's father left for America.

He glanced around the fabulous ballroom. His paintings rested on magnificent gilded easels placed with artistic precision around the massive space. The second story room was ablaze with light as Serena checked for shadows and glare that might hinder the viewing of his pieces.

"These are *magnifico*," she complimented. Tilting her head to study him, she asked, "Are you aware of the rare gift you possess?"

He judged her comment as sincere rather than flattery. "It feels that way at times."

She flashed a quick smile. "Conte Dolcini will love these. He is so proud of you."

*He is for now.* An ache in Gabe's chest limited his response to an appreciative nod with a murmured, *"Grazie."* He left the residence by the rear exit to escape the commotion—and the unsolicited childhood memories.

## 

While the inner soul of the palazzo flaunted the masters' paintings, the gardens outside boasted their own treasures. Trees and vines shaded and caressed the master sculptors' marble and bronze figures. Today, however, Gabe's mind was too preoccupied to let the garden's glory entice him. Today, he longed for sanctuary. He needed to center—to remind himself of all he had accomplished through diligence and hard work. *Why could one memory strip him bare so easily?*

As he meandered along a wide path that circled the large lawn, the beauty of the symmetry was nearly lost on him. Overhead, the tips of the ancient olive trees intermingled, providing a welcome respite from the unusual September heat. Statues of Roman women holding fruit or vegetables seemed to pause along the path. He had already bypassed most of them when the extended hand of a magnificent bronze reached out to him.

A bearded Greek warrior stood elevated on a round pedestal. The sculptor had wrought the realistic musculature of the chest and body in great detail. Gabe studied the rounded skull, certain it was once crowned with a helmet. He had seen two such statues on the cover of an art magazine in Louis' library. Divers had discovered them off the coast of Riace, a village near the toe of Italy's boot-shaped landmass.

"The Riace Warriors," he said aloud and shook his head in amazement. What were the chances his grandfather had purchased a third warrior, clandestinely rescued from the shallow water?

"Hey, man."

Gabe's head swung around to meet the wide grin of a red-haired man who looked vaguely familiar. "Do I know you?"

"You forgot your cousin, did you?"

Gabe's jaw dropped. "Ralph Witte?" He scanned the bizarre, silver-studded black jeans that clung to the man's long, skinny legs. "I haven't seen you since I was ten and you spent the summer with us." Raised without a father, or discipline, Ralph had proved to be a challenge for Gabe's parents. A one-sided smile dimpled Gabe's cheek. He had enjoyed the distraction and his father's frustration with someone other than himself. Where Gabe refused to take part in adventures, Ralph created one spectacular event after another. He even stole their neighbor's car and took out the trashcans instead of making the turn. A shadow crossed over Gabe's memory. His father had been less than gentle on Ralph's backside.

"Yeah, that was a good year, as I remember it." Ralph's dull green eyes darkened below the stiff spikes of natural red hair. "So, you still a good little chump?"

Gabe colored. Ralph had thrown that insult at him all that summer. But he was thirty-four now. All grown up. Ignoring the dig, he asked, "Do you still live in London?"

Ralph straightened. "Yeah mate, still in London. I'm a rock star now, you know."

Gabe looked at the wild hair and clothes and grinned. "You look like a rock star." *A hard-life rock star.* "What instrument do you play?"

"A mean guitar, but not the lead. Not like you, turnin' out to be a great painter an' all." His whitened teeth, too perfect to be real, sparkled from a narrow jaw. But Gabe could hardly call it a smile.

"What brings you to Italy?" Gabe asked.

"Got a gig. Then I finds out my cuz is here to get all glorified. The ol' man finally gets to hold up his *legitimate* grandson for the world t' see. It's all he's ever wanted."

Gabe recoiled. "I've just met him—I had no idea."

"That's the sorry part, ain't it? My mom and your dad, ignoring the ol' guy, but me growing up without nothin'. She wouldn't let me near him. And he wouldn't have nothin' to do with us, just because she *self-medicated.* Don't quite seem right, does it?"

"I'm sorry to hear that. My father cut us off from all of this."

Ralph eyed him. "Not your fault." He shook Gabe's hand. "I'm glad for you, with all this fuss and all. You turned out good, in spite of Angelica's accident."

Gabe's smile faded.

"You ain't past that?" Ralph smirked at the revelation. "Does Louis know yet?" Working to hide the sting, Gabe changed the subject. "Are you staying here while you're in town?"

"Right. My mum died and the ol' man let me stay here for awhile. Then kicked me out over a little misunderstandin'."

Gabe was silent. What could he say?

Ralph cocked his chin up. "Hey, just wanted to stop by before the big event. I ain't invited, but I'll see you around." He started to leave but turned back. "He hasn't been feedin' you any of that Templar lunacy has he?"

Puzzled, Gabe responded, "Haven't heard a thing."

With that, Ralph nodded, slipped through the iron gate, and vanished from sight.

Gabe stared after him. *Strange guy.* A moment later, Rinaldo emerged from around a precisely carved hedge. "Sir, would you give your grandfather a moment of your time?" He stepped back inside through the solarium door.

Why did it always come back to Angelica? Gabe was not interested in continuing the conversation. He strolled the perimeter walk, stretching out the time and keeping a lookout for more Greek bronzes. None showed themselves.

Arriving at a stone railing, he peered over and was astonished. Below lay a large seating area arranged like a small Roman amphitheater. A strong breeze blew up from the half-circle stage below and teased his black curls away from his eyes. He followed its direction and glanced back at the palazzo where his grandfather waited.

What would his life have been like without that fateful day?

The wind shifted. It was impossible to tell from which direction it came or to where it journeyed. Could it be that simple to change the direction of his life?

It was time. He trudged up the broad steps to the side entrance. Inside, the house was quiet. Rinaldo led him to the open door of a small chapel and left. Standing at the entrance, Gabe realized it had been ages since he had entered a chapel. The peculiar atmosphere here was different from anything he had experienced before.

The aesthetics of the narrow room were impressive. Its vaulted ceiling highlighted a magnificent glass centerpiece set high on one of its stone walls. Sun filtered through the five-foot rose window that displayed stained glass of every color. The soft light danced its rainbow illumination over seven rows of benches in the otherwise dusky room.

Gabe stood still. A gentle presence and distant singing filled him, causing a slow swell in his heart. He listened harder, but the song was not audible.

A movement in the front of the chapel startled him. Louis changed his weight on the altar where he knelt, head in hands. Gabe eased forward and heard his grandfather praying.

"Lord, my only son renounced me and is dead. And now, Angelica. Only You know the depth of my agony." Louis wiped the tears that dripped into his beard. "I cannot undo my willful actions, but please, deliver me from these spiteful accusations fettered to my soul." He pulled out a handkerchief and blew his nose, then rose from where he knelt on the padded altar and sat on the first bench.

Gabe grimaced at the grief his father's actions had caused this gentle man. He stepped forward and laid a hand on Louis' shoulder.

Startled, Louis turned. His face solemn, he patted the bench. "Come sit. Tell me about Angelica." His eyes probed for truth.

Gabe rubbed his forehead. The peace vanished. He hid a nervous swallow and sat on the other end of the smooth wooden bench, hesitating before beginning the story. "We were hiking in the Sierras, close to King's Canyon in California. The terrain was rough and wild, but Angelica was a gazelle, skipping from rock to rock, until a storm moved in without warning. Our father rushed us down the mountain in the torrent that followed." He looked down, unable to meet his grandfather's eyes and cleared his throat.

"I was able to wade across a place where the waterfall pooled, but when I looked back toward Angelica, a mudslide hit the place where she clung to the mountain." He sighed. "We never found her."

Gabe tried to shield himself from the loss and pain the memory caused—the part where she had always defended him from his father's brutal ranting. And from his schoolmate's taunts of *pretty girl* because of his beautiful features. He had returned her loyalty with treachery.

Shutting his eyes against the image, Gabe straightened. "He never spoke more than a dozen civil words to me after that."

"Your father was always full of blame," Louis moaned, apparently lost in his recollections. "I can see this was hard for you, but thank you for telling me. I need to rest now."

Back in his room, Gabe fell into the blue overstuffed chair. He snatched his wallet from the end table and fished through the dark pockets until his fingers touched the slick edge of the small photo. It had been a long time since he brought Angelica's sixth-grade picture into the light.

As he studied her confidant face, a new sensation grew inside his gut. Anger seized him, pushing out the guilt. If she hadn't been showing off—if she'd stayed with them… Her decisions ruined his life.

Condemnation rushed back. *Nice try*. Would he now blame her? He shrugged. *No*. There had been enough blame. He refused to step into his father's shoes.

Staring at nothing, he fought against the certainty that if the courageous Conte Louis Dolcini—master horseman and proud patron of his family—knew the rest of the story, he would cancel the art exhibit and send him packing. Gabe would have no way of paying his bills. His mother would be left homeless. His stomach knotted against the threat that hovered just out of his control.

# Chapter 6

Siena, Italy

When would his past stay in the past? Though a blazing fire added ambiance to the dining room, none of its warmth reached Gabe while he waited at the table for dinner. He glanced through the large carved arch and listened. Louis spoke on the phone in the library, giving Gabe time to collect himself from the distressing afternoon.

Rinaldo set another platter on the table. When the call was finished, Louis entered the room and commenced with dinner. He seemed at peace compared to his anguish in the chapel this afternoon.

*At least one of them was.* In spite of the nervous twinges in his stomach, Gabe managed to consume a good portion of each course. Having overheard Louis' prayer, he realized he still knew very little about his grandfather. After taking a long drink, he asked, "How did you injure your leg?"

Louis shrugged his shoulders and grinned. "As a young man, I had no common sense and thought I was indestructible. I took it upon myself to break my own horses, until one of them broke me." He bit into a crust of bread, chewed, and swallowed. "My pride suffered more than my leg."

The simple explanation caught Gabe off-guard. This man embodied everything his father was not. He took failure in stride. Did not cast blame.

Rinaldo cleared their dishes and left the room. Gabe met the old man's anxious eyes. Louis spoke in a low tone. "I know your father tried to poison your opinion of me. Nevertheless, I let you tell your story, now will you let me tell mine?"

Gabe nodded. He wanted to know what his grandfather had done that was so horrific his father had shut him out of their lives. Ralph had been mute on the subject when he had visited. As far as Gabe could see, Louis was kind and generous. *Do I really want to know?* His gut tightened. *The truth could ruin everything.*

Louis cleared his throat and began. "There is a hill south of Siena called Montesiepi. In 1185, the Pope ordered a chapel built on its crest around a miracle—the authentic sword in the stone." He must have caught Gabe's smirk, for he was quick to add, "You do not have to take my word for it. You could drive there tomorrow."

After letting that settle, Gabe asked, "When you say stone, you mean it was cemented into the ground?"

"No. The stone is solid and the story is of the purely miraculous variety—unless some scientist can explain how the solid rock melted in that one specific place just in time for Galgano Guidotti to stick his blade into it—then immediately became solid again. So far, no assertions of that kind have been made."

The confidence with which he spoke silenced Gabe's logical retort.

"Through the centuries, people have gone to Montesiepi to try to pull the sword out. The legend was added to the King Arthur tales—a year *after* Galgano's miracle. A few years ago, vandals used a sledgehammer and broke off the hilt. However, they were caught, and the sword studied. Scientists verified it as twelfth century and reattached it to the blade. It is now protected with a transparent cover and iron bars."

Banking on a scientific explanation, Gabe let it go. "That's fascinating. I never considered the legend beginning anywhere besides the British Isles—or that the idea could have come from some historical...*story.*"

"Of course, there is still a measure of disagreement on that issue." Louis' eyes twinkled. "However, that is only the starting place of my story."

Hmm. With the beginning this eccentric, Gabe braced himself for the rest and downed the last of his hot tea.

"As the patron of the family, all of these treasures have passed into my care." Louis gestured at the paintings and fine antiques. "Along with the tangible things, there are also the intangible. These are what matter most. The history of every family member—along with their deeds, good or bad—has contributed to who we are."

He peered at Gabe. "Your father was headstrong, as you well know. He wanted nothing to do with his heritage, nothing to do with fulfilling his responsibility and passing these glorious stories to you and to your children's children. Gabriel Russo Dolcini, it is vital that you know these things."

The conte looked so intent, that Gabe nodded his head. He let out the breath he had been holding and leaned forward. "Tell me."

With evident relief, Louis smiled, easing years off his tired face. Clapping his hands together with anticipation, he rose to his feet. "Come with me."

Gabe followed the straight-backed man through an arched entry. Steps led downward, disappearing into the shadows. His grandfather flipped a switch that lit the sconces lining the stairwell. A host of carved brass snakes coiled around metal torches that illuminated the steps. An iron rail, hammered into an elegant twist, supported Louis. Gabe readied himself to steady the older man should he falter, but he never did. Soon, they were in a subterranean part of the palazzo that he had not yet explored.

They reached a massive oak door somewhere below ground, and Louis unlocked the ancient deadbolt with a brass key. Short of breath, he turned. "I must ask you something of gravest importance." He studied Gabe's eyes. "Before I expound upon the mission entrusted only to our family as the *Custodi*, the *Keepers*, you must promise to hold secret all that I show you. Will you keep this vow of silence?"

Though it seemed a bit cryptic, Gabe saw nothing particularly sinister about the request. He had never been a gossip. "Certainly."

His grandfather nodded, and his broad shoulders relaxed. They entered a cold room furnished with dark antique furniture. Natural stone tables had serpent-like beasts carved on their wooden legs, creating the creepy sense of something slithering up one's shins.

Louis stopped at one end of the room in front of a huge mirror that covered a six-by-ten-foot section of wall. The frame sported gilded birds of prey, their talons and beaks aimed toward their unsuspecting quarry. Gabe shivered as a chill passed through the room and into his body.

Sliding the leather toe of his expensive Italian shoe under a section of the mirror's frame, Louis pressed upward, initiating a series of clicking noises. "Just like in the movies," he grinned, then pressed the place again. He moved aside while the mirrored wall swung outward, allowing them to step over the threshold and pass into a large hidden room. Once inside, he switched on an electric candelabrum and closed the door with a lever.

In the ample glow, the nearly empty, castle-like room seemed to swallow them. A desk, two chairs, and a large globe, floating in its iron support, huddled together in one spot. On one wall, tall wooden shelves stood empty except for a few dozen books, stacks of paper, and small art objects.

All the architectural elements in the room—the floors, walls, and arches that held up the domed ceiling—were made of icy stone. The room retained a constant chill, and Gabe imagined he had landed in the middle ages. It was sinister. *And fabulous.* "What is this place?"

"This is where I keep those valuables I was speaking of—our family ancestry, ancient legal documents, and histories of objects we have acquired…or protect." I added this outer wall for safekeeping some years ago. He touched a thick leather book on a near shelf. "Our military records are here, with all their history."

Gabe leaned his head to one side for clarification.

Pride beamed from Louis' face. "One of our ancestors served as a Templar Knight."

"You approve of the Knights? Weren't they responsible for the wars, greed, and heresy of the medieval period?"

A shadow of disapproval passed over the older man. "There was much envy leveled against the Templars. And it is true that some deviated sharply from their vows. Later, when they became rich and powerful, there existed even more self-interest and corruption. But who of us has not wrestled with that?"

Gabe cleared his throat. "Yes, but I don't go around killing, pillaging, and dealing in the occult."

Louis' eyes held Gabe's with firm conviction. "The heresy charges were invented by evil men to discredit the Templars and steal their fortunes."

Gabe masked a shrug of disbelief. No sense arguing, as neither of them had been there.

Continuing his story, Louis said, "The majority of the Templars, in contrast to the crusaders, were pious and humble. They were pure in their motives to protect Christ's people from bandits on their pilgrimage to the Holy Land. And to guard articles pertaining to Christianity."

Again, Gabe felt perplexed that Louis held such a biased opinion. "Where does our family fit into all of this?"

Louis leaned his forearms on the back of a chair and clasped his fingers. "Like other noblemen of the day, your ancestor, Antonio Dolcini, left his family to join the Knights Templar. Beginning in 1177, he spent two years defending the Holy Land, but was appalled at the violence he found there. To add to his grief, charges of heresy and pagan worship had been directed at the Templars. He wrote to his wife about the moral decay in Jerusalem.

Louis' eyes closed while he quoted one of Antonio's letters. "We guard a solemn secret. That which has touched our Lord fills us with the hope that our broken bodies shall also be caught up in the resurrection. Yet the very object we protect with our lives and secrecy brings these charges upon us."

"You're speaking of the Holy Grail or lost Templar treasure?" Doubt laced Gabe's words.

"Possibly."

Gabe parried. "My studies of ancient *myths* show that the Holy Grail—just an ordinary cup really—was tracked to Spain, long before the time you are speaking of. It was then moved to Valencia in the fourteenth century." He cocked his head. "Where it still resides."

His grandfather donned a patient expression. "Please, sit down." He motioned toward one of the burgundy and gold brocade-covered chairs. A screech reverberated off the walls as Gabe dragged the chair over the rough, mottled stone.

The conte sat down in the opposing chair and continued. "Many stories exist. The first Templers spent years digging under the Temple Mount in the bowels of the mountain. They were guided to the exact locations where many important items were hidden."

"You don't really believe they found the authentic Holy Grail?"

"I am saying that Antonio brought back from Jerusalem what he described as, 'the desire of every Templar.'" His grandfather held his head high.

Gabe turned his gaze toward the enormous stones, cut to fit precisely together in the walls of the bleak cellar. He considered the conversation. In the faculty room, he had listened to Howard's scorn when teaching classes on ancient religious art and relics. Gabe remembered pitying the excitable freshmen.

Howard had mocked, "I can't comprehend that there are still those who believe in the possibility of the Grail's existence—or God's existence for that matter." Howard described his delight in dashing his student's hopes and ridiculing their faith with the historical facts at hand. "You'd think we still lived in the age of superstition and idol worship."

Gabe agreed with Howard, but this was his grandfather, and a man who held his artistic career in his hands. He decided to use logic and questions to bring the deluded man around to reason. "When you said they were *guided*, what did you mean?"

A smile seeped out from under the corner of Louis' short, white mustache. "They had a map."

# Chapter 7

Seborga, Italy, 1113 AD

Hunched under a low ridge in the bowels of the tomb, Secundus Cerilius' gnarled fingers gripped the handle of a lantern and held it high for his visitor. Though the flame burned hot, its light was all but absorbed in the chilling pallor in the realm of blackness and death.

Abbot Bernard grabbed the wool of his monk's habit and lifted it, negotiating the seeping steps as he descended into the sepulcher. His white robe swayed like a ghost in the shadows.

The scent from the dank, earthy floor closed in around Secundus, making him glad this particular crypt had not been the recipient of a recent guest. "Just this way." His voice quivered with the same apprehension that infused his body. Praying this was a wise decision, he lifted an iron key from his worn leather belt and inserted it into the lock. It turned with a grinding screech.

"How did you learn of this tale?" the young Bernard asked.

"My papa brought me to this cemetery before his death and persuaded me to join the *Custodi*." Secundus' lips thinned into a grim line and he pulled back his shoulders. "Our family is worth less than the sheep to the men who own this land, yet *we* were chosen to guard this holy relic. "I am the last of my family to take the oath. The rest are dead. I must pass on the secret." Gripping the bars of the iron gate that separated an alcove of death from the main crypt, he swung it open and turned back. With a raspy voice, he whispered so as not to wake the departed. "Abbot Bernard, I have your word?"

The monk frowned his displeasure.

Secundus stood his ground. "I have no children. Own nothing. The whole of my life has become this one duty. If I should misstep now, I will have failed the one task entrusted to me."

Bernard's voice stung with impatience. "I am a servant of God, old man. I swore your oath. This is not something I do heedlessly."

Secundus wondered if the holy man had even believed that something of value could reside in this forsaken land. Stooping low, he grunted while struggling to pull a block out of the wall just above the floor. He reached through the narrow opening and extracted a long leather bag. Strips of rigid leather lashed the bag and resisted his tremulous fingers as he untied them. He drew out two scrolls and laid them on a dusty coffin next to the lantern, then stepped away for the monk to open them.

Abbot Bernard's face held a measure of anticipation. The centuries-old scrolls were stiff. Secundus was thankful for the reverent way the abbot handled them, his fingers applying only enough pressure to keep the edges from curling again.

When the scroll was fully unrolled, Bernard's head pitched forward with amazement. He stared for long moments. Tears welled in his eyes and rolled down his cheeks when he dropped his head with a mumbled prayer. Raising his eyes, he asked, "How did this come to be?"

It was time for Secundus to retell the story that had come down through generations of his family. When he finished, the priest's eyes widened. "Where is it?"

Reaching for the second scroll, Secundus held one side and helped Bernard unroll it. "It is safely buried in the Holy Land. My ancestor was a Roman soldier. When the Persians overran Jerusalem, he fled to our home and hid this map here." Secundus shifted his weight and watched the holy man in the flickering light. Would he protect it as he had sworn?

Silence filled the vault. Studying the ancient document, the abbot traced the lines and stopped. He tapped his finger on the spot indicated on the map. A smile twisted his lips.

# Chapter 8

Siena, Italy, Present Day

The chill of the cold cellar floor seeped up through Gabe's shoes. His toes stiffened and curled, matching the tension in his stomach. His perception of his grandfather assured him the man had a sound mind, yet an intelligent person would not fall for this kind of fairy tale. He appraised the man and challenged, "And where did they get this map?"

Louis did not flinch at the skeptical tone of the question. "We know that Saint Bernard, after leaving France, where he had taken a vow of poverty with the Cistercian order of monks, visited the small village of Seborga in the northwest of what is now Italy. He was shown something extraordinary.

"Immediately, he sent for two trusted Cistercian monks, Gondemar and Rossal, to help protect a *great secret*. Saint Bernard then had Edward, the Prince-Abbot of Seborga, anoint the monks, along with seven others, creating nine warrior-monks—the *first* Knights Templar!" Louis raised his eyebrows in excitement. "He then commissioned them to go to the Holy Land."

His grandfather's eagerness to tell the story grew—along with Gabe's resistance.

"They arrived in Jerusalem with the great secret—a map that revealed where the fleeing believers had hidden their most precious relics before the Persians razed the city."

A musty scent drifted to Gabe's consciousness, matching the stale story. "Did they ever tell anyone how a map from Jerusalem came to be in Italy?"

Interpreting his question as interest, his grandfather continued to expound on what he knew. "That remains unclear, but we have the proof that it did happen."

Fingering the layered threads of brocade on the arm of his chair, Gabe realized this must be what Ralph had meant. He wondered if his grandfather had also plied his father with this story. "So, you're saying they used the map and found the fabulous Templar treasure in the rubble under the Dome of the Rock."

Louis studied him. "The Templers were not after treasure—which they did find by the way. No, their objective involved something much more precious."

"Let me guess, the Holy Grail, the cross of Christ, the Ark of the Covenant, Longinus' spear, and what else, the Ten Commandments?"

Louis cringed.

Gabe regretted his sarcasm as soon as it came out of his mouth. He softened his voice. "I'm sorry, Grandfather, but these stories have abounded for centuries and have been discounted as we have learned the *facts*. No scientific mind would embrace the belief in their existence."

Sighing, Louis said, "Blessed are those who believe without seeing." He studied Gabe. "Do you believe Jesus lived on earth and died a cruel death to pay the penalty for our sins?"

Gabe flinched. *Where did that come from?* It had been a long time since he had considered his own beliefs. When Angelica used to take his hand and pray at bedtime, he had sensed a sweet presence. Even more so when their mother took them to church to hear the choir. He frowned. "It was hard to believe in a loving God when my father was so harsh." Anxiety tightened his chest as unwanted memories bombarded him. After Angelica died…after he watched her terrified mouth open and fill with mud…*there couldn't be a god.*

Gabe shook his head. "No. There is no proof that Jesus lived—only the hearsay of some ignorant fishermen playing on the gullibility of people who needed hope of a hereafter." The words rushed out with the force of resentment. He felt a rapid increase in his pulse.

Louis nodded. "I see." He looked thoughtful. "What if I could prove it to you?"

Gabe sat in silence, his lips tense with frustration.

Louis steepled his fingers. "The secret our family hides—is custodian of—is said to bestow courage *and* faith." Louis watched Gabe with hopeful eyes. "It was brought to Italy and hidden in 1179, its location lost until forty-two years ago. I found the documents describing where it is concealed—here, in this cellar. You can imagine my amazement to discover the great honor bestowed on our family centuries ago. Yes, we manage much wealth, but this, Gabriel, this is a divine assignment."

Gabe stared wide-eyed at the ecstasy in his grandfather's face.

Chagrined, Louis cleared his throat and reined in his fervor. "I know it must sound strange. It did to me at first. But the more I studied the documents, the more they made sense." He let his eyes fall to the stone floor and his voice quieted. "In my enthusiasm, I was not careful. My pride led to the death of my Christina."

His furtive glance fell short of meeting Gabe's eyes. "I have tried for four decades to unravel the mystery and fulfill my duty as a *custode*. Perhaps I am trying to vindicate my actions and prove I am not *pazzo*, crazy." His shoulders slumped. "But I am old now, and still no closer. It is time to pass this charge to you."

Shaking his head, Gabe objected. "Sir, this is not something I have any interest in. I'm sorry."

Anger flashed from Louis for the first time. "This is not some hobby that you choose or do not choose. It is not about twelve pretty paintings, Gabriel. People have been tortured and killed protecting this." His eyes blazed with passion.

Gabe stood. "So, my life has no value? My paintings are just cute wall hangings? Is that what you're saying?"

Louis' voice quieted. "That is not what I meant to say. But some things are bigger than ourselves." His grandfather shook his head.

"Enough. I need to rest."

Gabe fumed as he trailed behind Louis up the steep stairway. Why was the man so willing to destroy another relationship with his outlandish tales? Had he not learned a dire lesson? Resentment settled into disappointment over the downward spiral this ridiculous quest had imposed on their relationship. The last few days had warmed a frozen place in Gabe's heart. The door of trust had cracked open. Now he could hear it clanging shut again.

His mother was right. Louis was obsessed. His father's scornful voice chided Gabe from the grave for opening his heart to a lunatic. Gabe watched Louis struggle up the stairs, one at a time and wanted to reach out and support him. He cared greatly for this man, but they lived in separate realities.

Unlike his father, however, he would not reject his family because they were flawed. Rethinking his outburst, he realized that it was easier to say the words than to live them.

# Chapter 9

Siena, Italy

Anger and regret still lingered the following morning and took turns tormenting Gabe's emotions. He drummed his fingers on the dining table. Maybe Louis would be more sensible today. Rinado set a basket of croissants on the table, along with a plate of meat and cheese.

"Is Louis coming down for breakfast?"

"The conte frequently rests for hours at a time after over-exertion—or distress. His hopes have been quite high since you agreed to come see him."

Gabe glanced up. The servant's lips were tight with unspoken criticism. *Great. Get in line.* Tipping his cup, Gabe drank his espresso in silence. His thoughts moved through Louis' conversation. What did he mean about causing his grandmother's death? Surely, that was a figure of speech. Hearing the workers begin the day's chores of readying the ballroom, Gabe pushed back his chair.

Rinaldo removed his plate and asked, "What do you hope to gain here?"

Gabe's head jerked around. "What do you mean?"

"Just that."

It was an honest question as far as Gabe could tell. "I don't mean to sound arrogant, but I believe my work is truly exceptional. I suppose I want that validation from the professionals in my field. If I can gain

51

international status in the art world, the value of my paintings will increase substantially." He held Rinaldo's eyes. "I don't need to be rich, but I do need to pay off some pressing debt."

"What will you do after that?"

Gabe shrugged "Paint more canvases."

"And then?"

Gabe's lips tensed. "Then? I don't know."

Rinaldo nodded and left the room.

Heading toward the frantic activity on the second story, Gabe's feet echoed on the solid marble steps. He stepped into the ballroom and stared at the transformation. A frown accompanied his frustration. Rinaldo's questions irked him, but another stabbed at his conscience. Was it too much to humor the old man? *Look at all he's doing for you.* His frown deepened. *And all he can take away.* Dependence was dangerous.

Serena's upbeat voice pulled him out of his mental arguments. "Your main piece should be here, just as the guests round the corner and think they have seen it all, *eh?*" She raised an eyebrow for his approval.

He traced his steps back across the intricate cobalt blue and white tiles to the arched entry and started through the grand ballroom again. Imagining the position of each painting, he maneuvered around the twenty-foot ficus trees brought from the conservatory.

Hand-carved alabaster vases, some five-feet in height, held Cymbidium orchids, exotic bird-of-paradise blooms from Hawaii, plus other unfamiliar foliage. He touched one of the soft, glossy leaves and turned in a circle to take it all in. Bobbing in the fans, the plants toyed with the eye, creating friendly barriers to break up the space.

Serena had created a temporary courtyard in the center of the room where guests could find expensive *antipasti.* He grinned at the fascinating transformation. Strolling through the living maze, he came around the last corner where Serena stood. She was right. It was the perfect place to display *Il Viso.* He grinned, imagining the glory that would be his on Saturday evening.

"You are wanted at the front door," Rinaldo informed him. Half of his upper lip lifted in a distasteful expression.

Opening the door, Gabe was surprised to find Ralph slung over one of the marble benches that adorned the portico. "Hey, what's up?"

Ralph turned. "Hello, mate. Thought I'd come by to see your work, if the old man ain't around."

Gabe checked behind him. What harm would it cause? "Sure." He wondered why he felt sneaky as they climbed the stairs.

Stepping into the large ballroom, Ralph whistled. "Hey man, you're somethin'." He walked slowly around the room and stopped in front of *Il Viso*. His jaw dropped. "Where'd you get the idea for this one?"

"It just came to me."

Ralph eyed him. "Right." He raised his chin. "How 'bout I take you to town. Nothin' worse than being holed up with the old man and his ghosts."

Gabe nodded, noticing the tension that gripped his neck and shoulders. He needed to get out of here. They walked a few blocks in the September sunshine and entered a local bar.

Ralph ordered a few rounds of sparkling prosecco as they talked. Gabe gulped the sweet bubbly wine like water. It had been a long time since he felt so relaxed—quite numb actually. "What's the name of your band?" he asked, after Ralph filled him in on the gig he had just finished.

Ralph tipped his head back, cradling it in his clasped fingers. "We've been called, *The Street Gang*, but I'm thinkin' about renamin' us, *The Kestrals*, after a friend o' mine—you know, hunters of sorts."

A thick fog filled Gabe's mind. "*Kestral?* That's the name of that art thief."

Grinning widely, Ralph changed the subject. "So, how's Louis doing—his health okay? I'd ask him myself but he's hard as nails, that one. Reminds me of your dad in a big way—no quarter, no forgiveness."

Gabe's carefree mood slipped away. Why did Ralph always bring up his father? "He's resting...too caught up in the past, I think."

"I should've warned you about his stories." Ralph smirked. "What's he saying this time?"

After downing the last of his prosecco, Gabe laughed. "Says he's got a map where some Templar treasure is buried—something that makes you courageous."

The smirk left and Ralph looked deadly serious. Serious enough to sober Gabe up a bit. "Did he tell you where it is?" He leaned in and listened.

"Ah, come on, you don't believe that stuff, do you?" Gabe's voice was too edgy to cover his deception.

Ralph eyed him and sat back. "Na, just fun t' hear the old man's ramblin's." He looked past Gabe and out the front window of the bar. His nostrils flared and his lips tightened.

In the mirror, Gabe saw two men sitting at a café across the small *piazza*. The next door over, a thin, mustached man stood at a counter, reading a newspaper. *Why did he look so familiar?* The hair prickled under Gabe's shirtsleeve, but he was too numb to pay much attention.

Ralph pushed his chair back. "Need to get going, man." He slapped Gabe on the back—harder than necessary.

Still studying the mirror, Gabe watched Ralph step onto the stone street and turn quickly to his left. After a moment, the two men—one built tall and thin like Ralph, the other bulky—set down their cups and followed him. Gabe moved toward the door and caught his toe on the threshold. Grabbing the doorjamb to steady himself, he searched for Ralph and the men, but they had already disappeared from sight. The mustached man had gone as well.

Feeling self-conscious, Gabe held himself erect and watched his step on his way back to the palazzo. A nagging thought in the back of his muddled mind wondered why there was so much interest in a myth.

## 

Gabe awoke from a recovery nap and was the first to arrive in the library in time for *antipasto*. Uncertain how to face Louis, he picked up a carrot and mused aloud. "How did he get so involved in this obsession?"

"Perhaps our obsessions choose us?" Rinaldo's presence startled him.

"You sound like a philosopher."

Rinaldo shrugged, "It is an interest of mine."

"What did you mean?"

"There are times when destiny transcends coincidence. I believe your path has merged with your grandfather's for an important reason."

Gabe was about to ask him to explain, but Louis entered the library. Rinaldo set a plate of basil and cheese *bruschetta* on the delicate table and left. After finishing a slice, Gabe walked to a shelf where a wedding photo sat. "Is this my grandmother?"

"*Si.*" A troubled expression crossed Louis' face and he dropped his eyes.

"Sir, what did you mean about the Contessa dying because of the secret—was that symbolic?"

Louis sighed, his face sad. "No, Gabriel. It was a very real thing. It is the reason my children left and had nothing to do with me."

The grief in Louis' voice tugged at Gabe. He surveyed the spacious room, unoccupied except for the two of them. Before he arrived, even this chair would have been empty, leaving his grandfather alone with his memories. *For forty years.* Gabe's jaw clenched in bitterness against his father's cruelty. "What happened?"

Rinaldo returned with another *antipasto* dish. He set it down and dusted the crumbs.

"*Grazie*, Rinaldo."

The butler nodded, "*Si*, conte."

When they were alone, Louis answered. "I should start further back for the story to make sense. Would you indulge me?"

Gabe nodded, but apprehension tightened his gut. *Not again.*

"When the first Knights Templar arrived in Jerusalem, they dug to the locations listed on the Seborgan map. Some sights had already been looted, possibly when the Persians destroyed most of the Christian buildings and objects they found. Nevertheless, the knights were able to recover many silver and gold articles of worship, as well as secular items.

"Then in 1126, the Templars found something of even more value—that which they had been charged to find. That is the secret we are sworn to protect."

Gabe attempted patience. "You're saying they found the Holy Grail?"

Louis tilted his head to one side. "Faith, Gabriel. You will see." They finished the *antipasti* and he led Gabe to the dining room where sumptuous plates of food waited.

Resistant to the faith aspect, Gabe probed for more information after dinner. "How did our ancestor get involved with all of this?"

"Antonio trained with the other knights in Jerusalem and carried out his duties patrolling the roads." Louis pushed his chair away from the table and stood. "We will go back downstairs, *eh?*"

Fighting his resistance, Gabe conceded, determined to make up for his father's unconscionable behavior.

At night, a frigid hostility seemed to encompass Gabe in the chilly cavern. Once inside the secret room, they sat down, and Louis continued the story. "As I told you, in his first letters home, Antonio told of the disappointment he had in the lack of piety among his equals. Greed instigated unnecessary violence between the Templars and Crusaders."

Louis reached under the side of his chair and moved what seemed to be a latch. When he rose, the seat flipped open, and he lifted a fine leather sheath from the hollow seat. He looked up and grinned. "However, a year into his service, Antonio's wife received a letter with a different sentiment entirely."

Opening the leather folder, Louis removed several sheets of muted parchment. "These are letters from Antonio, which I have transcribed for you. He spread them for Gabe to see, then picked one up, dated 1178, and read it aloud.

*"My dearest Helena,*

*I know I have written tiresome letters of my outrage at the state of savagery that I have encountered in the Holy City, yet today everything has changed. At mass, where I am usually found in the dark before sunrise, a pious Templar took me aside to speak privately. I am not able to reveal to you what he said, nor what my eyes beheld, but let me say that before today I had not the faith that now so richly resides in me.*

*Previously I had only heard rumors about a secret that would increase one's faith, make one invincible in battle, a secret that had blessed the*

*Templars with wealth beyond measure. Helena, it is true!*

*Please show this letter to no one. Though I am convinced I have not broken a word of my vow by sharing this with you, it is my desire to keep this between us. I long to see you, my beauty.*

*With utmost devotion,*

*Antonio"*

"So why was Antonio chosen to bring back such a great secret?" Gabe was surprised at the hint of interest apparent in his voice.

The smug look on his grandfather's face showed his delight in being able to relay his fascinating story. He set the letter aside and lifted another, summarizing it. "By 1179, the Muslims solidified under Saladin, the Sultan of Egypt and Syria at the time. Saladin attacked the Crusaders at Jacob's Ford, a crusader castle built on the west bank of the River Jordan, north of the Sea of Galilee."

"I know this story, sir. The walls were breached and the crusaders were massacred."

Louis nodded. "*Si*, you know your history. But what you do not know is that your ancestor, Antonio Dolcini, was with King Baldwin when they arrived, too late to help. After Saladin's victory, Jerusalem was extremely vulnerable to capture. Baldwin made the decision to fulfill Saint Bernard's order, that if the relic ever left Jerusalem, it was to be transported to Seborga. King Baldwin disguised the relic and commanded Antonio to take it to Seborga where a stronghold of Cistercian Templars resided, ready to protect it."

"Then why didn't Antonio take it there?"

"He had every intention of doing so. After passing through Rome, however, he realized he was being followed. We only know this because another Templar sent word to Helena of their encounter—Galgano Guidotti, the knight who plunged the sword into the stone."

THE PROOF

# Chapter 10

Brindisi, Italy, 1179 AD

The journey from Jerusalem to Italy had been long and grueling, yet only one incident gave Antonio Dolcini possible cause for alarm. While exiting the boat in the port city of Brindisi, the hair on his arms raised in a tingling sensation. Pretending to be preoccupied with his luggage, he stole glances at the docks and caught sight of two men redirecting their attention away from him. *Crusaders.*

Antonio had seen one of them in Israel, north of Haifa Bay, then again when the crusader boarded at Acre in a second ship that followed his own to Brindisi. Both crusaders wore black surcoats emblazoned with King Frederick Barbarossa's black lion. The smaller knight's ruddy complexion and red hair revealed his likely kinship to the German king.

Alerted by Antonio, his two companions, also Templars, busied themselves saddling their horses while they kept their eyes on the strangers. The red-haired crusader and his companion soon disappeared. Still, Antonio and his men stayed on their guard for several days after departing from the port and throughout their time in Rome.

Once they left Rome, however, Antonio's shoulders relaxed, and he swayed in the saddle, matching the rhythm of his horse. He was in good spirits. In contrast to hot desert sands, a tempest-tossed ship, and nights spent picking sharp rocks from under his sleeping mat, he had slept on a real bed of straw in the holy city. Now, with new supplies and their bellies full, he and his knights rode toward their destination—their cargo cloaked and out of sight.

Three leagues outside the chaos that permeated Rome, Antonio expelled a long sigh. Reaching behind his saddle, he touched the sacred object for reassurance. The peace of his own countryside refreshed him after living two years in the parched lands surrounding Jerusalem. He could taste home.

Scanning the line between earth and sky, he noted that their path northward was clear. To the west, however, clouds obscured the horizon. As their journey progressed through the day, the ominous clouds thickened and darkened. Antonio studied the fortified village of Magliano Sabina that crouched on the proud cliffs to their right. Choosing to bypass the large commune, and possible questions, he led his men through the flat valley.

Less than a league beyond the village, however, he hesitated. Lightning bolted to the ground and the storm hastened closer. He glanced behind them, struggling to decide their course. Ahead of them, the sky looked foreboding. "We may as well turn back and take shelter in Magliano tonight."

Their horses reacted to the electricity in the air, dancing and tossing their heads while the men headed for shelter. The wind increased, whipping Antonio's hair into his leathered face. He reached to brush a tangled strand from his eyes when his horse shied.

Out of nowhere, six riders charged at them from both sides. Their roars accompanied the pounding of their horses' hooves as they neared. Drawing his sword in one swift move, Antonio twisted his horse around to face the attackers. *Crusaders!*

They reached one of his men first. The brave knight fought hard, but he was overwhelmed. He slew one ruffian before the others cut him down. His frantic horse reared and dragged him away from the fight.

Antonio cried out, "Lord, be our champion. Preserve *Il Testamento!*" Great courage filled him. He and the remaining Templar struck and turned, breaking the deadly thrusts of their assailants' swords. They were pressed into a tight circle, anticipating almost certain doom, when a war cry erupted from the direction of the village.

The attention of the combatants instantly diverted from the battle to see an unknown Templar charging toward them. Four of their enemies turned to answer the newcomer's charge, but one villain took the opportunity to thrash out at Antonio's remaining companion, knocking the man to the ground with a fatal blow.

With lightning fury, Antonio plunged his sword into the throat of his foe and charged after the men who were attacking the unidentified knight. He need not have bothered, for in the moments it took him to travel the distance, the bold knight had slain two men, while the others deserted the field of combat.

Whipping his horse around, Antonio scanned for the fleeing crusaders, but the darkened terrain masked their retreat. He drew in great gulps of air and rode to where the horse had dragged his friend. The knight lay dead.

Antonio crossed himself and prayed for the man—a faithful brother during the years he had spent in the Holy Land. He rose and held out his hand to the powerful knight who strode toward him. "Thank you, brother. I am Antonio Dolcini of Siena. You saved my wife from becoming a widow this day."

"Galgano Guidotti of Chiusdino," the knight said, and grasped the outstretched hand of friendship.

Antonio shook his head at the bodies. "I have not seen slaughter like this since leaving Jerusalem."

A crack of thunder heightened the havoc of the night. The clouds opened and sheets of rain drenched the scene. Antonio and Galgano searched the fallen crusaders, but found little to identify them. "Look at this," Galgano said. He wrenched the sword from one of the men. It was near one cubit in length.

"Blackhearts," Antonio said in disgust. The black cross on the steel pommel was easily identifiable. He turned the crusader over. A black lion emblazoned a gold background. "Barbarossa, the Holy Roman Emperor." They could have only wanted one thing. He wiped the steady rain from his eyes. "Let's leave these men for the scavengers, but I must bury my friends."

They worked late into the night, fighting the rain and mud. After laying the knights' bodies and their possessions in shallow graves, they covered them with stones. Antonio prayed over the two men, who had no family that he knew of. Brave souls lost into obscurity. Unseen, save by their God.

The new comrades returned to the village of Magliano Sabina and took refuge in a hovel that was warmed by the hearth in the gathering room below. They talked for over an hour. Antonio raised his eyebrows in surprise to learn that Galgano's family owned a vineyard near one of his own outside of the mountain town of Monticiano.

Though Antonio had not been active in the running of his estate, he enjoyed the fruit it yielded. From Galgano's tales of brawling throughout the countryside, it sounded as if he indulged to excess.

## 

"There were *six* of you—twice as many as them," Abbot Lorenzo Casselli raged. He glared down his beaked nose at the shamed faces of the two crusaders who had returned. Without the relic. The *Soci*, a distinguished order that had recently accepted him into their clandestine group, would not be pleased.

## 

The fair-haired Haydn, smaller than his companion and just fifteen years of age, stood tongue-tied. He studied Lorenzo's black slippers as they pressed into the patterns in the pretty rug and wondered how such thin leather survived.

Many strange sights had filled his eyes since he arrived in Palombara for duty. In his village, the priest wore the plain robes of a pauper, his feet shod with simple but sturdy sandals. He wondered how this abbot's footwear had lasted through the day's journey from Rome to his new position here at the Abbey of Saint John.

Oberon, his older companion, attempted to explain their defeat. Bad idea. The fist of Haydn's father had taught him to keep quiet in volatile times.

Abbot Lorenzo reached out and slapped Oberon's cheek. "That is for your failure. You are lucky I have not ordered you run through."

From beneath his bent head, Haydn chanced a furtive glance at the abbot. In addition to the fury, he saw fear.

"I assured Pope Innocent—and King Barbarrosa—that I would have possession of the relic in days, but now..."

A boastful knock on the abbot's door preceded the heavy tromp of a huge, black-bearded knight. The coat of arms of King Barbarossa adorned his black surcoat. His commanding presence caused Lorenzo to cringe when the giant confronted him.

"What do you mean by sending out a force before I arrived?" He scowled down, inches from the bridge of the abbot's nose.

"Sir Rafer, when I did not hear from you, the *Primo Consul* forced me to send out another company."

Rafer's eyes narrowed. "So instead of waiting, you sent out a band of incompetents and failed."

With an accusing finger, Lorenzo straightened and pointed at the two crusaders. "These are the cowards who failed to bring it back." Haydn wedged sideways an inch behind Oberon.

Rafer took a single stride toward them and peered down into Oberon's face. "What happened?"

Haydn admired Oberon's steady voice while he answered the scary face of Rafer. There was only a slight warble in his last sentence when he explained why they left the fight.

"Had we stayed, we would have perished without you ever knowing the location of the relic."

Haydn thought that a wise answer. At least it caused a pause in the shouting that had filled the abbot's fine office.

The king's knight pulled roughly at his black beard. He narrowed his eyes with a scowl. "Where do you suppose they are now?"

## ##

Dry and rested, Antonio rose to a magnificent sunrise framed by the hilltops of Magliano Sabina. He sold his knight's horses and tied his bundle to the back of his saddle. Then he and Galgano mounted their steeds and traversed the steep path down to the valley. They neared the crossroad that would take them north to Siena.

"Were you in the Holy Land?" Antonio asked.

"I was on my way when I came across you last night."

Antonio appraised the man and the situation, praying silently for guidance. "I need a strong knight to escort me on my task. It appears as though God has sent you."

Galgano studied the road that led south to Rome. Strands of his curly blond hair waved in the light breeze. Antonio understood his hesitancy. The knight had been on his way to Jerusalem for war and glory. Although Antonio's rank allowed him to command Galgano, he took the time to entice him.

"From the conflict last night, it is probable that more battles are to come. It will be a dangerous journey." He rubbed his chin. "My mission requires the utmost courage and secrecy. I perceive that you are not only a valiant fighter, but a man of integrity."

Galgano swung his head around. His puzzled brows wrinkled his broad forehead. "Do you mock me?"

Antonio held his gaze. "No, sir. You have already proven your worth."

Slowly, Galgano nodded his head. "I will join you."

Antonio administered the oath of the *Custodi* as it had been given to him, joining Galgano to the *Custodi Del Testamento*. Then he explained the secret he harbored. He opened his pack.

When Galgano gazed into the leather sack, the new *custode's* powerful legs buckled, dropping him to the ground. Mouth agape, his astonished eyes flew upward, full of questions. Antonio understood.

## ##

The Templars were two days from Siena, camped under the shelter of a thick, leafy canopy on the western side of a heavily wooded hill. In the morning, Galgano packed their horses while Antonio trudged through the brush to the top of a low mount to scan the terrain.

He jerked to attention when he spied the flapping black surcoats of several riders racing from the south. The crusaders were close. Too close. He dashed through the brush and over the rocks, down to their horses.

The two Templars secured the rest of their gear to their packs and fled. They had been fortunate in their first battle, but there were only two of them now. While they galloped away, Antonio shouted, "It appeared as though half a dozen crusaders are following us."

They had planned to stay in Siena at Antonio's palazzo before completing the last leg of their mission to the church in Seborga. This new threat, however, forced them to change their plans. *Il Testamento* had to be protected.

Leaving the main route north, they made their way west through the densely forested mountains, heading toward Galgano's home in Chiusdino. Hoping to elude their adversaries, they picked a path through oak trees, rocks, and brush, being careful to avoid the notice of any rural residents. They could not hazard drawing attention from anyone in these parts.

Under the blanket of night, they had sidestepped the killers. For now. They set up camp by a place Galgano called "Montesiepi." Galgano grinned and walked toward the side of the mountain. "As a boy, I discovered a cave to hide from my father. As a man, it became a place to avoid everyone."

Antonio followed him through a narrow opening concealed by dense vegetation. Inside, they explored a rocky grotto. Galgano shredded a rag, placed it on a stick of wood, and lit a torch. He led Antonio near the rear of the cave to a side cavern.

One section of wall was made of lighter colored stone than the rest of the cave. Some of the stones had fallen away, creating a niche large enough for their cargo. Antonio nodded. "This will do." He left to retrieve the thick leather hide that held the beloved *Il Testamento*, then carried it back to the hiding place. After setting the sack into the niche, the two guardians replaced the rocks and soil around it. Antonio glanced around, making note of the location. This section of white rock conjured the sense of a beam of light shooting down from the ceiling.

Still anxious, the men took turns sleeping during the night. Near daybreak, Antonio had just rolled over in an attempt to gain some relief from a persistent stone when Galgano called out a warning. The horses snorted, announcing the half-expected approach of strangers.

Antonio grabbed his sword, casting a backward glance toward his charge. He leapt out of the cave and emerged from behind the brush. One large crusader issued a final threat at Galgano and raised his lethal sword. Antonio rushed forward, bracing to meet the enemy.

## 

Flying furiously into battle, Galgano met the first attack in the early morning light. The extraordinary power with which he fought amazed him. Antonio joined the fight, protecting his back as the two Templars swirled in deadly grace, lunging and slicing their six attackers. The battle was quick. The less experienced foes fell easily. Five lay unmoving on the bloodied soil, but the sixth, a man with an enormous black beard, escaped.

The Templars fell against the side of the cave, gasping for air. Antonio winced and grabbed his leg where blood flowed freely from a slash. Galgano helped him lie down and wrapped it tightly. "Lie still while I dispose of this mess," he directed.

He stripped the men and used his horse to drag the naked bodies away from the cave for the evening scavengers. Gathering the clothing, swords, and shields into a heap outside the cave, he rolled a number of rocks down onto them.

After helping Antonio onto his horse, they led the crusader's horses away from the area before letting them loose. With only one able fighter, the two *custodi* left their priceless burden in the cave, planning to retrieve it after Antonio healed. No doubt, they would be ambushed again.

## 

In the modest, but comfortable home of Galgano's family in Chiusdino, Antonio waited through days of boredom for his leg to heal. Galgano's mother was kind enough to furnish him with parchment and pen. He wrote a letter to his wife, Helena, informing her of his injury and reiterating how much he missed her and his two sons.

Less than a week passed when a servant knocked on the door, reporting that a large bearded man had entered Chiusdino asking for the whereabouts of two Templar Knights.

Galgano explained to Antonio, "The villagers fear me. They will not cooperate with the stranger." Still, Antonio worried about their curiosity. Galgano's servants kept him informed as the stranger moved through the nearby towns, offering a reward for knowledge of the knights. Talk had begun about a holy relic carried from Jerusalem. Rumors began to spread that the Holy Chalice of Christ was hidden in their region.

Considering the looming probability of his death, Galgano left to see his fiancé, Polissena, promising to return within three days. Alone, Antonio fretted, occupied with his aching leg and dark thoughts. There was no way he could protect *Il Testamento* here. He needed a plan.

The following day, he grimaced as he mounted his horse and rode with great stealth back to the cave to carry out his strategy. It took all his strength to move through the cave and locate *Il Testamento* to complete his task.

Sweating from the effort and the excruciating pain in his leg, he pushed himself to travel the few miles from Montesiepi to his family's vineyard at Monticiano. He sent the unobtrusive caretaker to Helena in Siena with a bulky package and a map of instructions disguised as a letter. Antonio's strength spent, he returned to Chiusdino before Galgano returned.

## ##

"*More* men?" Abbot Lorenzo scoffed. "What was this—six to two?"

Rafer made a start toward him, sending the abbot stumbling back over a table leg. Gathering himself, Lorenzo remembered his position and attempted an offensive posture. "Pope Innocent waits—trapped in that fortress." He threw out his arm and pointed a shaky finger up the mountain at the fortified bell tower. "How long do you think his guards can hold, once that anti-pope, Alexander, sends his soldiers to dispose of him? You must get the relic. Pope Innocent's supporters will see it as a sign from God that he is the rightful pope. If the *Soci* do not produce it, I fear Innocent will be lost—and us with him."

Fury contorted Rafer's face. "Do you have the men?" he repeated through gritted teeth.

Distress evident in his voice, Abbot Lorenzo replied, "I will give you all I can spare, but we need every able fighter to hold the tower."

Rafer shoved several gold coins in front of the abbot's face, along with the note sent from him weeks ago. "More gold is to come?"

"Certainly. Not to mention the personal favor of our new pope and King Barbarossa."

Rafer nodded, crammed the gold back into his pouch, and stomped outside. A short time later, Lorenzo scrutinized the men he appointed to go with Rafer and frowned. A feeble lot, including the scrawny boy, Haydn. But with eight fighters and the element of surprise, the odds were on their side.

## ##

On an unusually warm October morning, Galgano's servant brought a disturbing report. Strangers had congregated with a townsman near Chiusdino the night before, then headed east. "Sir, my son heard the leader threaten to come back if he doesn't find his quarry. I followed them to a spot near Montesiepi."

There was no way around this threat. Desperate to comply with his vow, Galgano prepared for the battle. He rode out with Antonio to confront the trespassers. From a hill, they spied out the assassins, camped near the base of the mount.

"Watch out for that one." Antonio pointed out the bearded fighter who had deserted their previous battle. His frame stood large above the rest.

Galgano nodded, fire pulsing through his veins. He mounted his horse and kicked. They charged toward the waiting foe. Galgano was the first to feel the impact of the enemy's sword on his own. Antonio appeared to his right and fought with ferocity to avenge his fallen brothers and to protect their secret.

Five of their enemies were down. When Galgano drew back his sword to attack the last of his combatants, he saw the man was only a flaxen-haired boy, yet he continued his forward thrust, decapitating the youth.

He twisted around to see Antonio's brave attempt to ward off two attackers, one of them the huge black-bearded giant. In a moment, it was over.

The crusaders cut Antonio from both sides.

Grief, fear, and rage filled Galgano. "NO," he roared and rushed them. His sword moved like lightning, severing the smaller man's sword arm. The man cried out, eyes wide with shock and pain.

In the next instant, Galgano planted his heel in the giant's gut, throwing him off balance. The bearded man roared and charged forward again. Galgano bent away from the thrust of the crusader's sword, then whipped back around for the kill. The crusader turned and stared in surprise when Galgano's sword plunged under his ribs and out his back.

Ripping his sword from the dying man's body, Galgano grabbed a handful of the man's hair and exposed his neck. With a quick slice, it was done. He then stepped to the wounded man and ended his moans.

Sucking in great gulps of air, Galgano shoved their bodies aside and bent over his friend. Antonio's life eased out of him. With his last gasp, he uttered one word, "Helena." His eyes glazed as he left this world.

Grief overtook Galgano for the first time in his rebellious life. He looked at the slaughter. Around him lay his friend, the dead soldiers, and the headless boy. Groaning from deep in his soul, he rose and began to search through the bloodied tunics. A pouch dangled from the bearded knight's belt. Opening it, he discovered a letter folded around several gold coins. It confirmed the reason for the attack.

*...It has been made known to us that a small band of Templar Knights is in possession of a great relic, recently brought from Jerusalem...*

Galgano crumpled the letter and threw it on the ground. *Hired assassins.* So much bloodshed, yet what did it accomplish? How many more of these messengers would he have to vanquish? He looked toward the cave where Antonio hid the glorious object. What now? He had sworn to protect *Il Testamento*.

A sudden light blinded him. He plummeted to the ground. With shaking fingers protecting his eyes, he blinked. A mighty angel stood before him. Galgano's body trembled at the certainty of retribution for these deaths.

"I am the angel, Michael. Arise."

Immobilized with fear, it took long moments before Galgano could force his legs to support him. He kept his head bowed, waiting.

The angel was brief. "You are loved, but you have wasted the life your Father gave you."

When no other words were uttered, Galgano lifted his head and twisted around. No one was there. Though the noonday sunlight filled the sky, it seemed dull after the brightness of the visitation. Had he imagined the angel?

Seeing the dead bodies, he knew their blood was real. Their souls probably battled in hell at this moment. Over the course of his wayward life, he had caused a trail of pain. And now this. Leaving the scene, he took hours to catch the enemies' horses, strip them and scare them away. Away from the carnage.

Returning to the cave entrance, he knelt down by Antonio and closed his friend's eyes. He began to weep, his groans of regret breaking the silence of the early night until he rolled to his side, his strength spent.

## 

Galgano heard the morning before his eyes opened. He sat up. Mice rustled in the briars and birds jumped and flitted after bugs, or just sat in the trees to sing. His soul resonated with the song, a small note at first, but then it swelled like a choir. His lips turned up in a forgotten expression.

Had he ever smiled, not jeered or heckled? A sweetness he had not known poured like oil from his head to his heart. Humbly, he rolled up onto his knees, clasping his rough hands together to give praise.

He shuddered. Blood from yesterday's battle remained in dried layers on his fingers. He looked down at his white tunic. Dark stains eclipsed the red cross. Unable to ask for forgiveness, he hung his head and arose to bury the bodies.

He dragged the mercenaries past the grotto that held *Il Testamento*, down a steep slope to the back of the cave and deposited them into a low den. Laying them side by side, the boy was the last. Steeling himself, he lifted the young head, fear still frozen on his filthy face, and set it above the thin shoulders.

Sweat poured off Galgano's body. The stench of filth and death filled the cavern. Staring at the hole where they hid *Il Testamento*, he vowed, "No one else will die for the greed of owning this symbol of hope and faith."

Outside, he worked through the hot day. Stone by stone, he filled the narrow mouth of the cave, leaving all in perfect darkness to await the Judgment. Glancing toward the sun disappearing behind Montesiepi, he caught sight of a vulture soaring above the trees. He squatted by Antonio's stiff body and heaved it atop his horse. His brave friend, this valiant knight, this husband and father, was no more.

After securing the body, he reached down for the crumpled note and stuffed it into the saddle, then led Antonio's horse back to Chiusdino. He would write to Helena. Antonio had often talked of her sweet temperament and the gracious beauty of her face. Galgano hoped she had a stalwart heart.

Galgano had never fought alongside a finer man, one of more ferocious courage, who knew his way with a solidity that caused Galgano's heart to scream with envy. Shaking his head, he pondered a perplexing question. He had lived a worthless life. *Why should he live and Antonio die?*

As long as Galgano could remember, he had been frustrated. Was no one strong enough to challenge him? Yet Antonio had challenged him in a way far beyond his physical brutishness. He had challenged him to a higher calling, trusted him. And invited him into the inner sanctum of this great secret.

Once home, Galgano wrote to his friend's wife. He reread the ending and wondered at it.

*...Know that Sir Antonio Dolcini died in defense of the faith against the ungodly. He was a true bondservant to the Lord Jesus Christ, his Savior and King of a heavenly Kingdom, where all tears shall be wiped away.*

Knowing these lofty words had not originated in his mind, he rolled and sealed the letter, entrusting it with his servant to take Signora Dolcini the sad news. He would follow after Antonio's body had been prepared and loaded on a wagon.

# Chapter 11

Siena, Italy

Gabe's mind worked to connect the dots of the bizarre story Louis had related. It was obvious that his grandfather had obsessed over history and hearsay so intensely that it had all run together. The cold in the underground chamber, plus Gabe's frustration with this foolishness, added to his impatience.

Louis picked up the document he thought validated his crazy story. "It was great providence that God sent Galgano to aid Antonio, else we would never have known our ancestor's fate. This is the letter Galgano sent to Helena.

*To Signora Helena Dolcini, faithful wife of the most honorable Antonio Dolcini: by Galgano Guidotti, Order of the Knights Templar, Custode del Testamento:*

*It is with much sorrow that I send this tragic account of the death of your husband. The morning had broken clear, and Antonio, much recovered from his wound, talked of traveling the whole of the day and night to be with you and his sons once more. He spoke of regret at ever leaving his home and the vainglory he had sought. However, there was nothing to be done about that.*

*As we breakfasted, news arrived that covetous enemies were in pursuit of the precious cargo, which your husband and I had sworn to protect with our lives. Without second thought, we dressed in our armor and pursued them.*

*Our enemy saw our approach and readied themselves. Antonio flew at them, his white surcoat billowing in the wind. What a gallant knight was your husband, Signora. His face still shown with the thoughts he had of you that bright morn.*

*Before us awaited eight mean-spirited foes, save one, a young boy of fourteen or so years, which I, not your honorable knight, vanquished to eternity. The battle was quick, but I was not fast enough to fend off the two knights who thrust Antonio through.*

*If there is any comfort, know that he died quickly. In his defense, I dispatched those men to their judgment. Bending over my brother, I listened to him speak your sweet name as his last word.*

*I buried the savages beneath the mount, which now entombs the sacred and the perverse. Know that Sir Antonio Dolcini died in defense of the faith against the ungodly. He was a true bondservant to the Lord Jesus Christ, his Savior and King of a heavenly Kingdom, where all tears shall be wiped away.*

*God be with you. Your servant, Galgano Guidotti, Custode del Testamento.*

Louis let his arm fall with the letter gripped in his fist.

Confusion creased Gabe's forehead. "'*Custode*' means 'keeper,' but what does '*del Testamento*' mean, *exactly*?"

Louis stiffened. "I don't know, *exactly*."

Gabe rolled his eyes and stood. He had tried, but enough was enough.

Louis attempted to hold Gabe's attention with a quick answer. "It translates, 'Keepers of the Testament.'"

"If you don't know what it is, how do you even know it exists? Why are we going through all this?"

"Antonio fell by the hand of murderers to protect it. One does not do such things for a fantasy. Helena also, was at first overcome with grief, but then…then took up the cause."

"Which was...?"

"She took the vow of the *Custodi* as Antonio requested, to protect a treasure that infused the Templars with extraordinary courage and faith. A treasure so great that Templars died at the hands of King Philip, rather than break their vows of secrecy.

"Antonio's letter told her where to hide *Il Testamento*. Before the end of her life, Helena compiled all of his letters. She went to her grave with the hope that in an age when strife had ceased, the Dolcini's would be able to fulfill their oath to bring this treasure to Seborga for the benefit of all believers."

Agitation infused Gabe's voice. "So, there's never been a time of peace when it could have been taken there?"

"You tell me, Gabriel—you have studied history." Louis tilted his head for an answer.

Gabe huffed.

Louis continued. "Besides, it has been lost for centuries. The last time our family recorded any mention of *Il Testamento* occurred in 1308, when King Philip rounded up the Templars and handed them over to the inquisitors. Philip was in great debt, and enemies of the Templars told him about a hidden relic that would give him wealth beyond imagination."

Louis pulled at his mustache and frowned. "Those rumors initiated agonizing grief. When news reached Siena that the Knights had been tortured and murdered en masse, Benito Dolcini, our ancestor, commanded his son to destroy every document related to it."

"Obviously, his son didn't."

"Correct, but he did document the circumstances and hide them very well. I would never have found them, except for some renovations I was making in this cellar." Louis shared a hopeful smile. "Now we have the chance to change history and bring to light the most clandestinely sought-after object in history. With Helena's records, it is our responsibility."

A sour smile on his lips, Gabe rubbed the back of his neck at the absurdity of this situation. "So the real thing you want from me is to spend my life digging around, looking for the Holy Grail, or some unknown relic, which you don't know the location of?"

"No. That is not the plan."

"Oh, but there is a plan—one that involves me. Grandfather, I have a career in *this* century. What is past is glorious, but it is past. I don't mean to offend you, but…"

"There is more," Louis snatched up the bottom letter. "This is Antonio's map. See." He pointed to a line with the words, "*Il Testamento.*" With triumph, he lifted his chin. "This is where she hid it." Gabe took the letter and read it. He dropped his hand in his lap, his patience spent. "You call this a map? It's his dream of coming home, for Pete's sake."

Heat rose in Louis' face. "It is in code. In fear of its discovery by his adversaries, Antonio devised a clever cover for Helena to follow while hiding it. Don't you see? It is God's plan for us to find it."

Gabe stood, his voice louder than he expected. "How can you be this gullible to believe in an imaginary God and his plan?"

Louis yelled, "How can you stand there at thirty-four years of age and proclaim from your vast wisdom that there is no God? Are you that arrogant to boast you have no faith?"

"My art is my faith," Gabe shouted. He grimaced at the hollow reverberation. Forcing calm into his voice, he explained. "I believe in what I can accomplish with my own hands, what I can touch and feel." Blood pulsed against his temples. Breathing hard, he wondered how this conversation had escalated to this level.

Eyes closed, his grandfather's chin fell to his chest. "Okay. Okay. Let us stop this and go back upstairs." He replaced the letters under the chair seat and they left the room of secrets.

## 

The wooden door to Gabe's room shut out the echoes of discord. A solid barrier, it locked him in with resounding regret. He grieved at the words he had spoken in anger. But this was not his battle—was not even a reality as far as he could see. If the old man wanted to tilt at windmills, that was his choice.

"*Fesso!*" He punched his pillow. *Why can't Louis understand?* Art was the one arena where he excelled above everyone in his field. It lifted him over those who smirked at his short jacket sleeves or his second-hand car. This amazing gift was his transport to success. He did not have time to be sidetracked.

The pained expression in Louis' trembling lips burned through Gabe's tightly closed eyes. He gritted his teeth. *Not my problem.* Then why did he feel so unsettled?

Needing a distraction, he decided that tomorrow he would set up his easel in the garden and paint. But even that thought failed to bring its familiar joy. The clear plan he brought to Siena had blurred, replaced by this fractured bond with his grandfather. *Relationships ruined everything.*

# Chapter 12

Seborga, Italy

"Last warning." Within the confines of a windowless cellar, the angry growl threatened Reverendo Tito. Like a lion tormenting its prey, Niccolo's imposing physique hovered above him.

Tito gasped when the other man, Arturo, dug hefty fingernails into his bared arms like talons. A stinging tear rolled down Tito's cheek. Tied to a chair that wobbled with every movement, he cringed when his captor leaned closer.

Niccolo's stale breath was as vile as the rank wine barrels stored in this filthy vault. "Believe me, priest, we *will* find what we search for."

Tito's heart thumped behind the wooden cross that had belonged to his father's family for generations. Frustration and fear sent tremors through his icy limbs. He was a simple man, but when he had been contacted about the relic last year, he had felt important for the first time in his life. His head fell to his chest in self-condemnation. *Too important.*

Someone had listened to his prayers regarding the relic and informed the shadowy group known as the *Soci*. Tito swallowed. They wanted the relic, but all he had was a name. He was not a brave man, but he would not put another's life in danger.

Niccolo tightened the ropes that bound his hands. Tito screamed out when his finger snapped like a small twig. Blinding pain blanked his mind. He had heard rumors about the ambitious *Soci*, but kidnapping?

Torture?

"Again?"

The broken priest recoiled from the black eyes that glared in the near darkness. *Il cielo mi aiuti*, Heaven help me. Tito shivered. *Murder?* His mind refused to entertain that scenario. He grasped at sanity. Surely the *Soci* would not go that far. He lifted his chin in a tentative act of courage. "I hide no relic. I am but a lowly priest who cares for orphans. Brothers, do not do this. Do not be deceived, God is not mocked. Whatever a man sows, he will also reap."

Niccolo's eyes narrowed. "No. *I* will not be mocked. If you do not give me the relic, I have been ordered to make this your last day on earth."

"Who ordered this dark deed?"

"Our *Primo Consul*." Niccolo gave him a cruel grin.

Tito flinched. He believed Niccolo's menacing glare. Sensing he was about to die, his trembling lips whispered, "My life is hid with Christ in God."

Niccolo clenched his fists and growled, "Where are you hiding it?"

Refusing to let Niccolo see his fear, Tito twisted his head away from him. Too late, the priest caught sight of the powerful fist that headed toward his cheek. When it hit, it wrenched his head into an unnatural posture.

## ##

In an instant, the priest was dead. Arturo's angry glare matched his words, "Now what?"

With one slash, Niccolo cut the cord around the priest's hands. "Take his feet." They lifted the smaller man with ease. After checking outside, Niccolo opened the door wide and led the way toward a small rock wall that bordered the orphanage. He glanced over the edge to the rocky outcrop twenty feet below and indicated his intentions with a sideways jerk of his head.

Arturo nodded and they tossed the body to the rocks below.

Niccolo smirked, "He should not have been walking so near the edge during his evening prayers."

A one-sided grin drew Arturo's mouth up. "Should we search his office?"

"No. It is too late now. After he is discovered, we can arrange to *care* for his belongings." They left the orphanage as they had come and vanished into the night.

# THE PROOF

# Chapter 13

Siena, Italy

Tonight it would begin. *And end.* At this evening's gala, Gabe would make the contacts he needed from this trip. Then he would flee the ramblings of his grandfather. Relief mixed with remorse. Louis was kind and generous, like no man Gabe had known, but his ravings grew more intolerable every day. Gabe stared blindly out the window and reflected on his time here. So much of his stay had been good. *Grand,* even.

His attention refocused. This evening, a full moon added its special magic. Lights blazed from the palazzo windows, sending out a warm glow that bathed the tall rock towers and stone façades of the surrounding buildings in amber softness. Small, but expensive automobiles joined the chauffeur-driven models as they unloaded their finely-dressed passengers at the front gate of the Palazzo Dolcini.

It was time.

"We have a full house," Serena smiled and laid her hand on the sleeve of Gabe's custom-fitted tuxedo. She must have sensed his apprehension. "You look as *magnifico* as your work—every bit a Dolcini aristocrat."

Taking a deep breath, Gabe forced himself to relax and return her smile. A lot was riding on this night. "*Grazie.* You did an amazing job."

"Here is your grandfather," she said.

Gabe turned to see the elegant man stride toward him, with only a trace of weakness in his leg. Though the conte's eyes sparkled with pride at him, Gabe recognized the sad downturn of his mouth beneath his mustache. A pang of guilt pierced Gabe's chest.

"Come, Gabriel, let us feed the lions." He winked and they stepped through the grand arch into the magnificent ballroom together. The crowd hushed in respect when the Dolcini men were announced. Enthusiastic applause filled the ballroom.

Immediately, curious guests surrounded them. Louis handled every person with ease and grace, making each feel special and respected. Gabe noticed the admiration they gave him in return.

"Gabriel," Louis said, "may I introduce you to the honorable Detective Orsini."

Gabe was startled to see the David Niven look-alike from the airport standing in front of him. "I am pleased to meet you, detective." They shook hands, and Gabe noticed an austere glint in the man's eyes, probably from dealing with the seedier side of life.

A persistent fan grabbed Gabe's attention and insisted he explain the ambiguous details in one of his paintings. Gabe glanced back to excuse himself and caught Orsini's unreadable eyes.

After an hour of greeting the elite of Siena and receiving extraordinary praise for his paintings, Gabe's cheeks ached. Serena came to rescue him. "If we may, I think our artist needs a break." She smiled at the disappointed faces and whisked him over to the faux courtyard.

Handing him a glass of ice-cold sparkling water, they sat down on tall stools, and she clued him in. "We have the beginnings of a bidding war," she laughed. "I had not even made your prices known, but began to hear arguments from collectors. They are ready to outdo each other. Of particular interest is *Pacifica*. The sunlight sings off the ocean on your canvas. You will be a wealthy man after tonight."

Serena had pulled the whole thing together. He knew she would get a handsome percentage off his work, and he was pleased to pay it. The money was important, but more so was the reputation he was building.

Relief settled in. He leaned back and marveled as his eyes drifted over the decorative columns arranged around the central courtyard. Their

18-foot height was still shy of the perfectly preserved ceiling, frescoed in cobalt blue, gold, and the richest colors of the era.

Dropping his gaze, he was shocked to find Livia Ambrogi watching him. *What? How?* Thrilled to see her, he wanted to smile, but remembered her rudeness. Instead, he gave her an acknowledging nod. She did not respond, but continued to move through the crowd. He bristled at the lack of civility from this woman. *This beautiful, mysterious woman.*

Serena broke his reverie. "Are you sure you do not want to sell *Il Viso*? I am certain it would command a small fortune."

Gabe shook his head. "Not yet." Something about the painting connected with him on a level he had not before experienced. She shrugged her shoulders and left to greet another buyer. A moment later, Gabe sensed someone behind him and turned.

Livia perched on a stool next to him, scrutinizing a group of collectors involved in animated conversation over his paintings. She swallowed the last of her drink. "They are certainly cooing over you. How does it feel to be the Rembrandt of your day, *eh*?"

He resisted a defensive reaction and replied evenly, "After years of hard work, it's a moment every artist hopes for."

She raised a perfect eyebrow and attempted civility. "Your effort is obvious."

The coincidence of her being at the palazzo with him boggled his mind. "May I ask how you came to be here?"

"My family has connections in the art world of Tuscany."

He enjoyed the bits of information he was collecting about her. "I noticed you studying my work with more than a casual glance. Are you an artist also?"

"*Si.* Only an amateur. My expertise lies in collecting."

Gabe noticed his shallow breathing. This woman affected him like no other. "Perhaps you would be willing to show me your collection some time."

She glanced past him and ignored his suggestion. "Did you plan to become a famous artist?"

It was unclear if she was being sarcastic. Her steady gaze turned on him and he decided on honesty. "I knew at a very young age that I loved painting—loved everything about it. At the risk of seeming trite, I sensed it was my destiny." He waited for a curt remark and was surprised when it failed to materialize.

"It is good to know one's destiny." Her sight seemed to reach beyond the ballroom walls. "It is better if life does not get in the way of following it." A frown tugged on the corners of her mouth.

"Perhaps life's obstacles develop the perseverance to find one's destiny." He shrugged and gave a one-sided grin. "My apologies. It's a personal search I've been on."

"You must have conquered all those obstacles—it appears your exhibit is a great success." She turned to face him and their eyes locked. Sparks shot through him. A slight jolt of her head confirmed she felt it, too. The blush on her cheeks glowed in the soft light. Twisting her stool away from him to the bar, she speared an olive with a plastic toothpick.

Gabe glanced at the elegant indigo blue gown that capped her sculpted shoulders. Crimson-infused black tendrils escaped from the jeweled pins that held the rest of her shining locks high on her head and curled feather-soft against her face.

She would be a dream to paint. He studied the delicate collarbones that supported a slender neck. Her model-perfect face invited one to reach out and touch it. Gabe started. Had his fingers actually reached for her?

Her attention flew to his hand. He swallowed. It hadn't moved off the back of the stool, yet both of them experienced the impending touch. Her mouth opened in surprise. She fought to wrest her eyes away from his, then straightened and veered her attention back toward the crowd, biting the olive off the skewer.

Gabe leaned back, recovering from the moment, but wishing it had lingered.

Refusing to look at him, Livia was back in attack mode. "Why is it that you made no attempt to meet your grandfather until you needed his contacts?"

Gabe flinched. His search for a civil reply ended when Serena joined them. Ignoring Livia, she threaded her hand around his arm.

"There is someone you have to meet." Her eyes sparkled. Livia's clouded like a slow-moving hurricane.

Serena pushed through the crowd and led Gabe to a distinguished middle-aged man in an immaculate tuxedo. "Gabriel, may I present Signore Belvedere, curator for the Museum of Modern Art in Rovereto. Signore Belvedere, this is our talented, Gabriel Dolcini."

"I am honored," Gabe said.

The curator shook Gabe's hand. "Thank you. Serena was insistent that I come to Siena to see your work. After tonight, I have a new appreciation for her ability to recognize great talent." He nodded at her then turned back to Gabe. "Would it be possible for you to have lunch with me next week?"

Serena looked ecstatic and opened her mouth to reply for him, but an agitated waiter pulled her attention away. She excused herself and followed him to correct a problem.

The curator continued, "Since you are not letting go of *Il Viso*, I am interested in acquiring *Pacifica* as a permanent piece for the museum. Serena suggested a price that I could manage, but I believe she was working with another buyer to increase that amount. Of course, the sale would guarantee a one-man exhibit of your work. And, I would expect you to visit the museum next week to see where I plan to hang my acquisition."

Gabe hoped his pounding heart did not show through his shirt. "That is very generous. Consider it sold."

A smug expression hung on Belvedere's face as he reached out and shook Gabe's hand. "I will be back in Rovereto on Saturday. Send the piece ahead, and I will have it waiting for your arrival to discuss the details."

"Perfect." This was the first break into the massive European market. If all went well, collectors would soon scramble to own his paintings. He needed to get back to his studio.

The crash of breaking glass echoed through the room, followed by a loud commotion. Gabe rushed to the rear of the ballroom, where the now famous painting, *Il Viso*, hung. Waiters were picking up broken shards and mopping the floor.

His grandfather leaned against the medallion back of an antique chair. Gabe rushed to him. Serena asked the guests to clear a path while Gabe and Rinaldo escorted the pale man through a private door that led past the chapel to his suite. Gabe looked back and caught Livia's tense expression before the door closed, locking out the curious stares.

Sitting on the edge of his grandfather's black lacquer bed, Gabe jerked back in surprise when the man grabbed his lapels with strong hands and pulled him close to his furious face. "The painting, where is it!"

Gabe was at a loss. "What painting?"

"You deceived me. You stole my painting."

The familiar accusing expression of Gabe's father shot from his grandfather's face and sent twinges of fear and shame through Gabe. Fighting the indignity of the situation, he searched for a way to escape the man's clutches. "Sir, I don't know what you're talking about."

Louis let go of his lapel, dropped back against his silk pillow, and closed his angry eyes.

Rinaldo stepped forward. "Perhaps your time would be most useful with your guests. I will care for the conte."

Serena had smoothed the incident over, raising the music to move the guests back into party mode. Gabe rejoined the gala, ignoring the curious stares. He searched everywhere, but Livia had vanished. For the rest of the night, he felt off-balance, but with Serena's help, managed to smile and hold his own.

The tempo had picked up again, but Gabe caught fragments of a different subject of conversation. If the conte passed on, this handsome Italian-American would be the heir to the Dolcini fortune.

##

Hours after the gala ended, Gabe's head throbbed against the hard pillow. He kicked the silky-blue bedspread on the floor. Crisp white sheets tangled around his bronze body from constant tossing. Above, the midnight blue ceiling stared back at him. What in the world caused Louis' bizarre reaction? Recounting the events of the night, nothing gave him a clue.

In the hours closest to dawn, he finally fell asleep, only to be jarred awake much too soon by Rinaldo. "Your grandfather will see you in the dining room in fifteen minutes. He is quite shaken."

Gabe pulled on jeans and a sweater and headed downstairs in a daze of confusion. He passed workers disassembling the ballroom setting. Hammers pounded crates together. Entering the dining room, he stepped over the fringed carpet that covered the cold tile floor. Unsettled, he dropped onto the edge of a chair.

Recovered from the weakness of the night before, Louis stood to his full height and glared down. "What have you done with my painting?"

Gabe felt very small. That feeling had not invaded his mind for years. For the first time, the similarities between his father and grandfather were apparent. Angry, he rose and faced the enraged man. "I haven't done anything with any of your paintings."

"Then how did you copy it?" Louis shouted.

The conversation proved stranger with every sentence. Gabe attempted to calm himself and soothe the situation. "Grandfather, I demand to know what you are talking about." The tone must have done the trick.

Louis gripped the back of a chair. His teeth clenched and unclenched. At last he ordered, "Come with me."

Bewildered, Gabe followed the aged man up the stairs, past the ballroom. Inside, Serena worked on the shipments. Her smile faded at Louis' scowl. He continued to climb to the fourth floor and entered through a sturdy door. Crossing the floor, Louis unlocked and opened two dark oak doors to reveal an alcove enclosing a substantial chest. An empty frame hung on the wall above the chest and a yellowed sketch lay flat on the surface. Louis' breath came in rasps. He picked up the sketch and held it out with a shaking fist.

It was Gabe's turn to gasp. Though not exactly as he had painted it, the sketch was a near duplication of *Il Viso*. The woman held the same grief as she stared into the distance. "It can't be. This scene, the woman, they came to me." His hands spread wide, begging his grandfather to believe him. However, seeing the conte's disbelief, he dropped his arms.

"This painting was stolen from me a year ago. The thief knew exactly what he was looking for and had plenty of time to remove it from the frame." Louis lifted a fine feather, his eyes narrowing. "This was left in place of the painting."

"The Kestral?"

"If it was, Ralph was in here working with her. I have disinherited him for it."

Gabe's mind spun. "Did the police confirm that?"

"Our family does not need another scandal." His lips remained tight. "I am shocked by your connection with thieves, but I will not press charges against my family—no matter how disloyal." He finished his rant, stepped to the door, and turned to glare at Gabe.

Gabe was ruined. No doubt, the story of plagiarism would hit every tabloid once the painting resurfaced. Howard and the faculty would glance away from him when he returned to the university—if they would even have him back. His father's mocking eyes appeared. Heat advanced, threatening to overcome him. He had to get out of here.

As he stepped past his grandfather, the troubled man peered at him and squared his shoulders. "On your life, Gabriel, never share the location of the secret room or the things I have revealed to you."

Gabe nodded. *Gladly.*

Louis' proud bearing slumped. A sigh of despair escaped his somber lips and his voice quieted. "You *must* understand the dangers. For centuries, *Il Testamento* lay hidden away. When I discovered these letters forty years ago, Ralph's father, Kendrick Witte, found out and broke my Christina's neck. She knew nothing about their location."

Gabe's jaw dropped open in horror.

Louis' voice pitched higher. "I thought that was the end, but when I expelled Ralph from my home, he told me a shocking story. Last year, my daughter, Geneva, contacted the same men that Kendrick had. She told them I had the relic. She wanted me dead."

His trembling lips curled down. "I needed to talk to someone I could trust, so I spoke with a priest in Seborga and asked him if he had information that confirmed Antonio's letters regarding the existence of the relic."

Gabe cringed. He could not believe this man was crazy enough to expose his conspiracy theories to outsiders.

"After searching through the archives, the priest called back to confirm the existence of Saint Bernard's instructions. He was most anxious to receive *Il Testamento* when I found it." Louis' hand shook when he wiped his eye. "Yesterday, a child found the priest's body crumpled on the rocks below the orphanage that he managed. I received the news this morning. Tito was murdered."

Gabe forgot to breathe. Then sucked in air. What had he gotten into?

Louis moaned, "I must find the relic and take it to Seborga. If not, I fear for my family." His hand on his chest, Louis shook his head in misery.

Nauseated, Gabe struggled to make sense of the encounter. Having his painting called into question was the least of his worries. Louis was certainly crazy, imagining killers lying in wait for him. Gabe should have believed his mother. It was long past time to leave.

As he rushed downstairs, he passed the ballroom and caught a glimpse of Rinaldo's concerned expression. *Had he heard?* It didn't matter. Gabe needed to pack and get out of this house, this country, and this family.

## 

Rinaldo seemed contemplative while he negotiated the limo through the lunch traffic. They hustled to a hotel near the Florence airport where Gabe would await a flight booked for the following day. Still bewildered, Gabe sat, tense with anger. What had started as an amazing trip was ending in shreds.

The chauffer pulled in front of the hotel and sat the luggage on the curb. "I am certain when the conte has the opportunity to reconsider the matter, he will see that you had nothing to do with the disappearance of the painting. Perhaps you will attempt to clear up this misunderstanding, *eh?*"

Gabe had no idea what Rinaldo knew about Louis' abnormal state of mind. "Thank you, but he won't listen. He's just too...stubborn."

"In some ways I imagine he is, but you have more to offer each other than you might think."

Gabe thought otherwise. He grabbed his bags and escaped through the revolving hotel door. Once in his hotel room, his exhausted mind escaped into a deep slumber.

## 

In the library, Louis sat alone with his grief and made the call he should have made in the first place. "Livia, you must help me find *Il Testamento*. Please come to the palazzo at once." He hung up the phone and swallowed the lump in his throat. The familiar silence had returned.

Weariness overcame him, and he closed his eyes. The bright turn his life had finally taken had deteriorated into a storm of hard emotions. His consciousness moved from a fuzzy grey to black. His chin slumped to his chest.

A glimpse of Gabriel instantly gladdened his heart. But what was he doing? With a flimsy pallet knife, he was probing the lock in a massive door. An odd engraved symbol covered the door. When the lock gave, Gabriel turned and grinned. The door opened! Great joy surged between them...

"Louis?"

A hand touched his arm and gently shook him awake. Eyes bursting open, he started at Livia's smiling face.

"Would you like more time to sleep?"

Feeling disoriented, he straightened and rubbed his eyes. "Just one moment." He ambled to his desk and found paper to sketch the image he had seen, then laid it aside.

"What is it?" Livia asked.

Rinaldo entered the library and sat a glass of water on the table.

Wide awake now, Louis' eyes danced with excitement. "Gabriel knows the key to finding *Il Testamento*."

The smile left her face. "You are certain?"

Louis answered, "*Si*. I must get him back here."

"*Mi scusi*, Conte Dolcini," Rinaldo said. "Your grandson is very distraught. He may need some persuading before he is willing to help."

Livia bristled. "He lives only for himself and has shut out all others."

"Perhaps he feels that all others have shut him out," Rinaldo suggested.

Her brows furrowed at the unexpected support for Gabe. Nevertheless, turning her sullen face to Louis, she said, "If you are certain we need him, I will bring him back."

Louis nodded, "It is the only way." He smiled for the first time today, but a sudden thought darkened his mood. "You must be very careful. We have had another murder."

She gasped. "What!" Her eyes widened and shifted between the two men.

Louis related the details of the news he had heard about the priest's murder. Massaging his chest, he asked, "Rinaldo, would you bring me my medicine?"

"*Si*, and then I need to go to the market."

After the butler had left, Livia turned to Louis. "Tell me where the map is."

He shook his head. "Only Gabriel knows how to find *Il Testamento*." He watched her struggle through the resentment broiling inside. Frustrated, she stormed out of the room.

##

"*Buon giorno*," Detective Orsini barked into his phone. The greeting seemed at odds with his bristling intonation.

The caller said, "You need to send someone to investigate the priest's murder in Seborga immediately. And conduct a thorough search of his records. Apparently, Louis notified the unfortunate man about *Il Testamento*. If the *Soci* are behind the murder, they may have already discovered the link back to Louis."

##

An hour after he left, Rinaldo returned, not certain how to proceed. From the expression on Gabe's face this afternoon, only deft persuasion would ever persuade him to cooperate. He set his shopping bag on the kitchen counter and stopped. Pieces of the small dragon table in the dining room lay smashed on the floor. He ran into the library where he had left the conte. Papers were scattered across the carpet. A handwritten note lay on the desk.

*Gabriel,*

*If you want to see your grandfather again, find the relic. Be ready to hand it over in three days.*

There was no signature. After searching the house for Louis, Rinaldo slipped into his stately suite off the kitchen and dialed the police. "I need to speak to Detective Orsini." When the detective came on the line, Rinaldo shouted, "Conte Dolcini has been abducted."

# Chapter 14

Florence, Italy

Gabe twisted on the hotel bed and screamed as a searing brand sizzled his flesh. When the instrument pulled away, it left a capital "A" on top of a partial circle burned into his calf. Loud pounding startled him from his terrifying dream. He heard muffled shouts, "This is the police. Open the door."

*Which part of the nightmare was real?* Gabe frowned and switched on the light in the dim hotel room. The clock indicated it was only seven in the evening. He glanced at his burning calf for signs of the nonexistent brand, then opened the door as far as the chain would allow.

Two Italian police officers lunged at him, guns drawn. "Open up—now!"

Gabe shut the door and undid the chain. They burst through, shoving him onto the bed.

"What have you done with Conte Dolcini?" the leader demanded.

Fighting confusion, Gabe searched for an answer to the strange question. "Nothing. His chauffeur drove me here this morning. What's going on?"

The small man with fine features ignored his question. "I am Officer Santini, and this is Officer Romano. Get dressed."

At the police station, Gabe waited, stunned at the parade of bizarre events. Detective Orsini joined Officer Santini. Dressed in tailored street clothes, the severe-looking Orsini began his interrogation.

"Earlier this evening, Rinaldo Paravati, your grandfather's man, called me to the palazzo. He returned from shopping and found the house broken into, a table smashed, and Conte Dolcini gone. You want to tell me about it?" He leaned his elbows on the table and laced his long fingers together.

"I haven't seen my grandfather since I left this morning."

Disregarding his answer, Orsini nearly accused him of murder. "Rinaldo says you two had a falling out, and he booted you out. It is rumored that you were set to inherit the Dolcini wealth. I imagine being dismissed was quite a loss. So again, where is Conte Dolcini?"

Gabe explained every detail of the day since Rinaldo dropped him at the hotel that morning.

The other officer, Santini, did not seemed convinced. "If you do not produce the conte, you may expect your new home will be an Italian prison." Santini seemed set on terrorizing Gabe and used up several hours questioning him. He then left to make calls to Rinaldo and the hotel to check their surveillance cameras, leaving Orsini alone with Gabe.

Quieting his voice, but increasing the threatening tone, Orsini took advantage of the state of fear that gripped Gabe. "Rinaldo said a ransom note was left." He took out his notepad and read, *"Gabriel, If you want to see your grandfather again, find the relic. Be ready to hand it over within three days."* He tucked the pad back in his pocket. "Do you have this relic?"

Gabe gripped his hair with his fingers. Louis had gotten himself into real trouble now. "It is a myth," he seethed. "Louis is crazy, and his insanity has gotten out of hand, prompting a hunt for something that does not exist."

Orsini ignored him. "Do you know how to find this relic?"

Dropping his eyes, Gabe needed time to think. He had promised his grandfather not to speak of it. But it was Gabe's life that was on the line. He ground his teeth. "No."

The detective flew out of his chair, causing it to rattle on the cement floor. He leaned over him and hissed. "So, your grandfather will be killed.

Then you will find the relic and inherit his fortune. Rinaldo said you had financial troubles, this should solve them, *eh?*"

This was insane. Staring up at the furious detective, Gabe's mouth opened to protest, but no words came out.

Orsini grabbed his hair and pulled him off the chair. "You will not get away with this."

At that moment, Orsini's superior barged into the room with Officer Romano and intervened. He threw Orsini a savage scowl and barked at Gabe. "You are not to leave Italy until we get to the bottom of this. You may go back to your hotel, but Officer Romano will be on guard outside your door and will accompany you anywhere you go."

Orsini's eyes narrowed, enraged at his superior's interference, yet his voice communicated control. "Do you really think a guard is necessary?" His superior did not answer, but slammed the door on his way out of the dull grey room. Orsini glared at Gabe, then left, leaving Gabe alone with Romano.

Gabe glanced at his babysitter. The squat man glowered and grabbed his arm, shoving him out the door. Gabe looked around for some kind of sanity, but apparently, this was the norm.

"Get in," Romano said, propelling him into the back seat of a waiting car. Officer Santini drove while Romano struggled to turn his bulk and glare from the front passenger's seat. They drove through dark alleys, taking turns threatening him.

At one point, Romano pointed his gun at Gabe. "You know what this can do to a man's head? It leaves a nice clean entry hole, but the exit, that is a different story?"

Gabe dared not swallow, but could not control his eyes as they glanced frantically for a way of escape. Perspiration ran freely under his clothing.

"Enough," Santini murmured to his partner. They drove in silence the remaining distance to his hotel. Few people were in the lobby at this hour, but the ones who were, stopped what they were doing to stare at Gabe's handcuffs and the officers accompanying him.

His whole body shook with fear and adrenaline, wondering if they were really going to let him go. He almost cried with relief when he entered his room and Officer Santini unlocked the handcuffs and left.

Romano frowned and pulled out a half-eaten *panini* sandwich from his fanny pack. He grabbed the chair from the room's desk and pulled it outside to set up his post.

## 

From his second story office, Orsini communicated his instructions over the phone. "The young Dolcini needs a quiet place to contemplate helping his grandfather. It is obvious he did not abduct the conte. It looks like the work of the *Soci*. However, I am convinced he knows where the map is, perhaps the relic as well. I am handing him to you on a platter. Do not let your limey grunts mess this up."

"Right."

Orsini hung up, smug in the certain victory of his greatest challenge yet. He gloated at the destruction ahead and the infuriating hate it would produce in his longtime enemies, the *Soci*.

## 

Gabe fastened the chain on his door. His body shook uncontrollably. Would he really be sentenced to an Italian prison? If the police behaved like this, he could only imagine how it would be at the mercy of the guards. He paced the floor, pressing on his temples to relieve the stress.

Louis had warned him about new attacks on his family. Had his grandfather been murdered like the contessa? Gabe's trembling fingers splashed cold water on his face. He *so* wanted to get out of this country, but this fiasco had blocked that escape. Though he tossed on his bed for an hour, fear prevented him from closing his eyes. Louis' conspiracy had engulfed him.

A knock sounded at the hotel door, followed by a voice. "Room service."

*It's two in the morning.* Gabe had not ordered anything. He opened the door a crack and two men hit the door with enough force to snap the chain and knock him to the floor. He tried to push up, but a boot in the back flattened him. His head twisted sideways. *What is happening?* The scene outside the door choked him. Officer Romano slumped in his chair. Blood dripped from his neck over the edge of his white collar and pooled on the floor around him. A silent scream filled Gabe's mind—just before a handkerchief, filled with a ghastly chemical smell, covered his nose and mouth.

## ##

"Hey, mate." The cheery greeting was incongruous with the stench that surrounded Gabe. Smelling salts seared his sinuses, and he arched his neck backward in an effort to escape the acrid smell. His eyes opened, still blurry. An icy numbness invaded his cheek from where he lay on the cement floor.

"That's it, now. Come around." Ralph's white teeth glowed in the dark like a Cheshire cat's. Gabe shied away.

"Now you got it, mate. Sit up here, and let's have a little chat." His strong, sinewy hands hauled Gabe's torso off the floor of a dank storeroom and shoved it against a cold block wall. A tight rope bound Gabe's hands. Dampness had seeped into his pants and shirt. His head swirled and he thought he might be sick.

Above Ralph, a large man stood, faintly outlined by the flashlight he held. The scent of garlic and sour beer oozed out of him.

"Harry, point that on my cuz' face here," Ralph called to his accomplice.

"What are you doing?" Gabe gasped, wincing from the light glaring in his face.

Harry spoke from behind Ralph. "You got some information we need. The old man won't cooperate. He don't care if he's hurt or not, so it's up t' you now."

"What've you done with Louis?" Gabe gasped.

Ralph looked behind him at Harry and smirked. "We got him in safekeeping. Now, I promised Harry's boss I could deliver the relic. So, you get me the map and we go treasure hunting. Then you get Louis back. You're gonna give it t' me, right?"

Ralph held a knife in front of Gabe's face. It was stained dark red. *The blood of the officer? Of Louis?*

Gabe's eyes opened wide when he recalled the horrific scene. "All this for a myth? Ralph, the legend is bogus. We both know that."

Instantly enraged, Ralph jabbed the knife into Gabe's chin. He triumphed at Gabe's shriek. "Just like the blade of this knife's a myth." He stopped smiling and held the point against Gabe's nostril. "How would my pretty cousin look without a nose? Now where is it?"

The information flowed freely. "It's in a secret room at the palazzo."

"I don't think so, mate. I've been through that whole mausoleum, and there ain't nothin' there. Try again."

Ralph applied more pressure, and Gabe shouted, "There's a switch on a frame that opens it."

"Now we're making progress." After listening to the details, Ralph stuffed a rag into Gabe's mouth. He switched off the light. "We'll be back, chump," he promised. "You better be right."

Left in complete darkness, Gabe struggled against the rough rope that cut off the circulation to his wrists. No amount of twisting or pulling would budge it. Fear amplified the pounding pain in his head. *Your grandfather brings nothing but trouble to our family.* His father had warned him and for once, the tyrant was right. Despairing thoughts assaulted Gabe.

The image of his sister flashed across his mind. She screamed and clawed for a hold to keep from plunging down the sodden mountain amid the mud and debris, her slick shoes unable to gain a hold. Maybe he deserved this.

What seemed like hours later, a thin light pierced the darkness. *Ralph!* Gabe's heart thumped as steps neared. He could already feel the steel of the knife against his face. The image of the guard's blood-soaked shirt caused a new wave of panic. A light flashed in his face. The next second, a hand ripped the rag from his mouth.

"Are you okay?" whispered a woman's voice. Confusion fogged Gabe's mind to the point where she had to ask the question again. Her agitation grated in his ear. "Are you okay?"

"Yes." The light fragrance of lavender drifted to his nose. "Livia?"

She pushed him forward and cut through the ropes that bound his hands, then helped pull him to his feet. "Let's go."

His tingling legs cramped, causing him to shuffle along the uneven floor in the dark room. At her impatient sigh, he straightened and tried to increase his speed. She moved through a wooden door and out a hinged metal gate.

The cramps subsided and he jogged after her down a narrow path between ancient buildings. Above the tiled roofs that towered over him, night slowly gave way to the softness of dawn. The serene sight created a harsh contrast with the madness of the night.

Livia, dressed in tight jeans and a camel-colored leather jacket, flung herself into a small Fiat. He fell in beside her, subdued but relieved. She shoved the stick shift forward, and they sped away from the scene.

"Why are you here?" he asked.

"How about, 'Thank you for saving my life,'" she snapped. "There are many places I would rather be."

His head jerked back like a turtle's into its shell. "What does *that* mean?"

"It means you have complicated everything. You come here, get kidnapped..." She shook her head in frustration.

His impatience came out as sarcasm. "Yeah, it was my plan to have my cousin kill a guard outside my door to get to me."

"What?" She stomped on the brake hard enough to propel them forward while the car decelerated. Her eyes left the road for a millisecond to flash a fearful glance at him.

He swallowed back bile. "The last I saw, the man was sitting in his own blood." They rode in silence as she zipped around the narrow city streets of Florence, the ancient labyrinth mimicking the confusion in his mind. "So, how did you find me?"

She made another quick turn before answering. "Rinaldo told

Detective Orsini he had found a ransom note that said someone kidnapped Louis. Then…"

Outraged, Gabe shouted, "Orsini knew I was innocent, but let me take the heat for Louis' kidnapping." Anger instantly replaced the fear that had assaulted him over the last twenty-four hours.

Livia also fumed, but for a different reason. "Louis hates publicity. Rinaldo should have called me first. When he finally did call, I came to the hotel to pick you up, but the police were hauling you to the station. After they brought you back to your room, I was planning a way to get you out, but then Ralph showed up and carried you off to that warehouse. There was nothing I could do but wait for him to leave." She let out an exasperated sigh. "Now I am tired and hungry, and possibly on the wrong side of the law."

The Fiat's tires screeched as she negotiated several hairpin turns while they soared up a mountain, away from the lingering city lights of Florence. They came around a curve and entered a small, deserted *piazza* lined with ristorante and bar signs. The lights in a bakery fell across the narrow stone sidewalk that rose only an inch or two higher than the street. She dodged the cars parked on both sides of the narrow street. The rabbit's foot attached to her keychain flew in small circles.

He pointed to the puff of white fur. "Is that for luck?"

"My sister thinks so."

Gabe tightened his fingers on the door handle to keep from flying around. Still, she handled the car well. "Impressive driving."

"I test drive for my cousin's Fiat factory. He gives me good deals."

"How many cars do you need?"

"I hate dents."

Racing up the steep road, Livia downshifted and made a quick ninety-degree turn onto a narrow path between two tall stone buildings. The driveway ramped its way farther up the mountain. At the top, it leveled out. She swung around into a parking place and stopped with a jolt. "Let's go."

##

Ralph hid behind an oleander hedge that edged the gardens at the Palazzo Dolcini. *One day, I will buy this place—and tear it down.* His noble family was a sham. The last time he saw his mum, she was thrashin' on her deathbed, out of her mind from drugs. For forty years, the chemicals had eased her pain caused by his father's murder. When the good conte found out, he had cut off her financial support completely.

Instant fury shot through his jaw, and he jammed his thumb into the joint until the pain dulled. No tellin' what she woulda' done if Harry's boss hadn't given her money to live on the last few months. His mum had been wise not to them everything. Ralph smiled. But, she'd told him all she knew before she died. Now, that money flowed his way. The map and the relic were as good as his. Then he would get the jackpot his father had missed.

He watched while two guards prowled, checking doors and shining their flashlights at foliage that moved with the breeze. It would be light soon. He swore under his breath at the lost chance. He'd have to come back later.

Backing out, he rounded the tall brick walls of the neighboring villas and disappeared into the maze of alleyways. His feet hit the pavement hard as his torso sauntered from side to side in a haughty mode. Should he go back to Florence and deal with Gabe or go to his room to wait for dark?

Rounding a corner, he halted, then attempted to run. Two men grabbed him. Harry covered Ralph's mouth to stifle his scream. He pushed Ralph against the rough wall and held him.

Sam, equal in stature and strength to Ralph, choked him and thrust the point of a knife an inch from his eye. "Harry here told me 'bout your cuz. You give us the map, Ralphy, then we go get him."

Ralph gurgled a response, prompting Sam to loosen his grip so they could understand him. "There's coppers all over the house, Sam. I'll have to come back."

Sam motioned, and Harry pulled up on Ralph's arm.

Ralph groaned. "Just give me some time," he hissed.

"Time's all we've been givin' you," grumbled Sam. "I think you've been takin' my boss's money an' leadin' us on—the same way your mum did. That's what I think." He squeezed Ralph's throat, causing his jaw to open in searing pain.

"I know where it is—I swear," Ralph mumbled. His eyes darted sideways. "You heard him in the cellar, Harry. Gabe knew all about it—the old man's been tellin' him the stories he wouldn't tell me. I got it all out of him, I just need t' get inside."

"That's true Sam," Harry vouched.

"Did I ask you?" Sam shot at Harry. "You'd believe anything, you twit."

Harry's face darkened, and he released his hold. Ralph's smarting arm dropped to a somewhat normal position, blood pulsing back into his hand.

Sam kept the knife pressed against Ralph's cheek, the point feathering his eyelashes. "You got forty-eight hours, Ralphy, or it's over."

"Just let me explain to your boss," he pleaded.

"He don't want to meet you." Sam shoved Ralph backward, and the two thugs left.

Ralph rubbed his jaw, eyes focused on Sam. "Better watch your back," he whispered.

# Chapter 15

Fiesole, Italy

Livia tossed thin slices of *prosciutto* and cheese on a white plate and dropped it on the table in front of Gabe. He had watched her prepare the simple breakfast in silence. It seemed he offended her every time he opened his mouth.

"Café?" she asked, lacking the warmth of even the most obnoxious waitress.

"Sure." He wondered how such a beautiful façade could house such a disagreeable composition.

She stepped behind a bar and set a small cup under the espresso machine, hit a switch, and watched it empty a shot of dark, rich coffee. The liquid splashed when she set the cup in front of him. "*Zucchero* is there," she pointed to a small dish holding paper packets of brown sugar.

Gabe matched her frown and turned his attention to the dining room in which they sat. Several small tables filled the sun-bathed room. "Where are we?"

"We are at my family's hotel in Fiesole above Florence." Dropping to her chair, she snatched a croissant from a basket and began to cut off tiny bites with her fork.

"Thank you for saving my life. I'm sorry those weren't the first words out of my mouth."

"You are welcome, but I had no choice."

*There it was again.* Gabe closed his eyes and tilted his head to one side as though that would help him make sense out of this bizarre situation.

She slammed her fork down on her plate with a clink. "What did you tell Ralph?"

Gabe tensed and studied her. "How do you know I told him anything?"

"Do not think I am stupid like your solicitous patrons," she flung at him. "I know because I followed him and his friend when they kidnapped you and then watched Ralph drive off toward Siena—in a very happy mood. So what did you tell him?"

Gabe remained cautious. "I told him where something was hidden."

She flew out of her chair so fast, it tipped backward and crashed to the tile floor. "You told him where to find the map!"

"How do you know about the map? Louis said it was a guarded family secret."

"Because I *am* family," she spit. Louis is like my *zio*, my uncle. She reached down and righted the chair. "Antonio Dolcini had two sons. Your grandfather is from the eldest, my ancestors from the younger, but both of them were commissioned by their mother to become *custode* and protect *Il Testamento*."

"So we are not related?"

"Not for hundreds of years." She sat down hard and pointed her fork at him. "And now, you have handed it over to that *ratto*, Ralph. And for what, that nick on your chin?"

Gabe's hand flew up to the cut on his face. Dried blood had clotted with only a small drop on his shirt. Heat rose and he could feel it coloring his cheeks. "I didn't tell him anything—just lies to get him out of there." He threw back the shot of coffee and grimaced at the bitter strength of it.

Livia chuckled with obvious relief. She leaned her chair back on two legs and studied him, tapping the fork on her porcelain plate in a nervous rhythm. "So, you are not the coward your father thought you were, *eh*?"

Infuriated, Gabe demanded, "What do you know about my father—or me?" It was his turn to stand and glare.

She smiled benignly. "Ralph is my cousin also, distantly of course.

When he was staying with Louis, he filled me in about you." She eyed him. "He said you were afraid of everything."

Feeling exposed, Gabe focused on her. "Did your visit to Santa Barbara have anything to do with all of this?"

The smirk left her face. "*Si.* Louis summoned me in July and told me about his intentions."

"Why?"

A bleary-eyed couple dragged their suitcases passed the dining room into the hallway, probably still suffering jet lag. The host at the front desk smiled and conversed with them, then helped them get their bags to their room.

Livia bit her lip and stopped drumming. "He told you about finding the history of *Il Testamento*?"

Gabe nodded.

She lowered the chair so it rested on all four legs, then leaned her elbows on the table and spoke in quieter tones. "Until forty years ago, no one connected the relic to our family. But once a sliver of the mystery became known, the contessa was kidnapped to force the location from her."

Gabe's eyes narrowed, his tone bitter, "And my grandfather wouldn't hand over some stupid relic to save her? No wonder my father left everything."

"You know nothing," Livia snapped. "Your grandfather was never given the chance. It was a horrible business."

The unexpected rebuke hit him hard. Jumping to callused conclusions was something his father would have done. Not something Gabe wanted to emulate. Livia was right, he knew nothing about his family's history, or their motives. He cleared his throat. "Who killed her?"

Her defiant stare dropped to the miniature bouquet of yellow flowers on the table. "Greed is a horrible thing. Ralph's father, Kendrick Witte, heard whispers of the map. He and another coward kidnapped Christina when she was shopping in Florence."

Fury flashed from Livia's eyes. "Everything I have ever heard about Christina spoke of her kindness and love of life. She doted on her children, especially your father. Her sister found her body in a filthy basement with her neck broken. From the investigation, we know she had been beaten."

"Were they caught?"

Her grey eyes smoldered. "The bodies of Ralph's father and his accomplice were found in the Arno River. The police consider their deaths unsolved homicides."

Silence.

She continued, "Kendrick's death ended the assassin's trail that pointed to Louis and our family. For a while, at least. Last year, Ralph's mother, Geneva, died from lifelong drug abuse. Then Ralph came with a sob story and Louis took him in."

"Is that when Louis found him snooping and kicked him out?"

"*Sì.* When Louis demanded he leave, Ralph said Geneva had contacted the same criminal group his father had. She told them Louis had the map."

Gabe listened and watched Livia's knuckles go white as they clenched the fork.

"Louis revealed his desperation to me last year. I took the oath of the *custode*, yet he refused my help. When he told me of his plan to bring you into his confidence, I was doubtful." She shot a quick glance up at him and straightened in her chair. "During Ralph's stay at the palazzo, I spoke with him. From what he said, you were…overly cautious. I wondered how such a man could be capable of dealing with this volatile situation and guarding a secret of this magnitude. So, I came to Santa Barbara to see for myself."

"And?"

She frowned. "And I saw a soft, self-absorbed artist, caught up in his own little world."

Gabe pushed up from the table. "People see what they want to see. Not all of us are made in the form of Hercules." He threw his napkin on his chair and headed out the open door onto the patio. Anger constricted his throat. She knew nothing about him.

*Sure she does.*

He ignored the accusing voice and trained his attention on the view that stretched for miles over the surrounding hillsides. This was his calling. Dotted with centuries-old amber structures, the artist in him clamored to escape the drama of his family and spend the rest of his days painting every aspect of Italy.

"That is what I *thought*," she said as she came up behind him. "I am impressed that you did not tell Ralph, even though you knew he would be back."

When he did not answer, she added, "And I saw how seriously you take your painting. It is obvious you have worked diligently. The painting of Helena is profound."

Her contrite words helped curtail his anger. He turned around. "Who?"

"Antonio Dolcini's wife—the woman who inspired *Il Viso*. Surely you saw a picture of Louis' painting, catching her anguish just as she received news of Antonio's death?"

Gabe's eyes narrowed. "No. The first time I saw that painting was when Louis shoved a sketch of it in my face."

Her brow raised in surprise. "That is strange. Two nearly identical pieces painted over 800 years apart."

It *was* strange. Everything was strange in this perplexing family. "Who painted it?"

"Helena's brother. He wrote a notation on the back of each of his pieces. After he saw her, he fled to his studio to capture her grief. Your masterpiece is much more moving. I feel the intensity of her pain when I see it. It is beautiful." Her face softened.

Gabe rubbed the back of his neck. "The image of *Il Viso* came to me with such passion that I had to paint it. What is even wilder is that Louis' painting was stolen and he believes I had something to do with it." He frowned. The existence of that canvas could call his artistic reputation into question. The word *plagiarized* still stung his mind. "I cannot explain it."

Livia chewed her lower lip and looked out at the hills. "It would not be the first time that the unexplainable has happened in our family."

"Louis wants nothing to do with me now."

She touched his arm and smiled through a tiny chink in her abrasive armor. "He loves you and regrets his behavior."

Soft shades of yellow ochre reflected off the stones on the patio, enveloping them in a golden glow. He gazed down into her darkened charcoal eyes. For the briefest of moments, he felt a connection with this beautiful creature. Every romantic notion he had ever dreamed about Italy resided in her face.

"You need some sleep." She wrenched her gaze away and stepped back inside. After she showed him to a guest room, he closed the door and looked around. In his state of mind, the glory of the room's Tuscan ambiance eluded him. He fell sound asleep a moment after his head hit the pillow.

## ##

Ralph crouched in the deep shadows between a retaining wall and a large English laurel. Rinaldo had left earlier. At noon, one of the guards at the palazzo answered his phone and drove away. Monitoring the location of the remaining officer, Ralph used his key and slipped unnoticed into the rear of the villa.

He scaled the marble stairs two at a time, panting hard by the time he reached the fourth story room. Following Gabe's directions, he ran to the massive painting that hung on the left wall and felt for the button above the frame. *Nothing.* He started to panic. Maybe he had misunderstood.

He searched the other suites on this floor, but found no other paintings large enough to hide a room. Frantic, he flew back to the first painting and felt along the top with his hand again. *No trigger.* He slammed his fist into the wall as instant rage inflamed him.

Twisting back, he stared at the far wall. *Maybe?* He ran over and flung open the doors to the large alcove that had held the painting he had caught the Kestral stealing. Again, nothing. The coward lied! His eyes fell across the sketch of Helena lying on the cabinet surface. For the first time, he smiled.

Gabe was a fraud and now he could prove it. Now both his cousins could support him in the manner he chose. He grabbed the drawing and jaunted back down the stairs. "I'll get the truth out of him or he's ruined."

## ##

It was past noon when Gabe awoke to the sound of a vacuum cleaner. At first, the billowing white drapes made the walls appear fluid. He rubbed his eyes and got up to wash his face.

On the dresser lay a note that Livia would return in two hours. He picked it up, causing the cash she left beneath it to float to the floor. Frustration tensed his lips to a thin line. He was at her mercy. "No way!" He wadded up the note and threw it at the scattered bills, then wandered around the hotel. Red tile floors covered most of the area, while tall windows opened to the coolness of the mountains. No screens must mean the area had few bugs. So far, that was the only positive aspect of the day.

Outside, twisting lanes played hide and seek between the surrounding buildings, beckoning to him. Should he worry about the police up here? Livia seemed to think it was safe. He shook his head then returned to his room. After plucking the bills off the floor, he set out to make the most of the day. Under a clear blue sky, he exalted in a mind-clearing hike through the hilltop town of Fiesole and ended back on the *piazza*.

The aroma of freshly baked pizza awakened his appetite, drawing him toward the local pizzeria. He sat on an iron chair positioned in the welcoming shade of a large tree. A quiet sigh escaped his mouth. The last time he visited Italy, he had fallen in love with it, had imagined how it would be to share this romantic land with someone he loved.

A vision of Livia—without her attitude—invaded his imagination. A grin came to his face when he remembered the passion in her eyes. He was enjoying the stringy cheese and thinly sliced sausage piled on his pizza when Livia whipped past in her Fiat, saw him, and made a quick U-turn. She skidded to a stop near the ristorante. His fantasy girl had arrived. He pulled a second chair up to his table.

Without a greeting, she slammed down in the seat and launched in with desperate whispers. "I have checked every source I have and cannot find your grandfather."

He sighed. *So much for daydreams.* "What about where Ralph held me?"

She shook her head vigorously, absently rubbing the rabbit foot on her key chain. "I checked there first. There was no evidence left. Ralph must have come back for you."

A shudder passed through Gabe's body. "What now?"

"We must secure the map, find *Il Testamento*, and get Louis back. It is the only way to remove the danger from our family."

"I'm not going on an absurd grail quest."

Her eyes flicked back and forth in unison with the thoughts swirling in her brain. "Did you swear an oath to protect *Il Testamento*?"

"I *promised* to keep what I'd seen a secret."

She scowled and shook her head. "And knowing what you know, you still do not think it would be worth finding?"

Gabe shrugged. "I can't say that I *know* anything." He privately enjoyed how this conversation rankled her.

"You know it is important to Louis and that some people have no trouble stealing, kidnapping, or killing for it. Doesn't that convince you of its immense value?"

He refused to comment.

Anger made her wide-open eyes glint like steel. "Do you not understand that we need it to bargain for him?"

Gabe grabbed a handful of hair and raked it off his forehead. He'd had enough. "What we need is to take that letter to the police and let them find Louis."

"You would risk seeing your grandfather killed?"

"I didn't say that."

Chewing her bottom lip, she stood abruptly. "Let's go."

"Do I have a choice?"

Without answering, she headed to her car and drove him back to the hotel. Neither of them spoke, but nothing escaped his attention. Designer boots peeked out from under her chic jeans while she jammed on and off the brake, gas, and clutch. She had removed her jacket, revealing a simple scooped-neck white tee that made her olive skin glow.

He watched her long fingers shift the car and drive the narrow streets and steep inclines with the precision of a racecar driver. In a different scenario, this would have been an exciting excursion. As it was, her icy heart chilled his interest. *Almost.*

They came to a sudden stop in the space where she had parked earlier that morning. So far, his Italian adventure had been extreme, taking him from the highest hopes to the deepest despair. He almost longed for the boring routine of home.

Livia led him through the small hotel to the outside patio. She came back and set a cup of espresso in front of him, holding his attention with an intense gaze. "If you help me find *Il Testamento*, I will help you find Louis. You owe that to him."

"You mean give you the map?"

Her eyes brightened and she sat on the edge of an iron chair. "So you have it?"

His thoughts ran over all the data he had—and did not have. She knew about the map, but he could not understand why Louis kept him in the dark about her. There was no way to know who was telling the truth. Frustration fought against his loyalty. He let out a deep sigh and shook his head. "No, I don't have it. The police won't let me leave the country, so I might as well see what I can find—alone."

Through tightened lips, she hissed, "You are *stupido*—just like Louis was!" She stormed back inside, leaving him to doubt his decision.

##

Livia only had a moment to get her story straight. She had been stunned when Ralph hauled Gabe out of his hotel. Unconscious. She could not leave him in the storehouse at Ralph's mercy, but she dared not break her ties with Ralph either. If her cousin told his superiors about her involvement, they would be glad to pay her a nasty visit.

She looked heavenward and wished for another way out, but too many pressing financial obligations rested on her shoulders. This needed to be over. She dialed Ralph's number and hoped her voice held steady. "I followed you to the storehouse. I have Gabe." She sat perfectly still, holding her breath.

"WHAT?" Her cousin's foul mood leapt through the connection.

"You are going to do this my way—no more rough stuff," she said, sensing Ralph seething on the other end. She wound a strand of her black hair into a tight twist with her fingers.

"That was far from rough stuff, luv. Now where is he?"

The worst was over. She stood and paced, attempting to sound bold. "Promise me you will give him his head and we will follow him. I do not trust the people you work with. Once they have the relic, we are expendable. Gabe knows where it is. If you mess this up, it is over—the map is lost and we get no money. Then you will meet the same end as your father."

Ralph remained quiet for a moment, but then his words came out like acid. "Right. But if this don't work, I'm doin' it my way, and you won't be happy."

Livia hoped she could trust his greed. And fear. "I am putting a tracking device on his jacket and taking him to the bus station in Florence. He will want to return to the palazzo to get the map and find the relic. Follow him and keep a safe distance behind the bus in case he chooses to flee. I will be in touch. And Ralph, keep this between us. This is a golden opportunity and it is all ours—if we are smart, *eh?*" She ended the call.

This morning's image of Gabe's probing gaze pouring from those irresistible burnished bronze eyes, unnerved her. Too many times since she had met him, she imagined his lean, muscled arms encircling her, his soft, full lips pressing on hers. She swallowed and shook the image away. Too much was at stake for her to weaken her resolve.

She held her quivering finger above the phone, but it rang before she could dial the next number. Livia cleared her voice. "*Buon giorno.*"

"You put the tracking device on his jacket?"

"*Si.* It is all set."

"*Prego.* Now we will feed out the line and see what we catch."

## ##

Gabe finished his coffee with reluctance. When he entered the hotel lobby, he heard Livia's low voice speaking into her phone behind the front desk.

"What if he begins to suspect…"

His weight shifted on the wooden floor, causing the board to squeak.

She stopped in mid-conversation and spun around. Glowering at him, she clicked off her phone. "We have to get going."

"Where?" he shot. He glanced from her to her phone.

She ignored the question. "There are clean clothes for you in there." She pointed to his room and walked out.

Grabbing the back of his neck, he squeezed hard against the fear and frustration that had lodged there. He was at the end of his patience and still not out of danger.

He stepped into the shower and let the hot water soothe his tense muscles. Aware that time was ticking away, he refused to hurry. *Let her wait.* Afterward, he found the fresh clothes hanging in the closet. The white, long-sleeved shirt and ironed designer jeans fit perfectly. When he pulled on a navy blue blazer in front of the mirror, his reflection mimicked every fashionable Italian male he had seen since arriving in Italy—another pointed reminder of the loss of a dream vacation. For now, he had to be smart. Livia was in league with someone. Who had been on the other end of the phone?

She stood in the lobby when he came out. Their eyes met and deflected in equal aversion. He folded his arms across his chest at her haughty stance. "So, where am I being dragged to now?"

"To the bus station. Where you go is your decision," she said, grabbing her purse and keys.

He had not expected that. Again, they were silent while her Fiat flew through the streets. They shot down the mountain, dodging swarms of micro cars and Vespas. Gabe wondered how pedestrians stayed alive in the fair city of Florence.

Angry and perplexed, he did not trust himself to have a civil conversation with her. It was obvious he could not expect one in return. Instead, he focused on the architecture and landscape, hoping to burn it into his memory. It was not likely he would be returning.

They reached the bus station, and she shot into a tiny spot on the crowded curb. "Go."

"What about my grandfather?"

"You want to do everything on your own—then do it!"

He opened the door and she handed him his wallet. His eyebrows knit together. "How did you get this?"

"Not your problem. *Ciao.*"

# Chapter 16

Florence, Italy

He could get out. Now. Just fly home and away from the madness. Grasping his wallet in both hands, Gabe felt relief. And uncertainty. He made his way to the crowded ticket counter, rifling through his wallet for his credit card, and stopped. He had no passport.

Glowering, he weighed his options. He could take the bus to Rovereto and be ready to meet Signore Belvedere at the art museum on Saturday. Satisfaction laughed against the frustration of the last two days. At least his time would not be a total loss.

But the tender eyes of his grandfather crowded out his intensions. *Can I really leave him?* His jaw clenched. The man was trouble. Gabe pushed his credit card toward the attendant and hesitated. Finally, he said, "Siena," silently berating his own foolishness.

Time dragged while he waited for the bus. At last, he got up from the bench and stood in a long line. Before he could board, however, he felt a bump in his ribs. He turned, expecting to hear an apology. The piercing black eyes of a short, intense man, glared up at him. Gabe looked down at the barrel of a gun. His breath caught.

"Gabriel Dolcini, you'll have to come with me," the black-eyed man commanded. His voice communicated a chilling lack of emotion that contrasted with his singsong Italian-accented English. Gabe nodded that he understood and the man tilted his head toward the exit.

At the curb, a limo waited for them. The hair on Gabe's arms tingled. Glancing around, he spotted Detective Orsini at the far end of the terminal. But before he had the chance to call for help, the little man with the gun pushed him into the limo from behind.

Gabe ducked his head just before it would have hit the doorframe. He glimpsed the driver through the center window. His mouth opened as his mind tumbled in an effort to grasp the situation. "Rinaldo?"

The chauffeur said nothing, but sped away.

The gunman holstered his pistol and buttoned his jacket to conceal the weapon. He introduced himself. "I trust I did not make you wet yourself, but I had to be certain you would come with me without an incident. I am Firelli Dambrosi. Your grandfather hired me to keep an eye on you."

Gabe's head was spinning. "So where were you when Ralph conked me out?"

A grimace pulled Firelli's mouth down. "We underestimated how desperate he had become."

"Who took my grandfather?"

"No one. I found out about an attempt to kidnap the conte and spirited him away before they got to him. I have him safely hidden."

"I want to see him," Gabe demanded.

Rinado looked in the rearview mirror at Firelli.

"In time," Firelli said, "but first we need to get you to a place of safety away from Ralph and Livia."

"Livia?"

"She's not in the conte's court." His deeply lined face was grim.

Gabe was stunned into silence.

Firelli continued, "She and Ralph are working for a private collector—some kind of pseudo knight. They are hoping to get a huge price for the artifact."

It was hard to swallow that Livia was in league with Ralph. "If she is working with Ralph, why did she rescue me from him?"

"Good cop, bad cop," Firelli replied. "She hoped to get out of you what your cousin could not." His finger twitched against the seat.

Gabe glanced in the mirror at Rinaldo. "Where are we going?"

Firelli answered. "To wait for your grandfather."

##

"Who got him?" Livia screamed into the phone.

"Rinaldo was there with the limo, and some other guy had a gun on them," Ralph whined.

"A gun!" Her mind spun at the possible outcomes.

Ralph finished his rant. "Detective Orsini was hangin' out at the other end, so's I couldn't get anywhere near Gabe. This is your fault. I could 'ave gotten the location out of him by now." Ralph's venom traveled across the miles and hit home in Livia's ear.

She bit her bottom lip until it pinched. "Are you certain it was not one of your guys who picked him up?"

"Never saw 'im before."

None of it made sense. "Let's hope they are still headed back to the palazzo. Follow from a distance. The bug I put on Gabe will keep them in our sights. Let me know where you are and we can make our move when I get there. Do not lose them Ralph—this is worth a LOT of money."

She clicked off her phone, hands shaking. What if this guy *forces* the information out of Gabe? She shook the thought away. *No.* Gabe was unconvinced of the legend. It would not take much for him to give up the location of the map. She huffed. The end to this chase had been so close to her grasp. This mess was Louis' fault. He should have given her the information. Nobody would have had to get hurt.

##

"Wait! Aren't we going to my grandfather's home?" They had been driving for an hour and passed the sign at the roundabout that pointed to Siena.

"No. It's not safe for the conte or you. We have a better place to keep you until this storm blows over."

Gabe's nerves had been on edge for days. It was hard to trust anyone—especially this jerk. He struggled to keep his cool and focused on each participant. He trusted his grandfather, even if he was obsessed. Rinaldo seemed genuine in the way he cared for Louis—but he was with Firelli. Gabe had just met Firelli. What kind of guy sticks a gun in your ribs to make you go with him? Yet, Firelli was in opposition to Livia and Ralph. Gabe's musings continued to spin with no resting place.

Firelli instructed, "Turn here."

The car decelerated with a sudden lurch and made a sharp left-hand turn up the side of a large hill. Through the oak and cypress trees, Gabe caught glimpses of a ruin. "What's this?"

"A safe house," Firelli answered they stopped. He led the way up a path to a solid wood door. "In here." He moved to one side so Gabe and Rinaldo could step into the generous entry hall. They passed by a window that Firelli opened while Gabe went on to explore the main living area. Sunlight drenched the room, filtering in through tall, barred windows.

"Your grandfather will be along soon," Firelli offered before Gabe had a chance to ask. "Let's have some food," he called to Rinaldo. A disdainful smirk accompanied his demand.

Rinaldo's lips tightened, but he nodded and disappeared through the large entry to go back outside. He returned with bags of food and began to prepare a meal in the well-equipped kitchen.

Gabe scanned the ample room. Most of the second story flooring had collapsed, leaving a few remaining boards intact as a suggestion of a previous upstairs. A brick and wood ceiling hung twenty feet in the air. It looked in good repair. In fact, the whole place was disparate—outside a ruin, inside a refurbished home. "Who owns this?" he asked.

"I rented it," Firelli answered. "Louis asked me to secure a safe house for times such as these."

"Times such as what?"

"If the great Conte Dolcini and his family need to run and hide."

*He's trying to bait me.* Gabe collected himself, intent on getting some answers. "How do you fit into this?"

"I told you. I was hired to keep a lookout for you. I'm a bodyguard, you might say." He pulled a pack of cigarettes out of his jacket and swaggered outside.

In the kitchen, Rinaldo chopped tomatoes and toasted bread for *bruschetta*. Gabe walked around the tall blue-tiled bar that separated the kitchen from the rest of the room. He took the opportunity to question the butler alone. "Have you known Firelli for awhile then? I mean, my grandfather never mentioned him."

The servant continued to chop the vegetables on the wooden butcher-block countertop. With the tomato diced into small bits, he turned to Gabe. "All I know is that Signore Firelli assured me that your grandfather is safe and is being moved here this afternoon by an associate." He opened a package of meat. "I am preparing his favorite dish of wild boar. He has been through too much for a man of his age."

Gabe left the kitchen and stepped into the entrance hall to peer out the open window. Firelli was talking on his cell phone. Gabe leaned closer to listen.

"He is nervous, but that is to be expected."

Pause.

"*Si*, Your Excellency, but not too soon—perhaps after dinner. The special wine will get him talking. If not..."

Pause.

"Do you think that is necessary? He believes my story and expects his *nonno* to arrive here shortly."

Pause.

"*Si*, I understand." He flipped his phone shut and headed for the door.

Gabe escaped to the kitchen and was striding out with an apple as Firelli entered the living room. Dropping onto the sofa, Gabe asked, "Who is this guy that Ralph and Livia are working for? You said he was a collector."

"Of sorts." Firelli lifted a sap green wine bottle from the tiled bar. "No sherry?" he asked Rinaldo. The butler shook his head. Firelli frowned and perched his short body on a stool. He poured two glasses of wine and brought one to Gabe. "The man is part of a group known as the Dead Knights. They are intent on acquiring religious relics." He gulped a full swallow.

"Why?" Gabe asked, pretending to sip the wine.

"To destroy them."

That jerked Gabe to attention. "Why would they do that?"

Firelli stuck his bottom lip out as though pondering the question. "Their plan is to break the power that religious frauds hold over the gullible."

"But would they really *kill* to accomplish that? I mean, Ralph stabbed that police officer."

Rinaldo's head swung up. "What officer?"

"At the hotel. The police questioned me and then set a guard outside my door. Ralph attacked him early this morning when he grabbed me. I saw his bloodied body before I was drugged."

Gabe looked for a sign of recognition from either man. Firelli shrugged it off. Rinaldo frowned and looked like he would like to ask another question. He studied Firelli then returned to his cooking.

After taking another long drink, Firelli moved to the sofa opposite Gabe and said, "That sounds like Ralph's style. His family has been trouble to the conte for many years."

Rinaldo's lips were drawn thin and tight when he set a plate of sliced pears and cheese on the coffee table between them. Gabe watched him shoot a piercing look at the oblivious Firelli before returning to the kitchen.

As Firelli leaned to pick up a pear, Gabe glanced at the pistol through his open jacket. Fear gripped him, but he had to get answers. "What's this man's name?"

Firelli smirked. "The Scarlett Pimpernell, for all I know." He turned the conversation in a new direction. "Looks like your *nonno* has pulled you into a *ratto's* nest. The art exhibit was bait you could not refuse, *eh?*"

Gabe recoiled. "My grandfather extended a generous invitation."

Ignoring the comment, Firelli finished his glass and went to the counter to pour another. "I heard he got your *nonna* killed—no wonder your father left. Seems like trouble just comes looking for your family."

"How do you know all this?" Gabe worked to hold his temper in check.

Firelli was halfway through his second glass of wine. "Your *nonno*, of course. What I do not understand, however, is how he can keep holding out while his family gets murdered. Why not just give them what they want? The *Custodi* could get on with their lives, unharmed."

Gabe started at his words. Louis said no one except those who had taken the vow knew that name. It was doubtful his grandfather would share that with a hired bodyguard. He chanced a glance at Rinaldo, who seemed unaware of the conversation.

Firelli smirked. "What about you, Gabriel? You seem like a reasonable man. A pragmatist. Are you ready to risk your life to protect an old relic?"

Stalling to think out a plan, Gabe answered, "I think it's nothing but a trumped up myth, yet one that is very important to my grandfather. I'm not religious, but if it's of value to so many people, it needs to be displayed in a secure museum or church, not destroyed by fanatics."

An artificial smile crossed Firelli's face. "Well then, you are in luck. When the ARCC, the world's largest religious complex is finished in America, it will have the highest-grade security system. They will pay a king's ransom for the relic. I can help you find it, and you can sell it to them and become a rich man."

"How much are you talking about?"

A jar crashed in the kitchen. Rinaldo's clear, cool voice dripped with sarcasm. "*Si*, why not hand it over to them, let them create their circus and make a fortune." He bent to clean up the mess, then moved the green wine bottle from the tiled bar to the counter on the other side.

Firelli fumed at Rinaldo's outburst, his hand fingering the gun through his jacket. Gabe answered with care, "Louis' plan has always been to present the relic to the small church in Seborga. If it really does exist, that is my grandfather's decision, not mine."

A dangerous expression passed over Firelli's face. "We will see whose decision it is."

Gabe glared at the small man, but held his tongue.

Rinaldo interrupted the growing hostility. "I will return shortly," he said and strode out to the limo.

Firelli drained his glass and arose for a refill. He reached over the bar, picked up the green bottle off the wooden kitchen counter, and poured the remaining liquid into his glass. After gulping down the wine, he slammed the goblet on the counter.

Gabe jumped, watching his every movement.

A snide grin stole across Firelli's face. He mocked cheerfulness and glanced at Gabe's still full glass. "You don't care for that vintage? Let us try another." He grabbed a brown wine bottle off the counter, swayed, and plopped down hard onto the barstool. "We must pour you a special wine to celebrate your reunion with your *nonno*."

"I don't care for more wine." Gabe glanced toward the front door, hoping Rinaldo would enter soon. His fingers gripped the arm of the sofa.

Firelli shook his head and slurred, "Well then, how do we get Dolcini's secret from his grandson?" His mouth twisted to a sneer. Opening his jacket, his hand reached for the sidearm and brought the gun around. Gabe jumped up from the sofa, eyes focused on the gun. Firelli seemed to wobble. His fingers went limp and he let go of the weapon.

Rinaldo appeared from the entrance hall and stepped into the room at that moment. His eyes opened wide at the sight. Quick as a cat, he leapt and caught the weapon just as the bodyguard hit the floor.

"What happened to him?" Gabe yelled.

Rinaldo's anxious eyes flitted from Firelli to the empty green bottle. "He threatened you with a gun. I…I emptied the conte's medication into the wine bottle." Clearing his throat, he explained, "After his conversation, I was certain he was not with the conte. Besides, he knew about the *Custodi*. Very few know that word."

"What about you?" Gabe asked.

"I live with the conte." He gave a thin smile. "It is hard to guard all of one's secrets from one's staff."

Looking down at Firelli, Gabe reflected. "If he is not working with Ralph's Dead Knights, then we are dealing with another, separate faction. He seemed to be pulling for the ARCC. Do you know who is behind that organization?"

Rinaldo glanced down at Firelli and did not reply. He grabbed the small man's arm. "Please, signore, help me move him down here." They pulled the unconscious man down a set of rickety stairs to a dank basement and set him against a stone pillar. Rinaldo tied him to it with effortless efficiency. "We must go—now."

Once in the limo, Gabe asked, "Did you know he was working against Louis when you picked me up at the bus station?"

"No. He told me he had Conte Dolcini. I wanted to see if he really knew where he was."

"So I was bait? What if he'd killed me?"

"*Mi dispiace*, I am sorry, but you are still alive. I hoped he would bring your grandfather to us. Now, we will have to try something else."

"Like what—stake me to an olive tree and call for the wolves?" Blood pounded in Gabe's head. "How did Firelli know I would be at the bus station?"

Rinaldo shrugged his shoulders.

Gabe's mind thrashed at the intricate web entangling him. He could run, but someone had his grandfather. The last of the sun's glow was dimming, mimicking Gabe's limited grasp of this growing mess. "I've heard one version of the story. What do *you* know about Ralph's part in all of this?"

"If I make speak freely, signore. A year ago, the conte caught Ralph searching through the house and expelled him. In the altercation that followed, Ralph screamed that his mother told him everything—who his father had contacted, how much money to ask for, and that the conte was responsible for his father's death."

"Is that true?"

Rinaldo rubbed his chin. "No, but Ralph believes it. If *he* took the conte, I fear for him."

"What about Livia? Do you think she is working with them?"

"She is a *custode* and very close to the conte. I cannot believe she would do him harm." He turned the limo back down the hill. "Where would you like to go, signore?"

Gabe thought for a minute. "Can we get into the palazzo? I need to get the map and find *Il Testamento*. Firelli was lying about knowing where Louis is. I will trade it to Ralph and the Dead Knights and get my grandfather back.

Rinaldo smiled. "*Sì,* signore."

# Chapter 17

Near Siena, Italy

Livia fumed while she waited for Ralph to answer his phone. *What is he doing?* After the sixth ring, he picked up.

"Yeah?"

"Are you there yet?"

"Don't hand me that. I had to buy petrol and get some food. I'm entering the house now."

In the silence, she heard the door close and dishes clatter. "Did you find them?"

"The limo was gone when I got here. I don't see anyone—oh great, Gabe left his jacket here—with the tracker. Great plan," he bellowed. "Now we lost him and the conte. Who do you think took the old man, anyway?"

"I don't know, but we might be able to use this to push Gabe to cooperate."

Ralph grumbled, "If we find him again. They must have left in a hurry, there's a bunch of food sitting around."

Livia heard him munching. She worked to contain her impatience. "Anything else?"

"Wait a minute. Here we are. There's a guy out cold and tied up in the cellar."

"Just leave him and get out of there. We need to regroup."

"Just leave him in the dark? That's not nice."

##

After Ralph left, Livia followed the tracking signal and arrived at the ruin. She slipped inside the lighted room and peered around the wall into the kitchen. A door stood ajar. *That must lead to the cellar.* Her heart thumped against her chest.

The toe of her unsteady foot pressed lightly on the first tread. It creaked. She stopped and listened. It was too dark to see anything. Ralph did not know this guy, so who was he? And what side was he playing on?

She stretched her hand toward the light switch to her right. The tip of her finger flipped the switch, but the step gave way, tossing her forward. She grabbed both sides of the stairwell to steady her momentum. A squeal escaped her lips.

Nothing moved. Imagining a hand reaching for her ankle from below, it took all her courage to continue down the stairs. The dim ceiling light cast vague shadows across the musty chamber. Sitting on the floor, a man leaned against a pillar. Thin rope held him upright. His head hung to one side. *Still out.* She edged forward, bending to check on the prisoner.

Swallowing, she moved closer. Carefully lifting his jacket, she reached for his wallet. Her hands trembled while she rifled through the compartments. Wide with fear, her eyes flitted to his face several times. The name on the driver's license read "Firelli Dambrosi." A folded note, written on fine linen, peeked from behind a few bills. She read it quickly and bit her bottom lip while trying to ascertain its meaning.

"*Your Excellency,*

*Attached, please find the letters I uncovered during my visit at the Abbey of Saint John in Argentella, Palombara. After questioning the late Reverendo Tito in Seborga, I discovered he was in possession of a priceless document that has remained in the church's archives, also included. As always, you may count on my unwavering support.*

*Most sincerely,*

*Reverendo Bartolomeo Porta*"

*What did this Porta find?* She pocketed the note and reached back into the unconscious man's jacket, hoping to find the attachment. *Nothing.* She searched through the remainder of his pockets. *Empty.* Disappointed, she drew back and raised her phone to take a photo of him.

Firelli's eyes flew open. With a snarl, he lunged at her. Shrieking, she stumbled backward onto the stone floor and scurried backward like a crab. The man struggled violently and whipped his body from side to side. The cord began to loosen as he pushed to get his feet under him. *Will the rope hold?* She was not waiting to find out.

Racing back up the stairs, she flipped off the light and shut the door. *No lock.* She dashed through the kitchen and tripped over a stool. Muffled growls echoed up the cellar stairwell. Her fingers trembled when they grasped the front doorknob and tugged open the heavy door.

She jumped into her car and kept her eye on the open entrance while twisting the key to start her Fiat. Throwing it into reverse, she raced backward, then slammed on the brakes. The auto skidded to a stop, inches before it reached the wide trunk of a nearby oak.

A shadow darted across the entry window. Gears ground. The Fiat's wheels slipped on the loose dirt. Finally, they found traction. In a swirl of dust, she sped from the ruin, just as the man burst through the front door and ran after her.

*Who are these people?* Racing down the road, her high beams illuminated everything. Except what was relevant.

## ##

It was imperative that Gabe get inside the palazzo to use the map. *If it can be called a map.*

Rinaldo spoke through the divider window of the limo when he approached the massive residence. "From what you said, it is likely you are still wanted by the police, signore. Please, lie quietly on the floor and let me arrange this." He exited the limo to talk to the night guard.

Within a few minutes, the guard waved him toward the garage. Once the garage door was down, Gabe followed Rinaldo inside. "I told them there was no more need of their services," the chauffeur explained. Still, he closed the shades against possible watchers in the night and turned on only one small table lamp.

In the minimal light, Gabe took the stairs two at a time to his grandfather's room. He knew the massive suite would be empty, but wished desperately it had all been an explainable misunderstanding. The room's silence shouted the contrary. He slumped onto the black varnished chaise and clenched his hair in both fists. All at once, he felt tired. Exhausted.

He met Rinaldo outside the suite. "I have to get some rest before I can think anymore." Gabe made his way to the room he had first entered the week before. *Only a week.* Anxious thoughts filled his mind, but at last fatigue won out and he slept.

## 

Forming a rigid semicircle, a host of brilliant angelic beings waited for a decision. In front of them, a man with wavy blond curls quaked, his open hand pleading with frustration. As Gabe watched, it seemed very important that the blond man make the right decision.

One angel appealed to him. "For Antonio's sons."

Desperation flooded Gabe as the vision drew him closer, almost into the arena. Voiceless, he felt compelled to urge the man to do what had been asked.

As the blond man turned, Gabe saw a red cross on his white tunic—but the tunic was not white. The front was drenched in blood. The knight roared an agonized cry and wailed his answer. He raised his sword to strike the rocky hilltop. Gabe recoiled when the sword charged straight at the solid rock alongside the knight's foot.

The dream vanished.

Instantly awake, Gabe puzzled at the blue ceiling. He had thought he would have awoken on that mystic hilltop. The dream conveyed the sense that many lives were at stake, sending residual alarm racing through his veins. The feeling of urgency remained as he opened his door to Rinaldo's knock.

"*Buon giorno*, signore. Breakfast is waiting in the dining room."

Gabe jogged downstairs, not certain where to begin. He sat down at the expansive table and gulped his espresso. His dream superseded his strategizing. Who was that man and what did he need to do? No answers came. *Imagine that.*

Gobbling his food, he glanced over the morning paper that waited next to his cup. Written in Italian, he could only pick out the gist of the main story. Rinaldo returned with orange juice, and Gabe pointed to the photograph on the front page. "Isn't this that Cardinal who was at the airport?"

"*Sì.*" Rinaldo did not have to look.

"What's the story about?"

A frown creased Rinaldo's mouth and Gabe assumed he had already read the article. "There is a powerful group pushing an agenda for the very large and very expensive American Religious Cultural Center. They say their goal is to bring peace between all religions by creating a shrine of understanding. So far, they have raised hundreds of millions from the U.S. government, promising a payback in the reduction of religious terrorism."

"How could America's elected officials fall for that?"

"Perhaps it will be worth their while."

Gabe tilted his head. "You mean kickbacks?

Rinaldo shrugged and Gabe asked him to translate the article.

The butler cleared his throat. "Cardinal Vincenzo is working to calm outraged leaders from several denominations who are protesting what they say is the American Religious Cultural Center's purely political agenda—a reach for power in government. Vincenzo is quoted saying, 'Do not fret about man's futile schemes. If evil, they will come to nothing.'

"Other smaller religions are demanding equal influence in the leadership of the ARCC, regardless of the election results. A groundbreaking ceremony near Washington D.C. is slated for next year. Twice as large as Vatican City, it has been nicknamed, 'America's Vatican,' and is even feared by some to be a puppet of Rome."

Gabe's eyebrows furrowed. "What's this really about?"

"This is about taking humanity back to the dark ages of religious rule. Shall I continue reading?"

"Please."

"Under the democratic election process, nominations have been accepted to elect the Head Administer and other top officials to govern the ARCC. Registration for nominations closes in six days, followed by a vote of the registered clergy from every participating religion.

"Public speculation is widespread over which denomination will see their candidate rise to the top. Though no one is willing to go on record, rumors leaked that someone with major support has received an omen decreeing God's favor." Rinaldo set the paper down. "Imagine the influence an item like *Il Testamento* would carry in this struggle for power."

Gabe raised his eyebrows as Rinaldo left the dining room. Thoughts ran deep under the man's smooth exterior. Tapping his finger on the photo of Cardinal Vincenzo's sympathetic face as he addressed the concerns of angry protestors, Gabe felt heartened that *someone* maintained a sane perspective.

He recalled Firelli's comments. On the one hand, the most prominent religious leaders on earth were vying for leadership of the new religious center. On the other was his grandfather's obscure secret. Could there really be a connection? He shook his head. The gap was too wide.

Rinaldo returned with another cup of espresso. Gabe asked, "Do you know why Louis needed me if he has other *custodi* like Livia who are already in on this?"

The butler shrugged. "It seems it was an honor he only wanted to share with his progeny. However, it has caused other members of his family distress." He hesitated. "I believe they have been concerned about the conte's health, and stubbornness, for a long time. What would have happened if he had died before… "

"Before I got here," Gabe finished.

Rinaldo nodded. "I overheard Livia pleading with him to share his secrets with her, but he insisted you would come."

"No wonder she resents me."

Rinaldo raised one eyebrow. "Nevertheless, peace will only return to this house when *Il Testamento* is out of the conte's hands. I am glad you will help find it."

Both men jumped when the phone's loud ring disrupted the coffin-like silence of the palazzo. Rinaldo reached for it and answered in his monotonous tone, "*Buon giorno.* Dolcini residence." He listened, frowned, and then handed the phone to Gabe.

"How's the little chump doin'?"

The acid in Ralph's voice caused Gabe to jerk the phone from his ear before he yelled back into it. "What did you do with Grandfather? You bring him here—now!" Fury raced through Gabe's body.

"Oh, the *white* knight are we?" Ralph mocked. "Tell you what, mate. Why don't you bring ol' Ralphy the map and help me find the relic, and I'll tell you where your *nonno* is?"

"I don't have it! The whole thing's a farce, Ralph."

Ralph's voice sounded lethal. "You ain't a good liar. I know you got the map to the *testa* and apparently, you're the only one who knows how to use it. I got a real impatient *Dead* Knight fixin' to do me some serious harm if I don't hand over that relic. You got twenty-four hours to get it to me, or last week was the only memory you'll ever have of your dear *nonno.* I'll be in touch."

Gabe relayed the message to Rinaldo, who frowned while he cleared the table. "Did Ralph tell you where to bring the relic if you find it?"

"Not yet, but he just confirmed he's working with the Dead Knights Firelli told us about." Scowling, Gabe attempted to relax and allow random thoughts to swirl in his mind—an exercise he used to clear his head before painting.

"Excuse me," he said after a couple of minutes. He jogged up the stairs to his room, retrieved his computer, and returned to Louis' desk in the library. So far, all he knew about the Dead Knights was smoke and mirrors. There had to be some concrete information about them. He typed in "dead knights" and filtered through five pages of useless search results before finding an obscure mention in an old French book. He hit translate and was surprised at the outcome.

The book documented the 1717 formation of Freemasonry, which some of its members claimed was descended from the original Knights Templar. This claim had prompted an emphatic dispute from a shadowy figure, who insisted he was a member of a group called the "Dead Knights"—the *only* link to the famous Templars.

A summary at the end of the passage read, "After much investigation, the claims were uncovered as a hoax, breaking any connection of either group to the disbanded Knights Templar." Gabe noted that the summary did not discount the existence of the Dead Knights.

Further down the page, another search result caught Gabe's eye. In 1791, Jean-Paul Guarneri, a political prisoner, was released from La prison de l'Abbaye in Paris. Later, in his memoir, he wrote of a condemned man who begged him to arrange his freedom, stating he was a member of the Dead Knights and could pay him from the vast Templar treasure. Guarnier noted that during his imprisonment, inquisitors visited the man's cell regularly, demanding the location of an unnamed relic.

Gabe sat back and tapped a pen on the desktop. So, the Dead Knights had a history, but it was sketchy at best.

Rinaldo entered and handed him two envelopes. Gabe glanced at the return address on the first one and jammed his fingers through his hair. His bank. He caught Rinaldo watching him. "Thanks." He laid it on the desk without opening it.

The butler left, and Gabe opened the second letter, from his mother. He briefly skimmed her concerns, including a description of Sonia's distressing interview with an unrelenting investigator about Gabe's alleged sexual misconduct.

He crushed the letter and threw it across the room, then shoved the chair back and stomped over to pick it up. Outside the window lay the ancient city of Siena. Morning light caressed everything with a terra cotta glow. He sighed. So much beauty here, but it was untouchable.

He slammed back in his chair, determined to find a quick, sensible way to solve this crisis and get on with his life. Searching under "knights, templars, treasure," he found numerous references to the Templars and the supposed treasures they had discovered—the Holy Grail at the top of the list. He skimmed through the articles with no new revelations.

"Okay, let's see what anyone else may know." He typed in "custodi del testamento." *Nothing.* When he put the phrase into an online translator, it came up as expected, "keepers of the testament." He rubbed his forehead. Something niggled at his brain. He leaned back and replayed Ralph's message in his mind, "I know you got the map to the *testa*, and...." Had Ralph shortened the word, *"testamento"* inadvertently?

Typing "testa" into the translator gave him an unexpected result. *Testa* meant "head." His heart rate quickened, and he clicked back to the Templar article. Scanning down, his eyes widened when he read, "Under King Philip's torture, several Templars spoke of a head that was carried secretly by their leaders. The most common agreement held that it was either the head of the Templar's martyred heroine, Eugenia, or..."

Gabe's jaw dropped when he read the last line, "...the head of John the Baptist!" He leaned back in the leather chair. "Wow." Then, envisioning the relic, he wrinkled his nose at what he might uncover. With some credibility backing the mystique of the relic, Gabe's willingness grew.

He released a key from its hiding place in Louis' desk, rushed out of the library, and descended the steps toward the secret room. After glancing behind him, he unlocked the door and entered the outer room. Certain he was alone, he pressed on the bottom of the mirror where his grandfather had shown him. He waited a moment and pressed again, stepped through the opening, and switched on the light.

The seat of the chair opened easily. Once again, he extracted the letters. Picking up Antonio's map, he re-read it.

*"My dearest Helena,*

*I fear we shall not be together again in this life, but we shall spend an eternity side by side. I was so close to seeing your beautiful face once more, but assassins have followed relentlessly to discover our charge. We must protect it. I ask you to join me in the Custodi del Testamento and continue this sacred undertaking. Secure it as I have instructed below, and keep it safe until you can safely return it to Seborga. You will understand my passion once your eyes behold its worth, and you will comprehend what must be done.*

*How I long to enter the door to my haven, pass by the library, and descend through the narrow opening to the cavernous wine cellar. Oh, to enter the south room and taste the new wine that rests in the light of the eastern alcove. When one drinks of that ageless wine, one lays hold of his dearest treasure. This is my desire for you, my love.*
*Until I see you again,*
*Antonio*


Gabe spoke into the air, "She must have hidden *Il Testamento* in an alcove in this house—Antonio's haven." But who could want it badly enough to kill for it? He would have no problem exchanging a shriveled head for his grandfather. Now to find it.

He dropped onto the other brocade-covered chair. *Think.* "Begin at the beginning." He lifted the delicate letter and climbed the stairs to follow the directions. Mid-step on the second set of stairs, however, he halted. Livia's stern face met his. He scowled, "What are you doing here?"

She lifted her chin and clutched the iron railing. "Rinaldo let me in—family, you know." She glanced at the faded document in his hand. "What is that?"

Anger burned in his gut. "It's none of your business."

She retaliated, "It is certainly my business. You are the short-timer here. If Louis had not been so stubborn, he would not have been in danger and *Il Testamento* would be safe. Now look at this mess since you have arrived!"

"I had nothing to do with this mess. But I did promise my grandfather to keep quiet about it and that is what I intend to do—alone."

She quieted her voice. "You forget that Louis is like a *nonno* to me also."

"Yeah, you looked real concerned in Fiesole. All you could think about was getting your hands on the map and grabbing the treasure."

Her face contorted with pain and anger. A hint of a tear swelled in the corner of her eye. "That is not how it is. The death of the contessa caused a permanent strain of grief on my family. I grew up around an undercurrent of sorrow and fear that I could not comprehend.

"Last year, Louis told me he feared a new attack. Do you understand? My family is threatened. Who will be next? My father is in a wheelchair. Unlike Louis, we do not have the resources to hire a bodyguard."

"What bodyguard?"

"Rinaldo. Did you think he was just a butler?"

Gabe felt foolish. "I suppose I did."

"Well, in my family it falls to me, and I cannot allow this to continue. I am helping at Louis' request."

Gabe was suspicious. "When did that happen?"

"After you left to go home."

He countered, "I was *thrown out* for stealing a painting I didn't know existed."

She dropped her belligerent eyes. "Well, after you had gone, Louis called me to the palazzo to ask for my help, and…" She stopped.

"And what?"

"Nothing. He was desperate and I said I would help. But you are making that very difficult. Last night I barely escaped from a man who is stalking our family. This has to end."

In the seconds of quiet, Gabe was able to study the lines of her cheekbones. Tension constricted her mouth and strain shadowed her eyes. *Fear? Yes—great fear. And grief.* He softened. "I'm sorry you've had to live with that."

She inclined her head, coaxing him. "Louis showed you the map, but I have information that will be valuable for using it—if you let me help, *eh?*"

Livia was at his mercy. If she had the information, she would have bolted right through him to use it. Determination was a trait worth having on his side right now. Besides, Rinaldo seemed to trust her. Gabe managed a small one-sided grin. "Okay. Let's start over."

For the first time, a true smile, soft and appreciative, lit her face.

He breathed in. "What is that heavenly scent?"

"I make exclusive perfumes—with my own proprietary ingredients. Perhaps someday I will show you, *eh?*" She smiled up at him.

This was definitely the right thing to do. He handed her the map.

After a quick perusal of Antonio's words, she glanced up, her charcoal eyes now glinting silver with excitement. "He based the map on his home. *Magnifico.*"

"But, did Helena live here at that time?"

"Absolutely. The Dolcini's built this palazzo a hundred years before Antonio was born. His father was wealthy and owned an alabaster quarry near Volterra. She pointed to an exquisite statue. "He hired great artists to carve these beautiful pieces, most of them for the churches throughout the city-states."

Relief flooded Gabe as he listened to reasonable conversation. Watching Livia's animated face while relating the history of their family, he noticed this was the first time in a while that a real smile had visited his own. It felt good. "Then let's begin."

She handed the map back to him, and they climbed to the front door. He read, "I long to enter the door to my haven." They looked ahead from the entrance. "...pass by the library and descend to the cavernous wine cellar." Gabe led the way past the library and stopped at the top of the stairs that led to the secret room. "There is no wine cellar down there."

Eyes twinkling, Livia moved past him. "Of course there is. When I was a child, I accompanied Louis and my papa down these steps. I played I was a princess, guarded by the dragons under the carved table while Louis shared wine from his estate in Monticiano."

She rushed down the steps, straight into the room outside the secret chamber. Gabe followed her gaze. It swept over the habitat filled with predators hunting their prey on carved wooden legs of dusty furniture, peering from cornices on the support columns, and glaring out from a myriad of paintings. He quelled a shiver.

Turning to her right, she stopped. A quizzical expression anchored itself on her features. "Something is wrong." She moved toward the mirror, turned back toward Gabe, and let her eyes skip from antique to antique. "These chairs were here," she pointed, then turned back toward the mirror. "But beyond this, there were cases of wine from floor to ceiling. The walls were of large stones. It was a very cool room. I had to bring a sweater whenever I came with papa." She looked back at him, still puzzled. Her smiling mouth turned down in disappointment.

Gabe's hesitation did not last long. "You're right." He slipped his foot under the mirror. "Since you are already a *custode*, I don't see how this is breaking any confidence."

He was rewarded with her exuberant outburst, "This is amazing."

They stepped through and Gabe closed the mirror. She continued to move through the room. "It's so empty. The walls were filled with rows of wine. Racks sat in aisles—look." She pointed to a place in the ceiling where loops of rusted iron protruded. "I thought it was scary when Louis explained those hooks would keep his racks upright in an earthquake. I imagined all that broken glass, so preferred to stay in the other room on the soft carpet."

Pulling his eyes away from the wonder in her beautiful face, he read the next line in the letter.

. "Oh, to enter the south room and taste the new wine that rests in the light of the eastern alcove."

He had always been spot-on with direction. "This room faces south. Do you see an alcove?" They scanned the room, but nothing was apparent.

She bit her lip and let her mind wander. "I don't remember an alcove, but perhaps it has been walled up."

"I should warn you," Gabe grinned, "We're looking for some kind of preserved head."

Livia whipped around, "Head? What makes you so certain?"

Gabe explained. "We know that '*testamento*' means 'testament,' but I found out that '*testa*' translates to 'head.' It looks as though *testamento* was a code word for *testa*. The Templars were plagued with rumors about worshipping a head, possibly of John the Baptist. Maybe they did."

Livia pondered that. "It would not be so bad to hand over an old head." Gabe turned on the other lights so that the whole room was brightly illuminated. "The room is so empty," she repeated.

Gabe ran his hand over the bookcase. "Louis spent a lot of time looking for it in here. He moved everything out and constructed a barrier wall behind the mirror to hide his investigation." Gabe studied the stones in the eastern section and coaxed the bookcase farther from the wall. He pointed to several spots. "Look at these scratches and chips—probably where he tried to find a cavity."

Livia examined the damage that extended just inches into the fissures between the stones. "He did not get far—these stones are solid. It does not look as though they ever had an opening in them."

Gabe straightened after checking for any other possibilities. "Unless we are willing to tackle these monsters, I don't see how we would get to an alcove."

"So if there is no alcove here, then what are Antonio's directions about?" Frustration was evident in her voice.

"Perhaps the clues were written this way to mislead the wrong seekers. Maybe they only make sense to someone who lived here and was familiar with the layout." He reread the portion of the letter again. "...to enter the south room and taste the new wine that rests in the light of the eastern alcove."

"Wait," she exclaimed. "...the *new* wine."

"What?"

"This cellar held the aged wine. Did Louis mention the other cellar?"

"We didn't get that far in our conversation."

She raised an eyebrow and clamped her lips together, stifling what was probably a sarcastic comment, before continuing. "I remember being in there once. My father was about to open a bottle when Louis barked, 'Stop—that has just arrived from Monticiano.' I never saw them taste wine from that cellar."

"Where is it?"

She moved back through the mirror opening and outer room, into the hall. Looking ahead, she placed her hands on the cold stone. "It was close by. It should be here."

Gabe stood back and studied the hallway. "There *was* a door here." He pointed to the unmatched stone. "Louis must have had it closed off from this entrance. Perhaps to limit access to his secret room and Antonio's letters."

"I was only in the room that one time and entered from this hallway." Her eyes darted back to the stairs, trailed over the ceiling, and lit onto the walled-up entrance. She was still studying the ceiling when heavy footfalls and a crash in the rooms above wrenched their attention to the stairwell.

# Chapter 18

Siena, Italy

Livia cringed in apprehension. "It may be the police. It was on the news that they are combing the area to find you for the attack on your hotel guard. He is still in intensive care."

Gabe's eyes darkened. "Ralph did that, I can testify to it." He started for the stairs, but she stopped him.

"We only have a day to find *Il Testamento* before your grandfather is killed. The police will not believe you. Stay behind the mirror and I will go upstairs."

As much as he wanted to defend himself, he knew she was right. He stepped into the secret room and closed the mirror behind him. Fifteen minutes crawled by. Gabe wondered if he should venture up the stairs. No, he would be wise to remain here. After half an hour, however, the chill of the cellar had permeated his clothing, and the walls felt hungry.

He walked to the mirror and pulled the lever. *Nothing.* He pulled again, all the way to the bottom. Then he pushed on the mirror. Nothing budged.

He raked his hair and growled, "She locked me in." He struggled with the lever until his fingers cramped. Giving up, he collapsed into a chair. *Trapped.* His furious eyes scanned the desk. Where was the map? He threw himself against the back of the chair. "*Fesso!*" he screamed. *How did she know Ralph only gave Louis one more day?*

##

Livia rushed through the dining room. "I remember a wine cellar where they kept the new wine," she said, glancing at Antonio's map. "The old cellar door has been walled up, but the room should be just below the dining room."

"But that's way past the library," Ralph countered after reading the map for himself. "You sure 'bout this, *birdie*? Louis said only Gabe knew how to use it?"

She glared at him. "Nothing is *sure*, Ralph. If it was easy, Louis or someone else would have gotten to it by now." She was glad that shut him up for awhile. He had always been an annoyance. Still, she had to be careful. He was quick to move from irritating to deadly. She glanced again at Rinaldo, unconscious on the floor, and fear gripped her stomach. She could not think about that now. Ralph was desperate. And in a foul mood.

They entered the long dining room where she did a quick perusal. "There used to be a door..." The outline of a stone arch was just visible above a large armoire that held the china. After pulling and tugging on the cabinet together, it started to move. Then with one last yank, the armoire scraped against the tile, allowing a body's width to slip behind it. Dust and cobwebs covered the solid wooden door behind the heavy piece of furniture.

Ralph rushed in front of her, pulled the creaking door toward him, and tugged a chain that clicked the light on. He clamored down the stairs. "Where's south?" he yelled.

She shook her head. "To your left, Ralph."

## 

Fire torched Gabe's emotions as he paced up and down trying to warm his body. The image of Livia's beaming face when he shared his grandfather's secrets reminded him what a fool he was.

Raking his hair off his forehead, he decided to make use of the time. He set aside Galgano's letter regarding Antonio's death. The next document was a letter from Helena to Galgano. Gabe read the attached translation, which spoke of her gratitude for the knight's defense of her husband and…*interesting*. She expressed the desire to visit the place where Antonio died. *I wonder if she ever did.*

The third letter on the stack came from Signora Guidotti. *Galgano's mother?* Gabe studied it.

> …*I am sure you can understand our position. Galgano is engaged to a worthy maiden. His life is set out before him. Instead, he refuses to leave Montesiepi. He sits in the doorway of his hovel like a guard, watching the sunrise, with only the wolves to keep him company.*
>
> *We are disturbed to hear of pilgrims bringing him food and asking wisdom of him. Helena, I love my son, but wisdom was never in his wayward soul. Please, write to him. Tell him he need not grieve the loss of your husband or do penance any longer.*
> *With all respect,*
> *Dionisia Guidotti*

Gabe reread the letter. A question niggled at his mind and finally moved its way into the light. Why would Galgano stay guarding Montesiepi if *Il Testamento* had already been sent to Helena by Antonio? He smiled. "*If.*"

Enough. He had to get out of here. Brute force was not going to move that mirror. He opened the desk drawer. Pens, paper—aha. A silver letter opener. He grabbed it and flew to the mirror. Lifting the lever, he could see through the gap inside the mouth of the mechanism. The silver tip slid in. If he could just get the point on that gear. It wiggled and the mirror shimmied but stayed closed. Something was lodged against it from outside. He wiggled the mechanism again, this time pushing hard against the frame. It gave! A heavy carpet lay rolled against it.

Forcing himself through a narrow opening, he was free. He stuffed a book into the gap in case the lever was broken and stepped back inside to grab the rest of Antonio's letters. Now that Livia knew this secret, nothing was safe down here. He would use them to find *Il Testamento*. Catching a glance of himself in the mirror, he paused. Gabe Dolcini, professor at U. C. Santa Barbara, was caught up in a Templar treasure quest. As soon as he freed his grandfather, he was going back to America—and sanity.

Stealing up the stairs, he turned right and peeked into the library. *No one.* Muffled voices carried from the other direction. The soft soles of his shoes muted his steps while he crept across the finely decorated tiles that paved the entrance to the grand dining room. He peeked through the arched entry and ducked back. To his right, a piece of furniture sat askew of the wall. Quietly, he approached the armoire.

He stifled a gasp. Rinaldo lay beyond the armoire on the threshold that led to the kitchen. A gash on the side of his head had clotted with blood. When Gabe shook his arm, the butler released a low groan.

Heated voices argued through the open door behind the cabinet. Gabe's head shot up. Livia—*and Ralph!* "No way!" he hissed. He stepped over Rinaldo to the front of the armoire and leaned his shoulder into it with all his strength. It began to slide then caught, rattling the china.

"Hey!" Ralph called from below. His steps reverberated under Gabe's feet as he sprinted from the bottom of the stairs.

Gabe looked through the opening while he pushed with his shoulder.

"It's Gabe," Ralph yelled. "Hey, chump, you're gonna get yours now."

Gabe grabbed a different hold and pushed harder, straining the muscles in his arms and thighs. His cousin had scaled the first flight of stairs and was scrambling up the second. White teeth jeered from below. The ferocity in Ralph's eyes pierced Gabe's bravado. His heart thudded loudly in his chest.

Ralph clawed toward the opening with his outstretched fingers. At his last lunge, he tripped. "What're you doing?" he screamed behind him. He and Livia landed in a tangle on the stairs.

"Ouch," her voice raised in agony. "My foot caught under the step."

Ralph swore and flew up the stairwell again, hand outstretched toward the doorframe.

Gabe moved to the front of the armoire. Eyes closed, he set his back against the chest and pushed with all his strength. He would not give up. Suddenly, the large cabinet moved.

Ralph howled a curse when the armoire closed the door on his fingers.

Every muscle in Gabe's body quivered. He opened his eyes, and his head jerked sideways. Rinaldo had crawled over and leaned his muscular back into the other side of the cabinet, shoes braced against the heavy dining table.

Sinking down next to him, Gabe gave his heart a chance to recover from the adrenaline rush. Ralph continued to scream threats at him through the door.

"We've gotta get out of here and call the police," Gabe whispered.

"And very soon," Rinaldo added. "This wine cellar used to be an underground dungeon and has an exterior exit."

Gabe shot to his feet and offered his hand to Rinaldo. The man wobbled when he tried to stand. His fingers reached up to the top of his head. "Ralph will pay for this."

"Can you drive?" Gabe questioned as they hurried to the garage.

Rinaldo lifted the keys off the ring by the door. "I will be fine." He opened the rear passenger door before Gabe could grab the handle, then started the car, and sped down the alleyway, passing Livia's Fiat.

## ##

"It's no use," Ralph seethed, tired of pushing against the blocked door. He turned and glared at Livia. "So, what was that all about?"

A nervous flit of her eyes was all it took to put her life in danger.

"Oh, so that's how it is? Playing both of us. I think it's time we get some real cooperation out of you." He thrust his knife forward, slicing her shoulder.

She screamed and grabbed the wound. *God, what have I gotten into?*

He came at her, and she flinched again. "Get my meaning, luv? Now, where's the alcove?"

Livia's body quaked with fear. The searing pain from her shoulder made it almost impossible to think. Her wide eyes shot away from his chilling sneer and scanned the perimeter of the vault for an escape route. The south wall was void of any objects. With an unsteady voice, she said, "Louis must have started searching for *Il Testamento* in here also."

"Then get lookin'."

When her eyes swept the room again, she spied another set of stairs behind the ones they had come down. *They must lead to the outside.* Blood soaked her shirt and oozed through her fingers that held the wound. Fear moved to anger. She glared at her cousin. "This was not necessary."

He flew at her, pressing the knife to her throat this time. "I'll be the judge of that. Now you just do your job and get us to the *testa*—or the coppers are going to get an interesting tip on where to find the Kestral."

## ##

After they fled the palazzo, Gabe asked, "What happened?"

Rinaldo tentatively touched the bump on his head. "I came in from the garden and discovered the security guard unconscious—I am not certain of his condition. The kitchen door was ajar and a vase of flowers was shattered on the floor. I heard Ralph demand where you were. Then Livia took charge."

"What do you mean she took charge?"

"As I stepped around the corner, she moved past Ralph with the map in her hand. She said they did not need you, but she did need him to move that cabinet out of the way. I was suspicious of the old document she carried and tried to take it from her. That is when Ralph clubbed me," he scowled.

"She surprised me too," Gabe murmured. "You'd better call the police to help the officer. I doubt Ralph and Livia will still be there when they arrive, but I want the house checked and secured."

Rinaldo's voice held impatience while he waited on the phone. Finally, he said, "Detective Orsini, we have had a further incident at the Palazzo Dolcini. An officer is injured. The assailant, Ralph Witte, may still be in the cellar if you hurry." He nearly slammed down the limo's phone and glanced at Gabe in the mirror. "Where would you like to go now, signore?"

"Drive around until the police get there."

## ##

Livia held her stinging shoulder and blinked the tears away while her eyes worked to focus on the words of the map. Ralph was a monster, but she needed him for now. Something he said prompted her to take a chance. "So, how much do you think we can squeeze from the Dead Knights for the *testa?*"

"Took you long enough to figure out it wasn't the Holy Grail," Ralph mocked. "What would a group of knights need with a cup when they could have a spearhead?"

*Spearhead?* She hoped she covered her surprise. "Whatever—but you could have told me. I just want my share."

"You won't have time to spend it if you trip me up again."

The scalding glare he gave her was enough to make her a believer. Still, she deflected it skillfully. "We only have a moment, so keep looking."

Though the room was stuffed with an array of items, most of the east wall was visible. Her eyes slowed down, scanning it an inch at a time. It should be easy to find an alcove in this room, so why hadn't her family found it already? Helena would have known immediately where Antonio wanted her to hide *Il Testamento*.

Maybe Gabe's idea was right, and the clues were written to mislead the wrong seekers away from…the location. *Ah. Antonio was a fox.* Pretending to have some insight, she went straight to a corner of the cellar and checked behind a case of wine. "Here!"

Ralph pushed her out of the way and bent over. Raising a magnum bottle of champagne, she struck the back of his head. Hard. His forehead hit the rough stone. "That's for you, luv."

# THE PROOF

# Chapter 19

Chiusdino, Italy, 1180 AD

Sad business. It had taken Galgano three days to deliver his friend's corpse to his widow in Siena. Antonio's two young sons had clung to their mother, eyeing the bundled package they were told was their father. The knight had been gone two years, what did they remember of him? After returning to his home in Chiusdino, Galgano could not rid himself of his anxiety. Signora Dolcini, obviously a great beauty, was so transfixed with grief that her face took on the appearance of an old woman. Could he risk the same fate for his beautiful fiancé, Polissena? More assassins were certain to come. He could not vanquish all of them.

Dionesia Guidotti spoke with her son at dinner. "Galgano, this has been such a nasty business. I received word from Polissena's papa that she is sick with worry for you. Why don't you ride to see her?"

Galgano's thoughts were somber while he rode toward his beloved's home. He looked down at the luxurious robes his mother insisted he wear. He was a murderer, nothing more than a whitened grave full of death.

Without warning, a light blazed and his horse threw him to the ground. Dazed, he felt his body lifted from the soil and transported back to Montesiepi, to the scene of the carnage.

When he gazed to the top of the hill, he beheld Christ as a mighty warrior, yet with a gentle quality in his eyes. The apostles surrounded their King. Jesus bid Galgano to climb the mount. By the time he reached the top, however, the vision had faded. Still, he felt a powerful presence surround him and fell to his knees. His face sunk to the rocky soil while the images of those he slew—the men and the boy—marched across his mind.

A voice ordered him to stand, and he rose to his feet. Though he could see no image, he heard the tender words spoken by the Spirit to his heart. "Your life is nearly spent. What eternal good have you fulfilled?"

"Nothing, Lord."

*"Nothing?"*

The memory of defending *Il Testamento* and protecting Antonio flashed in front of him.

Again, the Spirit spoke, "You have a courageous spirit, but your strength is misguided. Turn to me and leave your brutal past."

Galgano shook his head. All of his days had been violent. He lifted his voice in agony. "That would be as easy as plunging my sword into this stone." Filled with anger and grief over his inadequacy for good, he drew his sword and thrust it at the rock next to his boots.

To his amazement, his sword slid into the rock, now soft as butter. His hand jerked off the hilt as though it were on fire. With mouth agape, he stared at the sword. Great tears swelled, blinding him. At once, his heart surged with glorious hope, and he bent his knee.

In the elation of the moment, the hard words he heard became easy. "Leave your life and live upon this hill. I will be your source and your defense."

Galgano wondered about the strange words. He raised his head and studied his sword. Only the hilt and a small portion of the blade remained visible, creating a cross—an altar for his prayers.

##

Dark spring months followed the vision. Galgano's mother beseeched him to come away from Montesiepi and marry Polissena. His friends and enemies derided him, but he prayed more earnestly upon the mount. When the soil warmed from the early summer sun, his mind felt strengthened with an unusual sense of peace. His enemies had tired of baiting him, and he experienced an extended time of serenity.

During his hermitage, a steady surge of pilgrims had thought him some sort of holy man and brought him food. In truth, the wisdom that poured from his lips continued to amaze and comfort him. God's Spirit seemed to dwell, not only in him, but also in the ground around the sword.

It was not an unbroken peace, however. One day, a voice hailed him, and he recognized Antonio's widow. Her countenance showed some renewal, but grief still plagued her. He rose to greet her and her sons. The eldest was gifted with Antonio's unmistakable sable eyes, the younger's, a strange charcoal grey. Helena's brother, a small man, had accompanied the family from Siena, along with one old servant.

Galgano listened while Helena begged him for *Il Testamento*, so she might take it to Seborga and finish Antonio's quest. "It will be protected by the Templars there," she insisted.

Anxiety drove the peace from his soul, dredging up old ghosts. "No, Signora Dolcini. I will not give you *Il Testamento*, nor show you where it is hidden. Go home and raise your sons." She protested, but he roared and pointed at the boys. "Do you want to see them slain? Trust me. You would not reach Siena before being cut down by the very men who sent their assassins to slay your brave husband."

When Helena's brother also insisted, Galgano sized him up. "Can *you* defend your sister and nephews?" The tender man lowered his eyes.

They stayed on the hill with Galgano until the next day and shared the food they brought. Helena did not ask again. In the morning, Galgano knelt near the sword, watching out over his charge. When he turned, he sighted Helena's brother sketching him. Later that morning, the visitors left. Galgano knew he would not see them again.

##

Galgano's words proved prophetic. It was not long after the signora's visit, that a huge red-haired crusader in black surcoat stormed up the mount to demand *Il Testamento*. The giant stood before him. "Today you will die, Templar—very slowly if you do not give me the relic." The assassin's voice was coarse, his mouth twisted with contempt.

Galgano sized up the crusader's strength and noted the sword, seasoned from battle. Yet, he was surprised that not a trace of his old fighting instinct charged through his limbs. Knowing he could not defend himself, he knelt to pray.

He heard the sword slide back into its scabbard, but then the high pitch of a dagger scraped against its sheath. Galgano bowed his head to the ground and prepared for certain death. He prayed for grace to die with valor and welcomed the glad release from this world.

A sudden, low growl caused his head to jerk upward. He expected to see his frequent companions—a common wolf pack. Instead, two huge white wolves stalked out of the brush from behind the hut he had constructed as a shelter.

They crept forward, heads down and hair bristling. He dared not breathe. They crouched on either side of him, ready to spring. He closed his eyes, shutting out the deadly focus of their amber gaze. The heat of their breath pulsed against his cheeks. For the second time in the space of a blink, he readied himself for heaven.

Behind him, he heard the assassin draw back. His ponderous steps struck the ground and reverberated up through Galgano's knees. As the man fled the mount, Galgano opened his eyes to the roars on either side of him. The wolves lunged toward the assassin, their powerful movements forcing the air into invisible swirling currents. Galgano spun around in answer to a scream and watched the intruder run.

With snouts drawn up and lips pulled back to reveal fangs of unbelievable length, the wolves' heavy bodies circled the crusader. They struck together. One of the beasts sank its razor teeth into the man's wrist. His dagger clanged on the rock when it hit. The second wolf, claws extended from its enormous paws, hit his shoulders, pummeling him to the ground.

The air exploded with vicious growls, breaking bones, and screams. One wolf's full weight held the crusader down. The second brute went for his throat. In one snarling bite, the shrieks fell silent. But not the growling and tearing. Galgano covered his ears and shut his eyes against the slaughter. When he dared to peek again, the mount was empty.

Sitting back on his haunches, it took a long time for his heart to return to its steady beat. He bent his head in awe and thanksgiving until the early hours of the next morning. After drawing his morning water from the cistern beneath the mount, he wandered to the brush where he last heard the wolves. Only the forearms of the man remained.

That was the last of the assassins. He never saw the wolves again.

## 

Abbot Lorenzo had failed his one glorious task. He sat in deep thought, his thumb and forefinger rubbing the shiny tip of his elongated nose. Rafer had never returned. Nor had Lorenzo's latest assassin, King Barbarossa's red-haired nephew. It was obvious they met the same fate as the other crusaders who had attempted to wrest the relic away from the Templars.

Lorenzo had no more excuses. Pope Innocent had dismissed him because of his incompetence. Finishing the last page in the chronology of his time spent at the Abbey of Saint John, Lorenzo laid down his quill. The parchment stared up at him.

What had begun as a promising venture, proved otherwise. It was only a matter of time before Pope Alexander's papal soldiers stormed the fortress. Pope Innocent would be fortunate if his life was not forfeit. How lenient would Alexander be? Lorenzo's fate was locked to Innocent's, unless...unless his decision to enter into a monastic life of solitude demonstrated his repentance.

A knock at the door shook him from his musings. "Enter."

Prior Timothy, second in command of the abbey, opened the door. He cloaked his exultant face with a solemn expression. "Forgive me, Abbot, but they are here for you."

"Thank you, Brother Timothy. I will be along shortly." Left alone, Lorenzo hurried across the room to the narrow door that led off his sumptuous office. He felt the soft padding of the thick wool rug through his slippers. *I will miss this.*

The bright clink of his keys clashed with his glum thoughts. Opening the door, he stepped past the heavy chests and shelves that housed the abbey's historical chronologies and important documents. He could not neglect adding his own contribution for his time spent here. No matter how incriminating.

However, there was no need to make it easy to find. If favor once again turned toward him, he would be able to produce proof of his loyalty to Innocent and his valiant attempts to secure the relic.

This last scheme caused Lorenzo to smile for the first time during this sorry business. He shoved rolls of documents to one side of a deep shelf. Wielding a dagger, he stretched across the shelf and pointed it at the wall. The blade would dull after chipping out the narrow stone. *Better it, than his own person.* Using both hands, he rocked the stone loose.

A knock on the door, more urgent than the first, interrupted his concentration. Beads of sweat rolled over his face. "One moment," he shouted. Rolling his scroll tightly, he flattened the document, stuffed it into the cavity, and returned the stone. His chest heaved with the effort. Pounding replaced the congenial knocking. Lorenzo scattered the scrolls back across the shelf to hide his handiwork. He had failed to capture *Il Testamento*. Now his fate awaited.

# Chapter 20

Siena, Italy, Present Day

Stark shadows hung in forlorn gloom over the façade of the palazzo, even in the bright daylight. Its master was missing, its walls breached. Gabe asked Rinaldo to slow the limo in front of the conte's home to see if the intruders, Ralph and Livia, were gone.

The bold rays of afternoon sun were blinding as they streaked through the blustery September wind and reflected off a police car. In the driveway, an ambulance waited for its latest victim. Gabe sat forward, straining to decipher the commotion.

After pulling the car over, Rinaldo stepped out. "Please stay here, and I will see what they have found." He spoke with Detective Orsini for a moment. The officer pointed to two attendants lugging a stretcher that bore an unconscious Ralph. They bounced him into the ambulance.

Gabe scanned the area in an anxious search for a dark-haired beauty, but there was no sign of Livia. *She locked you in the cellar.* He squeezed the back of his neck in frustration at his disparate emotions and rolled down his window to get a better look. A blast of crisp air stung his face.

Through squinted eyes, he saw flashing lights circling on top of the ambulance. The driver pulled away. The blare of a siren ripped through the streets, jolting Gabe's body. He recalled the fear that filled Livia's eyes when she had talked about the threat to her family. Was she in the ambulance, too? He slumped against the seat back and cast his eyes at the limo's carpeted floor, imagining the worst.

*You locked her in the cellar with a killer.*

He rubbed his forehead with his thumb and fingers, remembering Ralph's vicious sneer. Remembering how easy it was for his cousin to use his knife. What had Ralph done to her when she couldn't get *Il Testamento* for him? What if she was dead?

Old demons threatened from all sides with their accusations. *You should have stayed to help instead of running away.*

"But she was working against me," Gabe argued.

*So, that's your excuse for being a coward?*

Squeezing his bowed head between his hands, he tried to push the insidious razor of his father's words away, but it plunged in one more thrust. *Angelica died because of you.*

A hand shook his shoulder. "Livia escaped. Signore?"

Gabe's attention jerked up. Rinaldo withdrew his hand from the window.

"They found Ralph, but Livia is not here," he repeated.

She escaped! Exhaling the breath he had been holding, Gabe wiped the beads of sweat off his forehead. "What happened to Ralph?"

"She broke a bottle of champagne over his head. He is still unconscious." A flicker of a satisfied smile flashed across the chauffeur's face. Rinaldo slid into the driver's seat, speaking just above a whisper, "He will be fortunate if he makes it out of the hospital."

Now that Gabe knew Livia was safely away from Ralph, anger poured in to replace his guilt. "We need to find her and get the map back."

Once the police left, they entered the icy palazzo. Rinaldo leaned down to straighten the carpet in the dining room, rubbing the knot on his head.

"Why don't you get some rest," Gabe suggested. "I'm going to the library to make some notes."

Rinaldo nodded. "Thank you, signore. I phoned a locksmith to replace the locks on the doors at once. The police found a key ring in Ralph's possession with many of the keys to the palazzo on it. He must have stolen the originals when he lived here and had new ones made. No one else will be getting in unannounced." Gabe's shoulders relaxed. He had felt the palazzo's vulnerability ever since his grandfather's disappearance.

They both started at the sound of the doorbell. "I'll get that," Rinaldo said, striding to the door. Gabe heard muffled voices, then Rinaldo reappeared with a familiar well-dressed man in a wheelchair. "Signore Marcus Ambrogi," he announced.

Gabe smiled at Marcus. "It's a pleasure to see you again." He rose and shook Marcus' hand.

Clasping Gabe's hand in both of his, Marcus said, "*Buona sera*, Gabriel. I hope I am not interrupting, but I had to do something to feel like I was helping Louis and my daughter."

"Your daughter?"

"*Si*, Livia."

Gabe's mind reeled. Marcus was Livia's father? *She* was the daughter saddled with the responsibilities of three younger sisters and the family businesses? That explained a lot. How should he respond? Was Marcus a *custode*? Did he know his daughter was a traitor?

"May I offer you something to drink?" Rinaldo asked, giving Gabe a moment to pull his wits together. Marcus had the same grey eyes as Livia, but more subdued.

"Just water, thank you." When the butler left, Marcus got to the point. "You know by now why Louis wanted to bring you to Italy. He and I had a never-ending battle over this for the last year. Now, his stubbornness has gotten him into real trouble. I fear my daughter as well."

New vitality emanated from Marcus' broken body. Gabe opened his mouth to respond, but Marcus continued. "I came to ask what you may have learned about Louis' disappearance, and to find out if Livia is in danger." His jaw tightened as he waited for an answer.

"I'm clueless about Louis. But why do you think Livia might be in trouble?"

Marcus frowned. "It was Louis' dream to find *Il Testamento* with his son, or now, his grandson. After you, I am the next heir in the Dolcini lineage. He had no one else to turn to, so he brought Livia and me into his confidence. I have not heard from her." Strain showed in his tight mouth. "She might have become a target, like the contessa."

Gabe's eyes dropped to the floor. Even if he wanted to explain the events of the last couple of days, the convoluted circumstances refused to be unwound. "I'm at a loss of what to make of all this."

"I see. Are you as hardheaded as Louis, or are you willing to accept my assistance?" The man's eyes were steady, honest.

There was no harm in finding out what Livia's father knew, but Gabe was hesitant about giving away his grandfather's secrets again. "Sir, any information you can give me to help find the relic and free my grandfather is certainly welcome."

Pressing the tips of his fingers together, Marcus said, "I will do what I can. Louis has all the documents, only two of which I have seen. I assume you've seen this." Marcus handed him a note written in Louis' fine script.

Gabe read, "All who take the vow of the *Custodi del Testamento* must give their word, first, to guard it from its enemies, and second, to restore it to the whole body of believers at such a time as it will be safe. Until then, circulate it among the faithful in secret with utmost care." Gabe frowned. "Louis repeated the gist of it. Except the part that it was to be circulated. Did he tell you where this vow came from?"

Marcus nodded. "It was sent with other documents to Helena by Antonio before his death on Montesiepi. Louis has the original—which he said was dated 36 A.D.!"

"No way." That was too far to stretch. Gabe had not seen anything like it when he went through the papers. "He never showed it to you?"

Marcus frowned, "No. He is… reticent about these things."

"I see." Gabe wondered why Louis had not shown it to him either. "If this earlier directive was valid, it said to share it with everyone. Why then did Louis insist it go only to Seborga?"

Marcus shrugged. "Perhaps he felt Antonio's oath to deliver it to the Templar citadel overrode this first directive."

Gabe sighed, frustrated with all the unknowns.

Launching into what he did seem to know, Marcus said, "Louis told me of Saint Galgano's part in helping Antonio fight the crusaders at Montesiepi. From there, I took it upon myself to study the history in detail." He rested his hands on his knees. "Since my auto accident, I have too much time on my hands." A hint of sadness failed to dampen his enthusiasm. "Shall I give you the facts?" His eyes had taken on new vitality and changed to the color of luminous flint.

"Facts would be nice."

Marcus straightened in his wheelchair. "In my research, I discovered something very interesting. Do you know the story of Galgano's sainthood?"

"Only that he was considered a saint because of the miracle of the sword and his commitment to become a hermit."

Nodding, Marcus revealed what he had uncovered. "Montesiepi was located in a rural valley a fair distance from the pilgrim route through Italy to the Holy Land. Once Galgano's miracle took place, the hermitage became a favorite pilgrimage stop. In addition to the pilgrims, Saint Bernard's Cistercian monks swarmed the mount—looking for something very valuable." He grinned, "*Il Testamento.*"

"How would they know to look for it there?"

"Louis said Antonio wrote to Helena that he was coming home to fulfill Saint Bernard's last wish—to return *Il Testamento* to Seborga if it ever left the Holy Land. Bernard gave this order to his monks in Seborga."

"I don't understand the significance of taking it back to Seborga," Gabe interjected.

"Because Bernard's Cistercian Templars were princes of that village and would guard it. Now, of course, there are no Templar guards—a fact I have pointed out to Louis more than once—but he is very literal in his interpretation of Antonio's oath."

Marcus sighed and continued. "King Baldwin sent word to Seborga that *Il Testamento* was on its way, but it never came. In the meantime, rumors reached them that a valuable relic had been hidden on Montesiepi by Templars. That sent the Cistercians on a mission to recover it, prompting the building of the chapel and abbey. No one knew that Antonio sent the relic to Helena."

Gabe decided not to tip his hand and share his new theory. "Are you certain these weren't just legends created at a later date? Abbeys are pretty common all over Europe—without any sinister motivations."

Marcus raised his eyebrows. "Perhaps. But try to explain these facts. Galgano was from a common family. His funeral, however, was a huge event, attended by bishops and influential Cistercian Abbots. In the following year, the bishop of Volterra turned Montesiepi over to the Cistercians, who began to build the round chapel and two side chambers—one for Galgano's skull, and one for the arm bones of a thwarted assassin." Excitement sparkled from Marcus' eyes.

Gabe had seen the same expression in Livia's. He shifted in his seat. "I'm curious. Do you believe a sword encased in a stone and a vision that radically changed a man's character—as interesting as they are—would be enough to initiate all that construction?"

Marcus grinned. "Possibly—if rumors stated that *under* the sword rested the fruit of Saint Bernard's great secret. The excavations into Montesiepi extended for 90 years. As the pilgrims swarmed the area— bringing in greater revenues—the Cistercians built the grand abbey and a monastery to house the monks. With all that income, the monastery became one of the most powerful in Tuscany."

Gabe whistled. "Massive profits built on rumors. Do you think they were the ones who attacked Antonio and Galgano?"

Marcus was definite. "No, why would they? Antonio was bringing it to them. It was an opposing force. There were many religious and political factions who thought nothing of murdering and torturing to get what they wanted. Power struggles thrived as men used precious relics to claw their way to the highest rung of power."

"The papacy?"

"If they chose. However, there was one very powerful yet clandestine association that operated within and without of the church. Its members had aspirations far beyond the papacy. This group had nothing to do with faith. Its interest is power. I am inclined to believe that it was a group called the *Soci*, the Associates, who assassinated Antonio."

Gabe's interest intensified. "Do you think it is possible that the *Soci* from that era are still operating?"

"I am positive they are. They began as the Praetorians, a powerful guard created at the time of Caesar. Though not guards in this age, they maintain their lust for power. It is a little-known fact that they select ambitious young men and tutor them in their doctrines of dominance—religious and political."

Conversations with Rinaldo shot into Gabe's consciousness. "Do you believe it possible that they want the relic to influence their way into the ARCC?"

Marcus shrugged. "A relic of the caliber that I believe *Il Testamento* is could take a man as high as his aspirations. It is not hard to imagine what the *Soci* would gain, with it in their possession."

After considering this information, Gabe asked, "Do you really think there was anything under the mount?"

"There is. In my research, I found a reference that mentions a natural cistern Galgano used, fed by rain and an underground spring. It also spoke of a room below the sword. The Cistercians kept a vigilant watch and tight rein on all visitors, creating even more extraordinary rumors."

"Such as what?"

Marcus raised his eyebrows. "Such as, below that cistern was a fabulous chamber which housed the Holy Grail and the Ark of the Covenant."

Gabe smiled.

Understanding his skepticism, Marcus continued. "Anything is possible. Religious and political celebrities visited the site, including King Federico Barbarossa—The Holy Roman Emperor." He laced his strong fingers and rested on his elbows. "Why does an Emperor visit an obscure valley in the middle of Tuscany? To see a round chapel built over a hut where a hermit lived?" He sat back. "Rumor or not, it gave the Cistercian monks massive amounts of clout and finances."

"Do you think the Grail or the Ark were really there?" Gabe hoped for sanity.

"No. I believe the rumors were a cover. The inner circle seemed to know what everyone was searching for. From the maniacal way Philip of France tortured the Templars to uncover their secrets, I believe he knew of something even more important than the Chalice or the Ark." Marcus searched Gabe's features. "I believe they were looking for *Il Testamento*."

Gabe rubbed his forehead in exasperation. "I can understand the religious groups looking for a relic to bring in revenues and boost their authority, but I can't see the King of France going through all that trouble for a relic. History contends that he was after the Templar treasure—he was nearly bankrupt."

Marcus lifted his eyebrows. "But you have to remember the age in which they were living—one of great superstition. The secrets of the Templars were fodder for the imagination. Every retelling of the supposed magical powers of relics brought the frenzy for their discovery to new heights. I have read vivid accounts of an obscure object—which I am certain is *Il Testamento*—that was believed to be the cause of the Templar's great wealth. It was credited as the reason for their fierceness and victory in battle—even giving the possessor the ability to see his future. What king would not covet that? What would he not do to get it?"

Resting against the back of his wheelchair, Marcus sighed. "Louis told me of another document he found with Helena's collection. It was written by another of our ancestors, Conte Benito Dolcini, on his deathbed. After hearing of the arrests of the Templars throughout France by King Philip in 1308, Benito commanded his son to destroy all of the documents pertaining to *Il Testamento* and never speak of it again."

"Obviously, he disobeyed his father."

"That seems to be the case," Marcus nodded. "Benito must have known what Philip was searching for."

Running his hand through his hair, Gabe tried to gain a perspective. "So, starting with Antonio in 1180, until Conte Benito in 1308, you believe the Dolcinis protected the secret and location of the relic?"

"*Sì*. Beginning with Antonio's two sons, Russo and Gavino Dolcini, the task always passed from the fathers down to their sons. My lineage, through Gavino, stopped when no male heirs were born. The documents regarding the *Custodi* passed through Louis' ancestors down to Benito's son, who hid them. The information lay in darkness until Louis discovered them forty years ago."

Marcus frowned. "Perhaps Louis should not have found them—but he did. Then, his daughter and her husband learned of them. Both are dead. With the absence of your father and yourself, Louis brought Livia and me into his confidence—in case he died before finding it. We swore to keep the secret, and he promised that if he had not found it by his death, arrangements had been made for all the information to come to us."

Gabe considered Marcus and the responsible way he had handled the crumbs given him. "Do you know what *Il Testamento* is?"

Marcus' features fell. "No. Louis would never let us in on that knowledge."

Gabe grinned. "If it's any consolation, Signore Ambrogi, my grandfather has no idea either."

Marcus assumed a smug expression. "Wait until I see my dear Louis," he chuckled, then grew somber. "We must find him."

The shadows had grown long by the time Marcus was ready to leave. A refreshed Rinaldo entered as though on cue to escort the gentleman to his waiting vehicle.

Afterward, Gabe continued in deep thought. On the one hand, there was nothing Marcus had told him that could help him find Louis. But what about finding the object? It seemed that many historical figures gave credence to this legend. Still, how many other legends—Atlantis for example—stirred the imaginations and emptied the purses of gullible monarchs?

He gazed through the window at the stone towers and walls. Hints of vineyards striped the hills in the distance. A pang of longing sat in the pit of his stomach. There was so much to paint here, so much that stimulated his creativity. He could walk away from all this drama—just grab his bag and go. But the pride and love in his grandfather's eyes whenever he looked at Gabe...

A few moments later, Rinaldo entered the door to the library with a small plate of *antipasto* before dinner. "Sustenance, signore."

"*Grazie.*" His misery must have shown.

"You will find your grandfather and embrace your dreams. Then all will be put right, *eh?* The locksmiths will arrive soon and the police still seek you. May I suggest you retire to your room? I will serve your dinner there."

Gabe nodded. "I'd like to visit the new wine cellar in the morning—to see if Livia left any clue to where she was going. There is still the chance Helena hid it there."

"Certainly, signore, but may I suggest we use the outside entrance?"

Gabe was beginning to enjoy Rinaldo's dry humor. "*Sì*, that would be preferable."

# Chapter 21

Siena, Italy

The threat to Louis seemed surreal in the grey dawn. Gabe's stomach churned with anxiety while he paced from window to window in his suite. *What should he do?* He shuddered at the thought of going to the police. There was no doubt he would end up in prison, charged with the attack on the guard.

There had to be someone who could help. As he considered the options, the enormity of the challenge weighed heavy on his shoulders. Glancing around, he realized the dark blues of his room only served to accentuate the sense of foreboding. He escaped to the brighter rooms downstairs.

Still full from the heavy dinner Rinaldo served the night before, Gabe resisted the basket of buttery croissants on the dining table. Warmth infused his chilled fingers as they encircled his ceramic cup of espresso. The size of the room and the table dwarfed him, magnifying his loneliness.

Why had he really come here? Was it just about his career, or had he secretly hoped for more? The inner roiling of resentment, disappointment, and fear for his grandfather suggested the latter.

He shoved his wooden chair away from the table. His first stop was to check out the new wine cellar. The possibility still existed that the relic lay within a dark alcove underground. After calling Rinaldo, they exited through the arched door at the side of the palazzo and made their way around the sloping lot to the rear of the fortified foundation. Massive double doors squeaked open after Gabe unlocked the newly installed deadbolt. He peaked into the darkness.

"If I may illuminate your way, signore," Rinaldo stepped past him and switched on the electric lights.

Gabe was awestruck. From where he stood, the ceiling rose one full story above them while stone stairs moved down in a half circle to the brick floor below. Light diffused through three small amber windows and cast a golden glow over the cavernous chamber. The magical setting offered a brief reprieve from his worry. He grinned. This might be his favorite part of the palazzo yet.

He steadied his balance with his left hand on the wall that supported the stairs and moved down the steps into the chamber. His eyes swept through the captivating room, taking in the iron and wooden racks that stood in straight lines, twenty or so feet long. "There must be hundreds of bottles here."

Each rack supported shelves stacked with wine bottles of various shapes and colors. In other areas, terracotta cylinders lay on their sides, encasing individual bottles—probably more valuable than the rest. What did his grandfather do with all of this wine? Barrels, large and small, squatted in random disarray. "This is fabulous." Looking up, Gabe caught the butler frowning at the thick dust that a quick check left on his finger.

"*Si*, signore," he said without conviction.

Moving through antique items that crowded every corner and cubby, Gabe scoured the area. Only a small segment of bricks near the back and low to the ground looked slightly askew from the rest of the wall. He pushed against it and tugged on the bricks. It seemed solid. There was no sign that an alcove ever existed in here. If his new hunch failed, he could always come back and explore this again.

He moved to the center of the vault where a long wooden tasting table stood. The edge of its deep coffee-colored top displayed carved leaves, grapes, and blossoms. Simple curved legs supported it. He placed his hands on the table and shook, but it did not budge. "Sturdy *and* gorgeous."

Broken glass caught Gabe's eye. "This must be where Livia nailed Ralph." He bent down and tested the darkened grime. "It's still damp." He imagined her in here with Ralph, looking for their treasure. Huffing his frustration, he shook his head. "Let's go. I don't think there's anything here."

"Where, signore?"

"Do you know where Galgano plunged his sword into the stone?"

## 

The amazing countryside of Tuscany sped by. However, Gabe was too restless to enjoy it or the luxurious comfort of the limo's back seat. In another lifetime, he would be driving his convertible here. It would eat up this road.

He wished many things, none of them had to do with the task at hand. The day was too beautiful to be on a wild-goose chase. But, again, he saw the image of his grandfather's face when he had first toasted Gabe. It had held such joy, such hope.

Gabe straightened and stared out the window. Maybe if he put in a concerted effort, he could find the relic. It would be a good break if he proved right about the resting place of *Il Testamento*, alias, the head, or whatever. Could the map really show him the location?

Cringing, he could hear Howard's heckling laughter when he found out about this. So what? It could save his grandfather. He raked the black curls off his forehead as if it would help his vision. Where would Ralph be holding that dear, stubborn man?

After traveling south and west of Siena on *Strata Provenciale* 73, they arrived at their destination near noon. Rinaldo turned at the sign marked, *Cappella di San Galgano a Montesiepi.*

Lining both sides of the long driveway, Italian cypress stood tall like sentinels assembled to assist Gabe on his quest. A hill bearing lush green trees rose above a field of grey soil that lay in wait for the next step in the production of semolina wheat. His mind unconsciously worked out a mix of oil paint to match the taupe/grey color of the recently plowed clods.

The limo traveled up the paved drive that lifted them to the hilltop where the round Chapel of San Galgano squatted on the summit.

Rinaldo parked the limousine in line with the two other cars in the parking lot. Though not a stretch limo, Louis' vehicle was huge compared to the micro-minis that everyone drove.

"Wait here," Gabe said and walked up to the sprawling shrine complex. He looked south and shielded his eyes from the sun's position high overhead. A kitten wandered over to him. As he bent down to scratch its chin, an angry outcry resounded through the large open door of the chapel.

"No flash!" An aged woman stood in the doorway and rebuked a young couple within. The scolding continued under her breath while she stumped down the outside steps and yanked the purring kitten out from under Gabe's affectionate hand.

"Eleonora," warned a refined woman from the entrance hall. Eleonora turned and shuffled through an antiquated door farther down the side of the rectangular building attached to the round chapel. "My apologies," the pleasant woman offered. "My name is Barbara. I am afraid Eleonora is wary of visitors. Please come in for a brochure."

Gabe followed her into the entrance hall. They turned right and stepped through a doorway into a quaint herb shop where pleasant aromas wafted around him. He scanned the artistically arranged shelves of herbal concoctions. A familiar scent caught his attention. He picked up a bar of soap and sniffed. Lavender, mixed with the other scent Livia wore. Turning the bar over, he was amazed to see the name "Ambrogi" listed as the manufacturer. What were the chances?

His mind stuck on the image of Livia's smile when he had shown her the secret room. Those gorgeous grey eyes had opened to him. Yeah, then she locked me in and stole the map. *Wake up man, she used you. Just like Darla.*

Handing him the information, Barbara asked, "May I help you with anything else?"

"No, thank you," he answered. It was time to attend to business. He left the herbal shop and entered through the door of the circular mausoleum. There, in the center of the room, dwelt the famous sword. Something about the story finally solidified. He gazed through the glass cover and past the sturdy iron bars that served to protect the hilt. As advertised, solid stone held the black metal tightly in place. He bent closer.

A round pommel topped the grip that Galgano's hand had held. A metal hand guard crossed in front of the grip. Gabe shook his head at the imagery. What was once Galgano Guidotti's weapon for sending infidels to their final judgment, now protruded as a peaceful cross. Its bloody edge was forever imprisoned—a testament to the man's transformation from a violent knight to a repentant hermit.

Saint Galgano's simple story had been embellished and retold in many cultures, but Gabe had proof—of sorts—that the tales were a distraction from the real events that occurred in, or around, this building.

Enthused by actual history, he pivoted in the shadowy room, examining the concentric circles of red brick and white stone on the dome's interior. The brochure said it was an unusual design for this period—usually found in early Etruscan or Roman structures. And round chapels were used extensively by the Cistercian Templars, Gabe remembered from his reading.

His eyes studied every possible crack or stone that could hide an entrance to a cave or room below. Uneven bricks protruded from the floor, the joints filled with powdered soil from generations of pilgrims and tourists who made their way up the hill to gaze at the miraculous sword embedded in stone.

Did he really believe he could just saunter into this shrine, pull out a loose brick, and find the opening to a cave that held *Il Testamento*? For 800 years, men sought it here. But they didn't have what was given to him. Again, he wondered at how he came to be entangled in this strange task.

The leaflet noted the supposition that Galgano's remains at one time lay buried under the stone. When Gabe walked back to the sword, he noticed someone had dug around it. Marcus said the Cistercian monks had appeared right after Galgano died in 1181 and began to build and then expand on the original cylindrical chapel. He examined the walls. Thick and heavy. They would need massive foundations to support them. How far underground had the Cistercians dug?

Sensing he was being watched, Gabe swung around toward the door. *No one.* Yet the hair on his forearms stood at attention. He checked out the many holes and cracks where someone might spy on the room. Finding nothing obvious, he headed for the door to ask Barbara a few questions.

The herb shop appeared vacant, but he had not seen the shop owner come back out. He glanced around the fragrant room. Hanging behind the counter, a thick, red velvet drape waved softly at him. *Should he?*

A quick sweep of the empty room assured him no one would witness his unusual sense of impropriety. He stepped behind the counter next to the cash register. His heart pounded while he pulled aside the heavy fabric an inch. The darkness behind it provided no answers. Perhaps a bit more…

"*Fuori, fuori, fuori imbecille!*" Eleonora rushed from behind the curtain into the shop screaming at him.

All he could say was, "*Scuzi, scuzi.*" She advanced on him like a hornet, backing him up the stairs and out into the courtyard. Once there, her tirade continued, accompanied with infuriated gestures. The young couple stopped taking photographs and watched the scene.

Gabe's face burned with embarrassment. He turned and stumbled down the rocky path toward the abbey. Once out of sight of the old woman and his audience, he stopped. "*Fesso!*" he chided himself. With an introduction like that, he would never glean any information.

He leaned against a tree to regroup. A clear, blue sky stretched overhead. He let his eyes drift over the gently rolling hills that lay to the southeast of the Chapel. On the next hill, pine trees and small oaks fought for supremacy. They stopped in an abrupt line where a rectangular plot of soil slanted down the hill and nurtured emerald green and gold grape vines. The clusters of fruit were heavy, ready for the knife.

At this time of day, no workers were visible. He checked once more, then crushed down a crude wire fence that skirted the path, and stepped over. Trudging through the brush across the top of the vineyard, he stayed near the cover of trees. A squirrel scolded him, reminiscent of Eleanora. Done with verbal abuse for the day, he stamped his foot at the creature, which dove into a nearby opening.

Curious, Gabe knelt down to check out the hole, too circular to be natural. He brushed the soil and leaves away. An irrigation pipe. After running his hand around the mouth of the broken stone protruding from the hillside, he studied the exposed rocks gathered on the slant below it.

When flowing, water would empty into the rocky swale and be diverted around the vineyard.

He stood on the mount directly east of Montesiepi and glanced uphill. The culvert appeared to follow a direct angle through this hill, toward Galgano's chapel. Perhaps Galgano *did* draw water from an underground spring on Montesiepi—one that Etruscan or Roman farmers had tapped for their crops.

"Signore?"

Gabe spun around and encountered an unsmiling laborer. Reining in his surprise, he attempted to shift the man's suspicion, pretending interest in the irrigation. Using hand motions, he asked, "Do you use the water from these pipes to irrigate the grapes?"

Still frowning, the man shook his head. He drew a wide arc around the vineyard with his hand, explaining that the water coursed away from the planted slope.

"*Grazie*," Gabe nodded and began to walk back to the path. The laborer walked with him. Gabe assumed it was to make certain he refrained from sampling the ripe grapes. He stepped back over the bent fence, his face coloring. The worker frowned while he tugged the wire back into shape with strong, jerking motions.

Anxious to be away from a second *faux pas*, Gabe jogged down the trail and let his forward momentum accelerate away from the chapel. However, a few meters down from the top of the hill, he skidded to a stop. A vision he had never imagined greeted him. Low in the valley stood the ancient Abbey of San Galgano. "*Magnifico.*"

He finished his descent into the valley and wandered past the huge abbey walls to the entrance on the far side. While he paid his entrance fee, he could not help feeling that selling tickets in a building of this stature seemed beneath its dignity. He shrugged. Perhaps the money they collected would be enough to keep the magnificent ruin from further decay. The young female guide smiled and handed him a pamphlet with a brief history of the Cistercian monks who built the structure.

Sixty feet above the dirt floor, pigeons fluttered across the roofless sanctuary and landed in one of the broken stone frames of a rose window. Gabe shook his head in admiration. The hand-carved opening nestled in a crumbling wall that strove to protect it.

He could only imagine the glory that had flamed within these walls when its roof enclosed dozens of glowing torches. Or when the daytime illumination was limited to beams of light that streamed in through the intricate windows, creating moving patterns against the brick walls. An unexpected mix of glory and sadness overcame him. This was not the first mausoleum he had witnessed—the skeleton of a dream that had died and decayed along with the men who dreamed it.

Forcing himself to leave the mystical nave, he stepped into a side room. Multiple vaults hovered over the space, noted as the "Chapter Hall." Moving deeper into the empty room, he was in awe of the elegant rust-colored vines and emblems painted on arches that sprung from sturdy columns planted deep into the floor below. He moved closer to inspect the artwork, then stopped abruptly and slid behind an arch. *Firelli!*

Gabe's enemy stood outside the open gothic window. Soon a plump, white-haired priest joined him. Gabe glanced back toward the attendant, busy at her desk. He pretended to study the ceiling while inching his face toward the window.

"Abbot Porta," Firelli nodded and reached to shake the priest's hand. "I must admit my surprise to your choice of meeting locations." He glanced back up the hill at the chapel. "You have not found the relic on your own I trust?"

The abbot did not smile, but greeted the two other men who joined them, "Ah, Niccolo, Arturo." Dressed in athletic clothes, both men stood a foot higher than the abbot and looked like bodybuilders. Niccolo wore his bleached blond hair short like a mercenary in an action thriller. His wide-set dark eyes scanned the area like an eagle's.

Arturo, slightly shorter and built like a tank, wore an olive green t-shirt that stretched over his bulging chest and biceps. With jet black hair, he looked like he could crush any mere man with his extraordinarily large hands.

"You sent for us?" Niccolo asked.

"*Sì.* I summoned you and Arturo to introduce you to Firelli

Dambrosi. He is a resourceful associate whom our *Primo Consul* believes will help us deliver the relic in a more *expedient* timeframe." Mild scorn twisted Abbot Porta's lip.

Firelli ignored him. "You have information for me?"

Abbot Porta nodded and Niccolo stepped forward with a small spiral notepad. Gabe noticed that he nearly forced Firelli to pull it from his strong grip.

Porta explained, "My good brothers here retrieved this from the office of Reverendo Tito in Seborga. He had a habit of writing down his phone messages—before his demise."

Gabe's heart stopped. *They killed the priest!*

Firelli studied the notepad. He read the priest's brief scribbling aloud, *'Conte Dolcini. Map is at palazzo.'* He scrutinized Porta. "How would Tito come by this information?"

A smug smile broke the austerity of Porta's expression. "Read the date. It seems that Conte Dolcini contacted him last year."

Gabe ducked back, his breathing quickened. They knew about the relic. And about his grandfather! He peeked around again and listened as Firelli replied with an even tone to Porta's criticism. "So why have you been searching the mountain again? For the missing cave?"

"I have my reasons."

"And?"

Porta looked away, his cold eyes expressionless. "We have found no cave. And nothing that could ever have been a cave."

Firelli nodded. "Then it must be at the palazzo."

"Really? It is obvious why our *Primo Consul* suggested I work with you on this crucial assignment," Porta said, disdain evident on his pale lips. "He intimated I could rely completely on your professionalism—and your discretion. As you are aware, more depends on our retrieving this lost icon of power today than at any other time in our history."

"I understand the *Primo Consul's* urgency to lead the flock to the new Center. The sheering should be bountiful." Firelli's voice was cold as steel.

"I am gratified to hear that you realize the importance. The timing is critical. When you need assistance with your preparations, my associates here are skilled in *anything* that might become necessary to secure the relic."

His face impassive, Firelli assessed Niccolo before he answered, "No, *grazie*. I prefer to work by myself."

Niccolo glared down at Firelli. The abbot's lips twitched, and Gabe saw the closest expression Porta ever got to a smile. "I will entrust this assignment to your leadership, but my *Soci will* work with you."

Gabe jerked at the mention of the *Soci*. His movement alerted Niccolo. In a slow sweep, the huge man scanned the area between him and the windowless opening where Gabe hid. Holding his breath, Gabe realized he dared not risk being found out. If Firelli captured him for the *Soci*, he could not give the Dead Knights what they wanted. Gabe could not allow himself to fail his *nonno*.

The shutter creaked when he ducked behind it, and he groaned inwardly. When he chanced a peek through a slit in the wood, Niccolo had started in his direction. Gabe checked the distance between himself and the entrance. The attendant was gone. Could he make it before this guy stuck his head into the Chamber Hall?

Forcing his trembling body to move, he sprinted across the hall, ducking through the door, and flattened himself against the outside wall in the courtyard. His heart pounded, but he heard no footsteps following him. What kind of medieval game was he involved in?

He stole out of the entrance room and jogged up the trail as fast as his legs and lungs would allow. Arriving at the limo, he flung himself inside. "Firelli is talking to an abbot about getting *Il Testamento* for the *Soci*," he huffed. "I think you were right about the new religious center."

Rinaldo's eyes narrowed, and his lips formed in a grim line. "*Sì.* Whoever leaps to the top of that tower will wield significant religious and political power."

Gabe's mind swirled with the implications. These were powerful enemies—far beyond any punks like Ralph and Harry. What had Louis gotten him into? He glowered out the window at the inconspicuous mini cars parked next to them. They stood out too much. They drove out of the chapel parking lot and had just made the wide sweep past the Wine Bar, when Gabe spotted Livia's Fiat approaching them. "Stop her!"

# Chapter 22

San Galgano, Italy

Providence had finally smiled on him. Gabe pointed at the Fiat, and Rinaldo swung the limo across the oncoming lane, where the heavy vehicle skidded to a stop. Livia's car lunged off the road and smashed into the brush. Pushing her door open against the stiff branches, she raced toward the trees. Gabe rushed after her and tackled her in a bear hug.

"Let me go!" she screamed.

"Well, what brings you up here," Gabe huffed.

"None of your business. Let go of me—now!"

"No way, you're going to show us where Louis is."

She continued to struggle while Rinaldo grabbed her kicking feet. Gabe noticed blood on her shoulder and changed his grip. When they reached the limo, he fell into the back seat through the open door, pulling her in with him. Rinaldo stuffed her lashing feet inside and closed the door.

"See if the map is in her car," Gabe said.

Rinaldo jogged to her Fiat and held the prize in the air. He swung back into the driver's seat and raised the divider window halfway. When he locked the doors, Gabe let go of Livia.

"How dare you," she screamed.

Gabe smirked. "How dare *me*? You have a lot of questions to answer, but let's start with where you and Ralph are holding Louis."

175

Through angry, gritted teeth, she seethed, "I am not with Ralph, and I do not have Louis." It did not sound convincing. She wrapped her arms around herself and winced when her hand touched her shoulder. Blood continued to spread.

"How did this happen—trying to escape from a cellar?" Gabe goaded, trying hard not to care.

"Ralph cut me, *after* I kept him from getting to you on the stairs." She turned her head to the window.

"So, you're a little with him, and a little with me, whatever gets you closer to your goal. We'll let the police unwind this."

"No," she pleaded. "Ralph says we have to bring him *Il Testamento* or Louis will be killed by the Dead Knights."

Rinaldo glanced back through the mirror.

"What do you know about them?" Gabe asked. He wanted information—now.

Her chin sank in resignation. "They formed in 1314, when DeMolay, the Grand Master of the Knights Templar, was burned at the stake."

"Modern day Templars? I don't think so."

She rolled her eyes with impatience. "They are not Templars. Just the opposite. After the pope allowed King Philip to kill their leaders, many Templars turned against the church and committed their wealth to destroy its power."

"And relics were a major source of their power and revenue," Gabe finished.

"How do you know that?"

"A gunman named Firelli told me. Right before he was about to blow me away. He also told me that you were planning to sell the relic to them after you used me to find it." His sable eyes flamed bronze. "I was kidnapped—again!"

"I didn't plan for you to get hurt." She bit her lip. "I put a tracking device on your jacket to follow you to *Il Testamento*."

His lips stretched to a thin, venomous line. "So you could get your hands on it. If it wasn't for Rinaldo, I might be dead. Does any of this sink in? This is not a game."

She turned away from his glaring face. "*Mi dispiace*—sorry."

He leaned his head back against the seat. "So am I. Rinaldo, please drive us to the police station so I can turn her in for assault—and theft."

"No." Livia shook her head in defeat. "I will take you to Louis. He is at his vineyard near Monticiano."

"I knew it," Gabe seethed. "Are we going to run into another gunman?"

"No. I was just headed there."

He was so furious he couldn't speak. To think she, a member of the family, held his grandfather hostage was more loathsome than he could comprehend.

Less than an hour later, Rinaldo turned onto an unmarked dirt road and drove down a winding drive that ended in front of a large stone villa. "What shall I do with the signorina?"

"Leave her locked in the limo for now. I don't want her interfering." He started to get out and caught Livia's angry eyes spitting darts at him.

Rinaldo moved around the car. "I am a professional body guard. Please allow me to handle this, signore." He strode quietly over the flat stone pavers in front of Gabe. Nothing seemed sinister. They listened at the door and heard rustling. Both men jumped back when the door opened a crack.

A middle-aged woman spoke, her face strained. "Oh, Rinaldo, *buona sera*."

"*Buona sera*, Maria." They spoke in rapid Italian while Rinaldo peered into the room over her head. Gabe gathered the gist of the conversation as Rinaldo asked to use the kitchen to make lunch for the conte's grandson.

Her face blanched. "*Sì*." She glanced behind her and slowly opened the door.

Rinaldo stepped cautiously inside. Gabe followed. Maria seemed to be the only occupant in the grand villa. Gabe's eyes swept over the rustic tile floor and up the wide wooden staircase to the loft where doors hinted at a number of bedrooms. *Wow, right out of a movie.*

At his feet, plush rugs grouped overstuffed furnishings into conversation areas. Books, whose covers enticed their readers to adventure, rested on the desktop, and…a wine glass sat on the table next to an ashtray. He recognized the familiar scent of Louis' cigar. He glanced at Rinaldo, who had also noticed it.

"Where is he?" Gabe grabbed Maria's shoulders, whose eyes went wide with fear.

"Stop!" Louis demanded, stepping into the room.

Gabe let go of her and turned to his grandfather, not comprehending. The old man looked fine—surprised, but healthy. Checking out the room behind him, Gabe realized no one was there. A slow rumble began to churn in his gut. "What are you doing here?"

Louis dropped his eyes to his feet. "*Mi dispiace*, Gabriel. I owe you an explanation." He sat down on the overstuffed sofa. "Come, sit."

Gabe had heard too many apologies in one day. His words were controlled, much more so than his emotions. "No, I won't sit. Tell me what's going on."

Louis' anxious eyes searched Gabe's. "I thought you had deceived me and had something to do with the theft of my painting, but I have learned since that you are innocent. You cannot imagine my grief at treating you so harshly."

"And?" It felt like Louis was sidestepping.

"And I had an idea how to get you to change your mind. I hoped that if you thought my life was threatened, you would come back…and be motivated to find *Il Testamento*." He cast Gabe an uncharacteristic sheepish glance.

Closing his eyes, Gabe fell onto the sofa. "Do you realize what you've done? A guard from the hotel is in critical condition after Ralph attacked him—I think his throat was cut. And who knows what he did to the other man guarding your house, while you…while you play at some ridiculous game! Livia is out in the limo right now, bleeding. Did your bright idea include that?" He stood up, shouting by this time.

Louis jumped to his feet. "Is she all right?"

Rinaldo rushed to Louis, who was massaging his chest. "Conte, it is just her shoulder."

"Bring her in," Louis ordered.

"Not on your life!" Gabe countered. "She locked me in the cellar then stole the map and stood by while Ralph smashed Rinaldo's head—it could have killed him, too."

Louis looked at Rinaldo with sad eyes. "You must know I never meant for this to happen." He motioned to Rinaldo who went outside to retrieve Livia. Then he turned to Gabe. "She is not to blame in this. It is my fault."

Gabe's rigid body smoldered with furious emotions.

When Livia entered the room, she ran to Louis and wrapped her arms around him. He looked down at the fresh blood on her shoulder, his eyes wide. "What happened to you?"

"I was so frightened, Louis." Tears drained over her cheeks. She wiped her eyes and pulled away from him, anger overtaking her fear. "Ralph cut me with his knife"

Louis' chest swelled. "That *criminale* could have killed you."

"It was a chance I had to take to find *Il Testamento*." She darted a sideways glance at Gabe.

"That was a brave but foolish thing you did," Louis scolded. He squeezed her hand.

"Yeah, well done," Gabe jeered. "You guys go ahead and play your cute little games—I'm out of here." He jumped up and headed for the door. "Rinaldo?" The chauffeur looked to his employer.

Louis' jaw held firm. "Not quite yet, Gabriel. Why don't you eat and settle down a bit, *eh*?"

Seeing he had no options, Gabe stomped outside and glowered at the vineyards. The fruit hung heavy on the vines, a sight he would have enjoyed immensely, save for the sudden angry tears that stung his eyes. How could Louis betray him like this? He had feared he would never see him again. *Just like Angelica*. He kicked a stone. "Foolish man!" he spit, swiping at a tear.

Louis came up behind him. "Gabriel, I am sorry. I deceived you and exposed you to great risk." He laid his hand on Gabe's shoulder. "I do not know what I would have done had anything happened to you, son. Livia has told me of all that has gone on. Come back inside, she wants to explain."

Nothing Livia could say was of any interest to Gabe, but staying where he was did not put him any closer to the airport.

They sat at the rectangular dining table, which Rinaldo and Maria were covering with simple dishes for lunch. After a few sips of wine with cheese and bread, Gabe felt the tension ease, but not his anger. He glared at Livia. She was a willful, spoiled user. Darla's deception had not come close to hers.

"Much of this is my fault," Livia said after awhile. She dropped her eyes but lifted her chin. It was apparent she was not used to admitting blame. "When Louis refused to let me see the map, I was angry and took matters into my own hands. Why should he show it to an outsider—one who had no interest in being part of our family, no commitment to finding *Il Testamento* and getting us out of danger?"

Gabe flinched. That's how she saw him?

Louis defended his actions. "For over forty years, this burden has weighed heavily on my shoulders. I do not take an oath lightly. When I first discovered our family's obligation, I dreamed of finding *Il Testamento* with my son and taking it to Seborga, to the Church of San Bernardo, for all of Christendom to embrace."

Livia frowned. "And why should our family live in terror because of your dream of glory to have your family deliver the spearhead? We could have…"

"What?" Gabe and Louis said in unison.

She glanced from one astonished face to the other and nodded. "*Sì*. That is what we are looking for. Ralph said the Grand Master of the Dead Knights told Harry they were looking for a spearhead, so I did some checking on prominent Templar treasure. A spear was purportedly found and protected by them. The Dead Knights want Longinus' spear—the one that pierced Christ's side on Calvary."

Louis' mouth dropped open. "That *is* something."

Livia jumped on that. "*Sì*, it is a precious thing, but did Christ come so people could kill each other to own bits of crosses and spearheads? To bow and worship such things as though the objects themselves are God?

180

"Louis, I know you are partial to the Templars because of Antonio, but Jesus said, '*If* this were my kingdom, my servants would fight for me.' This is not His kingdom. He would not have approved of knights and crusaders slaughtering in his name or providing relics used to trick believers out of their money."

"But this is different, my dear. We are talking about *protecting* the relic, not killing for it."

Maria entered to set a tray of figs and cheese on the table, and the conversation hushed. Livia pushed her chair back, using the opportunity to break from the conflict. She stepped to the buffet where Rinaldo filled the water glasses. He handed one to her and whispered, "Well said."

Gabe's eyes narrowed. "Speaking of stealing and nearly killing, how do you sync your actions with your words? You are working with Ralph against Louis and you almost got me killed to get your hands on the relic. Is the money that important that you would risk our lives?"

Livia's eyes widened at the serious accusation. She glared at him and slammed down into her chair. "I love Louis. After you left for the airport, he called and asked for my help in finding *Il Testamento*. I wanted him to go to a safe place until we could figure out who was targeting our family. So I suggested he disappear to get you to cooperate. I drove him here."

Rinaldo gasped. Gabe's mouth dropped open in shock. "This was *your* plan?" He felt like these people were winding a sticky web around him.

She tilted her head and shrugged her shoulders. "It seemed like a good idea at the time. And you were making progress. I am truly sorry it became so dangerous for you." Anger and frustration seemed to get the best of her. Latent tears streamed down her flushed cheeks.

She covered her bent face with her hands. "I just want peace for my family. The contessa is dead, and we are threatened again." She grabbed a napkin and wiped the moisture away. "Ralph is in league with the Dead Knights. I made him think I was desperate for money and was working with him to sell the relic. I hoped he could lead me to them before they got to us. Again."

Gabe shook his head. "How did you expect to get away with your story? Ralph's not stupid, and I doubt the Dead Knights are, either. They would have seen through you in a minute."

She bit her lip. "I used the cover identity of an art thief—the Kestrel."

"*You* took my painting," Louis snapped.

Livia grimaced. "I knew Ralph was snooping around the palazzo, so I arranged for him to catch me stealing the painting of Helena. I needed to gain his confidence. He thought he was blackmailing me so I would help him find the relic." Her eyes pleaded with Gabe. "I am sorry you were blamed." She turned to Louis, anxiety tensing her face. "You must believe that I planned to give your painting back as soon as this was over."

Louis wagged his head. "Okay. Okay." He reached for her chin and squeezed it in a pretend reprimand.

"Wait." Gabe was not at all convinced. "What about leaving me in the wine cellar and conking Rinaldo?"

She straightened her shoulders, back in attack mode. "When I went upstairs, Ralph was on the way to find you. I had to think fast and turn his mind away from you, toward looking for the relic. Rinaldo tried to take the map from me, and Ralph hit him. But when Ralph was climbing up the stairs to get you, I tripped him—earning me this." She punched her finger toward her shoulder.

Gabe glanced at the red stain on her shirt and shuddered, remembering he had locked her in the cellar with a killer. Louis sat across from him, safe, not dead. Gabe touched the knife cut on his chin and swallowed hard. The terrifying things his mind had imagined had not happened. Suddenly, he felt ravenous. He stuffed a cheese-filled fig into his mouth, needing time for his emotions to adjust.

They ate in silence, until he spoke to Livia, "I owe you an apology." He looked at her shoulder. "I didn't know you were hurt when I grabbed you, but after I did...I didn't care. Well, I didn't care as much as I should have." He dropped his head and closed his eyes. "I was just so worried about..." He glanced at Louis and his throat constricted. This crazy man had gotten into his heart. Excusing himself, he left the room for a few minutes.

When he returned, he found an array of vegetables, cured ham, and rich cheeses. Rinaldo had retrieved Antonio's letters from the limo. They lay spread out on the table, with Livia scouring over them.

"Come, Gabriel," his grandfather said. "The secrets are over. Come see the rest of the story—together. We will plan a safe way to find the spear or we will hand it all over to the church authorities. They are better equipped to keep it safe than I am."

Livia's eyes shot up with a start. "I do not think that will be necessary—now that we are all working together." She cast a dubious glance toward Gabe.

He dropped in his seat.

"Look at this," she coaxed, gently holding up a brittle letter to Helena from Galgano. She read a portion.

*"I am most grieved to add this to your pain, but the valiant horse your husband rode into battle was injured beyond remedy and needed to be destroyed. Please inform my servant if you want the saddle returned to Siena or left at Monticiano…"*

She looked at Louis and laid the letter down. "Do you still have Antonio's saddle?"

Louis shrugged. "I remember seeing it as a boy, but it was in very bad repair. Maria's father complained about having useless things lying around. I do not know if my father ever gave him permission to dispose of it." He grinned, revealing his deep dimple. "It may have more historical value than it ever did as a saddle."

# Chapter 23

Monticiano, Italy

Hours into the conversation, and stuffed with too much food and information, Gabe groaned. He pushed his chair back from the table and yawned. "I need to go for a walk." Outside, he stood on the porch and took in the sunset.

While he listened to the voices coming from inside the villa, born of familiarity, he felt more alone than he ever had. A nearby peak caught his attention. He imagined Galgano sitting on his hill looking out at the sunset, left alone to guard the spear that had pierced his God. His whole life had boiled down to that one task.

"May I join you?" Livia's voice sounded soft, melodic even. It was a pleasant change from most of their encounters.

"Sure." He had no fight and no emotion left for this day. As he started to walk across the top of the vineyard, she moved in step with him. The sky darkened and bats swooped in and around each other to catch their share of insects. Crickets filled the quiet void with their chirps.

"I really am sorry," she said. "I was so caught up in my desire to end all of this that I almost caused the very thing I fear most."

"Which is what?"

"More loss. And never having a normal life—one not caught up with secrets and villains." She sighed. "And responsibility. I had grand plans for my life, but everything changed. My mother died in the accident that paralyzed my father's legs. I had just turned nineteen and ended up with three younger sisters depending on me, each of us trying to work through our grief." She grew silent.

He understood death and loss, but his troubles seemed small after listening to hers.

Her eyes skimmed the path, and she continued. "It was impossible to study full time, let alone study abroad. The farthest away from home I traveled for my education was Florence—for only two years. Even then, Papa needed me to come home on weekends. Then a year ago, Louis' daughter, Geneva brought our family under this threat again." She hugged herself, and Gabe detected a shiver. "I cannot remember the last time I felt safe."

He glanced sideways at her somber face, cast with the last touch of sunlight, and wished he could change that for her. Watching the path, he resisted the urge to console her with a hug. Her disposition had proved too volatile. "Perhaps Louis will find a way to end all of this and our family can find its way again."

She shrugged. "My father told me that when Christina died and your father left, Louis lost interest in all the things he loved. His one obsession became finding *Il Testamento*."

Gabe pondered her words. "Perhaps he believes it will absolve him."

"Hmm. That would explain his stubbornness. Poor Louis, *Il Testamento* is his blind spot, robbing him of life. He needs to be free of it, for his own good."

"That would be a good thing. I would like to know him without this lunacy." Gabe chuckled.

Livia turned to him with a gentle smile and nodded toward the villa. "He has so much to enjoy. If all of this were mine, I would eat, sleep, and breathe it." Scanning the vineyard, she added, "When he is gone, it will all be yours."

Though Gabe didn't say it, a skeptical place in his mind whispered, *And all yours should anything happen to me.* Instantly, he brushed away the sour notion. She had explained her motives.

Continuing in a lighter tone of voice, she said, "I am glad you came to Italy. Are you?"

He pulled his gaze away from hers. "In some ways I suppose I am, but it's certainly not what I expected. I thought I'd be painting every day and meeting other artists. And getting to know my grandfather," he laughed. "I was looking forward to enjoying my life outside of the university."

She nodded. "Do you miss teaching? All those pretty, young students?"

"The teaching? Yes and no. I would prefer to instruct gifted students who are serious about their work—give them the opportunity that I had to sell my soul to get. As for the ladies…," he grinned and remained quiet for a few steps. She pretended to be offended. He glanced over, "Honestly, they never interested me."

"Right. I saw them melting at your feet."

He laughed and caught her eyes. "Since we're getting personal, do you have a man in your life?" She drew back, clearly not expecting the direct question. He enjoyed seeing her off balance for once, but the pleasure was short lived.

She didn't smile. "I have had suitors, but with my father's needs, my education, and my financial obligations, there is no time for a love life." Her lips tightened and she cast her eyes into the distance. "I did not have time for this drama."

They strolled in silence, their bodies moving in a rhythmic gait. Being this near, he felt the weight that she carried with fervent determination. The night continued to reveal new insights. It became obvious there was nothing superficial about her life. That she cared deeply for those she loved.

Her hair swung gently as they walked, her exotic scent drifting around them. Though his heart sounded a warning, he reached for her hand anyway. She didn't resist. Sweet sensations coursed through him at the long awaited connection. When she looked up and smiled, he squeezed her soft fingers to let her know it would be okay and then let her hand drop.

In that instant, life seemed lighter, regardless of the crushing burdens they carried. A door of understanding had finally opened. Renewed energy lifted his steps. After passing several rows, he picked a cluster of grapes, offering her a small handful. Crushing the fruit between his teeth, intense flavor flooded his mouth. "Do they do all the picking themselves?"

"No. A crew comes in for the harvest. They cut the grapes by hand, cull out all the inferior fruit, and throw the good clusters into the crusher."

"What, no dancing feet?"

She raised an eyebrow and grinned. "It can be arranged."

"No, thank you." They smiled freely at each other. She was gorgeous when she was like this. He caught a glimpse into the vitality usually suppressed under her demanding life.

Circling around, they turned up a row of vines that headed back to the villa. She said, "I have always enjoyed this place. My father used to bring me riding here." She pointed ahead to their left. "The stables are there. Louis kept wonderful horses. The villa is full of medals his thoroughbreds won at the track. His mixed breeds were a favorite choice for the *contrade*—the races in Siena."

An unexpected snort caused them to jump sideways. Staring at them from the top rail of a five-foot fence stood the tallest horse Gabe had ever seen. "Where did he come from?"

She chuckled. "That is *Selvaggio*—the 'Wild One.' He is Louis' prized sire. Many of Italy's champions have come from his line. Breeders throughout our country consult Louis on a regular basis."

How could Gabe not know that about his own grandfather? The man was famous, nearly a legend, for Pete's sake. He scowled at the image of his father who had robbed him of three decades of life with his family. There had been so many years of feeling isolated, years where no one knew what he was going through. Then Gabe thought of Louis' broken-hearted prayer in the chapel, his fear of dying alone. If there was a way to make up the loss for both of them, Gabe determined he would find it.

Livia continued. "This is the only stallion left." A light glowed in the barn ahead of them. "There are two other horses that Maria's husband,

Stephano, and his helper use in the vineyard. Would you like to see them?"

He nodded, surprised how natural it felt when she reached for his hand. Natural, but electrifying. After a quick glance at her, he examined the barn ahead and tried not to grin. They entered through a wide, vine-covered brick arch and stepped into a large paddock. A host of stone columns supported its wooden roof.

The perfect symmetry of the architecture filled him with admiration. Someone skilled in perspective had built this. It needed to be captured on canvas. He recognized the flag that dangled from the rough wooden ceiling. A large tortoise with daisies decorated a yellow and blue background. "*Tartuca.*"

"*Sì.* The Tortoise—the neighborhood flag of our Sienese ancestors," she said with obvious pride. A horse reached its head out of a stall. "And this is Celia." Livia dropped his hand and scratched the white blaze of the large red mare with wide-set eyes. Celia seemed to enjoy the gentle stroking.

As he lifted his hand to pet her, Gabe felt something nuzzle the back of his shoulder. He jumped and swung around to see an even larger horse staring at him.

Livia laughed. "And that is *Sansone*—Samson. He is our gentle giant."

"What do you mean *our*?"

She reached to scratch the gelding's ear. "Just a figure of speech. Though we are from different ancestral lines, we all grew up together as family. It is not an expression of ownership, but…connection, *eh*?"

He considered that and cast a sideways glance. Even in the dim light, he could see the love that glowed from Livia in this place. He stroked each horse in turn, studying the jaw lines and wide eyes of their noble heads. His shoulders began to relax in the cool, serene setting. "I've never been around horses."

"You seem natural with them. They are prey animals, you know, and can tell if they are with someone they can trust." She grinned. "They trust you."

The smile fled from his face. With his defenses down, his father's cruel words inflicted their latent accusations with as much venom as ever. "I should never have trusted a coward. Because of you, your sister is dead."

Gabe dropped his hand and backed away. "I need to go."

A pout showed her disappointment. "But why?"

"I just do." He cut her off and disappeared into the villa.

## 

Detective Orsini closed the door to his office, shutting out the nighttime commotion of the police station. He waited for his associate to answer his call.

"*Buona notte.*" The greeting was tense when it came through the phone's tiny speaker.

"Can you talk?" Orsini asked.

"*Si.* I am going over the information I have gathered. The backers of the ARCC are starting to swarm like disturbed bees."

"What has happened?" Orsini blew smoke into the air above his grey desk.

"Cardinal Vincenzo is taking some of the wind out of their sails. It looks as though he is trying to broker a peaceful compromise between the organizers and the religious zealots by excluding Christianity from the Center. The investors are incensed." His associate's bitter laugh rang through the phone.

Orsini smirked. "That would eliminate the lion's share of their profits. Perhaps they will need to go back to their old ways of shearing the sheep."

"Their greed has moved them beyond that. Have you heard anything on the Dolcinis? They seem to have vanished."

Frowning at the delay, Orsini said, "I expect I will hear something soon."

"Keep me in the loop."

"*Si.*" Orsini closed his phone. He should have received an update by now.

##

Early, just as the sun began to illuminate the eastern sky, Gabe left the villa and its sleeping inhabitants. It had been a beautiful September, and the brisk autumn air greeted him as he made his way back to the horses. Livia's words echoed, "They trust you." He wanted to embrace that, use it as evidence against the guilt he battled. It was easier in the light of day.

Once again, Sansone poked his head out, whinnying for attention. Gabe smiled and scratched the horse's neck. Picking a metal comb out of a green plastic bucket, he began to untangle the wiry black mane of the huge bay.

Gabe's mind was free to wander in the backdrop of the vineyard and stable. For years, he had worked to prove trustworthy to his students, in his relationships, and through his art. The accusation regarding Sonia had called his integrity into question. Had yanked up the lid of that trap door of guilt. Shifting his weight, his foot ground heavily onto the wooden floor. This time, the accusation was a lie.

Sansone's warm brown eyes gazed at him. Trusted him. Before long, his father's accusation shrank back into the black hole of the past. Peace soothed away the recent days of anxiety. He must have stayed with Sansone for an hour while the horse rested his head on the top of the gate, his lower lip drooping low.

"If he were a cat, he would be purring." Livia's lilting voice broke the silence of the morning.

Gabe smiled without looking around. "I think you're right." Without any reference to last night, they moved into easy conversation about their lives.

"…So, with a family history such as ours," she continued, "it was obvious that my studies would focus on Italian history—especially art history. When this is over, I plan to intern at the Uffizi Museum, then open my own gallery. My family owns several masterpieces, and I am developing a contemporary collection of my own."

Gabe peered at her over Sansone's head. "You have a lot of interests. Aren't you spreading yourself a bit thin?"

Her eyes instantly clouded, and she dropped them away, but not before he caught the uncertainty lodged within them. "The resources will come." She lifted her chin. "In the meantime, I learned how to make perfume, and run a hotel, and drive fast cars, *eh?*"

Their eyes linked and he drank in the hope and the anticipation of success that radiated from her. "You amaze me," he said. They laughed together, discussing the thrill of launching their dreams. "Will the family connections help with the Uffizi?"

Her smile faltered. "I have been counting on it. Louis' influence is huge in the art world, as you have discovered. Perhaps, when this is over…" She let the thought remain unfinished.

He understood the helpless feeling of dependency. Thankfully, Louis' contacts had proved a tremendous assistance for his career. "I have a meeting with Signore Belvedere from the museum in Rovereto on Saturday. He purchased *Pacifica* at the gala for his collection."

Her head jerked up. "He bought it?"

"Yes, and as good as promised that a solo exhibition came with the sale." The craziness of the last few days had prevented Gabe from enjoying the partial reprieve from his financial fears. "That will help repay some of the money I foolishly borrowed." Relief peeked through a half smile.

Livia covered a frown and turned her attention away. She scratched Celia more vigorously.

Gabe assumed she was thinking of her own financial difficulties. Moments passed in silence until he asked, "Isn't Louis' art collection fabulous?"

"*Si*, it is enviable. When I was younger, my family visited his home for parties. I felt like I was in a famous museum."

Imagining his own family's fun and laughter, without being able to be a part of it, dampened his mood. "So you have family gatherings often?"

"When my mother was alive, it was grand for my sisters and me. The year was a whirl of excitement with the festivities of the holy days, the horse races, and the grape harvest. And of course, birthdays, weddings…and funerals."

She shook her head, a subdued expression taking the place of the carefree time they had been enjoying. "As a child, the contessa's death was not discussed in front of us. It was not until later that I realized the cause of the deep sadness I sensed in Louis." Her shoulders physically drooped. "Back then, my father was strong and happy. Life was good, and we visited the palazzo often, but then everything changed." She sat on a bale of hay, her gaze falling to the ground.

"Papa suffered physically. And emotionally. After the accident, he could no longer work. The medical bills were enormous. We still own the villa, but we have no resources to maintain it. And Louis, well, he has his own troubles. I have watched him become increasingly reclusive, a shadow of the striking man I grew up admiring."

"I would like to have known my grandfather back then."

"At least you have him now, *eh*?"

"I suppose." Gabe wondered how much Louis' grief had altered him.

"I have not seen him this animated in years. He was especially down last year when he caught Ralph sneaking around the palazzo—just like Kendrick had. It brought back all the pain of losing Christina."

She spoke into the distance. "Louis has paid a high price because of *Il Testamento*. I understand his noble intentions, but he does not deserve more trouble. He needs to let go of this foolish quest." A jealous Celia whinnied, pulling Livia's attention back. She stood and grabbed a brush to stroke the horse's neck.

Gabe brought the conversation back to art. "I noticed an exceptional piece that hangs in the library above the fireplace. Who painted it?"

Her eyes lit up. "Helena's brother. It is entitled, *Eremo di San Galgano* and is a rendering of the hermitage that Galgano built on top of Montesiepi. There is a notation on the back written by Helena. She claimed Montesiepi as a shrine to her husband's bravery—where he fell protecting *Il Testamento*."

Gabe pondered that. "I read her letter about wanting to visit Montesiepi. Her brother must have gone with her. He obviously painted it then. His work is stunning."

Livia winced when Celia's nose bumped her shoulder.

"How's your cut this morning?" He touched her arm below the wound.

She lifted her head to meet his eyes and moved into his touch. When he gave her arm a gentle squeeze, she rested her other hand on top of his. Her eyes took on a violet hue, their desire drawing him in. Closer. She tightened her grip on his hand, lacing her fingers into his.

It was too late to heed the warning signals sent by his thumping heart. Bending the last inches between them, he kissed her soft, warm lips. His breathing stopped as he wrapped his other arm around her and pulled her close. Their lips melded, exploring rich, sweet sensations. Highly charged electricity passed between them. The tensions that had repelled them since they had met, magnetized, drawing them together. What he had imagined with Livia did not come close to this reality.

Sudden fierce shouts broke the moment, interrupting the pleasure of their first kiss. A commotion sounded from the direction of the horse arena. Concern overrode Gabe's frustration as he and Livia broke apart and raced around the trees. They halted at the astonishing sight.

The powerful stallion, *Selvaggio*, bucked and twisted—while Louis rode him, gripping its body with his legs! Gabe watched as his grandfather, hindered on foot, rode the raging horse with elegance and ease.

Stephano lay dazed inside the arena. The infuriated beast stormed toward him. There was no time! Gabe ducked between the rails to grab the injured man. "Ouch!" Gabe's leg caught on a protruding nail, tearing the flesh.

"Stay back," Louis shouted, but Gabe lunged forward and dragged Stephano toward the fence. Almost on top of Gabe, Louis thrust his heel into the stallion's side, forcing him to turn. They missed Gabe by inches. Gasping, he pulled Stephano the last few feet to safety.

*Selvaggio* flew to the far side of the arena, but slowed as he neared the rail. Louis used the moment to slide his right hand down the rein toward the horse's mouth. He wrenched *Selvaggio's* nose back toward his boot, causing the animal to turn in a tight circle. Round and round they went, stirring up clouds of dust and nearly plummeting to the ground.

Fear clenched Gabe's heart as he watched. The horse struggled to maintain its footing while fighting the immoveable force on top of him. It seemed an eternity until the stallion tired. *Selvaggio* tossed his head one last time, then stood still, his powerful lungs heaving, nostrils flaring. He was beaten.

Louis sat up straight and let the rein relax. He nudged *Selvaggio's* flanks, and they walked to the rail. After he slid from the stallion's bare back, he patted the beast's sweaty neck. The horse twitched nervously. "Whoa, son," he said. The horse dropped his head and stood quietly.

Stephano sat up, rubbing his elbows.

"Are you hurt?" Louis asked.

"No, Conte Dolcini."

"What happened?" Livia's wide eyes shown out of her ashen face.

Tugging at his beard, Louis shook his head. "I put his bridle on as usual and mounted him from the rail. Stephano stepped into the arena to remove a rake he had been using. For some reason, *Selvaggio* charged him and knocked him down. He reared as though he would attack, but I was able to pull him around."

Louis scrutinized the arena, but there seemed to be no indication of what had startled the horse. A concerned expression deepened the lines in his forehead. "I would hate to destroy a good horse, but I will not have a man-killer on my land."

He started to lead the horse toward the gate, favoring his left foot, when *Selvaggio* shied away again, his wild eyes trained on the foreman. They all looked toward Stephano, who had just dusted his hat and flopped it back on.

"Is that a new hat?"

"*Si*, Conte Dolcini. It is a gift from my brother. He visited last week."

Louis frowned. "Did he ride *Selvaggio* when he was here?"

Stephano studied the ground. "*Mi dispiace*. Against my instructions, he attempted to mount the horse. When I came out, he was waving my hat to get *Selvaggio* away from him."

A relieved sigh escaped Louis' mouth. "I see. That will not happen again." His exhortation was straightforward, but Gabe detected no sting in it.

"*Si*, Conte Dolcini."

Louis spent several minutes calming the horse. Afterward, Livia followed Stephano and *Selvaggio* back to the paddock. Stephano without his new hat.

Louis turned to Gabe and grasped his shoulder. "That was a brave thing to do. You could have been hurt helping Stephano."

Gabe shrugged and followed Louis toward the villa. "I've never seen anyone handle a horse like that."

"Hmm."

"There is so much power in that stallion." He glanced at his grandfather.

"*Si.*"

They arrived at the villa and Louis reached for the door with a trembling hand. He looked up at Gabe. "The answer you are looking for is *si*, I was afraid. In fact, I was terrified. When I was younger, I relished that kind of excitement. But a fall from that horse at this age could…well, it could end my useful days."

"Then why did you do it?"

"I was on the horse when he attacked Stephano. I had to act. Courage had nothing to do with it." He stepped inside and looked down at Gabe's leg. "You should ask Rinaldo to give you some antiseptic to cleanse that wound."

Blood oozed from his calf onto his jeans. Gabe nodded. "*Si*, signore."

After Rinaldo cleaned the grime out of the cut and bandaged it, Gabe headed in the same direction that Stephano and Livia had taken. He ended back at the horse barn. The unbridled stallion stood quietly in his stall, while Stephano spoke in rapid Italian to Livia.

Her mouth dropped open, and she turned to Gabe. "He says Antonio's saddle is in a closet off the tack room."

Following the stocky man, they entered through the only solid door leading off the paddock. Stephano hung the bridle on a hook, then passed by rows of saddles. He opened an interior door and left them alone. Gabe felt for a light and switched it on.

They gasped at the sight revealed before them. What was left of Antonio's deteriorated saddle rested on a low rail. Livia stepped forward and ran her hand over the saddle's rough leather and ancient metal. Cracks and rust had all but eaten it up. "This is history—our history—and it has been waiting for centuries for us to find it."

Gabe stepped closer. "So, Helena must have told Galgano to bring it here when he wrote to her." When he reached forward, he brushed against Livia's uninjured arm, dividing his attention. His heart pounded at the greatness of this discovery. And Livia's nearness.

She slid her arm around his waist. In an instant his arms encircled her. Drawing her close again, his dreams exploded into reality with a kiss. When he drew back for air, he shook his head while he gazed into her eyes. "With such a rough start, I'm amazed that we ever connected. It's nice to be on the same side."

She dropped her eyes. "*Sì*." She let go of him, and they turned their attention to the saddle. When Gabe gently pried open the saddlebags, the leather tore like paper. "Empty." Pursing his lips, he explored the saddle with more care.

A shudder went through his body as he experienced the odd sensation of connecting with Antonio's violent end. The knight had been close to his own age, yet larger than life. After lifting the stirrup over the top, Gabe's eyes caught a glimpse of something through a crack in a compartment.

With deft fingers, Livia pulled out a crumpled note. "It looks centuries old."

"Perhaps Antonio's own hand put it here." His family's history was certainly colorful. Two weeks ago, he complained about the boring routine of his life. And the solitude. He looked down at Livia and thought about Louis' genuine smile whenever they met. How could life change so abruptly?

They walked out into the sunlight and Gabe watched Livia's gentle fingers straighten the vellum. She translated the faded words while she read it. Her eyes widened and she whispered, "This is why Antonio was killed."

# Chapter 24

Monticiano, Italy

As facts began to substantiate Louis' flimsy tales, Gabe felt his resistance wane, but his anxiety increase. They raced back to the villa, Livia's jaw clamped hard with determination to solve this mystery. There was no telling where this pursuit would lead them or what danger lay ahead.

A strong desire urged him to pull her close and protect her, but in many ways, she possessed strength far beyond his own. Instead, he gave her hand an assuring squeeze, wishing he could ease her worry and entice a glorious smile from her lips again. When they entered the front door, the intense smells of coffee and breakfast hit them. Gabe broke into a grin when Louis' eyes fell to their clasped hands and his eyebrows rose.

"Look!" Livia showed the letter to him.

They sat and Louis read it aloud.

*"To Rafer Abito, most loyal Knight of the Crusades: By Abbot Lorenzo Casselli, Abbey of Saint John in Argentella, Palombara: Greetings:*

*It is under the strictest confidence that I write to you concerning our most Holy Father, Innocent III, whom our Holy Roman Emperor Frederick Barbarossa and I are anxious to see claim the support he merits. At present, he is safe here in Argentella, fortified against the forces of Alexander, but it is a precarious existence. We are in dire need of a miracle.*

*It was made known to us that a small band of Templar Knights is in possession of a great relic recently brought from Jerusalem. I believe a treasure of this magnitude would not only benefit the Soci, but would speak against that usurper, Alexander.*

*As indicated by this initial token of my sincerity, it would be in your favor to return the relic to me at any cost. I send this to you by the hand of my servant and look forward to word from you."*

Louis' hand fell to his lap. "This Lorenzo sent the crusaders to kill Antonio."

"And he was with the *Soci*—centuries ago!" Livia marveled.

Gabe tilted his head. "But who were Innocent and Alexander?"

"They were competing popes in the twelfth century," Louis explained. "Lorenzo must have believed *Il Testamento* would bring enough favor to Innocent that he would gain support over Alexander. It appears, so did King Barbarossa." He stroked his beard.

Livia's eyes were wide with apprehension. "It sounds like the *Soci* were ruthless even then."

Gabe tensed. "And still are. Maybe more so than the Dead Knights. Louis, I think you should remain here." Though Gabe longed to put a stop to this insanity right now, the intention in Livia's face was clear. There was no stopping her. The only way to protect her and his grandfather was to share what he knew and get them through this as quickly—and safely—as possible. He swallowed against the dryness in his mouth. "When I went to the Chapel of San Galgano yesterday…"

"*Sì*, why did you go there?" Louis interrupted.

"Because I believe Antonio never sent *Il Testamento* to Siena as we suspected."

"But his map," Louis argued, "it tells her where to hide it in the palazzo. He sent the relic to her."

"That was what I thought, too," Livia said. "But either he failed to send it with the map, or she was meant to come find it, using the map, and take it to Seborga herself."

Gabe added, "Also, in Galgano's letter to Helena, he talked about burying something important. Listen." He sorted through the letters and read the attached translation, "...I buried the savages beneath the mount, which now entombs the *sacred and the perverse*."

Livia raised an eyebrow and listened intently to Gabe's revelation.

He continued, "I went to Montesiepi because I wanted to see if there was any indication of a tomb or cave, but didn't find anything. Then, I met a crabby woman there..." Livia inclined her head, but he decided not to expose his embarrassing antics. "Anyway, I hiked down the path to the abbey and overheard a conversation between Firelli and an Abbot Porta—a member of the *Soci*!"

"Firelli? What was he doing there?" Astonishment flooded Livia's face.

"How do *you* know him?" Gabe felt a pinprick in his trust bubble and stiffened. Her involvement seemed to appear and disappear behind the shadowy details as they uncovered them.

She hesitated, eyes flitting sideways. "I followed you to the ruin and found him in the basement. He got free and chased me."

Gabe studied the genuine alarm residing in her eyes. Those gorgeous, cloudy eyes. A knife of fear pierced his heart and he blurted his concern. "What if he'd hurt you—or worse?" Anguish intensified his words and stung his eyes.

Laying her hand on his arm, she said, "But he didn't."

Struggling to gain control, Gabe turned and picked up a letter. Shaking his head, he murmured, "Firelli is no one to play games with. The *Soci* have already murdered once."

"Reverendo Tito," Louis whispered sadly.

Nodding, Gabe said, "When Abbot Porta asked if Firelli needed any help dealing with us, he said no, he could handle it. He patted his gun."

Louis' shoulders pulled back in nervous determination. "It is time to enlist Marcella."

"Who's Marcella?" Gabe asked.

Groaning, Louis explained, "She is Christina's younger sister. When Christina died, Marcella blamed me for exposing our family to those thugs." His jaw tightened. "Then Kendrick was found in the river. So was his co-conspirator—a member of the Dead Knights. Thankfully, their deaths broke the link back to our family. Until recently."

Livia turned to Gabe. "Marcella suspected the Dead Knights' involvement again, but then things became confusing with the presence of a second group—the *Soci*. A month ago, just after Marcella alerted us to be on our guard, a strange man approached my sister, Delia. He frightened her when he questioned her about a relic. I immediately called Marcella. She did not have an answer for us, but has been checking it out."

"How does she do that?" Gabe was almost unwilling to hear the answer.

"She is the head of an elite section of the *Guardia di Finanza*, the Italian agency that investigates crimes, from smuggling to terrorism."

A light went on in Gabe's head. "Is that how you got my wallet back from the police?"

Livia fidgeted in her chair. "*Sì*."

Gabe drew back. "What does she know about all this?"

Livia's eyes flitted between the two men. "Marcella told me the Dead Knights have been operating for centuries throughout Europe. Their current Grand Master is known as DeMolay."

"Didn't you tell me DeMolay was the Templar burned at the stake by King Philip?" Gabe asked.

"*Sì*, but since his death and the formation of the Dead Knights, all their Grand Masters take that name. Recently, officials in the UK have been tracking the group's involvement in the vandalism that killed the Thorn Tree in Glastenbury, England."

"Thorn Tree?" Gabe was lost.

Louis interjected. "Joseph of Arimathea, the merchant who came for Jesus' body after his death, often traveled between England's tin mines and Jerusalem. After Calvary, he brought back a staff from the thorn tree that produced the thorns used in our Savior's crown. He planted it 2,000 years ago, and it has bloomed every Christmas since. It was a travesty to see photos of it hacked down."

Gabe marveled at the ease with which his grandfather spoke of Jesus' life, as if He had really existed. At home, if you wanted to stop a conversation in its tracks, all you had to do was mention Jesus, and people looked away or scattered. These stories of the miraculous were foreign. He preferred concrete facts.

Livia chewed her bottom lip. "From Delia's description of the man who questioned her, I think it was Firelli. After I found him tied up in the basement of the ruin, I called Marcella to tell her we may have found a member of the second group."

"Do we know how Abbot Porta is involved in this?" Gabe asked.

Livia looked from Louis to Gabe and reached into her pocket. "I think I know. I took this out of Firelli's pocket in the basement of the ruin." She unfolded a note and read the message.

*"Your Excellency,*

*Enclosed, please find the documents from Abbot Lorenzo Casselli, a twelfth century Soci brother, which I uncovered during my visit at the Abbey of Saint John in Argentella, Palombara. They speak of instructions left in Seborga concerning the relic. After questioning Reverendo Tito in Seborga, who unfortunately suffered a fatal accident, I discovered he was in possession of a priceless document penned by Saint Bernard—also enclosed. As always, you may count on my unwavering support.*
*Most sincerely,*
*Abbot Bartolomeo Porta"*

Gabe pursed his lips. "Does that abbey sound familiar?

Livia nodded, "The letter from the saddle." They set them side by side and she read the salutation, "To Rafer Abito, most loyal Knight of the Crusades: By Abbot Lorenzo Casselli, Abbey of Saint John in Argentella, Palombara..."

Amazement brightened Louis' face. "The same abbey. The item they are referring to is definitely *Il Testamento*."

Gabe raked his fingers through his hair. "Abbot Porta is working for a *Soci* leader he calls, the *Primo Consul*. No doubt they are all involved in Reverendo Tito's murder. We need to uncover their leader's identity. Soon."

Louis reached for the letters. "Leave those with me, and I will see what I can find out when I return to Siena." He tapped his fingertips together. "Before we miss any other vital information, we should comb through all of Helena's documents in light of what we know."

Rinaldo appeared and brought out a plate of chocolate croissants. Extraordinary smells of cocoa and espresso wafted up from the table, causing a temporary break in their sleuthing.

Livia exchanged a glance with Rinaldo, her hand accidentally knocking Porta's letter to his feet. Gabe watched the servant take his time as he bent to recover it. Livia seemed intent on the food and closed her eyes as she tasted one of the flaky pastries.

Gabe only nibbled at the food, his mind alternating between trust and distrust. No doubt, there was a conspiracy, but who were all the players? And what team were they playing on? For now, everyone was moving in one direction—find *Il Testamento*. He worried about what would happen afterward. There were too many sides vying to obtain it. He hoped his family did not get crushed in the middle.

With great care, they sorted what they could and set the documents in order, but some had no date on them. Seeing a familiar letter on the table, Gabe held it up to tease Livia. "Well, look at this, we have Antonio's map back."

She shot a smile at him and shrugged her shoulders.

He held her eyes. "I need to thank you for running interference with Ralph, but don't ever put your life in danger for me again."

She raised her chin. "Am I now a porcelain doll?"

"No, but there are real killers out there. *Nothing* is worth a life." He held her eyes.

She gave a half nod to his warning then sifted through the documents. Picking up each in turn, she summarized it for significance. "Louis, you wrote that the oldest reference about Saint Bernard finding the map in Seborga, was around 1178. Where did you get that information?"

"Marcus. He found a mention on the internet and tracked down an out-of-print book that contained the information. His research has proved invaluable."

"He never told me." She frowned and laid down the reference. "We have several letters sent to Helena from Antonio while in Jerusalem; Antonio's letter to Helena where he tells her he is returning a secret to Seborga; Abbot Lorenzo's order to Rafer to capture *Il Testamento* from Antonio two years later; and a letter to Helena from Antonio after he was wounded, asking her to come get the relic and hide it at the palazzo." She studied it. "He included the vow of the *Custodi* in it.

"Next, we have Galgano's letters to Helena, telling her of Antonio's death and asking what to do with his saddle; Galgano's mother's letter to Helena to encourage her son to leave Montesiepi; and Helena's letter announcing her visit to Montesiepi."

Gabe gently tapped one of the letters, his eyebrows furrowed together. "I don't see much else to go on here."

Louis straightened. "I am going to follow up on Abbot Porta. I have friends in high places who can tell me what kind of intrigues are going on in Rome and elsewhere." He seemed satisfied at being able to help.

Gabe said, "You might want to look into the activity surrounding the ARCC. I imagine there are a lot of power plays going on behind the scenes."

## ##

"You do not want to disappoint me," the *Primo Consul's* words from earlier that morning constricted Abbot Porta's throat as he sat at his dining table and swallowed a lump of pork. He wiped his mouth as Niccolo strode in. "I need you to rent a room in Siena."

"When?" Niccolo stood at attention.

Porta studied him, gloating on the strength of this young man who served him. He would go far in the *Soci*. "As soon as possible." Porta chewed the rest of the fat off the rib bone, then wiped his fingers on his napkin. "Our *Primo Consul* has lost patience with the situation. Monday is the last day to announce his bid for the leadership of the ARCC. That only gives us five days. Then he must make a decision, with or without the relic."

"Do you have a date for us to move in?"

"Soon. However, if we are rash, the information could be lost for another thousand years. Wait for my orders and be ready to seize it." Porta leaned back and folded his hands on top of his bulging stomach. "If the *Primo Consul* wins this bid, the future appointments he makes will elevate all of the *Soci* who supported him."

Niccolo nodded. "He will have the relic."

The greasy corners of Porta's lips lifted. "It is a pleasure to work with someone who will not fail me."

## ##

As glorious as this place was, they could not hide out here forever. Gabe stepped out on the porch of the villa and stretched his arms high into the afternoon air. It was hard to believe so many different colors of leaves could grow on the same vine, filling the vineyard with crimson, yellow and orange flames. He agreed with Livia. If this were his, he would eat, sleep, and paint here. For now, tension underlined all they did. The danger threatened to escalate in the coming days.

Louis joined him, chewing on the end of his cigar. "I try not to smoke these."

Gabe nodded. "Good. Now that I know you, I'd like to keep you around for awhile." His grin fell when he studied his grandfather's troubled face.

"Look at this land, Gabriel. So much time lost—we could have done so many things together. I would have shown you the world." His voice cracked when he looked at Gabe. "News of your father's death came through an attorney. I always saw myself as a man of courage, but I could not write to you."

"Why not?"

Louis' jaw tightened against the grief. "I feared your rejection. When you were in Siena and refused my invitations, it seemed you had accepted his judgment of me."

206

Gabe shook his head. "I shouldn't have listened to his tainted advice. I wish it had been different."

Staring at the horizon, Louis was contemplative. "Before you came, everyone I loved was gone. Christina loved me in spite of my harsh ways. Our children were difficult, but they were children, and that is a hard time of life. I never thought they would hate me with such vehemence. Your father left, then died. Geneva was lost to drugs." He bent his head. "God helped me change, but it was too late. I was left alone."

"Did you consider remarrying?"

His lips tightened. "There was no way to invite another to share my life without endangering hers."

Gabe shook his head in anger at the pain Louis' children had caused him. The next moment, guilt flooded his own heart. "I'm sorry for not contacting you."

Louis patted Gabe's hand where it rested on the porch rail. He straightened his shoulders. "Enough looking back. It is good that you are here now. And who knows, when this is over, perhaps I will think about a bride." He grinned, his white mustache lifting.

Gabe put his arm around his grandfather's shoulders and hugged him. Even if Louis was peculiar, Gabe realized he loved this man, and that love had turned his world upside down.

He had come to Italy with a clear goal, but his career was stalled by this quest. Worse, the focused drive he had used to climb toward the top of his profession had dissipated like a vapor, leaving him unsettled. He dropped his arm and stared at the fruit-laden vines. For now, his course was set. He would stay and help his desperate family in this outlandish situation.

Worry wrinkled Louis' features. "I do not want you endangered while trying to find *Il Testamento*."

Gabe nodded. "We will find a way, *nonno*."

They moved back inside and sat with Livia on two facing loveseats. Gabe leaned back and crossed his ankle over his knee. He revealed the last piece of information he had gathered. "When I overheard Abbot Porta, he stated that the Cistercian monks built the Chapel and Abbey of San Galgano to hide the excavation while they looked for *Il Testamento*—

and they dug a room below Galgano's sword."

Livia's eyes widened, and he watched while this news searched for places to connect with information she already had.

Louis stared at the cut and sprang to life. "There is something I have not told you, but your discoveries have confirmed the truth to me."

Gabe tensed. *What now?*

"After you left for the hotel, I had a vision. I saw you using an artist's knife."

"A palette knife?"

"*Sì*. You unlocked a large bronze door, engraved with a special symbol. When the door opened, light beamed through the opening, but I could not make out what was inside." He sat forward and reached in the pocket of the wool cardigan sweater he was wearing and laid his sketch on the coffee table for all to see. "I knew from the vision that you were the one destined to find *Il Testamento*, not me."

A faint gasp escaped Livia's lips. "Is that all you meant about Gabe knowing where it was?"

"*Sì*," Louis beamed.

Gabe avoided the absurdity of the remark and asked, "What do you mean I am *destined?*"

"I saw you open the door with this symbol on it." Louis' eyes were hopeful.

"You can't be serious about a dream connecting me to some ethereal destiny?" This kind of thinking threatened to undermine their common reality all over again.

"If I may," Rinaldo studied the drawing and said, "This is the symbol for…"

"Alpha and omega," Louis cut in.

"And?" Gabe asked.

"Jesus said *He* was the Alpha and the Omega—the Author and Finisher of our faith. He sets a seed of faith in us, then gently brings more understanding. When this world passes, He will open our eyes to *all* the Truth. Then we will no longer need faith," Louis explained, his countenance glowing. "It is definitely a sign."

Gabe decided not to say what he felt. "So, do we know what I'm supposed to do with this sign?" The group fell silent.

The phone rang, and Rinaldo answered it. The distressed tone in his voice caused everyone to turn and watch him. He listened for a few moments and blanched. His face tensed with anger. "*Sì*, I understand." He did not offer to hand the phone to the conte, but hung up instead.

"What is it, Rinaldo," Louis asked.

The servant came close and laid his hand on the older man's shoulder. "Signore, it is very grave news. Detective Orsini called to say that Ralph escaped from his hospital bed…"

"What!" Gabe exclaimed.

"…and they pulled his body from the Arno River. Just like his father." Rinaldo grimaced. "His head was not found."

Livia and Gabe gasped.

Louis' hand covered his mouth. He bowed his head. "So much tragedy." After composing himself, he grabbed the arms of his chair and stood. "It is time to go home and find an end to this."

# Chapter 25

Siena, Italy

The family determined to close ranks. When Louis arrived home on Wednesday night, he phoned Marcella, who smoothed over the *misunderstanding* of his disappearance with the authorities. Before Livia left, Louis asked her to come to the palazzo the following day to formulate a plan. He also put Rinaldo on high alert, who offered to call Detective Orsini for backup if needed.

They all spent a restless night. Several times, Gabe started awake, certain he heard voices and doors opening. In the morning, he rushed downstairs when Rinaldo announced that Livia was waiting for him. Thoughts of her softened the undercurrent of dread he had felt since Ralph's body was found.

"*Buon giorno*," Gabe said, taking Livia's hand and kissing her softly on the forehead.

She smiled up at him. "Let's go outside, it is a beautiful day, *eh?*" She led him to the formal garden of the palazzo, where they sat on a marble bench. Gabe's arm encircled her as she sat next to him. Above them, an umbrella of alizarin and amber leaves clung to their branches. This was the Italy he had dreamed of.

"If you could, I bet you would be purring," she teased.

He kissed the top of her head. "I am."

He slid his fingers through her silky hair and the next moment pulled her face toward him, pressing his lips onto hers. Fiery sensations tingled through him, and he could think of nothing other than spending his life with Livia *Dolcini*. He pulled back and gazed into her loving eyes. "I wanted it to be like this the moment I saw you."

She laughed, "You were so full of yourself that evening."

He straightened in protest. "I certainly was not. The cleaners ruined my jacket, Howard was throwing barbs at me, and..."

"It is okay, you are here now, and you have settled into a nice sense of humility." She kissed him lightly.

"Having one's life threatened a few times can have a humbling effect." He leaned back on the bench. She turned and settled against his chest. The amazing scent she had conjured in one of her test tubes floated around him. He sighed. "This is like the calm before the storm."

She trailed her fingers along his arm, her voice tentative. "I wish life could stay this simple."

"It never does."

"Do not be such a skeptic," she teased.

"I call it realistic."

A bird flew off a branch above them, drawing Livia's attention after it. "Do you ever wish you could just pack all your responsibilities into a box and hand them to someone else? Or wish you could fly so high that your problems seemed miniscule?"

He laughed. "I did, and came here. Only they followed me—and quadrupled."

Her smooth fingers caressed his hand. "I am sorry you got caught in the middle of this. But it is really a simple process now. We use the map, find *Il Testamento*, and deliver it." Her voice sobered. "Then this will be over. Soon, I will have the money I need to help Papa and my sisters. Then I can fly as high as I choose."

Tension gnawed at him and he sat up straighter on the bench. "And this money will just fall from the sky?"

"No. I have risked everything to make it happen. You know how that feels, *eh*?"

"Hmm." He was not sure where she was going.

Her voice carried a tentative edge. "Would you be opposed to the relic *not* going to Seborga?"

Cautiously, he asked, "Where else would it go?"

Louis' voice called to them from the palazzo steps, hindering her answer. He was smiling. "You will be impressed by what I discovered."

Livia sat up, instantly alert.

Gabe glanced at his grandfather's dancing eyes. "What did you find out?"

"I spoke with Bishop Roberto."

The frown that had started with Livia's cryptic conversation turned Gabe's mouth into a full-blown glower. "Why would you bring the clergy into this again?"

Louis pulled his head back in defense. "Just because there are weeds in the wheat field, do you refuse to eat bread?

"So far, all I've seen are the thistles."

Livia narrowed her eyes at him. "That may be, but the community of faith here is sincere. This negative element we are dealing with is a rare exception."

Gabe rubbed his forehead in frustration. "I can only speak of my experiences. So far, we have religious men in the highest places hard at work killing their own people and trying to kill our family. So excuse me if I don't think it's a good idea to share our secrets with them."

Louis was firm. "I understand, but as Livia said, our family of faith is trustworthy—and ready to help. Now, shall I tell you about those weeds growing among the wheat?"

Gabe huffed, but nodded.

His grandfather pulled over a wrought iron chair. "There is an unusual amount of politicking occurring between several ambitious members of the religious clergy—Catholics, Protestants, and too many others to name. They are all vying for the leadership of the ARCC. Cardinal Vincenzo is trying hard to keep things civil, but the whole world seems to be in an uproar. Many groups do not want the center at all.

"What's the big deal?" Gabe's brows wrinkled. "As I understand, it's just a religious museum of sorts."

Louis' expression sobered. "It is more than that, I am afraid. I saw the plans online. The main building in the complex is a colossal, contemporary cathedral—though nondescript in its architecture. It not only houses religious artifacts, but each religion will have worship areas for their deities recessed off the central gallery, one after another."

"What's wrong with that?"

Taken aback, Louis inclined his head. "You truly have no understanding, do you?" Though his words were not cutting, Louis was definite. "The message of Jesus is that there is one God. He warned us about worshipping created things instead of the Creator. Can you understand how God and His followers might feel about listing Jehovah as *one* of many gods, and setting up a place of worship among a myriad of idols?"

Foreign to this notion, Gabe could understand the concern of people who believed that way. "That might be true for other religions as well."

Louis sighed. "*Si*. Most of the others, however, do not seem to mind having a plethora of objects and personages to call god." He leaned on the back of the iron chair. "There is another strong objection among the religions, although the ARCC refutes the claims. Through the sheer size of its projected membership and profitability, the center will have more religiously-based political sway throughout the entire world than any other organization, at any time in history."

"How so?" Gabe's skepticism peaked.

"With more than twice the representation of Rome and the involvement of all religions, imagine the influence a *Soci* leadership of the ARCC would have. They could sway governments to enact laws that affect, even limit, the religious rights of those who oppose them. History has painted a pretty grim picture of what happens when governments dictate religion."

Gabe raised his eyebrows. "And when religion dictates to government."

Livia moved the conversation back. "Did the Bishop say anything about Abbot Porta?"

Louis shook his head. "He could not say directly, but it is obvious Porta is attempting to buoy support for his candidate by providing him with the famous *Il Testamento*."

"What do you mean by famous?" Gabe asked.

"I am afraid just that." Louis frowned. "Lorenzo's letters to Rafer demonstrated that this search began hundreds of years ago. These monks write down everything—which then gets squirreled away to either be found or lost into oblivion."

"In our case," Livia added, "I think every stone was pulled up looking for information about *Il Testamento*."

Nodding, Louis expounded. "The legend is as potent today as it seems it was then. People are talking about 'Saint Bernard's relic,' or the 'secret Templar relic.' They aren't calling it by name, but there is a growing expectation." He sighed. "The point is that tension is high within the ivory towers. There is only a week left before the elections, causing a frenzy of speculation about who or what will tip the scale for the leadership position."

"Sounds like more power-mongering," Gabe accused.

"*Sì*. Unfortunately, more thistles. It is more important than ever to find the spear and take it to its rightful place."

Livia protested, "But Louis, those with more authority will just take it. Surely, the *Soci* have powerful members within every major religion. It would be an easy task to get their hands on it to add to their carnival show."

He smiled and winked. "I have already thought of that. I asked myself who is the most powerful and worthy man in the church who could protect *Il Testamento* from the *Soci*."

"The pope?" Gabe guessed.

Louis pursed his lips. "Perhaps, but he does not busy himself with these things. No. Cardinal Vincenzo. I have been following his efforts to bring a fair and peaceful solution to this religious center, and he has made great progress protecting the sanctity of our faith. And, as Vicar General, he is in charge of the relics for the Vatican. I called his office and spoke to him personally this morning."

Livia gasped. "What did you tell him?"

"I explained what I know about *Il Testamento*. Cardinal Vincenzo was fascinated. I said I have found the map to where it is buried, and that my family and I are very close to uncovering its location. He assured me he would protect it to the fullest extent possible." Pleased with his report, Louis left them alone and made his way inside.

Gabe and Livia were speechless.

She rose. "Let's walk." Gabe reached for her hand, but she withdrew it and wrapped her arms around herself.

"Are you cold?"

She ignored his question. "He does not realize what he has done," she moaned. "*Il Testamento* was never supposed to be in the hands of an organization. There was a reason the early Christians circulated it in secret."

Gabe smiled to reassure her. "This was Louis' responsibility, and he's made his decision. Did you see the delight and relief in his face? It's out of our hands now." He took her hand and pulled her to him. "Let's find this thing and start creating our own dreams, *eh*?" He grinned, but she did not.

She studied his face and touched his cheek. Tears filled her eyes.

"What?"

She shook her head and looked away. "Nothing. I need to leave." Her expression turned cold. Distant.

Alarm tightened Gabe's chest. "But why?"

"I just do."

## ##

In spite of the fair autumn weather, Abbot Porta shivered in the morning shadows of the regal villa owned by the *Soci*'s second in command, *Consul* Bizzarri. If Porta posed the strategy just right, Bizzarri's lust for power would convince him to join Porta's bold scheme against the *Primo Consul*.

Porta went over his reason for such drastic measures. They were sound. A growing uneasiness was circulating among the *Soci* at the ruthless brutality of the *Primo Consul*—a useful rumor that Porta had started.

He tapped at the small arched door that hid inside a vine-covered brick alcove. Only a narrow streak of light penetrated the windowless interior when it opened. Once he stepped inside and closed the door, he heard a match scrape across the surface of a box and watched the flame move to light the wick of a candle. He swallowed. This was the most daring risk he had taken, but it could gain him the world.

*Consul* Bizzarri's elongated face peered at him, unsmiling. "What is this about, Abbot Porta, and why the secrecy?"

Lifting his chin, Porta poured out his reasons. "I have come because I am concerned about the widespread violence our leader is employing to find the relic. If we are not careful, the ensuing investigations and heightened exposure could topple the *Soci*."

"And what would you have me do about this?" One eyebrow rose, almost imperceptibly.

Porta worked to make his voice even. "Forgive my frankness, *Consul*, but the rift between the *Consuls* is common knowledge."

"Sit down." Bizzarri pointed to a chair, his piercing eyes scrutinizing Porta's.

Porta returned his assessment. They had a right to be nervous. This conversation dripped with treason. "Shall I continue?"

Bizzarri nodded, and Porta expounded on what he knew about the relic and the *Primo Counsel's* plans. "You have always ruled with wisdom, preferring finesse over brute force—a vital aptitude that could be used to manage the wealth of the ARCC, should I gain the appointment. The relic is the key. My associate will deliver it to me once he obtains it. After that…" He stopped short of jeopardizing his safety.

Studying his manicured fingernails, Bizzarri was silent for long moments. Porta held his breath, knowing his future pivoted on this man's response.

The *Consul* lifted his narrowed eyes. "You seem most anxious to betray your *Primo Consul*. I perceive you would be equally ready to plot against me should I gain his position."

Porta's self-assurance disintegrated. His throat tightened. "Not so, *Consul*. It is only the *Soci* I am concerned about."

A mocking smile played on Bizzarri's mouth. "Then let us approach our *Primo Consul* with your concerns. He will be most interested in our conversation."

The pounding of Porta's heart had increased with every minute of his visit. Drops of perspiration tickled his temples. "But Consul..." Bizzarri put up his hand to silence him, then withdrew a phone.

Feeling under his robe, Porta felt for the dagger he brought with him in case this plot failed. He bowed his head in submission and gripped its handle. Bizzarri drew back his finger to enter the last number in the phone. This was the moment.

Porta leapt from his chair to strike, but Bizzarri's hand flew up and grabbed the thick wrist holding the deadly blade. Both men groaned in the struggle. Porta's arm twisted free. He caught the *Consul's* throat with the sweep of his knife. Bizzarri's horrified face tensed, then fell flaccid as his body slumped to the floor.

Porta shook violently. It had been awhile since he had to carry out the physical responsibilities of his position in the *Soci*. He glanced around the room and wiped the blood off his knife. Standing over the corpse, he said, "I warned you. We need to put an end to this sensational killing."

# Chapter 26

Siena, Italy

*Why would she just leave like that?* Gabe shook his head in frustration shortly after Livia abandoned him in the palazzo garden. Detective Orsini arrived wearing an enviable cashmere trench coat that could have come straight off the runway in Milan. Gabe sank back in a leather chair in the library, frustrated with Livia, but glad to be on the right side of the law again.

Orsini wasted no time. "Conte Dolcini, Ralph Witte has been accused, posthumously, of assaulting the guards at the hotel and the palazzo. We arrested an English lowlife who had been seen with him— Harry Smythe. But with no hard evidence, we had to release the man. *Mi dispiace*, Conte Dolcini, but this will most likely be added to our list of unsolved homicides."

Louis was stoic, his lips firm. It belied the distress Gabe sensed. No matter that Ralph had been disloyal, he was still family. His grandfather demonstrated loyalty foreign to Gabe's upbringing.

Orsini arose, and Rinaldo escorted him to the front door. They conversed in low tones for a brief moment before the door closed.

Afterward, Louis stood and gazed through the library window. "I never knew what to think of that boy. He never had a conscience, never was right—but then neither was his mother." He sighed. "After Christina died, Geneva—like your father—hated me even more. She had always rebelled against anything good for her." Louis collapsed onto the sofa.

"That is how she ended up with Kendrick, a brawling alcoholic. They never married, even when she learned she was with child.

"After Kendrick's body was found, I felt there was at last a chance for... Well, had he lived, I believed he would have been a horrible example for Ralph. Still, growing up without a father can be hard on a boy."

Gabe nodded, "So can growing up with one."

His grandfather studied him. "There seems to be more than you are telling me about your family." He motioned to the chair across from him. "Come. Tell me about this wound you have worked so hard to bury."

This was unexpected. Gabe's breath caught in his throat. Heart beating wildly, he fought the part of him that guarded his secret. His shoulders rounded in an attempt to cover the shame that burned in his breast. *Don't, don't, don't.*

"Gabriel?" The tenderness in his grandfather's voice wove its way through chinks in the walls Gabe had built, past years of accusations—his father's and his own. It cooled the blaze of bitterness in his core, causing tears to swell. He had to discharge this festering wound. A wound he feared would burst if he did not slice it open to relieve the strain.

A violent shudder shook Gabe's body. He kept his face low. It was time. If he could not trust his grandfather, who else? Gabe stared at nothing, seeing only that fateful day. The words tumbled out.

"My father and Angelica were two of a kind. They lived for the outdoors, always searching for higher highs, bigger adventures. I was just never into it." He swallowed. "As a boy, I was scared—scared of heights, bullies, water—you name it. I could see the disappointment in my father's eyes and hear it in his voice.

"He kept pushing me, knowing I hated it." The corners of Gabe's trembling lips turned down. "He seemed to take pleasure in that. One time, Angelica came to my rescue. I wish she hadn't. He humiliated me in front of his friends—said he had a tomboy and a little girl."

Anger swelled. "My mother was out of town for the weekend, so I couldn't stay home while Dad and Angelica went camping. I begged Angelica to stay home, to say she was sick. Dad would have listened to her.

"She said it would be fun, I would see. I was so angry. I wanted her to know what it felt like to…" He shook his head. "I sat in the backseat with the tent and rain jackets. All during the drive, I dreaded what lay ahead. Once we got to the mountain, it was worse than I imagined.

"Higher and higher, we climbed giant boulders beside a massive waterfall. Dad never used a trail. I was eight and Angelica was twelve. I remember resenting her agility—she just seemed to float when she pushed off from one rock to the next. It was a struggle for me to crawl over them, even with my hiking boots. She was already much higher on the mountain than we were. Dad kept screaming at me to catch up."

He swallowed. "It happened so fast. A low moan swelled into an all-out roar as wind whipped through the branches of the pine trees. Almost at once, they bent under the unseen force. I watched the sky above the mountain and saw ugly black and green clouds edge over the top. They came out of nowhere.

"Dad jerked his head up and his face turned white. He got Angelica's attention, and she started back down. Heavy drops of rain began to pelt me. Within minutes, I was soaked. It was even harder to keep my balance on the slippery rocks. The waterfall roared. Dad was screaming to hurry—not to me, but to Angelica.

"Water started gushing from above, swirling and gaining speed, dragging everything it could down the mountainside. Dad and I were near a place where the waterfall flattened and calmed enough to wade across the torrent. He could, but I couldn't. I looked at that rushing water and froze in my boots. The more he swore at me to go, the more frightened I became.

"He ripped a rope from his pack and tied it to a small tree, then half swum to the other side to secure it. He yelled for me to hold onto it and wade through the water to him."

Gabe broke into a sweat and looked at the tension in his grandfather's face. "I was stuck with fear. I couldn't hold the rope, much less climb across it. The wind was whipping around my face and blowing rain into my eyes. All I could do was crouch down and cling to that tree."

Gabe tried to swallow the lump in his throat. "He screamed and cursed at me, but it was useless. '*I* was useless,' he yelled. In a rage, he stalked back across and slapped me. Then he grabbed my shoulder and yanked me into the water.

"He thrashed through the whitewater close to the ledge, suspending me in midair by one arm. The surge flowed over my head and into my nose and mouth. I was terrified by the sight of the sharp rocks fifty feet below."

Jagged intakes of breath punctuated Gabe's story. "When we reached the other side, he threw me to the ground and started back. A deluge of water had gained momentum and was shooting down the mountain. Fearless, Angelica laughed and jumped to a lower boulder, but this time, her foot slipped. She dove headfirst down the steep incline. Over and over she struck the rocky slope. I can still hear my father as he screamed her name over the roar of the water.

"When I saw her again, she clung to a tree root on a steep section of the mountain. Her feet slashed at the rocks, trying to get a grip. But all she had on were tennis shoes. Those slippery tennis shoes.

"We heard her cry out when the mudslide hit. Mud flooded her open mouth and tore her hands away from the root." Gabe looked up. "In a moment, she was gone."

Horror struck Louis' face. His lips trembled under his mustache.

Gabe bowed his head. "I struggled to keep up with him while he tore down the mountain. I knew he was hoping the same thing would happen to me. It should have."

Louis laid a hand on Gabe's shoulder. "Nonsense. There is no shame in being frightened."

"I was more than frightened. I was a coward."

"Son, you were an eight-year-old boy. Could a child of that age fight those massive forces of nature?"

Anguish contorted Gabe's face, twisting his mouth downward. He whispered, "That's not all. Before we left home, Dad and Angelica searched the house for her hiking boots. But *nonno*, I hid them so she couldn't go so fast. I killed her." Gabe's shoulders shook with sobs.

His grandfather's voice held steady. "No, no. Enough of that. You did not kill your sister."

Shame accompanied the truth Gabe had never told a soul.

Louis rose and stood behind Gabe, kneading the tense muscles of his neck. "Tell me, if a bird stopped flapping its wings and fell to the ground, would it blame the other birds, or blame God for creating gravity?"

Gabe sniffed. "No."

"You said your father had packed the car with rain gear. He must have known you were in for bad weather, but he pushed ahead anyway. Then he blamed you. And God. How can simple birds be so much wiser than men when they suffer the consequences of their actions?"

When Gabe did not respond, Louis added, "Would you blame your son for this kind of tragedy?"

A latent protest surged from inside of Gabe and released in an agonizing cry, "NO!" The floodgate holding back his grief burst. Tears poured out freely. Unthinking tears. Cleansing tears. With great relief, he stood up and embraced his grandfather. The conte's strong arms held him firm. This man of strength and character did not blame him. Knew of his fear, but did not reject him.

Gabe wiped his face and collapsed into the chair. Other memories, buried for years, came to the surface. Now he *wanted* to think of Angelica, to speak of her. They reminisced for a long time. "She loved music and could remember the words after hearing a song just one time. We would leave church and she would still be singing when we got home."

Gabe's brows furrowed as a new consideration hit him. "She would have had teenagers of her own by now. I miss her, *nonno*," he whispered.

Louis shared his grief, cried when he cried, and seemed to absorb every image as Gabe recounted them.

Studying his clasped fingers, Gabe said, "I'm sorry you never got to meet her."

His grandfather nodded. "I will, son, just not in this world."

Gabe shrugged, too tired to compose an answer. "I'll be in my room for awhile." Hours of emotional turmoil made him feel like he had struggled with that waterfall all over again.

##

The two *Soci* assassins ducked under the doorframe and entered Firelli's extravagant quarters in Siena. Firelli had just finished his lunch and was enjoying a glass of his favorite Oloroso sherry, one of the fringe benefits of working for the wealthy *Primo Consul*.

"What is your plan?" Niccolo's eyes bore down into Firelli's.

Attempting to demote the challenging tone, Firelli reached his hand into his trouser pocket and let his jacket swing away from his revolver. "If our sources tell us that Conte Dolcini has not discovered the relic within the next two days, we will pay him a visit. He handles no business on Sunday. No one will miss him. If we arrive early, we will have the whole of the day to hunt for the relic—and tear the palazzo apart if necessary. The *Primo Consul* must have it by Monday noon."

"When we find it, what do we do with the Dolcinis?" Arturo blurted. His large, hairy fists stretched and clenched alternately.

"I will let you know. Until then, I will contact you if I need anything else. You may go."

Arturo's mouth twitched while he stared down at Firelli's smaller stature. Feigning tedium, Firelli leaned over a small table to busy himself. In an instant, Arturo's hand flew to Firelli's throat and threw him up against the glass closet door that rattled in the frame. "You will show us some respect, *eh* little *ratto?*"

Firelli gagged out a warning. "I work for the *Primo Consul.*"

Arturo jeered at him and slid him down the door until his feet hit the floor. "So do I."

"Come, Arturo," Niccolo ordered. They exited the room and slammed the door.

Firelli collapsed into the wingback chair and massaged his neck. Fury and adrenaline throbbed through his body. "They might be surprised at what the little *ratto* is capable of." He glanced around his opulent room and thought of the cramped, temporary quarters these *Soci* lived in at San Galgano. That might appeal to monks, but he preferred his luxurious suite in Siena. He put his feet up on the leather ottoman and eased back against the chair's softness, black eyes gleaming with the vision of planting those men in the ground.

##

After revealing his part in the tragedy, Gabe's heart felt raw. An hour later, a light rap on the door drew him out of his reflections about his childhood. When he opened it, Louis stood before him.

"I should have said this earlier, but I would like to make amends for my actions. I knew that Ralph had taken the painting of Helena. The thought of you, my only other grandson, being in on it was too much. I feel I must apologize. Will you forgive me for this?"

Gabe studied the older man. *Can it really be this easy for a man to apologize?* "Of course."

Louis smiled. "Let's go have a real look at your painting before lunch, shall we?"

In the ballroom, *Il Viso* still sat on the gilded easel. Gabe looked around. The other decorations had been removed on Sunday morning, before Louis' disappearance. *Pacifica* had already been shipped. Others waited in their crates for Gabe to decide what to do with them.

The two Dolcini men neared the grand *Il Viso*. Livia had returned Louis' *Helena*, which now leaned on a smaller easel. "Amazing likeness," Louis said while he stroked his beard and studied the larger painting. He pointed to a spot. "What is this here?"

Gabe looked closer at *Il Viso*. Beyond the tragic face of Helena, he had painted a window that looked out over a distant, muted landscape. He took a step back to gain a better perspective. "That is… that's Montesiepi as depicted by Helena's brother in his painting of Saint Galgano—look!"

He gently touched the canvas. "How could I have known to place those brush strokes there? I can make out the form of a man watching the sun setting over the next hill. Incredible."

Taking in the details of the scene, Louis shook his head. "That has to be the sunrise. There are no hills to the west of Montesiepi for the sun to set behind."

Gabe trained his eye on the light coming over the hill through Helena's window. The detail was obscured, and yet… "What is that dark patch on the hill that Galgano is looking at?"

Rinaldo entered, and Louis stopped to take a glass of water and his medication. "Thank you. Would you please bring the painting of Saint Galgano on Montesiepi from my library?"

The butler returned within a few minutes and set the painting on an empty easel on the other side of *Il Viso*.

Louis waited for him to leave the room before he turned his attention back to the painting. "*Molto sorprendente*, very surprising," he whispered. He looked at Gabe and raised his eyebrows, "What do you think?"

In both scenes, painted over 800 years apart, a black brush mark had touched the canvas in identical places. Gabe stepped closer. Excitement rifled through his body. "It's the cave—not on Montesiepi, but like Antonio said, *near* the mount. It's at the base of the hill directly to the east!" Louis was jubilant. He moved even closer to *Il Viso* and blanched. "Gabriel, what do you see on that cave door?"

Squinting, Gabe's mouth dropped open. He whispered, "I can make out the fine lines of the Greek alpha and omega." He looked down at his arm. Louis held his forearm alongside. The hair on both stood straight up. "Electricity?" Gabe grinned.

He dropped his arm and scrutinized the details of the paintings, making a mental note of the distance between the two hilltops. Excitement electrified the air between them. "The foliage shows it must be in the fall. And see how the sun is rising in relation to the cave?" He turned toward his grandfather. "I think I can find it. I explored that area and the footpath leading from the Chapel of San Galgano down to the abbey."

Louis' enthusiasm grew. "The one thing in our favor is the position of the sword—it has never changed, so we know exactly where Galgano kept his prayerful vigil."

"You're right! I have to get to Montesiepi and find that cave."

"Don't you mean *we* need to find it?" Livia said as she stepped into the ballroom. Her face held the same cool distance as it had since leaving the villa. She reached out a stiff hand to Gabe. "*Buona sera.*"

It was as though nothing had ever happened between them. He tried to catch her eyes, but she stepped to hug his grandfather, "*Buona sera,*

Louis. What are you looking at in here?" While Louis explained what they had discovered, Gabe watched her eyes widen in awe.

"Of course I will be going with you. We can pretend to have a picnic on the chapel grounds, and then go for a hike in the hills."

Insides twisting, Gabe decided he could play the game as well as she. He shook his head. "The land is privately owned, and I saw several workers tending to the grapes."

"Then we could ask permission."

"No. It's their land. They might claim it."

"*Si*," Livia said. "Who knows who they will sell it to. We must find a reasonable excuse to be there."

Rinaldo entered and handed Louis a newspaper. "Did you see this, conte?" His agitation showed through his smooth veneer.

Louis read the heading and first few lines. "Cardinal Approves ARCC Changes. Cardinal Vincenzo reportedly says he has been given a holy sign from heaven, which his supporters interpret to mean he should be the one to head up the ARCC." Louis fumed. "What kind of a trick is this?"

"Do you think he views your phone call about *Il Testamento* as this holy sign? A sign that he should be the leader?" Livia asked.

"Absolutely." Rinaldo was firm as he explained the rest of the article. "He worked out an agreement where Christianity will still be included in the cultural center, but in its own building—taking up two-thirds of the whole center."

Gabe huffed. "That plays right into hands of the *Soci*. There are more Christian relics than any other religion. They'll rake in a fortune."

Louis sat down in shock. "Cardinal Vincenzo will have a fight on his hands from the *Soci* for the leadership position."

Livia's eyes sprang wide with fear and anger. "The Dead Knights know about us, and now Cardinal Vincenzo knows who and where we are. It's only a matter of time before the *Soci* find us. Gabe, we are not safe."

"And it is all my fault. Again." Louis closed his eyes against his regret.

"What about using Marcella's resources to keep the *Soci* at bay and locate the relic?"

"No." Livia's protest was out instantly. She darted a glance toward Gabe and softened her voice. "Marcella will not have anything to do with hunting for the relic. She feels this quest is what killed her sister."

Gabe tilted his head and watched her trying to backpedal. *What's going on?*

She glanced away and took a breath. Her next words were deliberate. "Besides, she told me she is having trouble with a mole on her team. Sensitive information has been leaking out. When we met at lunch, she was very concerned that her involvement might actually cause us problems. We have to do this alone."

She kissed Louis on the cheek. "I just stopped by for a moment. I need to tend to business."

He smiled. "Come back for dinner, though."

After she left, Gabe glared out the window. He knew as certainly as if she had told him outright. She was still after the relic for her own purposes. *What did he expect?*

## 

Livia shoved open the heavy door of her villa in Radda and threw her purse on the table in the entry hall. She rubbed her temples in an attempt to push the headache away. It was all too much.

Marcus leaned back in his wheelchair and peeked around the doorway. "*Buon giorno.*"

"*Buon giorno*, Papa." She walked over and rubbed the tops of his shoulders. "How is your day going?"

He laid down his pencil, the house designs sitting in front of him. "Better than yours, I think. What has happened?"

She shook her head. "Too much to repeat. I have to tend to some pressing business."

Enthusiasm lit her father's face. "Is this in relation to the remodel?"

She looked past him. Out the window, piles of building materials screamed for her attention. She stopped rubbing his shoulders. "*Si.* Soon we will have the money, and you can complete your project. She leaned down and kissed him on the cheek. "I have been expecting a package."

"It is on the dining table."

A smile lit her face for the first time since... It faded as she remembered Gabe's tenderness in the garden. She was certain he was lost to her. A tear escaped, and she wanted to claw her way out of her entanglements. When would she get to choose her own life?

In the dining room, she opened the package. On top of a stack of papers was a check. The smile returned with full force as her financial burdens flew away. She read the contents of the agreement. Wings seemed to expand from her sides. "Half down and half after the delivery."

THE PROOF

# Chapter 27

Siena, Italy

That night at dinner, Gabe had little appetite as he watched Livia engaging in normal conversation with Louis. She was some piece of work. Rinaldo served the *primo* course—a plate of savory risotto. When he left for the kitchen, the rich scent of pork stew promised the *secondo* course would be even heartier.

Dabbing at his mustache with his napkin, Louis waited for Rinaldo to exit. In a low voice, he said, "I realize that Cardinal Vincenzo was not the right choice to protect *Il Testamento*, but I cannot wallow in my mistakes. I will decide what to do when we have possession of it. In the meantime, we must be extremely careful that everything we know or do stays between the three of us. Agreed?"

Gabe nodded, but his eyes narrowed at Livia. It was now obvious to him that she had wheedled her way into their plans—and his heart—to find and sell the relic. As he ate, he considered his next move. If she succeeded, Louis would find out about her betrayal. His feelings would be hurt, but then it would be over.

Actually, Gabe could really care less. His only concern was for their safety. A black thought hit him. She would be a rich woman if he and Louis were dead. *No.* He unconsciously shook his head. She cared too much about family. As for their relationship, he drove a bitter nail through the remaining hope. The pleasant dream was dead. Feeling another loss, he steeled his mind against his heart's protest.

Louis asked, "What do I tell Cardinal Vincenzo—that I was mistaken?"

A second wave of despair passed over Gabe. Didn't Louis realize how much danger he was really in? These powerful men were used to playing hardball. Gabe cleared his throat. "Leave him in the dark as long as possible. The *Soci* have already searched Montesiepi, so they won't be expecting us to search for it there." He held Louis' eyes. "They will all come looking for it here." Louis nodded his understanding.

Livia interjected, "We are the only ones who know the cave is in the other hill."

Gabe pierced her with a glance. "Let's hope it stays that way."

She tilted her head and raised a questioning eyebrow, but Gabe ignored her.

Fear tensed Louis' features. He stroked his beard as he thought. "You said that Porta's two men were housed in the chapel complex. The hills are so close—it would be just as easy for you to be spotted on one hill as on the other."

Gabe shook his head. "Actually, the smaller hill is thickly forested, making it easy to move around—if we are discreet…"

"…and if there is a distraction," Livia finished Gabe's train of thought. She cast a quick glance at him with a tentative smile.

He did not return it. They had frequently finished each other's sentences since they had kissed, but this time it drove the dagger of betrayal deeper into his chest.

Louis laced his fingers together and rested his forearms on the edge of the table. "What kind of distraction."

"I looked into that after I left this morning," she said. "There are regular concerts held at San Galgano Abbey, but they are over for the season. However, I found out about a wedding that takes place there on Saturday. It only gives us a day and a half to prepare, but a wedding means a large number of guests."

"And?" Louis furrowed his bushy eyebrows.

"And, Gabe and I will attend, as guests, so to speak."

"You mean crash the wedding?" Gabe asked.

"We will bring a gift, *eh*?" she argued.

Gabe frowned and speared an asparagus tip. "I don't like it. It puts a lot of people in the area who could easily spot what we're doing."

"But that's the point." The grey in her eyes darkened and her mouth tightened. "The festivities will provide the distraction we need. With so many people, we will not stand out."

Gabe shrugged. It was not a horrible idea, but would make it harder for him to detect if someone was watching them. His stomach knotted. "If there are professional killers where we're going, I'd like them to be visible."

Louis let out a deep sigh. "The *Soci* are not the only ones we have to watch for. Even though Ralph was murdered, the Dead Knights are still out there, waiting to make their move at the first sign of *Il Testamento*."

Livia shivered. "I sense them all the time."

Gabe considered her. It was almost believable that she had only pretended to work with them. "Then why are we even going through all of this? Let's just give it to Cardinal Vincenzo and we can be done with it."

She looked as if she had been struck. Her head popped back, and she bit down on a nasty response. Closing her eyes, she seemed to be trying for patience. "If this is the spear that pierced Jesus' side, if the stains of his blood are on it, then I agree with this one tenant of the Dead Knights—it cannot be used for profit or to bring power to verminous men. Jesus said to be greatest in the kingdom was to serve, not be served. Give, not take. Can you understand how contrary to the meaning of Christ's death it would be to give it to them?"

Gabe scrutinized her expression and saw a glimpse of spiritual fervor for the first time. It only added to his confusion. Deceit flowed out of her mouth with every other breath, yet here she sat with her chin lifted in defiance, ready to go to the mat with assassins because of her faith. *Or her greed.* He closed his eyes and stretched his neck from side to side. Regardless, there was no leaving the game now. Neither she nor Louis would back down.

It was certain these murderous adversaries would continue their assault—if not directed at the three of them, then at other members of his family. This was not just a local gang of bullies. Even his mother could be at risk. He clenched his teeth against the growing fear and remembered his grandfather's words. "I had to act. Courage had nothing to do with it."

He held Livia's eyes. "No, I can't understand. But I am committed to getting the heat off my family."

She crossed her arms, a puzzling pout turning down the corners of her mouth. "Can we agree on one thing, that it is our mission to keep *Il Testamento* from the *Soci*."

"Without loss of life or limb," Gabe added.

"Agreed," Louis said. "What shall I do while you two go to San Galgano?"

"Stay safe. Rinaldo is here to guard you." Gabe reached over and squeezed Louis' shoulder.

"*Si*," Louis tried to smile encouragement.

Gabe made it through the dinner, but the betrayal exhausted him. He watched Rinaldo come in and close the front door after escorting Livia to her car. All Gabe wanted to do was get some sleep.

Louis stopped him on his way up the stairs. "Gabriel, may I see you in the library?"

Gabe rubbed the back of his neck and turned around. "Sure."

Once seated, Louis said, "You are embarking on a dangerous journey tomorrow. This is not just about *Il Testamento*. Your faith is being tested."

Thoroughly fatigued, Gabe frowned. Louis saw everything through his faith.

Louis held his eyes and entreated him, "Gabriel, it is a gift to believe, but you must desire it. There is an enemy of your soul who would keep you from knowing the living God."

"So, Satan is out to get me with his pitchfork?" Gabe gave a derisive chuckle.

"Not with a pitchfork. With lies, criticism, and false speculations about God—these are his tools. But none of these change the truth of who God is. He has always loved you. He is on your side, fighting for you. Can you believe that?"

A warm sensation swelled within Gabe's heart, melting his defiance. He rubbed the stubble on his chin. "I used to believe that. It was the one happy thing that Angelica and I shared." He met his grandfather's eyes.

Louis nodded. "Who stole your God?"

"Pardon?"

"You used to believe. What happened to your faith?"

Misery tensed Gabe's face. "I lost it when Angelica died—or shortly after. My father beat it out of me." He hung his head. "I don't see a way back."

"You must forgive your father."

The words sliced through Gabe's heart, slamming the door that had cracked open. His head jerked up. "Never. There's no way I'm letting that monster off the hook."

After a considerable silence, Louis said, "Let me tell you about your father."

Gabe rubbed his tired eyes and leaned against the back of the sofa. Louis went to his desk to get a framed photograph and handed it to Gabe. The picture was of a young boy on his mother's lap, gazing up at her. There was no doubt as to the love between them. He held a sleeping black puppy on his lap.

Louis' mouth twitched with emotion. "This is Christina with your father and the pup she bought for him. Russo named her *Valentina*—his brave little protector. She followed him everywhere." Louis sighed. "It aggravated me. I had never had a dog in my home—my father had never allowed it."

Tension wrinkled Louis' brows. "When it chewed up an expensive shoe, I demanded that it be removed from the palazzo. I did not want the mess of a dog in my beautiful home. Your father pleaded with me. Christina pleaded with me. But I would not relent. Russo hid Valentina somewhere and I had to...I had to *make* him tell me where it was. It took over an hour before he gave up the location." Louis' eyes misted. "It crushed your father to show me the hiding spot."

Sickened, Gabe drew away from the grandfather he thought he knew. He wanted to flee the room and forget what he had just heard.

"I took the dog to the vineyard and gave it to my foreman to use. But..."

Gabe eyed Louis with alarm. "But what?"

"It was such a small little thing, it wandered off." He bit his lip. "My man reported that the wolves got it."

Feeling the anger and sense of loss as though it were his own, Gabe's heart hardened against the conte's cruelty.

"From that moment, Russo hated me. Christina tried to coax him out of his bitterness, but his resistance and sullen attitude continued. After a time, I sent him away to school, away from his mother. I believed the strict discipline would accomplish what I could not, but it only fed his anger toward me."

Louis cleared his throat. "Russo was twenty and in college when Christina was murdered. He came to my house and swore at me. He said, 'You killed the only two things I ever loved,' then spat on the floor at my feet. That was the last I saw of him." A tear escaped Louis' eye and fled down his cheek.

Jaw set, Gabe stared at the broken man in front of him, but this time he felt no sympathy.

Louis shook his head. "Gabriel, I needed forgiveness, but my son never gave it, never let me apologize. The grief almost killed me. But then, in my despair, I cried to God. Through His Spirit, I have received the love and forgiveness I craved the whole of my life."

"So you got off scot free with your little prayer?" Fury at the injustice tainted Gabe's response.

The fiery dart hit its mark. A pained grimace passed over Louis' face. "I am not perfect, but I was never the same. The kindness of the Lord helped me overcome my intolerance. This is what I want for you, to be set free from the hatred that seems to follow our family."

Anger burned in Gabe's head. "How can you call your God *kind?* He let Angelica die!"

Grief contorted Louis' face, but he worked to explain. "God does not cause the accidents and wickedness. He picks up the pieces and gives us strength to get through. Angelica is in a safe place, but we are still here, in need to receive—and offer—forgiveness."

"I don't believe in that fairytale," Gabe spat. He jumped up. "You did the same thing to my father that he did to me. NONE of you should be forgiven. I would NEVER treat my son this way."

Louis' eyes filled with tears, but Gabe didn't care. Forgiveness was out of the question. Scowling, he escaped to his room. Once he slammed the door shut, he collapsed on his bed and tucked his knees to his chest. Pain clawed at him, opening new wounds. Was there no escaping the betrayals of his family?

*What about your own?*

Gabe screamed into his pillow to stop the accusing voice. Only after hours of anguish and thrashing around in his bed, did sleep silence it.

## 

"Do you have it?" the *Primo Consul* whispered.

Abbot Porta knew the soft tone was a farce. This man could silence a mob with his booming voice, yet took great pains to render a compassionate façade to the public. However, his enemies had come to know the depths of malice when facing his displeasure. With wide-set eyes and a thick neck, he could appear as a teddy bear, but gave the impression of a raging bull when angry.

Porta swallowed. "Our strategy is in motion, and our opponents are moving into our snare. It will require just a few more days." The *Primo Consul's* wrath was notorious among the *Soci*. If only *Consul* Bizzarri had listened to him.

"The chain that binds my supporters together has a missing link. I pledged they would behold my miracle from God. Doubt gathers in their eyes with each passing day, and I hear veiled threats of losing their support in favor of my opponents. Before his unfortunate death, *Consul* Bizzarri had been one of my most powerful supporters."

Porta cringed. He had done everything possible to make certain Bizzarri's death would remain a mystery, but the *Primo Consul* seemed to see through walls. Porta dropped his eyes so as not to reveal his guilt while being lectured.

"We have lost this generation. They do not respond to guilt or old traditions." A pleasant smile eased across the *Primo Consul's* wide mouth. "They want to create a god of their own design. We will give that to them—they can pick and choose." He tapped his fingers together. "They are also fascinated with history and cultural artifacts. What we have lost in offerings, we will more than make up in ticket sales."

His eyes narrowed, and his voice rose in a crescendo. "I must have the relic before the election in three days." Nostrils flaring, the *Primo Consul* finished in a quieter, but no less forceful tone. "If not, I may have to demonstrate my displeasure with my colleagues who are inclined to renege on their promises. I *will* have the support I need to head the ARCC." With great calculation, he stood tall and loomed over Porta. "Where are we now?"

Porta straightened his spine and made an attempt to suck in his paunch. "Niccolo and Firelli continue to observe the Dolcinis. It is imperative that we bide our time."

At his window, high above Rome, the *Primo Consul* looked out over the tiny crumbling kingdom. "I have coveted ruling this city most of my life." He glanced back at the architectural plans of the massive American Religious Cultural Center on his desk and smiled. "But thanks to Conte Dolcini's fortuitous phone call, this elegant, state-of-the-art campus is a more worthy prize." He seemed lost in his vision.

In the silence, Porta sought to reassure him, "My associates will know exactly when to remove the Dolcinis."

Keeping his eyes focused on his future kingdom, Cardinal Vincenzo, the *Soci's Primo Consul*, said, "Then trust their instincts."

##

Friday, Gabe sulked in his room. At breakfast, the conversation had been strained. Still, the plan needed to be discussed. As soon as possible, he retreated upstairs, unwilling to have anything more to do with Louis.

Gabe had decisions to make about the coming day. Saturday was their best chance to look for *Il Testamento*, but it also meant he had to reschedule his noon appointment with Signore Belvedere at the museum. He clenched his teeth in frustration. You do not put off someone in the position to offer you a one-man exhibition.

On the other hand, time was closing in. Louis was anxious to expedite the plan. The threat of the Dead Knights or the *Soci* launching another attack on his family had caused him to add a second medication to his regimen. Everyone else's nerves were suffering as well.

Gabe squirmed in the large chair, unable to get comfortable. Except for selling one painting, he had made only a minor splash on the Italian art scene. He shut his eyes and ran his fingers through his hair. It was time to look at the glass as half full.

The money he would receive from the sale of *Pacifica* almost paid his critically overdue loan. If he could sell one more, he could save his mother's house. He would be able to look at himself in the mirror again.

He took out Belvedere's business card and made the call. Perhaps there was a chance that another of his paintings had appealed to the man. "*Buon giorno*, this is Gabriel Dolcini. Signore Belvedere asked me to meet him for lunch…"

An energetic young woman interrupted him. "*Si*, Signore Dolcini. He has been expecting your call. Please hold."

"Whew." He wondered how many cups of espresso she had consumed today.

Gabe recognized Signore Belvedere's voice, but was instantly alerted by the tension it held. "Signore Dolcini, what is the meaning of sending me an empty crate? Was the feather an American prank, because this is not something I find humorous."

Gabe was stunned, as in a stun gun. "Signore, I do not engage in pranks of this kind. What are you telling me?"

"We opened the crate this morning. I was there myself. We unwrapped the frame but there was NO *Pacifica*. I lifted the frame out and a feather floated to the floor."

Gabe's mind was beginning to catch up. *The Kestral?* "Signore Belvedere, let me make some inquiries regarding the packing from this end. I think we should postpone our meeting tomorrow…"

"*Sì.* Definitely. *Ciao.*" He hung up.

Laying his phone on the nightstand, Gabe fell back in the blue velvet chair that offered to wrap comforting arms around his rigid body. But he would not be comforted. No *Pacifica*. No check. He closed his eyes. The timing had been too tight. The door was slamming shut.

He bolted upright. "Livia," he growled. She probably stole it on Tuesday after she conked Ralph over the head. And had it sold before…before they were at the villa together. *Great performance.*

His mind spun out a hundred scenarios for evening the score, but none would work, at least for now. He would deal with her treachery after they found the relic.

# Chapter 28

Siena, Italy

Walls, thick and solid, seemed to close in around Gabe, pushing him into a narrowing path. The palazzo's new wine cellar, once so engrossing, felt claustrophobic. He was too tense to enjoy the eclectic room today. Having Livia here with him, and knowing she was a thief and a liar, further troubled his mood.

Livia set an intricately woven basket onto the vine-carved tasting table. Clothes for their excursion lay folded neatly on the table next to two sets of hiking boots. She arranged the tools in one side of the basket and packed her boots. She attempted to break the tension. "This is an amazing place."

Gabe turned and scrutinized her face. A thin smile tugged at her lips, but sadness ruled her eyes.

"I wish this were over." Without warning, she pulled his face close with her hands and gently kissed his lips.

Surprised, he forced himself to play her game for one more night. His angry arms surrounded her agile body, and his lips responded. At first, with disinterest, but the attraction between them was too intense. He pressed harder on her mouth. His mind screamed, *She's a traitor*! He jerked back and released her. "We've got work to do."

Stunned, she pushed away from him. Anger burned behind her tight lips, but she said nothing.

He turned away, grabbed his new boots, and shoved them into the large basket. Disheartened, the foolish part of him still yearned for something special between them. Would he ever learn to read a woman?

Her fingers jerked a ribbon into shape while she tied a fancy bow on the basket handle. "This strain has been hard on Louis."

Gabe shoved the lid down. "He's strong enough to manage."

"Yes, I am." Louis' bold voice accompanied his stately bearing as he descended the cellar stairs one at a time. He reached the bottom, face somber and his eyes pensive. "I came to give you my blessing."

An arrow stabbed Gabe's conscience. Even after the vicious things he had said, Louis still loved him. His grandfather embodied all a conte should possess: courage, wisdom, humility.

Gabe fought the word *humility*, but it was true. It was hard to see anything of the intolerant self that Louis had described last night. Gabe cleared his throat and shook those thoughts away. No matter. Louis was still the man who had ruined Gabe's father's life, shaping him into a monster. Gabe would not apologize.

Louis stood before them, his gaze moving from Livia to Gabe. "I want you to know how proud I am of both of you. Thank you for completing this worthy task, one that I devoted my life to." Livia lowered her eyes. Gabe swallowed a hard lump and tensed when Louis placed his hands on each of their shoulders and bowed his head.

"Holy Spirit, Jesus sent you to comfort, strengthen and defend us. Please go with my children and direct their steps. Show yourself strong on their behalf. Increase their faith and open their eyes to see You."

Conflicting emotions battled inside Gabe as Louis prayed. He shrugged out from under his grandfather's hand as soon as he said, "Amen."

Avoiding Gabe's eyes, Livia picked up the basket and started up the stairs. He caught her chewing her lip, and anger hit him. Would she really betray them? His stomach churning, Gabe reluctantly followed her. At the top of the stairs, he glanced back. His grandfather's hand covered his bowed head, sobs shaking his shoulders.

##

Saturday afternoon, Firelli sped from Siena toward Montesiepi. He turned into the parking lot of the bar that rested halfway up the road to the Chapel of San Galgano and hiked through the trees to the far side of the chapel. Caterers scurried around the grounds, setting up the decorations as far from the chapel complex as possible. Firelli smirked and disappeared through the creaking wooden door to the room Porta had given him when he first arrived.

He held his handkerchief tight against his nose. The dead rat he had stashed under a floorboard in the janitor's closet yesterday had overpowered the fragrant herbal shop and chapel, as well as the other rooms of the hostelry. It guaranteed that the women who ran the concession would not be working today. All other guests had moved out late last night. There could be no witnesses to this assignment.

A rap at the door startled him. He opened the door and returned Arturo's scowl. "You are early."

Arturo covered his nose with his hand. "Something's dead."

"*Si.* A stinking *ratto.*" Firelli looked pointedly at Arturo when he pronounced each word. It was all the huge man could do to hold his anger. Smirking, Firelli stepped out past him and shut the door. "Come down to the chamber. I found something of great interest to the *Soci.* Something even you could appreciate." Firelli led the way, relishing the other man's obvious hatred.

Arturo followed him through the hidden stairwell into the far side of the herb shop. Firelli unlocked the ancient door behind the counter, keeping Arturo in his peripheral vision. "I told Porta I didn't need a grunt around to mess things up. I am sure you must have something else of value you could have been doing." The huge man's neck and face flushed red with rage, sending Firelli's instincts into high alert. He savored the adrenaline rushing through his body.

Opening the door from the herb shop, Firelli slipped into the darkness without lighting the way. He felt the edge of the stone landing with his toe and counted the steps as he descended into the room below Galgano's sword. Once at the bottom, he calculated that Arturo would be on the middle stair.

"Don't trip," Firelli joked, then leapt away from the bottom of the staircase.

Flashes from Arturo's weapon lit up the nearly black chamber from the stairs above. He missed.

Firelli's hand flew up to fire his pistol. Surprised roars pierced the air as the bullets accurately hit their mark. He heard Arturo's body tumble off the stairs onto the stone floor below. Afterward, only the sound of labored breathing filled the dark chamber. Firelli beamed a flashlight onto the face of the struggling man. Arturo's angry eyes focused on the barrel of the gun.

Firelli grinned at the helpless, bleeding man. "So, you thought you would murder me? Perhaps you should not have shot your mouth off. Your walls have ears." He pulled out the listening device he had retrieved from Arturo's room and dangled it in front of his victim. "Amateurs. Your friend will get his later."

Stepping closer, Firelli finished the job—one shot into the forehead of the defeated giant. "Just like David and Goliath," he mocked. He felt elation at the elimination of one of his competitors. "Like I said, I work alone."

## 

Watching the clock on the library mantle, Louis paced across the room. The hour hand struck six o'clock. It was time. He picked up the phone and dialed the number. This time, there was no mistake. Soon, the palazzo would be breached by Louis' enemies, tearing at its foundation. Better the bricks of his house than the body of his grandson.

"*Buona sera*, this is Conte Louis Dolcini. I wish to speak with Cardinal Vincenzo."

## 

Rain clouds threatened the afternoon wedding as Gabe and Livia drove toward the magnificent Abbey de San Galgano. Livia parked under a row of sycamore trees along the crowded drive leading to the ancient structure on the valley floor. Gabe studied her. Did she know what they were getting into?

He could still turn around—go back to the US and forget all this. *"Fesso,"* he uttered under his breath. It was the only way to protect his family. The rumors that the Dolcinis possessed *Il Testamento* were now too widespread. These adversarial forces would never stop their assault. He felt some of what Antonio and Galgano must have experienced when they tried to protect *Il Testamento*.

There were so many things he wanted to ask Livia, but he kept his jaw locked to prevent any further arguments. He couldn't count on her telling the truth anyway. Instead, he flashed a quick, phony smile. "You ready?"

"Absolutely," she snapped across the small space. She hopped out of her Fiat and slammed the door with extra vigor. "Are *you* ready?"

He stiffened. *"Sì."*

They walked up the long drive and watched the soft blue of the afternoon sky change as roiling clouds blew into the Val di Merse. Livia interrupted the silence with nervous chatter. "I hope they have a big tent for the reception. There must be five hundred guests here."

"All the better for us to disappear."

Even wearing a drab green pantsuit, Livia was stunning. She walked ahead of him and followed the other guests across the lawn. Her steps were deliberate, but could not suppress the feminine sway of her hips. Though he tried, he could not will away the longing she stirred. *Think Darla.* But that only added to his misery.

A gravel pathway led the visitors from the lawn to the imposing structure. The roofless abbey was even more dramatic with the brooding clouds swirling in a powerful, slow-motion eddy behind the immoveable tonnage of stone and brick. "It's breathtaking," she said.

Soft electric lamps lighted the paths and stone walls. When they neared the 800-year-old façade, Gabe tilted his head up. His mouth opened in a silent gasp. The clouds, darkened to an ugly green, leered down at him from the edge of the abbey's decapitated wall. A chill ran down his spine. He tried to seize hold of the threatening fear. *It's just a storm.*

They waited without speaking in a long line at the entrance. Cheerful babble grated against the apprehension clawing at Gabe's gut. He shifted his weight from leg to leg. High above, wind whistled as it looped in and out of the carved skeletons of the rose windows. He was relieved when, at last, one of the ushers welcomed them.

"This way."

"*Grazie*," Livia said, and they surged with the crowd toward the great nave. Rustic arches, like proud, defeated gladiators, endured the frivolous layers of ribbon, intent on civilizing the awesome power encased in every column and wall.

The wide nave overflowed with white plastic chairs and hundreds of candles. Delicate garlands of miniature white roses dipped from row to row down the central aisle. The feeling was otherworldly, like a genuine fairy tale. In the north transept, a quartet played a stirring baroque piece. Gabe wished he knew as much about music as he did about art.

A smiling usher arrived to take them to their seats. "Bride or groom?"

"Bride," Livia answered, and took the arm of the handsome escort. Gabe followed, ignoring the antagonism between them. He needed to center himself if they were to be successful. It didn't help that the man covered Livia's delicate hand with his own while he made small talk. Her light laughter caused Gabe's jaw to grind. She could turn the charm off and on at will.

The wedding started a fashionable half-hour late, but no one seemed to mind. Sweet music swelled within the walls, announcing the arrival of the bride. They stood to honor the procession. The radiant young woman approached, controlling a tremulous smile. When she swept her large brown eyes up to meet her father's, his proud countenance faltered. Controlled tears mingled with his smile.

Gabe stood behind Livia. His arms longed to encircle her as he breathed in the scent of her hair. The bride, the candles, the roses— Gabe's emotions played havoc with his mind as he battled the image of Livia coming to him in a flowing white dress. It was impossible to think clearly when she was this close.

When it was time to sit, he finally exhaled. Her hand brushed against his. She glanced up and caught his eyes. Had she felt it too? He frowned and distanced himself. As far as he knew, she was working with the enemy.

She pulled away and watched the wedding.

As always, the ceremony seemed much too brief for all the effort. In no time, the laughing couple marched back down the aisle and out to a waiting car that whisked them away to the reception. An usher announced that the guests could walk up the hill or wait for a shuttle. The caterers had fashioned a magical kingdom on the grounds at the top of the hill, outside the Chapel of San Galgano.

"Let's go," Livia whispered. They followed the raucous crowd toward the shuttle, then made a quick detour back to the car. She unlocked the hatchback, and Gabe pulled out the heavy picnic basket, dressed up like a gift. She avoided his eyes.

He glanced toward the chapel. This was it.

## ##

Though ready to execute his plan, Louis still jolted when the doorbell rang. Impatient knocking ensued. Before Rinaldo reached the door to let in their visitors, Louis motioned the frowning butler into the library.

"That will be Cardinal Vincenzo's men. I called and told him we had found the location of *Il Testamento*."

"Did you?"

Louis pulled on his beard. "There were only three possibilities. No one has found it on Montesiepi, so this is one of the last two places. Please follow my lead."

Rinaldo's brows rose at the new information. He nodded at Louis and strode to the door. Louis stood with a slight waver, hoping he could withstand the storm he had unleashed.

As soon as the door opened, Niccolo burst in. His narrowed eyes bored into Rinaldo's, then turned to Louis. He towered over him and pulled out a gun. "You have something for the cardinal?"

Louis looked behind the armed man in surprise. *Only one?* He had hoped to lure all of the cardinal's men here, away from Gabriel. Chin held high, he ignored Niccolo's intimidation. "I will escort you to the cellar where we believe the relic is buried."

"Believe? You told Cardinal Vincenzo you found it." Niccolo watched him carefully, his empty hand tightened into a huge fist.

"There is only one place in this palazzo that coincides with the map and it…"

"Let me see it."

Louis limped more than usual toward his desk and brought a copy of the map to Niccolo. "See for yourself. It begins at the front door."

Moving back to the entrance, Niccolo studied the instructions, then moved the twenty-five feet to the top of the stairs. "What is down there?" Suspicion ruled his countenance.

Louis stepped forward and pointed to the floor. He drew an imaginary line to an area under the dining room. "The new wine rests under here. The entrance is through the rear foundation wall."

Niccolo glanced at Rinaldo, then back at Louis. "Show me."

Rinaldo stepped forward, but Louis said, "I will lead." He limped forward and led the way out the rear entrance and down to the giant cellar doors. His body felt weaker than he had in months, yet his senses were acute.

After unlocking the heavy deadbolt and opening the door, Rinaldo turned on the light. Louis nodded his reassurance at the anxious servant, who stepped to one side to help him down the stairs. This was the third time Louis had visited the cellar today. All afternoon, the stab of Gabriel's anger refused to lessen, making Louis' labors more difficult.

Rinaldo assessed the room below and gasped with surprise. He whispered softly, "You found the alcove?"

Louis said nothing, but continued to the floor of the cellar. He then collapsed on a small chair. "Behind that wall," he pointed. He had cleared away boxes and wine from the wall in one area. Bricks lay scattered on the ground, along with a crowbar and hammer.

"What is this?" Niccolo snarled.

"It is where *Il Testamento* lies—read for yourself. The alcove is on the eastern wall."

"It does not look like you found it," Niccolo said and started toward the conte's chair.

Rinaldo moved closer to Louis, who tilted his head to look up at Niccolo, but did not react. "All I can do is follow this map. Do you have a better idea?"

"Your grandson should be helping us. Where is he?" Niccolo waited for his answer.

Louis seemed to falter.

Rinaldo volunteered, "He and Signorina Livia went out this afternoon on a picnic and left no information as to when they would return."

Niccolo studied him then pointed toward the wall with his gun. "Get to work."

Rinaldo stepped forward and grabbed the crowbar to wedge out more bricks and chip at the mortar. Though he worked with determination, the progress was too slow for their captor. Niccolo holstered his gun and grabbed a sledgehammer. He held it like a weapon as a warning, then started digging.

They worked for an hour. Shards flew as they pushed through three layers of bricks and then into a wall of irregular stones, obviously set in place centuries ago. Dust stuck to the sweat that covered both laborers. Rinaldo backed out and wiped his face on his white shirt sleeve.

Though slumped in his chair, Louis watched the progress with great interest and thought, *Il Testamento* could *really* be here.

Clunk. Niccolo's hammer hit something new. Louis jumped and Rinaldo scrambled back into the hole. The two men increased their efforts, scraping debris out of the way.

Rinaldo turned back toward Louis. "It is a stone box."

.

# Chapter 29

San Galgano, Italy

Most of the younger wedding guests were already in high spirits and took the rocky footpath that led from the abbey up to the chapel. Gabe and Livia joined the procession. Passing the vineyard on their right, Gabe tried to appear nonchalant in contrast to his struggling emotions. A shiver passed through him.

"Can you do this?" Degrading doubt laced the tone of Livia's voice, adding to Gabe's own apprehension. He nodded, but the sense of imminent danger, and another glance at the menacing clouds closing in over him, conjured up powerful old memories.

Near the top, the path circled to the left toward the north entrance of Saint Galgano's Chapel. A huge oak tree dripped with sparkling white lights. Except for the darkening storm, the tiny white specks would have been indistinguishable until later in the evening. In fact, the chapel grounds were dazzling.

"Looks more like a restaurant than a sacred chapel," he scoffed.

"A lot of the sacred disappeared when people found out you could make money from the pockets of the curious."

"Maybe the Dead Knights have another point."

She glanced sideways at him. "Perhaps they do."

They lingered near the top of the hill. Gabe held her arm as she balanced, pretending to have a stone in her shoe. The last group of guests passed them, laughing and tripping up the rocky path. "Need a lift?" a large, amiable guest offered.

"I've got it handled," Gabe grinned. When Livia bent to slip her shoe back on, he kissed the back of her neck for good measure. She whipped around and glared at him. The big guy laughed. He hauled one of the young women up in his arms, causing the rest of the group to cheer as they moved on.

Gabe's heart raced while he searched the path for stragglers.

"That wasn't necessary," Livia hissed.

"It sold the story."

She continued to glare, but they did not have time to argue. He bent the wire down, and she stepped over the old fence between the random stick-posts. They ducked behind a tree and crouched in the brush until they were certain no one had seen them.

Farther down the hill, he set the basket on the ground and took off his jacket. They pulled out oversized black sweat suits and struggled to pull them over their clothes. He appraised her bulky figure, "Stunning."

Still fuming, she did not find the remark amusing. She stuffed her shoes inside the basket.

Gabe grabbed his boots. Hesitating before he pulled them on, he realized he had not worn hiking boots since the day Angelica died. Guilt started its attack, but this time, it held no sting. Louis had forgiven him.

*You want forgiveness, but refuse to give it?*

He tugged hard on the laces, tying them with quick, jerking movements. He wasn't about to take on more guilt—especially about someone who deserved to be despised.

Above him, the wind caused the trees to bend and moan. A sense of foreboding circled around, sending a shiver of fear up his spine. He stashed his dress shoes in the basket and willed his hands to stop shaking. They headed due east for the cave. It was a short walk to the bottom of Montesiepi and onto the base of the next hill.

Stealing through the brush, he stepped over a tree root, but it caught his shoelace. He flew headlong toward an unyielding tree. Arms out,

Gabe let the basket fly to the ground. He grabbed hold of the tree to stop his fall. Air shot out of his lungs when his torso hit the trunk.

"Whoa." Livia whispered.

Too shocked to speak, he struggled to catch his breath. He released the tree and stared. Rough bark protruded from his scraped palms. The image of Angelica shot through his mind. This was becoming *too* familiar. He plucked out the wood, fear looping through his body. If he kept messing up, they would not get through this. After waiting for his heart to settle, he recovered the basket.

Reckoning his location again, he moved along the invisible line he had drawn from the chapel to their target. Crouching, he pulled out two small penlights. "These shouldn't be large enough to attract attention." He barely kept his voice from shaking. Glancing at Livia, he hoped she had not let her Dead Knight friends in on their plans. With Ralph dead, he wondered if she had made another contact. If so, it was too late to do anything about it.

## ##

"Pull the box out," Niccolo ordered.

Rinaldo swung his head to catch Louis' surprised expression. The old man leaned forward and nodded.

Niccolo's eyes flew from one to the other. "It looks as though you were not expecting this." His face became grim and dangerous. He waved his gun at Rinaldo. "You, dig."

Rinaldo crawled in with his crowbar. He used it to dig fragments out from around the box. "There are markings in the stone," he called back over his shoulder.

Louis swallowed and stood to watch. This was the spot the letter had indicated, but neither Gabe nor Livia had considered it seriously enough to check it out. He massaged his chest. If it really were the relic, it would soon be taken from him. So might his life.

Niccolo crawled in next to Rinaldo, and they increased their efforts, creating a cloud of dust. Rinaldo climbed out and bent over, coughing vigorously. Niccolo grabbed the two-foot stone container with his powerful hands. Kneeling, he moved it from side to side, dragging it over the rough surface. He backed out to the edge of the alcove, feeling for the floor with one foot.

"Enough!" Louis shouted and brought the end of the crowbar down on Niccolo's skull. The man slumped to the ground.

A very surprised Rinaldo studied Louis with admiration. "Well done, conte."

Louis' breathing became erratic. "Help me move him and tie his hands with this rope." Rinaldo secured the man then turned toward the box. Louis collapsed onto his chair, while Rinaldo set the box onto the floor of the cellar. Using the crowbar, he pried open the lid. It slid off easily. He shook his head with disappointment. "It holds the remains of a child."

Louis looked into the container and crossed himself. "There were rumors of a Dolcini baby buried within the palazzo, but I thought it just rumor. Please, put the lid back on."

Rinaldo replaced the lid and wiped the dust from his hands. "What should I do with him?"

Louis looked at the assassin with disgust. "Leave him tied up in here until Gabe returns with *Il Testamento*."

Rinaldo's eyebrows lifted in surprise. "*Sì*."

## ##

After helping Louis back inside the palazzo, Rinaldo escaped to his room and placed a phone call. "Louis called Cardinal Vincenzo, who sent Niccolo to the palazzo to pick up the relic."

"Did he find it?"

"No, but Louis said Gabe knows where it is and went to get it."

"On Montesiepi?"

"No. They seem to have discovered another possible location. I will try to get it out of him."

"Do not try. Do it. And then silence him." Rinaldo's superior hung up.

Rinaldo studied his face in the mirror, reflecting on the man he had become. Although, he had hoped this kind of thing was behind him, he knew what he had to do. Setting his jaw, he took the bottle of potassium cyanide from its hiding place in the back of his drawer and slipped it into his pocket. In the kitchen, he opened an expensive bottle of sherry and set it on a tray with two *copita* sherry glasses. He filled one glass, then poured the cyanide into the bottle, trusting the sherry's walnut scent would overpower anything the poison might emit. A scowl crossed his features. "For my old friend."

After preparing a plate of *antipasti*, Rinaldo set it down with a glass of red wine next to Louis' chair. "For your nerves."

"*Grazie.*" Louis accepted his kindness without smiling.

Rinaldo picked up the day's unread newspaper. "It is almost nine o'clock. Should Gabriel be home soon?"

Louis shook his head. "It will take time to search the hill."

"Montesiepi?"

Rubbing his tired eyes, Louis said, "No, the next mount over."

Relief caused a smile to threaten Rinaldo's expressionless lips. "May I bring you anything else?"

"No. That will be all for now."

Rinaldo left to make the call his impatient superior had been expecting. *No answer.* He would have to try later. His jaw tightened. The Dead Knights planned to eliminate all loose ends once this was over.

## ##

The growing darkness swallowed the thin white beam of Gabe's penlight. He flicked the light around and searched the base of the hill as far as he could see. Livia moved ahead of him, pushing back brush and kicking loose rocks with the toe of her boot in the area that should have been the cave. It was difficult maneuvering around the thick trees and boulders in that spot.

"I see nothing," she said.

"Well, it has been over 800 years since Antonio and Galgano were here."

In the distance, a shout pierced the air. Gabe and Livia squatted. Their minds went on high alert until they heard bits of laughter that drifted from the wedding reception on Montesiepi.

Gabe let out his breath, and they rose to continue their search. "We'll leave the basket here to mark our starting point and go thirty feet in each direction. If we check two yards up the hill with each sweep, nothing should get by us." They began the arduous task of rolling rocks off the side of the hill, hoping to uncover the cave. At this rate, it would be a long night.

Bodies shaking from their labor, Gabe and Livia stayed diligent in their search. They scrutinized thirty feet on the first level of the hill, and then moved up two yards to start another sweep. Halfway back, Gabe thought he saw lights coming down the hill toward them. He motioned for Livia to turn off her penlight, and they crouched behind a bush.

Branches broke as footfalls came closer.

*The basket!* Gabe could see the light colored straw clearly, even with the darkening sky. Anyone coming this way would be certain to see it. His breathing was shallow and uneven. Whoever was out there, they were advancing. "Stay here."

Threatening lights flashed through the woods and up into the trees—still forty feet from the basket. Gabe eased out of his hiding place and crept as quietly as he could toward the straw traitor that sat out in the open.

*Really thinking ahead, idiot,* his father's words taunted.

Gabe took one last look through the trees and leapt for the basket before a flashlight moved his way again. In one smooth motion, he grabbed the basket and rolled under a bush. At the last moment, however, his back slammed hard against a pointed rock. The impact knocked the breath out of him.

"What was that?" A man's voice spoke, clear and very close. Steps quickened toward Gabe and three flashlights whipped furiously over the area. "Are you certain you saw them come this way?" a stern English voice questioned.

"I'm sure, mate. They popped over the fence and headed down the hill."

Gabe's heart pounded. *Ralph?* He squinted through the leaves but could not make out a clear image. Three men stomped aggressively through the bushes. Gabe stopped breathing when they reached the bottom of Montesiepi. Rain began to pelt his face.

"They must have circled 'round the mount lookin' for the cave."

The flashlights turned north, and the cracking of brush quieted. Filled with pain and fear, Gabe's body was slow to respond to his signals to move. Perspiration streamed over his face and mixed with raindrops falling from the canopy of trees above him. He battled to get his breath.

"There you are," Livia whispered, pulling a low branch away from his face. He could not respond. "Gabe?" She squinted at him. "Here, let me take that." She pried his hands off the basket and helped him slide off the rock and into a sitting position, then pulled a rock away from the hill and helped him lean against the slope.

He managed a full intake of breath and shuddered. "Thanks."

She sat next to him in the light rain while they strained to listen for the stalkers' approach. In the near darkness, she reached under her and pulled out another stone. Her fingers smoothed out the soil and tugged at a root. It pulled easily out of the rocky soil, breaking in small pieces. "Look, it's a string of sorts. There's something else. Shine your light on it."

Gabe strained to see what she had discovered, but was unwilling to turn the flashlight on again. "No, they'll see us."

"Then I'll kneel in front of it and block the light." She pushed herself onto her knees, then clicked on the penlight.

Gabe reached down and held onto the object while he dug around its edges with his other hand. "A leather pouch." The rotten object split in half. "An *old* leather pouch." He handed it to her and scratched at something else that was barely visible. Then, he grabbed a small camping shovel from the basket.

"The bride and groom would have wondered about this if they had opened their gift, *eh?*"

"Just keep an eye out," he said and scraped the soil around the area a bit at a time. *Ping,* the shovel hit metal. They crouched and turned off the light, waiting for a response. All remained quiet. He set the shovel aside and clawed at the earth.

Following the straight outline of the object in the dark, bits of wood and leather disintegrated in his fingers. He brushed more debris away and felt something straight and hard. Struggling to keep his excited voice soft, he said, "It's a sword. Help me clear these rocks."

They squatted and hefted a heavy rock to another spot. After moving several more, Gabe grabbed hold of the exposed edge and jimmied it slowly from side to side. It let go of the soil, but a six-inch tip broke off in his hand.

Livia directed the penlight, and they examined the rusted edge. She pointed to another object that had been unearthed—the outline of a rotten wood shield was unmistakable. She could not contain her excitement. "This could be from the crusaders who killed Antonio!"

"Shush," Gabe warned, slipping the sword point into his pocket. He had to think. "Galgano told Helena that he buried the savages beneath the mount, which now entombs the sacred and the perverse." He drew back. "This could be their grave."

# Chapter 30

Tripping backward over the stones she had moved, Livia struggled to right herself. "Then this is the hill where *Il Testamento* is buried."

"And the cave must be right here." Gabe was hesitant to trust his senses. Had they really found it?

Picking up the rest of the sword, she said, "We did it!"

"And the Dead Knights thank you." The bold voice of an Englishman spoke out of the darkness.

Livia shrieked. Gabe jumped and turned to meet the three flashlights that hit him in the face.

"Hello, mate. All we needed to do was give you a bit o' time, and you got right to it."

"Ralph?" Livia shrunk back, eyes wide with fear. "I thought you were dead?"

"Sorry, luv. Harry is kind'a partial to me. That was ol' Sam, wha' ended up w'out no head."

She muffled a cry with her hand.

"Right, luv. Oh, was you grieving your old cuz' early demise? Did ya' send flowers and all? No. I don't imagine you did. Well, no one's even gonna find your body."

She straightened and stood her ground. "We had a deal, and I have kept my part. In another hour, I would have had the spear, but you had to bring your hoodlum friends. Good luck collecting now." Her attempt at bravado confirmed the truth to Gabe. She glanced at him and dropped her eyes to shield them from his violent glare.

Ralph sneered. "You soured our deal when you got Marcella involved. Did you think I didn't know about your Kestral impersonation? Get her!"

Livia screamed as Harry grabbed her. Instinctively, Gabe lunged at him and wrestled the assailant's arms away from Livia. Ralph's strong hands grabbed Gabe from behind and thrust him to the ground. Gabe managed to pull free of Ralph's grip and land a solid kick into his gut, knocking him backward.

"Enough. Just get him," their leader ordered. Ralph had dropped his flashlight, which now illuminated the man's face.

"Firelli?" Gabe's mind worked to untwist the facts. "You're with the Dead Knights?" His perplexed words were muffled when Ralph caught his throat in a headlock.

"We don't need nobody else down here, so shut your trap."

After attempting to run from Firelli's grip, Livia raked his face with her nails. He growled and grabbed her arm. Wrenching it high behind her back, her shoulder dislocated with a loud pop. She screamed out in agony.

"Quiet," he hissed, then shoved her to the ground where her head struck a stone, silencing her. He looked up as though nothing out of the ordinary had occurred.

"Surprised to see me?" he said, without a trace of his Italian accent. "I imagine Cardinal Vincenzo will be equally surprised when the *Soci* fail to turn up with *Il Testamento*. Porta was very generous with his information about his plans." Firelli's voice was grim. "The *Soci* have no soul, but are very good at hiding that fact. We will do anything to keep this relic out of the hands of that fraud, Vincenzo."

"But we weren't planning to give it to him," Gabe pleaded. "Louis called them as a cover to give us time to find it here."

"And take it to Seborga. That is the same as handing it over to them. The *Soci* are insidious, with far-reaching tentacles. They can get to anyone they wish, but we are collecting quite a list of names that we intend to cross off, thanks to Abbot Porta."

"So the Dead Knights are equally ready to kill." Gabe's eyes held steady.

"Our mission requires it."

Gabe curled his lip in disgust, "The end justifies the means." He lifted his chin. "Machiavelli's quote continues to fail in its quest to validate violence."

Ralph tightened his grip on Gabe's neck and put a knife to his ear. Gabe felt the pressure of his pulse pounding against his temples. Ralph had already cut his chin once, would he really cut his throat? Feeling the shaking hostility in Ralph's body behind him, Gabe had his answer. Ralph *wanted* to kill him.

Firelli acted bored. "I can do without the drama, Ralph. Now get to work—I do not want to be out in this drizzle the whole of the night."

"Right." Reluctantly, Ralph released his hold and shoved Gabe toward the hill. "You're gonna find the cave so I can get my money."

Trembling, Gabe took a step toward the hill. Livia lay sprawled in a tangle where she had fallen at the feet of Firelli. Gabe wanted to believe she deserved this, but his heart wrenched at seeing her unconscious body. Rivulets of water were building quickly and flooding the ground around her. Taking another step beyond her, he gasped.

Livia's mouth lay open in the mud, conjuring up the scene from years ago—before the whole hill slid away and buried his sister. He wanted to lift Livia and carry her to safety, but Ralph would be at his throat again. The old terror twisted his gut.

A black shadow closed around his mind. It compressed his vision to one narrow tunnel, too tight to get through. More panic. Somewhere in the distance, Ralph was kicking him. Gabe was at the waterfall, his father screaming at him to move across. But he couldn't move. *Help me.*

Born somewhere deep in his being, a tiny surge of strength began to seep into his veins. Soothing heat melted the despair. His vision began its slow return. It expanded a few feet at a time. The trees and rocks and rain came into focus again. Though fear still dominated his emotions, a sliver of hope pierced his will. *There has to be a way out of this.*

He stood unsteadily. A strong hand rested firmly on his shoulder. Gabe jumped around, ready to fight off Ralph, but his cousin was four feet away. Next to him, however, the faint image of a man with compassionate eyes gazed at him. *Jesus?* Gabe stared harder.

"Get moving." Firelli held an umbrella and a flashlight. Gabe, Ralph, and Harry worked on the spot where Gabe had pulled out the sword. They pushed back the foliage, digging their fingers into the mud to dislodge small boulders. Rain slicked the area, causing their feet to slip. There was no sign of a cave entrance.

After an hour, Ralph fell back against the hill. "This is useless."

Firelli flashed his light in Gabe's face. "What makes you think the cave is here?"

Between the exertion and the cold, Gabe's mind had numbed.

Ralph slapped his face. "You were asked a question."

Gabe recoiled and held up his shaking hand to avoid the glaring light. "That sword was there," he pointed. "I thought it might belong to one of the assassins who killed Antonio. Galgano's letter said he buried them beneath the mount that holds the sacred. We assumed that meant *Il Testamento.*"

Heaving a frustrated sigh, Firelli bowed his head and stared at the ground. When he did, the flashlight dropped out of Gabe's eyes, allowing him to see Firelli's face. He taunted his captor. "Did Ralph tell you he left you tied up in the basement of the safe house?"

Firelli glanced up. "Neither he nor Livia had ever met me. Ralph was recruited by another, then he enticed Miss Ambrogi with the promise to split a large reward. Ralph has a very promising career. He understands total dedication to a cause—and my style." Firelli pushed Livia's leg with the toe of his boot. "She, on the other hand, is conniving, playing both sides against the middle." A mocking smile turned his mouth up. "I guess you are the middle."

Gabe gave him a scathing glance.

"Angry, are we? Too bad," Firelli sneered. "Harry, take Dolcini and Ralph and check out the rest of the area—thoroughly. If there is any suggestion of a cave, explore it." Firelli's phone rang. After listening for a moment, he said, "I know, we are on the other mount right now."

Ralph pushed Gabe as they trudged farther around the mount. They stumbled over bushes and rocks, while Ralph assailed him with intimidating remarks. A sudden cloudburst released its pent-up threats in earnest, drenching them in seconds.

For the next two hours, they followed Gabe's theory that the location lay east of Montesiepi, but it yielded no result. They made their way back to their starting point. Gabe spotted Livia's unconscious figure getting drenched in the rain and shivering in her sodden black sweat clothes. "Can I move her?"

Firelli motioned to a place on higher ground under a canopy of brush. She cried out when Gabe moved her arm to lay her down under the dense foliage, but at least her face was out of the pelting raindrops.

"That way." Firelli directed them to continue their search on the opposite side of the mountain. The icy shower increased, spilling down the mountain around their feet and racing toward the vineyard. After another hour, Ralph slammed a stone to the ground. "I don't see nothin'! Nothin'!" Miserable, he grabbed Gabe's jacket. "Where is it?"

Teeth chattering, Gabe said, "It's all a guess. The letters are hundreds of years old. Who knows what could have changed over that amount of time."

Firelli interrupted the altercation. "I do not see any possibilities here. The thread of evidence is too slender to think the cave is anywhere besides on Montesiepi. Soon, I will have the rest of the letters. No one will ever think to look here without them. We will let the dead lie with the dead."

"What do you mean?" Gabe jerked his head around.

Ralph turned on Gabe "Funny you should ask. Why don't you pick up missy, here, and we'll just take a walk back up to the chapel—or should I say mausoleum? Isn't that where they put dead people?"

The night could not get any bleaker. Gabe's energy was spent. Hours of drudgery under constant intimidation had desensitized him to Ralph's threats. He stooped down and gathered Livia in his arms as gently as possible, his anger toward her relenting. She was freezing, but still breathing.

"Thank God." The words escaped his mouth. It had been years. A warm presence buoyed him in this unfathomable situation. Gabe raised Livia's head and rubbed his face to her wet cheek. *Please, keep her safe.*

A torrent flooded the hillside, blurring Gabe's vision. Beyond weary, he worked to find his footing in the sludge on Montesiepi. He slipped, nearly dropping Livia. Harry grabbed her, carrying her with no thought for her comfort. *It's a good thing she's still unconscious.*

They reached the chapel grounds, long deserted by the merrymakers. Gabe tried to see through the downpour, hoping someone from the chapel staff was on duty—even Eleonora would do. Everything, however, was deserted.

Above him, water sheeted off the lofty bell tower. Ralph pushed Gabe forward, causing him to stumble under one of the powerful streams. Its force pushed Gabe to his knees. Panicked, he scooted away from the flow. He rose and huddled against the solid stone wall of the round chapel. Ground water pooled over his feet, building up and pushing through inlets set around the building's foundation.

Ralph shoved him again. "Move it."

They waited under the cover of the entrance hall while Firelli turned the lock and opened the door to the herbal shop. He stepped in, making room for Harry to carry Livia inside before Ralph pushed Gabe through.

A sickening stench hit them, and they grabbed their noses. Heading behind the counter, Firelli searched an oversized ring for the right key. He flung open the curtain, revealing a small door with a rounded top. Symbols were engraved deep into the wood—the most pronounced being a Templar cross that divided it into four segments.

Firelli unlocked the door and pushed it inward, then flipped on the light. His men followed him with their captives, down several steps to a large room, bare except for the wide stone column in the center.

Gabe shivered uncontrollably from the wet clothes that sucked the heat out of his body. And from the menacing thoughts that bombarded him. He blinked his dull eyes. "We're below Galgano's sword."

"Good observation, Sherlock," Ralph needled.

Like a snide schoolmaster, Firelli explained. "This is where the Cistercian monks dug for *Il Testamento*. They believed, like we did, that Galgano buried it in a cave on Montesiepi and then became a hermit to guard it." He pointed above him. "Upstairs, there is an interesting display. Abbot Lorenzo, also one of the *Soci*, sent an assassin to kill Galgano and take the relic. The bones of the forearms are all that is left of the abbot's man." He scoffed, "Looks like all their pious giants fall with the same ease."

After unbolting a heavy, sealed door, Firelli had Ralph tug it open. The sound of crashing water battered Gabe's eardrums while they descended a short flight of steps into a large circular room. Firelli lit a fat candle that sat sheltered in a deep alcove. It cast a subtle light, revealing a low ceiling with pipes emptying powerful streams of water into a large cistern in the center of the room.

Gabe noticed iron grates attached to the wall at floor level on five sides of the round room. They covered openings that led to dark tunnels. *Irrigation canals?*

Firelli motioned for Ralph to bring Gabe forward. "This is where the Cistercians ended their digging for *Il Testamento*—not the head of a martyr, as many supposed, but more likely, the spearhead that pierced Jesus' body. Or, it could have been one last secret that died with our Grand Master, Jacques de Molay."

The roar of the roiling water increased, and Firelli raised his voice. "Whatever it was, it would give undeserved power to the unholy man who finds it. I am not going to let that happen. This is one more relic that will be lost in history."

"But what if it proves Jesus lived," Gabe cried out.

"He did. As a man. Goodbye Gabriel. We cannot leave any loose ends. This cistern has long been forgotten." He checked his watch. "Your grandfather is dead by now, but I would not count on meeting him on the other side. There is no *other* side."

Grief punched Gabe hard. Tears mixed with the water dripping from his hair. He yearned for the chance to apologize, but he'd missed it.

Ralph pushed him toward the cistern in the center of the room, which was at least twelve feet in diameter. He grabbed Gabe's neck and shoved him over the edge. Gabe gasped and clawed for a hold. Surprised, he landed on a narrow step, three feet below the lip.

Beyond the step's edge, he peered into a black hole, thirsty for the tumultuous surge pounding its way off the roof. Like a deadly waterfall, the powerful flow shot into the deep stone container. He crumpled against the side wall and shut his eyes. He was eight again. He couldn't breathe—couldn't move.

*Together Gabriel. Trust Me.*

Ralph screamed from above, "...I said get up Gabriel, or she dies."

Opening his eyes, Gabe saw Harry toss Livia into the hole. Terror struck his whole being. Her unconscious body floated into midair before it sank out of sight. It took an eternity to hear the splash.

"No!" Gabe screamed. He clung to the stones and cried out, "Livia!"

"She's right down there, mate. Go save her." Ralph's cruel lips quivered in their excitement. "Now's your chance to show your dad and the whole world that you're not a coward."

Livia was drowning. Gabe's body was rigid, yet he felt a sudden infusion of strength.

*Jump Gabriel.*

Inexplicably, he stood up and stepped over the edge.

Ralph shouted from above. "Idiot!"

# Chapter 31

Siena, Italy

Louis pushed back his leather desk chair and stood, unable to sit still. How would he endure this night? He glanced at the clock again. It was ready to strike eleven and still Gabe was not home. With a trembling hand, he pinched the bridge of his nose to ward off the headache that was threatening. "Rinaldo, have you found where I laid my glasses?"

The man did not answer. Louis huffed. Had he gone back down to check on their prisoner? Louis attributed his own impatience to the stress of Gabe and Livia going after *Il Testamento* and the danger they could be facing.

That, and the super storm that had inundated the region with a monsoon-like effect had put him on edge. He had to do something. He had waited long enough for them to get home. When Rinaldo's steps finally echoed from the dining room, Louis announced, "Something has gone wrong. I am calling Marcella."

"No, you are not."

Twisting his head around, Louis' eyebrows furrowed. "What do you mean?"

His butler strode passed him and yanked the phone cord from the wall. "I have deceived you. My real name is Rinaldo De Paola. I work with the Dead Knights."

"How..." Louis sputtered at this revelation.

"Sit down before you make yourself sick and tell me where the other documents are regarding *Il Testamento*."

"What have you done with Gabriel and Livia?"

"Firelli is waiting to see what Gabriel finds. If your grandson is correct, Firelli will take *Il Testamento* off his hands."

Louis fell into his chair. *Killers have Gabriel.* "What if he doesn't find it?"

A flicker of uncertainty crossed Rinaldo's face.

Louis sat back and grabbed his heart. "They wouldn't hurt him?"

## ##

Gabe wondered if the scream had really come from his own mouth. The whole scene was surreal. As he descended deeper into the pit with the wash of runoff, the candlelight dimmed. After a split second, he was underwater. All sight and sound stopped. The icy wetness hit his ears and eyes, waking him.

The same calm voice whispered, "Livia."

Gabe shot to the top and gasped for breath. He sucked in a stream of cold water that set off a desperate coughing fit. Partially recovered, he splashed around in a circle. The faint light washed over Livia, struggling to reach her head up for air. She was on her side, unable to right her body with her wounded arm.

He pushed off the side of the cistern and grabbed her head, pulling it out of the churning water. "Livia," he cried.

Her wild eyes darted around. She seemed panicked, unable to comprehend where she was.

Gabe held her and shouted toward the top of the cistern, "Ralph, get us out of here!"

"No one will hear your screams," Ralph laughed as he yelled into the hole. "Just like no one heard mine when your dad beat me. Every night. With a belt. Never thought to come to ol' Ralph's rescue, did you chump?"

Twenty feet below the top of the cistern, Gabe worked to keep Livia afloat. The bleary figure of Ralph disappeared, leaving only the sound of crashing water.

## 

Firelli toweled off in his room that was attached to the chapel. He blocked out the shouts he had left behind in the cistern. Drowning was not his style. Recalling that suffocating feeling, he sucked in a deep breath. Just put people out of their misery and get back to the task.

He put on dry clothes and dialed his associate. "It is time to clean up the loose ends, starting with Niccolo, tied up in the cellar at the palazzo." Firelli had proven all his adult life that big guys were just big. Nothing to fear, anymore.

"Did you find the relic?" his associate asked.

Firelli threw the towel on the floor. "I do not believe it ever existed."

His associate's voice stung. "You mean you failed."

Anger heated Firelli's freezing body. "Perhaps. Just do your part and destroy the documents. Soon *Il Testamento* will be forgotten."

## 

Water crashed from the ceiling inlets. The tumult bellowed and echoed in their murky prison. Attempting to keep Livia afloat with one hand, Gabe clawed at the sides of the cistern with his other, but was unable to hold a grip on the wet, slimy stones.

He struggled to keep his head out of the water, yet keep his face down so he could breathe without taking in the plummeting water. It wasn't working. Water splashed up his nose. He coughed and tried to suck in air. More water gagged him. Thrashing wildly with one hand, he knew he was losing it. Livia was sinking. There was no way out.

Recalling Angelica's scream, just before the force hit her, plunged Gabe back into the horror of his sister's death. More pictures flashed.

His father's fierce shouts bombarded him. *You killed Angelica.*

Desperate for air, fear gripped Gabe's body. His own guilt responded. *I deserve to die.*

Plunged into despair, he stopped fighting. He lost his hold on Livia. His legs ceased kicking. All the failure and guilt of his life engulfed him. All his striving. *For what? Twelve pretty paintings?*

Water rose over his head as his body sank. *He had wasted his life.* Gabriel Russo Dolcini blew out the last of his air. He had just closed his eyes when a sudden flash of certainty shot into his consciousness. He would soon be called to give an account.

*I'm not ready.* Panic stabbed at his lungs. His eyes flew open, and he slashed toward the dim light above him. His mind screamed, *Help me!*

Soothing words called to him. *This is not the waterfall. You know how to swim.*

The fear released him. With renewed energy, Gabe kicked hard and shot to the surface. Water plunged over his head, and he gasped for air. He blinked, looking for the one who spoke to him, trying to make sense of it.

Then he saw the face of Jesus, but not with his eyes. *You are real—Louis' God was real.* He wanted Louis to know he believed, wanted to see the delight in his grandfather's eyes.

But, regret was quick to crush his jubilation. The image of his grandfather's silent sobs, in reaction to Gabe's stinging words, kicked him in the gut.

"Gabe." A hand gripped his shoulder and tugged lightly. Squinting, he jerked around. *Livia.* She tilted her head to direct him to the side of the cistern. He could see that to his left, the downpour was not hitting the surface of the water. A stone extended from the wall above them, diverting the stream to the center.

He grabbed hold of Livia's good arm and kicked. It was a good decision. Wedging his fingers into a small crevice in the stone wall, they were able to catch their breath and steady themselves. If he got out of here, he owed his rock climbing instructor big time.

The water rose inches by the minute. There was no way to know how deep this cistern was, but they were now only ten feet from the top.

Perhaps they could get out. He looked up. *No. They would drown.* With the exit door locked, the water would be forced out the grated openings, smashing their bodies against them.

Regardless, he was not giving up. They were almost even with the overhanging stone now. Gabe lunged at it, grabbing a handhold. The pressure of the water beat on his fingers. His body quaked with adrenaline and cold.

Livia trembled as well. He tried to talk to her, but the racket drowned out his voice. Gathering her near him, he felt her sobs while the surging water pushed and pulled at her dislocated shoulder. His mind whispered, *Please, numb her pain.*

# Chapter 32

Siena, Italy

"Rinaldo, do not hurt Gabriel. He never wanted to be part of this. I tricked him."

"Yes, you did trick him. And the sooner you give me the rest of the documents, the sooner Gabe will be returned to you."

Feigning heart trouble, Louis asked, "Please, my medicine."

Rinaldo studied Louis' ailing body.

Louis gasped for air and clutched more violently at his chest.

"Relax and stay put," Rinaldo said. He holstered his gun and left.

As soon as Rinaldo was out of the room, Louis crept across the library to his bookshelf. Without his glasses, it was difficult to read the title of the volume he sought. He was certain he had the correct shelf, but where was the book? He squinted and ran his fingers over the row. It must be farther along the shelf.

Rinaldo was returning. His steps grew louder as they hit the floor tiles in the dining room.

Louis had only moments left to save his family. He touched each book with a brief perusal until he found the one.

Steps reached the carpet on the hall floor.

Louis ripped the book off the shelf and pulled his pistol from the fake volume. He lunged forward and fell back into his chair, just before Rinaldo stepped around the corner carrying a tray.

Rinaldo studied Louis' labored breathing and set a glass of water and his pill onto the inlaid table. "Take this." He set the tray containing the sherry and two glasses on mantle.

Reaching for the water glass with his left hand, Louis obscured the pistol grasped in his right. Rinaldo was just taking a seat on the sofa across from him, when Louis issued a terse demand, "Where is my grandson?"

Rinaldo's eyes flew open in surprise. He stared at the narrow gun barrel. Louis took the butler's gun from his holster, then ordered him into the dining room. He dialed Marcella's number from his other phone. The brief explanation he gave was enough to pull her out of bed and put her in high gear to get to the palazzo.

When they were back in the library, Louis again demanded, "Where is Gabriel?" The face of his friend had become the face of his enemy.

At Louis' direction, Rinaldo sat on the sofa. "You know where he is. You sent him to Montesiepi. I imagine he is still there, digging."

"Why do you want the documents?"

Rinaldo spoke with great conviction. "Man will contrive an idol out of the simplest of things. Even a *record* of *Il Testamento* carries great mystery and intrigue. The dark minds of the *Soci* know this. Whether they produce the treasure it is purported to be, or even your amazing documents that track its history, people will worship the *Soci* for their discovery. They will pay to see it, revere it. You of all men should understand that."

"Why do you say that?"

"Look at you. You obsessed over it, lied, and endangered your own grandson—the last in your line—for the possibility of gaining praise for yourself."

Louis' anger faltered. "But I was charged to take it to Seborga."

"By who?"

"King Baldwin ordered Antonio, who passed that charge to our family."

"Yes. King Baldwin. A murdering invader, leading ruthless men to butcher men, women and children. Using, of all things, the banner of Christ—the very one who gave his life because he loved those people."

"But Antonio was a man of faith, not a butcher."

"My point exactly. Power deceives good men. Cardinal Vincenzo is just the latest in the line of the *Soci* who desire to be worshipped and live as kings. The relic will pave the way. If he presents it, the glory will pass through the object and shine on him.

"Louis, I read the documents. *Il Testamento* is no ordinary relic. The effect it had on the Templars, and the zeal with which men coveted it, are unsurpassed. It is just the symbol of power the ARCC needs to validate its spiritual authority. I cannot fathom how you can collaborate with the most detestable plan yet devised to enslave the soul of humanity— stealing the truth of God and replacing it with a hollow, powerless form of religion. The *Soci* will have achieved their purpose."

Louis resisted. "What purpose?"

Rinaldo's fervent gaze pierced Louis. "You know that Emperor Constantine filled prominent Roman positions with Christians, *sì?*"

Nodding, Louis tilted his head. "And?"

"And the leaders of the pagan religions simply moved their practices under the banner of Christianity. Eventually, those who were greedy for absolute control, melded political and religious power into one. They gave themselves the power to murder those who disagreed with them. This is not Christianity. I believe this was the direction the *Soci* are taking the ARCC."

"So, the *Soci* came out of the early church?"

Rinaldo shook his head. "Not necessarily. Constantine also disbanded Caesar's Praetorian Guard. It had grown so powerful, its members began to oust noncompliant leaders and replace them at will. The disbanded members secretly formed the *Soci*."

Louis murmured, "They were murderers from the beginning."

"*Sì.* The *Soci* found they could use this new state religion to their advantage and infiltrated the church leadership. They defamed Jesus by leading the church into murderous wars and conquests for their own purposes."

Rinaldo glanced at his watch. "Louis, you *must* give me the documents. Your stubbornness in keeping them makes your family a target."

Marcella burst through the front door and charged into the library. "Where are they?" Relief hit Louis hard. "They are on Montesiepi."

Her dark eyes flashed at him, her words vehement. "Digging for your treasure?"

"*Si.*" He dropped his eyes from the judgment in her glare.

Shaking her head, her lips stretched to a thin, tense line, and she turned back to Rinaldo. She jammed the muzzle of her gun hard onto his kneecap. Her eyes were vicious. "While playing chess with other people's lives, you ridiculous men killed my sister. I have a license to kill, and I will not hesitate to miss a few times. Now what have you done with them?"

Louis understood her passion. The Dead Knights were responsible for years of anguish. Still, this would just add violence to violence. He closed his eyes and prayed, *Not like this, Lord.*

## ##

Gauging the rate of incoming water, Gabe knew the time was critical before it reached the ceiling and trapped them. He pulled himself up and sat on the outcrop. Livia held onto it above her head with her good arm. He pushed up to a stand. Water splashed into his face when he reached above to find the lip of the cistern. He squatted back down, ducking his head. Soon Livia floated up, even with the overhang. He held onto her, shielding her face from the flow with his body.

When the water was two feet from the top of the hole, Gabe grabbed the edge and kicked, landing with a splat on the room's floor. He rushed over to the door. *Locked.* He peered around the small room and spied the grates on the wall. There were no other exits.

Soon, water bubbled over the lip of the cistern and plowed through the grates into the irrigation tunnels carved through the mountain to the valley below. A piercing scream invaded his numbed mind and drowned out all the other sounds. He jerked his head downward.

Livia's face held pure terror as she thrashed her legs at the water, trying to get away. Gabe strained to see what had terrified her. The vacant stare of a dead man gaped at them from just under the water's surface. *Arturo.* His ghostly white arms and legs waved in the surge, as though reaching for her.

Gabe knelt down and pulled her away from the body, then heaved her onto the slippery floor. She stood and clung to him, gasping and shivering as they watched the churning water pull the body down again. "He was one of Abbot Porta's assassins."

Livia buried her face in Gabe's soaked chest. "I never wanted this."

"I know." He wrapped his arms around her. Though she had been foolish, he was certain she meant no harm to anyone.

She sobbed, "I need to sit down." He let go of her trembling body and she sat in a pool of water, pulling her knees against her chest. She moaned when her injured arm tilted at an odd angle. Water gathered over her ankles and crept up the sides of her legs.

"There has to be a way out." Gabe pushed and kicked at the door again, but with no better result. Studying the door and the room, he pointed to one of the grates. "East." He sloshed to the iron bars that caged them in and shook hard. They were rusted but sturdy. However, the wall around the grate was crumbling. Digging into his pocket, he pulled out the fragment of rusted sword and chipped at the stone with a frantic effort.

The edge of the sword crumbled, but the core remained intact. His fingers bloodied as the rust scraped against his waterlogged skin. At last, a large chunk of the old stone came loose and sank to his feet. *In minutes, the water will rise above this outlet.* He tried wedging the sword into the crack made by the chipped stone. Another chunk fell. Water continued to gush through the grate with increasing volume, creating a suck that pulled him against it.

"What can I do?" Livia's determined voice spoke in his ear. She had come up behind him and pressed her cheek against his back. She wrapped her good arm around his chest. "I am sorry. I care about you. I want you to know that in case we…"

"We are not going to die," Gabe said, hoping his words sounded reassuring. "If I can get this grate out of here, we may be able to…"

"It is too small." Livia pushed away. "We cannot go through there. We will get stuck and drown."

"I have to try." Gabe turned and gazed into her clouded eyes. "I'll chip, you pray." While the water rose at ever-increasing speed, he struggled in a frantic attempt to dislodge the barrier that kept them pinned in. He could faintly see the rounded, narrow hole on the other side of the grate. The diameter of the ancient clay pipe could not be over eighteen inches. It extended only a short distance from the bars. Beyond that, it became a rock-lined hole. Livia was probably right. It was too small, and they would drown, but he was not giving up.

Fatigue slowed his movements as he struggled to wedge the makeshift tool under the stubborn stones. The water was now three feet above the top of the grate. He cast a doubtful look at the ceiling and the gallons of water that continued to pour in through the gathering holes set at ground level far above them.

He took a breath and used the bars to pull himself under the water to hack out more stone. The hard suction hindered his movements. It took all his strength to jam the blade under the edges of the jagged rocks. He clawed his way up to grasp another breath. "The grate is moving. It's free from the wall, but the water is keeping it in place."

"I want to help."

He frowned at her distended arm, but nodded. She watched for his signal and took a breath. Pressed against the wall, she grabbed the grate from above with her good arm and they pulled upward. It did not budge.

*Pull down.*

Without argument, he dove down and followed the odd instruction. It gave! The grate slid out of the upper mounts. Livia helped pull it sideways. The barricade moved! They pushed to the surface and gasped for air.

With a creaking rumble, the stones of the irrigation canal dislodged. The water seemed to sink around Gabe. A whirlpool formed and pushed out through the hole with massive force. Losing his footing, Gabe gulped a frantic breath.

He caught a last glimpse of Livia before the torrent swallowed him and forced him down the hole. Rough stone scraped his body. Then all went black.

## ##

Louis watched as Marcella cocked the gun, absolute in her determination. She shoved the barrel harder into Rinaldo's knee. He flinched. "Did your comrade, Firelli, follow them?"

"I am sure he did."

"How long ago," she demanded.

"Three hours, perhaps four."

Keeping a watchful eye on her captive, Marcella called the station for help. "Orsini, I want you here at the Palazzo Dolcini—and get a team to Montesiepi—NOW!"

She turned to Louis. How are you holding up?"

"I will be good as soon as I know Gabriel and Livia are safe."

Sorrow filled her eyes as she studied him. "As much as you have brought this on yourself, I am sorry for all you have been through." Louis leaned back, massaging his heart. The strain in Marcella's face eased as she gazed at him. "It is almost over, and we will have caught these murderers."

Less than half an hour later, pounding on the front door jolted both of them. Marcella signaled for Louis to get it while she watched Rinaldo.

Louis limped to the entryway and shouted for the visitor to identify himself.

"Detective Orsini." When Louis unbolted the lock, the detective pushed inside. "Who is Marcella holding?"

Anger flooded Louis afresh. "My butler, Rinaldo."

Orsini's eyes widened. He followed Louis to the library and stopped when he saw Marcella's gun pointing at Rinaldo. "What happened?"

She stood, her gun outstretched. "He is a member of the Dead Knights. Louis' daughter, Geneva, told them about Louis having the map, but she had no idea where they might find the object. Rinaldo has been spying on Louis for a year, waiting for him to expose it. My nephew

279

and niece may be…" She glanced at Louis. "Rinaldo's companions may have captured them at Montesiepi."

"May I question him?" Orsini walked passed Marcella toward the sofa. With a quick movement, he grabbed her weapon and threw her to the floor.

"What are you doing?" Louis demanded.

"My mission." Orsini pointed his firearm, fitted with a silencer, at Louis. "Rinaldo, get his pistol."

Rinaldo's face tensed with apprehension as he glanced at Orsini's outstretched gun. He took Louis' pistol and stepped back. "Now, where are the documents?"

Fury and fear battled for Louis' emotions. This man had been his friend. "Upstairs. In my safe."

Rinaldo took the combination and shot up the stairs. He returned a short time later with the papers. "We have them," he announced, handing them to Orsini. "At last, it is over. Will you join me for a glass of sherry in celebration?"

Louis' lips trembled with anger. "You have what you want. Now take the relic and leave my family alone."

Expressionless, Orsini said, "Too late for that, I am afraid. We cannot leave witnesses to our identity." He aimed his gun at Marcella. "It has been a pleasure working you."

"You are the mole," she hissed.

"Stop!" Louis yelled.

Orsini's face held grim satisfaction. He cocked his gun.

"That is not necessary," Rinaldo shouted.

Orsini rounded on the former butler. "Firelli told me about you. We would have been done by now if you had not drugged him at the safe house. Your mission was to destroy the relic, not get cozy with the Dolcinis. Their deaths are on your head." He swung the gun toward Louis. Before he could fire, Rinaldo jumped on him, wrestling for the weapon. In the struggle, Orsini fired two wild shots.

Without warning, a burning sensation inflamed Louis' side. He collapsed on the floor. Blood immediately soaked his shirt and pants.

One bullet pierced Orsini's leg, splattering his overcoat and the blue sofa with blood.

Leaping for Orsini's gun, Rinaldo grabbed it. He threatened Orsini and Marcella. They backed off, but still looked ready to pounce. Rinaldo knelt by Louis' side and put pressure on the wound with his other hand. Louis cried out as severe pain shot through him.

"Bring that tablecloth and bind this," Rinaldo ordered Marcella.

She scrambled for the cloth, ripped it and tied a tightly folded wad of fabric to the wound. Louis moaned. "We need to get an ambulance," she screamed.

Rinaldo ignored her. "Now, tie Orsini's hands."

She pushed the detective forward and secured his hands with the telephone cord from Louis' desk phone. Shoving him back, she thrust her knee into his bleeding leg. Louis heard Orsini screech, but was in too much pain to savor the retribution.

Rinaldo's voice sounded ruthless, "I am taking Louis with me. If you value his life, do not try to follow." Rinaldo shoved his arms under Louis' armpits and lifted, causing Louis to clutch his heart.

Keeping the gun pointed at Marcella, Rinaldo pulled Louis to his feet and dragged him backward toward the garage. Groaning in pain, Louis felt dizzy when Rinaldo laid him in the back seat of the limo. The door slammed and the car started. It was all too much…

## 

As soon as Rinaldo was out of the driveway, Marcella called her office to have him apprehended. She glanced at the carpet, soaked with Louis' blood. He would not make it far. Her rage was tangible as she glared at Orsini. She was barely able to keep from putting a bullet into the detective's head.

Assuming a haughty posture, the disdain in Orsini's voice did not ease the situation. "We have men in places higher than you could ever imagine. None of this will stick, and I would not count on keeping your position."

He had gone too far. Her weapon arched downward and struck him hard on the side of his head. He bellowed curses at her while a stream of blood coursed down his cheek. Her rage refueled and she raised her weapon to strike again.

"Hold it right there."

She swung around to face a small, beady-eyed Englishman. He had come in through the rear of the palazzo and stood at close range with his revolver directed at her torso. She dropped her weapon and kicked it behind her. "Who are you?"

"Another Dead Knight, at your service. Enough of this nonsense. Now back away from Orsini. After she moved out of the way, he lifted Orsini's chin to examine the cut.

"Firelli, untie me," he demanded.

"In due time. What happened here?" His eyes swept the room, studying each detail. He strode to the fireplace and lifted the bottle of sherry to his nose. A smile lifted the edge of bitterness from his mouth.

Orsini barked, "Rinaldo turned on us as you suspected. He took Dolcini and fled. Marcella has other officers on the way. Now untie me!"

Ignoring Orsini, Firelli poured the expensive sherry into the empty sherry glass. He swallowed a mouthful of the liquor, then lifted the glass in a toast, "To the good life." He smiled and downed the rest.

Marcella fumed. "Where are Gabriel and Livia?"

Firelli poured another glass. "Louis' grandsons are dead, along with the young woman. Also, I left a rather large dead man by the name of Niccolo in the cellar downstairs." Firelli moved toward the sofa and leaned to reach Orsini's bonds. He swayed and grabbed his stomach. "What the…"

Enraged, Marcella took advantage of Firelli's difficulty and lunged at him. Knocked off balance, the assassin struggled to point his weapon at her. Marcella was indifferent to the danger as she sought to bring down the enemy who had caused her family so much anguish.

Firelli tried to push her away, his weapon flailing in the air. He fired several bullets before Marcella broke his wrist and pried the gun from his useless fingers. She fired the last two rounds into his chest. His spinning body fell on top of Orsini.

She rushed to the sofa. Shoving Firelli to the floor, she drew back. One of his bullets had pierced Orsini's head. Her grim lips tightened. Standing to her full height, she assessed the situation.

Two members of the organization responsible for forty years of terror and loss had fallen. Bitterness imbued her ironic words. "Dead knights."

# Chapter 33

San Galgano, Italy

Burning lungs and panic aroused Gabe. He awoke in a muddy grave. Coughing and spitting, he tried to rid his body of the congestion that saturated him. *Hell?* No, it was some other place. Light filtered in from a small opening below him.

Livia lay on her side, breathing steadily. Images flew at him. *Water. Choking—Firelli!* He was wide-awake now. The rocky cistern wall that held the grate had broken from the volume of water. Their bodies had been dragged through the loose rocks and soil, dislodged by the flood.

When he pushed to sit up in his shadowy surroundings, he cut his hand on a sharp object. Feeling gingerly around it, he dragged out a stick—no, a rib. His hand jerked, dropping the bone. As he scurried away, his feet stirred up more bones. *A mass grave!* Gabe grimaced, his heart pounding.

Livia moaned. He crawled to her on his hands and knees and lifted her head out of the grime. Her skin was coated with silt from the torrent that had dragged them into this tunnel. When he touched her cheek, her eyes fluttered open.

"We made it." He tried to smile. "How about let's get out of here? Do you think you can move?" She attempted to sit up but cried out and collapsed. "I can't, Gabe. I know I'll faint again."

He cringed at her pain and stroked her hand.

She lightly curled her fingers around his. "I know it looks like I deceived you, but I need to explain."

"Explanations can wait. I need to find a way out of here." He wiped mud off her cheek. "Just be calm."

His eyes darted around the area. Below them, a small amount of light entered through an irregular hole. They were in a tunnel, about thirty feet up from the opening. It looked as though they had been deposited in an offshoot from the main irrigation canal. He worked his way down and tried to kick the boulders out of the way, but the hole was too small to get out. He crawled back up through the muck to Livia.

The upper portion of the tunnel disappeared into blackness about forty feet above them. Pointing in that direction, he said, "The water must have pushed us down from there then flooded out. We seem to be in some sort of…"

"Cave?" Livia's voice held a hint of life.

The thought jolted some life back into him. "I'll be right back." Scrambling upward through the slush, he grabbed onto roots and pulled himself through the soggy tunnel. He had never been so cold. It seemed to reach the core of his body and emotions, numbing everything except the thought of getting out of here.

A prayer ran through his mind. *If You are still here, we really need You.*

To his right, he felt the edges of a larger tunnel connected to this one. Feeling the rock formations with his shivering hands, he climbed onto a ledge and found himself in a dry area. It was pitch black except for a pinhole of light ahead. Bent over, he followed the contours and scaled another ledge, drawn to that single ray of hope in the distance.

Stretching gingerly to his full height, he reached up and traced the ceiling and walls with his hands. It was a cavern. After taking several steps, he felt another opening to his right. In front of him, the point of light beckoned. He stumbled ahead over a rough floor and stopped when he reached the wall of rocks surrounding the bit of light. His heart began to race with hope. Only inches away, freedom waited on the other side of this barrier.

Feeling the rocks, he found one he could grasp. Yanking it from side to side, he worked hard to loosen it. It moved toward him. He grabbed a better hold and pulled with all his strength. It fell to the ground, bringing others down with it.

Gabe jumped back and watched the wall open. He squinted at the brightness, pushing other rocks down until the opening was large enough to step through. "My God." Directly above him sat the Chapel of San Galgano.

Tears of relief sprang to his squinting eyes. His legs trembled and he leaned against the remaining cave wall as waves of emotion hit him. They had made it. They were alive. But not his grandfather. Firelli had him killed.

He crumbled to the ground and covered his face with his hands. A longing that he had never known pressed his chest until he thought he couldn't breathe. He desperately wanted to talk to Louis. To share how sorry he was. A violent shiver racked his body. He had to move.

Swallowing his grief, Gabe stood and stepped away from the hill. He studied the area. *This must be Antonio's cave. Il Testamento* was near. Threading his hands through his filthy hair, he closed his eyes to shut out the image of Louis' enthusiastic face. There was no time to dwell on this. Gabe was freezing, and he needed to get Livia out.

The extra light allowed him to scurry back down the tunnel. In one place, he picked up too much speed and slipped. "Whoa." Placing his feet with more care, he re-entered the tunnel where Livia lay.

"This is it!" he announced. "This is Antonio's cave—it opens up right at the base of the mount next to Montesiepi."

Livia's teeth chattered violently. "Then *Il Testamento* is nearby." Her voice was weaker than when he left. Her fingers brushed his arm. In the darkness, he heard her confession. "Gabe, I told Rinaldo I would turn *Il Testamento* over to him. He is working for the Dead Knights."

Gabe jerked his arm away. "Then Firelli had him kill Louis. Why would you do this to us?"

A congested wail escaped her throat. "You cannot possibly understand."

Heat washed out the chill that infused his body. He did not want to understand anymore. "You need to get out of here." He pulled her legs out of the mud and scraped the debris away from her injured arm. "I'm going to lift you."

She screamed. "No. I can't."

"Gabriel Dolcini, are you in there?" An unfamiliar voice called up through the small hole below them.

Gabe's heart jumped. "We're here!" he choked. "Livia's hurt."

Something blocked the light and he could hear scraping and grunts coming from the lower opening. More and more light found its way into their tunnel. Finally a rescue worker crawled up the narrow tunnel and reached them. "You are lucky to be alive." He moved toward Livia. "Where is she injured?"

"Her shoulder is dislocated. I can't move her."

The man assessed Livia and the surroundings. "It's too small for us to get a stretcher out down below. Is there another way out?"

"Up there," Gabe pointed. "The entrance is just below Montesiepi, in line with the chapel." The man scooted back down to take his crew around to the larger entrance.

Gabe couldn't touch Livia. "It won't be long now." His words of comfort sounded like they were made of tin. Her mouth stretched into a constant grimace, but her pain seemed worlds away from him.

Several minutes later, a man called down for him to move away. "We will take it from here, signore." Two workers scrambled into the small space, dragging their equipment behind them. Gabe hardened his heart against Livia's scream when they moved her onto a stretcher.

The medic provided Gabe with water and a warm coat until they could check him out. Then they began the long process of drawing Livia up the rough passage to safety. Gabe followed them out the crumbling entrance, up the mount and into a waiting ambulance. He refused treatment for his minor scratches and bruises.

An attractive, but disheveled older woman rushed over to him in the parking lot. "I am Marcella. I am Louis' sister-in-law, your great-aunt. We have been searching for you for hours." Her eyes were intense, in spite of the fatigue that drained her face of color.

Bitter tears filled Gabe's burning eyes. "They killed Louis."

Her face tensed with anger and grief. "Orsini shot him. Then Rinaldo used him as a shield to escape."

"Rinaldo." Gabe's anger at the butler and Livia swelled to fury. Louis left this world surrounded by treachery. *Including mine.* He dropped his head in his hands.

Marcella swallowed her emotions. "Firelli said he killed you, Ralph, and Livia."

"He tried to, but Livia and I escaped." Gabe glanced at the ambulance driving away.

"You were fortunate, Ralph was not. We found his body in the woods not far from the chapel." She surveyed Gabe's filthy state and dazed reactions. "I will take you home to clean up and rest."

Gabe nodded. *Home.* His throat choked. Louis was dead, Rinaldo and Livia proved to be traitors. The palazzo, once so full of discovery and friendship, was now an empty shell.

# Chapter 34

Siena, Italy

Gabe took a shower and put some food together for lunch. His cuts burned and kept him from the nap his body needed. So did his angry thoughts. The longer he tried to comprehend the situation, the more troubled he grew. He needed answers.

A taxi took him to the hospital. When he peered into Livia's room, it was no surprise to see a triangular bandage draped from her neck to support her arm by her side. The blackened eye and head bandage, along with intravenous tubes, however, were a shock.

Her body leaned back at an angle. When her eyelids lifted, a smile started to light up her face, then stopped. He was sure he looked anything but happy to see her. She turned her face toward the wall. "Go away."

With more control than he thought he possessed, he said, "I can't fathom your motives. I can't understand why you would put our lives at risk, no matter how much money you stood to make."

When she said nothing, his self-control ended. "Are you that cold-hearted? You talked about me being self-centered, but this surpasses everything. You betrayed the man you called *nonno*."

She remained mute.

Gabe's teeth ground in frustration. With seething venom, he spit out, "He is dead because of you." Frustration followed him out of the

291

hospital. And a newfound sense of shame. His father's words had become his own.

## ##

On the fourth floor of the palazzo, Gabe sat in a hard chair near the window, trying to gain perspective. Everything that had been on solid ground now swirled like a vapor, daring anyone to nail it to the floor. Pressing his hands against his face, he stretched the tension out of his cheeks and rubbed his weary eyes. As if that would help.

Looking toward the grey sky, he prayed, "Now that you've cracked open my heart, it hurts more than ever." He closed his eyes. "I hate my father, but I am sick to death of that hate. I want to be free."

Livia's face, lit up with her glorious smile, filled his vision.

"NO." He pushed out of the chair and paced hard on the wood floor. She had joined the list of those bent on thrusting their blades through his heart. There was no one he could trust.

*No one?*

He flopped back down. Louis had been constant in his love. Grief struck anew at the great loss. Gabe grabbed a small chair and slammed it against the wood floor, crushing it to pieces. Like his life.

## ##

The painful coughing intensified as Livia sobbed miserably. Strong antibiotics dripped into a tube that ran to a needle piercing the back of her hand. Gaining some control, she stared out the dull window, made duller by half-closed blinds. She knew none of her motives could ever justify the loss. Marcella had been gentle, but not understanding. A great sigh heaved from Livia's aching chest.

"May I come in?"

Pain pierced her heart when she recognized the voice of the man who had taken all she loved. She glanced behind Rinaldo, her voice spewing acid, "I hoped the police would have caught you by now." She broke into a new fit of labored coughing.

The confidence that had exuded from the former butler was absent. He stepped into the room and closed the door. "Pneumonia?"

She glared at him. "*Sì.*"

Eyes cast down, he sat across from her in a simple plastic chair. "I owe you more than I can pay for your loss."

She did not wait for him to continue, but blasted him with a seething rant. "You have no idea what it was like—knowing it was *my* fault that Gabe and I were drowning in that cistern. And later learning Louis was dead. You promised me they would be in no danger. What happened to that promise, *eh?*"

Her voice escalated. "It was for *nothing*. We did not find it. The *Soci* will be back. My family is estranged from me. And Gabriel… You've left me *nothing!*" She swatted at the angry tears burning her cheeks.

"Regardless of what you may think, I care about Louis and your family deeply."

"Liar!"

The word hit hard enough to jolt him. "I understand." He rose and left her alone.

## ##

There were "too many bridges under the water," as Darla used to say. Gabe lay back on Louis' chaise in his suite. The loss of his grandfather pained him with every turn in the palazzo. His almost-romance with Livia was dead, as was his hope of making a big impression in Italy with his art. Nothing was left of the life he had dreamed of. No one was left. His body felt like sludge, matching his mind.

The front door opened, disrupting his thoughts. Low voices filtered up from the foyer. He jumped up from the chaise. Had Rinaldo come back? Gabe was in the palazzo alone. He grabbed his phone and started punching in Marcella's number. His heart pounded. *The Soci? Dead Knights?*

From the stairwell, a phone went off. He heard Marcella's voice answer, "*Buon giorno.*"

Gabe stuck his head out the door and peered down the stairs. Relief flushed out his fear. Marcella stood in the entrance hall. He rushed down the marble stairs. And stopped.

"Gabriel." His grandfather's eyes misted as they had done the first day they had met.

"*Nonno!*" Gabe let out a sob and reached for him, strangling him with a gripping hug. Was this a dream? He looked to Marcella then back at Louis. It was true! Gabe gripped harder as tears flowed from both men.

Louis groaned, causing Gabe to pull back. He searched his grandfather's face. "What happened to you? Where have you been?"

Marcella helped Louis limp to a chair in the library. He supported his side and sat with a moan. "I passed out in the limo while Rinaldo took me to the hospital."

"Then why didn't they call?" Gabe gripped his hair between his fingers. "This is inexcusable." *All this time…this grief.*

"I was unconscious, with no identification. Rinaldo must have realized they would think he was the one who shot me. He told them he found me on the street near the hospital." Louis' face grimaced with pain and sorrow. "He protected me from Orsini."

Gabe tilted his head in confusion. "He did?"

Marcella nodded. "With the net that was surrounding our family, it is fortunate that any of us survived."

Gabe stared at her. "So Rinaldo called you?"

She shook her head. "No. Livia did. Rinaldo visited her in the hospital. He left but called back with the information early this morning. It won't be long before we catch him."

A frown wrinkled Gabe's brow. "Why would he risk calling?"

Sadness aged Louis' features. "He was my friend."

Marcella rested her hand on Louis' shoulder. "When I arrived at the hospital this morning, I waited for your grandfather to wake up from his pain meds and brought him home." She massaged the tense muscles in Louis' neck. "Your grandfather was lucky. The bullet passed right through the soft tissue. Still, he will need to be cautious for the wound to heal properly."

Gabe's eyes shot to Louis' side. A bulge under his shirt suggested a bandage. "Are you certain you should have left?"

Marcella answered for him. "*Sì*. I can protect him here much better than in a hospital with so many strangers."

"What do you mean?"

"The Dead Knights are murderers. They seem to have scattered to the four winds, but we are making progress in rounding up the leaders. The *Soci* as well. I have an arrest warrant out for Abbot Porta in connection with several murders, although I doubt we will ever find him."

"Why not?"

"Word is that the *Soci* are after him for killing one of their leaders, a man with important political connections. They do not like losing power."

"What about Cardinal Vincenzo?"

A peeved expression tightened her lips. "He has diplomatic immunity from the Vatican, although they don't seem particularly interested in helping him, since his true colors have been exposed."

Watching Marcella hovering protectively around Louis lifted Gabe's spirits. For the first time in many days, he felt like smiling. He leaned down and kissed Louis on the top of his head. "I am so sorry for what I said about you and my father."

Shaking his head, Louis replied, "I forgave you before the words were out of your mouth. I love you, son."

A knock on the door caused Gabe and Louis to jump. Marcella went to answer it. She called over her shoulder, "I hired a temporary cook while waiting at the hospital with Louis this morning." The woman followed Marcella to the kitchen to prepare lunch.

After they ate, Marcella took a phone call and rose to leave. "I have a lead regarding Rinaldo." Gabe saw the blood drain back out of Louis' face.

When they were alone, Gabe took the opportunity to tell Louis the secret he had been holding close to his chest. "I found Antonio's cave."

Louis' eyebrows lifted in astonishment. "You found *Il Testamento*?" Hope seemed to make him younger.

"Not yet, *nonno*." Gabe choked on the words.

A tremulous grin crumpled Louis' face. "I had hoped to find it with you."

Gabe grinned, "Shall we uncover the resting place of *Il Testamento*?"

A smile turned up the quivering corners of Louis' mustache. "*Si*. We will go tomorrow."

# Chapter 35

San Galgano, Italy

Anticipation made Gabe lightheaded one moment and frustrated the next. He drove the limo while Louis sat next to him in the front seat. Sometime during the night, Rinaldo had cleaned it out and delivered it to the palazzo. That contradiction kept Gabe's anxiety level high. *What was the man up to? Did he plan to come back?*

Gabe shook off the worry. He glanced at his grandfather's beaming countenance and smiled. Marcella had things under control. Last night, she and Louis had talked for hours. It had done wonders for him.

It had only taken Marcella two phone calls to clear the way for them to explore the cave today. Clout came in handy. Halfway to Montesiepi, the brooding clouds thinned. By the time they reached the Abbey of San Galgano, glorious sunshine poured over the Tuscan setting.

On the north side of the abbey, a worker stood next to an ATV that had been reserved for them. Gabe parked along the cypress-lined drive and opened the door for Louis. "You're certain you are up to this?"

Louis waved off his concern. "I have never felt stronger."

Still, Gabe was careful driving the ATV on the bumpy road. The short drive paralleled the vineyard, and he was able to park close to the cave entrance. His heart beat faster by the moment. He glanced at Louis' expectant face. It was radiant.

297

"Let's go." Gabe grabbed the flashlight from his backpack and helped Louis through the tunnel entrance. He grinned and let out a huge breath. "This is it."

Louis squeezed his arm with a strong hand and said, "I am ready." Having committed Antonio's map to memory, he quoted the words, "How I long to enter the door to my haven, pass by the library..." They passed by the opening to a room off the main cave.

"...and descend through the narrow door to the cavernous wine cellar..." The cave narrowed. Gabe strengthened his hold on Louis' arm. They clambered over a ledge and descended into a large, cavernous room.

"Oh, to enter the south room and taste the new wine that rests in the light of the eastern alcove." Gabe looked back to where they had come from. He turned and pointed to one of the two small rooms that opened off the larger one. "South."

Stepping inside, Gabe shined his light on the eastern section of the cave. His eyebrows knit together. "This is the south room, but there is no way light can get in." A mound of rocks lay on the ground below a breach in the wall. When he shined the flashlight on the wall and ceiling of the cavern, he smiled. "This vein of rocks is *light* in color compared to the rest of the wall. Looks like these rocks tumbled out sometime in the last 800 years," he chuckled.

He tossed some of the stones out of the way and edged closer. "*Nonno*, take my hand." They moved close to the opening, and Gabe flashed the light. "I see a leather bag!"

He started to pull a stone away, but Louis grabbed his arm. "Do not go any farther."

"Why?"

In the glow of the flashlight, Louis' eyes glistened. "In one translation, *Il Testamento* means *The Proof*. Before we remove it, tell me Gabriel, do you believe that Jesus lived?"

So many bizarre things had happened in such a short period that Gabe had not considered all the ramifications. Awe and faith had replaced skepticism and unbelief. "*Si, nonno*. As glorious as this discovery may be, I need no other proof."

A smile lifted Louis' mustache. "Then let us do this together." He took the flashlight from Gabe and pointed its light at the rocks.

Careful not to cause a slide, Gabe pulled out some of the stones and let them fall to his feet. He reached through the opening and tugged on the thick leather, but it was too heavy.

"Why would it weigh so much?" Louis asked. "A spearhead would be light."

"A preserved head?" Gabe suggested. He hoped not. After moving one last stone, he used both hands and lifted the cool, dry bag out through the gap. His fingers tingled when he clutched the load. Heart pounding, he squatted, laying the unknown treasure at his grandfather's feet. "Why don't you open it?"

Louis stroked his mustache and swallowed. Bending down, he balanced the flashlight on a rock so its beam fell across the bag. With trembling fingers, he grasped the edge of the flap and pulled it back. A large white stone nestled in the bag. His brows lifted in question.

Gabe squatted and clutched the icy stone. When he rolled it over, both men gasped. Gabe released it and fell back on his haunches. "My God." He stared, blood pounding in his ears.

Louis knelt before it and crossed himself. Tears coursed down his cheeks and dropped to his chest. Captured by the spectacle that lay before them, it was several moments before they could move or speak.

There, in the semi-darkness of an obscure cave in Italy, the tortured face of Jesus stared out of the white stone.

"Someone has captured his face in stone!" Louis whispered.

The image shocked Gabe. The Savior's swollen cheek and numerous gashes were testament to the beatings he had received. Across his forehead, jagged punctures from the crown of thorns extended deep into the stone.

Gabe's chest tightened with a sorrow he had never known. *What would compel people to do this to someone?* Though stunned by the brutalized face, it was the expression that tugged at Gabe's heart. Jesus' eyes had been captured open. They gazed steadily with a mixture of sadness, compassion, and serenity.

In the cistern, Gabe had experienced the power of God. Why would Jesus allow Himself to be killed like this? He shut his eyes against the answer.

"Listen." Louis choked on his emotion while he translated an inscription engraved on the stone. "Jesus, Son of God, Courageous Soldier." He cleared his throat and pointed. The Greek letters, *alpha* and *omega*, had been carved into the base of the stone.

Gabe met his grandfather's eyes. "They are set one on top of the other—just as you drew the symbol.

"*Sí.* Just as I saw them. But what is this?" Louis pointed to an unusual oval imprint that protruded from the stone.

Gabe shrugged and moved his attention back to the face of Jesus.

Louis touched Jesus' cheek caught in the cold stone. Speaking the last line of Antonio's letter that he had written to Helena, Louis said, "When one drinks of that ageless wine, he lays hold of his dearest treasure. This is my desire for you."

Louis sobbed. "He is my dearest treasure."

## ##

The following Sunday was different from any in Gabe's life. Sweet music and the rise and fall of singing met him as he made his way toward the small amphitheater in the gardens of the Palazzo Dolcini. Louis had invited close friends from his church to an outdoor service at his home. Gabe approached the upper wall and peered over. More than a hundred men, women, and children stood, joy radiating from their faces in the soft grey morning.

Louis stood up from the back row and caught Gabe's attention. Together, they made their way toward the front. Gabe offered his arm to Louis for support as he limped down the steps.

"This is *so* beautiful," Gabe said.

Louis beamed, "We have an awesome God."

They were almost to the front row when Gabe stopped.

Below them, *Il Testamento* sat prominently on an alabaster table. Louis grinned at him and whispered, "It was meant to be shared."

Glancing over his shoulder for danger, Gabe had to remind himself that their enemies were gone. *Mostly.* They continued down the steps to the front. As Gabe moved closer to the stone, Jesus' tender eyes seemed to follow him. A lump formed in his throat.

The song ended, and they sat down. Bishop Roberto stepped forward. "Today, we unite our hearts together in the most unique of ways. We can understand what our brothers and sisters experienced two thousand years ago. Jesus came to testify of the truth—teaching them to love one another. When he was killed, their hearts were broken, but the Comforter was given to them."

He glanced down at the stone face of Jesus. "Another gift was given through the providence of God. Though we walk by faith, this bust of his face—made by one who witnessed His death—is special beyond belief…" A sob caught in the bishop's throat. He motioned to another man. "Pastor Green, will you join me."

A man with thinning blond hair and a white beard and mustache stepped forward. He put his thick arms around the bishop. Unspoken joy flowed between them, then the bishop sat down. Pastor Green wiped his cheeks, his blue eyes gazing in love at the crowd. "What a moment. The joy we feel in our hearts is the presence of the Holy Spirit—Jesus' gift to guide and strengthen us. He did not leave us alone." Pastor Green turned toward *Il Testamento*. "I never thought to see His face this side of heaven." His voice broke, "This is glorious."

Spontaneous praise and clapping broke out. The sun picked that moment to peek through a small hole in the cloud cover and stream down on the gathering. Without hesitation, Gabe raised his eyes upward and whispered, "Thank you for opening my eyes."

##

Rinaldo twitched in the chair as he sat in Livia's dingy hospital room the next day.

She had felt better, until he arrived. Her mind still seemed fuzzy from the multiple injuries and medications they were feeding her. Her words burned with sarcasm. "How is it you can move so freely without fear of the police?"

A grim smile tightened Rinaldo's lips. "Let us say I have temporary diplomatic immunity." He came and stood by her bed. "They found *Il Testamento*."

Amazement filled her as he explained the excellence of the treasure. "No wonder it was so pursued," she said.

Rinaldo nodded. "It still is. We have not yet succeeded."

Her eyes opened wide, and her jaw dropped at the unbelievable words he had just uttered. "I am done with this." Her hands began to tremble.

"Louis thinks he is being careful, but Cardinal Vincenzo or another of the embedded *Soci* will most certainly find out. They will persuade any authority they need, legally or illegally, to take *Il Testamento* from Louis." He held her eyes. "We must finish this, Livia."

Another piece of her heart shattered. It screamed *NO*, but her mind and her word won out. "What do you need from me?"

"Do you know where Louis would keep *Il Testamento*?"

Shock stopped all thoughts but one. "You are not still planning to destroy it? You know what it is—you cannot go through with this." His silence told her everything. Livia shook her head in disbelief.

Rinaldo forced his argument. "If Louis keeps it hidden at the palazzo, it will not be long before he is attacked and it is stolen."

She was back where she had started. Yet, she had already lost everything. "There is a mirror in the cellar."

# Chapter 36

Siena, Italy

"It's GONE!" Louis bent over Gabe, holding onto his side and gasping for breath.

Awakened from a sound sleep, Gabe tried to grasp the situation. "What's gone?" Had the Kestral stolen another painting?

"*Il Testamento*," Louis wailed. "Last night, I locked it in the secret room downstairs. When I went to visit it this morning, the mirror was open, and it was missing." He sat gingerly on the overstuffed blue chair. "Who would do such a thing?"

Gabe considered the possibilities. The Dead Knights who knew about the cellar—Ralph, Firelli, and Orsini, were dead. That left only Rinaldo. And Livia. Only she knew how to open the mirror. *She wouldn't.*

The arrow of betrayal pierced Gabe's chest with a slicing pain. He squeezed his forehead with his thumb and fingers, trying to blank out what he knew in his heart. *She would.*

After a quick breakfast in the dining room, Louis called Marcella. His face grimaced in pain. When he hung up the phone, he said, "They caught Rinaldo an hour ago, but he refused to speak of *Il Testamento*."

Scowling, Gabe jumped up from his chair. He could not rest until he confronted Livia. He drove the limo with Louis next to him. Monday morning's traffic was normal for this time of day, but Gabe still leaned on his horn several times.

The two Dolcini men stormed into the hospital room together. As soon as Livia looked at Gabe, he knew. Even knowing, it was inconceivable. "Why?"

"It *had* to be destroyed. Let me explain," she started to plead, but shrunk back at the explosive intensity of fury and disgust in their faces. Her expression crumbled and her uninjured hand flew up to cover her shame.

"You mean, you needed the money so you had to steal it." Venom poured from Gabe's lips. "Just like *Pacifica*. I wasn't going to tell them who stole it, but you're a thief—expect to do some jail time."

Grief wrinkled the sallow skin of Louis' face. Hours of contemplating the huge loss had darkened the skin around his eyes. "Traitor," he spit and turned his back on her.

Gabe dragged his eyes away from his grandfather's face and Livia's sobs. He could not escape the loathsome scene fast enough. Following Louis, he charged out the door to drive his distressed grandfather home.

## 

They arrived at the palazzo, Gabe still shaking with rage. He slammed down into a chair in the library and stared at nothing for an hour.

Stooped, and looking older than when Gabe had first arrived, Louis stepped into the room. "My insurance company called. They found *Pacifica* on the premises of a suspicious collector and are working to find the thief that sold it to him."

Gabe was tempted to call them back and tell them where they could find her, but decided against it. At the hospital, Livia's face had exposed the depth of grief she already carried. Gabe had his painting. He rubbed his eyes, then reached for the phone and left another message for Signore Belvedere at the museum. So far, the curator had refused to return his calls.

"You also received a letter." Louis handed him a thick envelope.

Gabe glanced at the parcel. It was from his mother. Shaking his head, he said. "I'll be in my room." He trudged up the stairs and flopped into the blue chair. When he tore open the envelope, a second one fell out. It was from the bank. His mother had already opened it. After a quick perusal, he crumpled the demand letter and threw it across the floor. They were just days away from foreclosure.

Unfolding the second letter, he cringed at the anger and fear that permeated his mother's harsh words. He didn't blame her. This was his doing. All his hope had been wrapped up in his paintings. Maybe his pride had blinded him to the realistic value of his work.

Gabe tapped the letter on the arm of the chair. Louis would give him the money in a second. But dependency had put Gabe in this situation. He felt more determined than ever to solve his own problems. It would take some doing, but he could do this.

He rubbed the back of his neck and began to pace. At least *Pacifica* had been found. If he offered the rest of his work at a steep discount to scrounge up sales, it would permanently decrease the value in the collector's eyes. He sighed in defeat. There was no other choice than to contact his agent in Santa Barbara for a fire sale. As he raised his phone to punch in James Hefner's number, it rang in his hand.

"*Buon journo*, this is Signore Belvedere, it seems we have been missing one another's calls."

Gabe knew better, but was cordial. "Yes, it seems that way. What may I do for you?"

Belvedere's voice revealed a change in tone. "I am pleased I was able to contact you. I understand you have located *Pacifica* and must remind you of our agreement. May I also make an inquiry about the trio of pieces you painted with the lyrical theme. Are they still available?"

Disbelief was slow to move aside for the relief that flooded Gabe. A tremor shook his hand as it held the phone. Still, he did not want to appear too eager. "I am fairly certain they are still available. Let me call my agent and confirm."

"Certainly. I look forward to hearing from you. *Ciao*."

Exhilaration swirled in Gabe's chest. He was free! He didn't need to contact James Hefner, besides, in California, he would be sleeping. After an appropriate amount of time, Gabe returned Belvedere's phone call and settled on a price for his other paintings. At the end of their conversation, Gabe said, "I will pick up *Pacifica* from the police and bring the crates personally." There was no way he was taking any more chances of valuable objects slipping through his fingers.

Excitement sizzled in Belvedere's voice. "Then allow me to send my vehicle tomorrow. There will be ample room. As soon as you deliver them, I will wire the money to your account."

They hung up, and Gabe checked his watch. The bank would not be open yet, but he could email them to expect payment. After that, he left his mother a message on her phone to alleviate her worry. He wondered how he could make this up to her. A sudden idea brought a hint of relief.

Louis appeared at the door, his face ashen. "Rinaldo is dead. It was on the news. He was hit and killed by a car while attempting to escape." He slumped onto the end of the bed and covered his face with his hands. Tears dripped onto his lap. He moaned, "No matter what, he tried to save me. I *know* he was my friend."

## 

The following day, Belvedere sent a limousine to carry Gabe and the paintings to Rovereto. Gabe knew he should be happier about his success, but the losses had been too great. Anger resided under the surface of all he did. Louis had declined to come out of his room for breakfast, choosing to remain alone for the rest of the morning.

Gabe remembered Louis' face, so full of joy at Sunday's service. *If it wasn't for Livia and Rinaldo…* Massaging his tense neck, he knew he had to switch off this hatred or his body would pay for it.

His mood elevated somewhat when he arrived at the museum. A contingent of reporters met the car, snapping photos and taking notes. Once inside the lobby, a magazine writer interviewed Belvedere about his new acquisitions. "Signore Belvedere, your reputation for recognizing emerging talent is unprecedented. Where do you place Gabriel Dolcini's work?"

For the first time since Gabe had met Belvedere, a broad smile broke across the arrogant man's face. "It would not be an overstatement that these four paintings may prove to be the most significant additions to the museum in this century."

Gabe's jaw dropped as the statement registered. He had made it.

The distinguished director posed and shook Gabe's hand as flashes snapped and the small crowd clapped. Without condescension, Belvedere leaned over and whispered, "Your work is truly remarkable. We will set a date for a proper reception soon."

After the press meeting ended, Belvedere offered the limo for the return ride, but Gabe wanted time to decompress in the fresh scenery. Autumn was in her glory. Crimson and yellow ochre, vermillion and olive green—brilliant splashes of colored leaves painted the hills and dotted the streets. As he walked through a small park back to the bus station, he heard his name called. Turning, he halted.

Rinaldo hailed him from a bench and strode toward him carrying a brief case. "I have something for you."

Instant anger flamed inside Gabe. "You! I want *nothing* from you. Louis is devastated. He grieves the loss of *Il Testamento*. And his *friend*." Gabe scowled, "The news said you died trying to escape. You should have."

Rinaldo flinched. "It seems I am more useful to Marcella if the public thinks I am dead."

Gabe's mind snapped to attention. "What do you have to do with her?"

"As you have experienced, the Dead Knights have spun out of control. Though I agreed with their original intent, what is left is a vigilante organization. I had already determined to do what I could to stop their violence, so I have agreed to work with her. Perhaps we can expose the criminal activities of the *Soci* as well."

"But you destroyed *Il Testamento*." Gabe felt his heart break all over again.

Dropping his eyes, Rinaldo rubbed his hand across the beginning stubble of a beard. "If Cardinal Vincenzo had acquired it before they elected a leader to the ARCC—and he would have—the damage to Christendom would have been incalculable. I disagree with the idea of a religious center, but at least for now, they have a man who is against it becoming a place for worshiping multiple gods. A man who is *not* with the *Soci*."

A sad smile engulfed Rinaldo's face. "I would like to explain this to Louis. It was a crushing deception for him to endure, but you must understand that no one can know I am alive, except you."

"Why me?"

"Louis becomes confused, not realizing what he is saying. I was able to secure a very special item from the Dead Knights' headquarters when we raided it yesterday. A copy needs to go Louis. Come, walk with me."

Curiosity opened a small window through Gabe's anger. As they proceeded slowly around the grassy *piazza,* Gabe asked one of the questions that had plagued him. "How did you get mixed up with the Dead Knights?"

Rinaldo motioned to a bench. He sat down in the sun and crossed his legs. "My parents were worldly and wealthy, until an ambitious priest convinced them that they could buy their way out of hell. They were persuaded to assign all their earthly goods to the church at their death. There was no inheritance. Nothing."

His mouth twitched. "When the representative of the church drove up in a new Mercedes to collect the check from the auction company, I snapped. I ripped the check in pieces and joined the *Col Moschin,* an Italian special forces unit. When my military service ended, I spent time in France where I heard a rumor of a secret society, one that played havoc with the religious establishment. It struck a chord.

"Orsini approached me a year ago and briefed me on this assignment. When he explained the situation between the *Soci* and the ARCC, I felt I must intervene before more people were duped. At the time, I had no idea what *Il Testamento* was, but I knew it was important. I had to destroy it before the *Soci* used its leverage to insert their guilt-based lies between believers and God."

"I thought the Dead Knights were all atheists."

A smile played at Rinaldo's mouth. "After living with Louis and witnessing the validity of his faith, I came to understand the *real* Jesus." He sighed. "I cared deeply for Louis and became extremely conflicted. I had to enlist Livia. Exploiting her fervency to protect her family and her faith, I convinced her to help me find and destroy the relic. She took great risks."

Gabe glared at the mention of her name. "Like what?"

"She knew how much Louis was counting on retrieving the relic. Yet, she agreed with me that it could not, under any circumstance, fall into the hands of the *Soci*. Even if it meant risking Louis' love—or yours. Once she found out what it was, it devastated her to tell me about the secret room."

Sarcasm laced Gabe's words, "And here I thought it was all about the money."

Narrowing his eyes, Rinaldo's voice sharpened. "It was never about the money. That was a ruse. If anything, this cost her. She lost a time-sensitive contract for her perfumes because of this pursuit. That money would have gone far to help her father, who was depending heavily on it. No, she was telling the truth—just as she said."

Guilt seeped into a thin crack in Gabe's armor. "But she betrayed her vow as a *custode*."

"On the contrary, I reminded her that keeping it from Christ's enemies fulfilled her oath to protect it. From the beginning, that belief gave her the strength to play a dangerous role with Ralph and the Dead Knights."

Rinaldo's eyes softened. "She realized that keeping her vow doomed your relationship. She had fallen in love with you, Gabriel. This was the price of her integrity." He gazed up at the colorful leaves and mused, "She is very courageous for one so young."

The revelation punched a hole in Gabe's pent up anger. He fell silent as he reflected on this new information. Livia had risked everything and lost it. All of it. He ground his teeth, ashamed of his cruelty. He hated that part of his father that was still so embedded in him. "The things I said to her…"

"I truly wish there had been another way." The muscles in Rinaldo's lips tensed to hold his emotions in check.

Gabe shook his head slowly. "It was a losing situation for her no matter what she did." Anger roiled at the circumstances cast upon them. "We didn't stand a chance."

"That remains to be seen. This was a traumatic experience. For all of us. Perhaps you can all put it behind you."

With that minute possibility, Gabe's despair relinquished some of its hold. Had she really loved him? That hope created a frightening sense of vulnerability. He changed the subject. "Do you think you will ever see Louis again?"

A sad note in Rinaldo's voice betrayed his smile. "Not this side of heaven. The local authorities and *Soci* think I am dead. I will leave it that way." Suddenly, his face tensed with alarm.

A man approached with a purposeful stride. Just before he reached them, however, a smiling woman rushed over to meet him, and they entered a busy restaurant. Rinaldo continued to scrutinize pedestrians as they moved around the busy *piazza*. Several men sat alone, but all seemed preoccupied.

Rinaldo's shoulders relaxed. With furtive movements, he reached to open his briefcase and slid out a manila envelope. Glancing around again, he subtly pushed the envelope across the bench to Gabe. "I want you and Louis to have this so you know the whole story. Just say it came from a mysterious friend."

Gabe studied Rinaldo's steady brown eyes. Smiling for the first time since they met today, Gabe said, "It's true. You are mysterious." He followed Rinaldo's lead and eased the envelope inside his jacket. "Will you continue in the relic-destroying business in your undercover role?"

"No. I understand now that God is big enough to take care of his Church without me." He stood and reached out his hand.

Gabe never imagined he would see Rinaldo in a positive light again. Yet, against all rationale, the man had proven trustworthy. They shook hands. Swallowing a lump in his throat, Gabe felt certain this was the last he would see of him. "Stay safe."

# Chapter 37

Siena, Italy

Strolling across the broad expanse of lawn in the palazzo gardens, Gabe contemplated all that had happened. Faith was new to him, yet indescribably strong. Louis had tried to help him understand, but how does one explain an invisible God? And now, how did he live out that faith?

*Forgiveness.*

He stopped, grinding his teeth at the remembrance of his father. Forgiveness felt impossible. He reached into his pocket and pulled out the small New Testament Louis had given him. For the third time today, he read the scripture Louis had underlined. "For, it is God who works in you, both to will and to do of His good pleasure."

Looking heavenward, he prayed, "You know how much my father hurt me. You also know the hurt I've caused." He swallowed, "I need the will and Your power to forgive."

A breeze caught the remaining leaves of a massive sycamore tree. One moment they were falling, the next, their path shifted, and they were carried heavenward, beyond the height of the four-story palazzo.

Gabe's jaw dropped in amazement at the revelation. His life *had* changed direction. Just like the wind. He trusted that what had started would continue its upward momentum.

##

Gabe paced on the street in front of the Ambrogi villa in Radda. Glancing up at Livia's door, his false accusations against her screamed in his mind. She had been innocent, yet she had borne his hostility with silence, adding it to her despair. The gracious image of *Il Testamento* came to mind. He cringed. This was useless. He shook his head and reached for his car door.

"Leaving so soon?" Marcus called from the far side of the porch.

Jerking his head up, Gabe swallowed. Now, he would have to go through with it. He advanced up the steps. "*Buon giorno,*" he said, reaching out his hand to the unsmiling man in the wheelchair.

"*Buon giorno,*" Marcus said without warmth. "Please come in. We need to talk about my daughter's broken heart."

"I know, and I'm sorry…"

Marcus held his hand up. "Do not apologize to me. I am not the one you have hurt."

Gabe remained silent as he followed him into the dining room. Marcus turned his wheelchair. "Now, tell me why you are here before I allow you any farther into my home."

Gabe took in a sharp breath. "I came to apologize for my behavior."

"And?"

Holding Marcus' steady eyes, Gabe said, "And it is my hope that Livia will forgive me, at least enough to become friends again."

"At least?"

Gabe changed his weight from one foot to the other and cast his attention to the wooden floor. "I love her. But I can't imagine she could ever forgive me that much."

"I can do anything I want to." Livia's clear voice held most of its former strength.

Marcus wheeled out of the room as Gabe swung around and gazed into Livia's eyes.

She held her head and shoulders with dignity, yet, her lips trembled.

How he wished he could take back the pain he had caused. When tears swelled in her eyes, he rushed to her. "I am so sorry." Holding her gently, he felt her rigid body soften. "You were so brave. Please, please forgive me."

She held him tenderly with her uninjured arm. "I do."

He took Livia's hand. "We discovered that Serena stole *Pacifica*. I am so sorry I believed you were the thief."

"It wasn't too much of a stretch, since I had been posing as the Kestral."

Her eyes drew him in. Their lips met, and the full force of their love fused their embrace. Not ever wanting to be apart again, their passion drew them closer still. Sweeter sensations than he had ever known thrilled his heart. He had found his love.

Breathless, Livia drew back. Her stern gaze pierced him. "But next time, trust me."

He buried his face in her silky hair. "There won't be a next time. No more quests."

She smiled her glorious smile, "*Sì*. Just a normal life."

## ##

Livia lay propped against a blue and gold chaise that rested near a roaring fire in the palazzo's grand library. Strands of glossy black hair escaped from her ponytail and framed her soft features. "I cannot seem to get warm." She shivered against the morning chill and tugged the sleeves of her thick white sweater over the hand that protruded from her immobilized arm.

Gabe stepped toward her, glad that Louis had softened his resistance to her, and glad for a reason to stay as close to her side as possible. He grabbed a second blue velvet blanket and tucked it around her legs, then lingered over her upturned face. Gazing into her violet-grey eyes, he whispered, "If I have anything to do with it, you'll never be cold again."

"Promise?" She pursed her crimson lips as an invitation. He was quick to respond, pressing into the softness of her mouth. He sat on the chaise and drew her into his arms, imparting his warmth. Drawing back to take in the beauty of her love, he kissed her eyes, and cheeks, and neck.

"Ah-hmm," Pascal, the new butler, came in with a tray, followed by Louis.

Gabe jerked back and ran his hand through his curls. Heat flushed over his cheeks.

Livia laughed, "Caught us." Still grinning, she wiped her lipstick off Gabe's mouth and tucked her hands back under the throw.

"*Amore*," Louis chuckled and sat down across from them.

Gabe basked in gratitude for the turn his life had taken. His grandfather pulled a chair closer, joyful eyes twinkling at the love in his home. They held pride as well.

"Espresso," Pascal announced formally, situating Livia's cup on the alabaster table where she could reach it.

After he left, Louis' smile faded. "Pascal is a good man—I had him thoroughly checked out. I am still in shock about Rinaldo though. I feel a knife is stuck between my shoulders. For forty years, I dreamed of restoring *Il Testamento* for all of Christendom to see."

Livia raised her cup and focused on her coffee.

Gabe glanced between the two of them. Hoping to alleviate the tension, he smiled, "At least, many members of your church were able to see it."

Louis' mouth tensed.

Following Gabe's example, Livia brightened and sat her coffee down. "They already have, for centuries."

Gabe tilted his head, "What do you mean?"

She picked up one of Louis' intricately decorated art books lying on the table and began to flip through the pages. "We know that *Il Testamento* was shared with the early believers and kept a secret. However, in 527 A.D., under the rule of Emperor Justinian, Jerusalem was restored to a Christian city. Look at this." She pointed to a photograph.

"That's a painting of *Il Testamento*," Gabe exclaimed.

"*Sì!* Look at all of these." One after another, the paintings and drawings carried strikingly similar features to those from the stone image. "I believe that whoever was guarding the bust felt the time had come to share it with the world."

"But then the Persians overtook Jerusalem," Louis interjected, "and we know what happened after that." He changed his tone and smiled at Livia. "Enough of the past. We need to move forward."

"Yes, we do," Gabe nodded.

Louis raised his coffee like a toast. "To new beginnings."

Gabe arose and picked up an envelope he had carried into the library earlier. He handed it to Louis. "This is for you."

Louis reached for it. "What is this?"

Gabe shrugged.

On opening the package, a note fell out. Louis read it. "Before his death, Reverendo Tito had found a brief mention of *Il Testamento* cloistered away in the church's archives, then discovered this document sealed in a tomb near Seborga. I am sad to say that after the *Soci* killed him, they stole the original of this." Louis' eyes darted to Gabe. "Where did you get this?"

"It arrived mysteriously."

Louis lifted the second page and scanned it. His hand flew to his heart. Incredulous, he said, "This is a letter from Longinus—the centurion who pierced Jesus' side—to his brother!"

Gabe stood next to him and pointed. This oval mark—it is Longinus' seal from his Roman signet ring!"

His grandfather's jaw dropped. "The same seal was on *Il Testamento*!"

"*Sì!*" Gabe's heart pounded at the discovery.

With great reverence, Louis turned the document over, to the translation typed on the reverse side. He read it aloud.

*"To Florentius: by Gaius Cassius Longinus: Greetings brother and fellow soldier:*

*My heart is fresh with terrible awe and I must share this wonder with one who understands death. Recently, I was guard to yet another crucifixion. However, the prisoner, Jesus of Nazareth, was most extraordinary. Many astonishing occurrences surrounded this man's death, too many to relate at this time. But Florentius, this was no mere man.*

*After his death, I had him carried away to a cell. My men fled the ill-omened scene, leaving me alone in contemplation. Though inadequate for such a man, I honored Jesus as we do our mightiest soldiers and captured his last image. My hands placed the wax against his skin, still warm. Later, a godly believer made a stone image from the death mask."*

Louis gasped, his hand shaking. "*Il Testamento* was a *death* mask— the *very* face of Jesus!"

Livia's hand flew to her anguished face. "And it is my fault it was destroyed!"

Gabe's jaw started to tighten in agreement, then stopped. He refused to add more condemnation to her sorrow. That feeling was all too familiar.

Once Louis composed himself, he finished reading the letter.

*"Many of his followers, of which I am now one, have already given their lives because of their faith. Seeing His face, fresh from death, has given me great boldness to preach the message: that God came to earth in the flesh; that through Him we can be assured of our eternal future; and that, although we are poor here, we shall lay hold of the riches of the kingdom of heaven.*

*Florentius, these past years you have asked for my pardon for your betrayal. Yet I did not have the strength nor will until now. Having received such love and forgiveness, I in turn must offer the same. I forgive you.*

*Though we have been careful to conceal our treasure, rumors have prompted evil men to seek and destroy it. As the keepers of this proof of our Lord, we have taken a vow of silence to protect its location.*

*As much as I desire to keep Il Viso, the face, of my God near me, I have instructed the leader of a small group of the faithful to move it from house to house, that the brethren might take courage.*

*I send this letter with great care as it may endanger precious souls. Yet your soul is equally precious. I ask you, Florentius, to believe my testimony and commit your trust to the One who truly is the Son of God.*

*Peace be with you my brother, Longinus"*

Silence filled the room for many minutes. Gabe was the first to speak. "Rinaldo and Livia were right. Every day we have demand letters bombarding us. It would not have taken long before we would have been forced to turn it over—most likely to *Soci*-connected officials. *Il Testamento* is too precious for that." He squeezed Livia's hand and wiped a tear from her cheek. "We have the living Proof, right here." He touched his heart.

Awe pervaded Louis' voice. "Longinus called the bust, *Il Viso.*"

Gabe took the letter and reread it, his eyebrows raised in astonishment.

Louis smiled. "The providence of God."

# Chapter 38

More rabble than usual plagued Jerusalem's streets. Longinus spat on the dust. The chill of the morning air struck a sharp contrast to the heated flames of brutality aimed at one lone figure—Jesus of Nazareth.

The centurion studied his captive, whose bloodied body displayed the wrath of the high priests and Pharisees, as well as Pilot and Herod. The man looked common enough, yet the powers he had demonstrated, and his extraordinary teaching, had prompted the multitudes to follow wherever he went.

Longinus scrutinized the riotous quarter. *Where were they now?* A grim sensation turned his insides—more so than usual for a crucifixion. He hated cowardice. In his mind, these puffed up religious leaders hid behind their laws, using and twisting them to bend the masses to their will by fear and threat. He ground his teeth. That was the way of every leader he had served. The Romans talked about rule of law—but it was *their* law, and they imposed it on every culture they subjugated.

Jesus tripped on the stone step ahead of him, causing the rough beam to fall sideways. "Grab it!" Longinus ordered.

His men let it scrape across the condemned man's scourged back before reaching to steady it. Longinus grimaced at the excesses in cruelty that permeated this city. What a backdrop for one such as this to come preaching the love of God. Longinus looked around at voracious faces.

319

Before this man was even dead, the love professed by thousands had vanished, trampled into obscurity by their unquenchable thirst for blood.

It became obvious Jesus was too weak to bear the heavy wood. Longinus' men grabbed one of the onlookers and thrust the cross piece onto his shoulders.

They progressed again, through the throng that lined the rocky road leading to Golgotha. Longinus peered into their eyes. The loud ones shook their threatening fists at the victim, their faces contorted with an incomprehensible rage. *What had this man done to them?* But there— Longinus spied a small group, huddled together, hiding their tear-streaked faces in fear and great dread. *At least they came.*

When the guards ascended the hill, they ripped off Jesus' tunic. Even being the seasoned soldier that he was, Longinus flinched at the punishment ravaged on the flesh of his prisoner. He wanted this over. "Get on with it!" he ordered his men, now caught up in the frenzy of the mob as they raised two other prisoners on their crosses.

With cruel insults, the soldiers threw Jesus' body against the slivered wood. His head shot forward when the razor-sharp thorns in the makeshift crown gouged his skull. Longinus waited, but heard no sound of complaint. Nor was there one when the heavy metal spikes were driven through his wrists and feet.

The soldiers grunted when they lifted the heavy cross, letting this infamous instrument of death slam into the waiting hole between the two other victims. Jesus opened his mouth as it twisted in agony, but no torturous cry arose from his throat.

Longinus was obliged to watch the slow progression of the crucifixion. Jesus' eyes fixed on a single man standing with a trio of women who mourned for him. *One* man, Longinus noted. Pilate had expected an attack from his followers. How easily they swayed from teacher to teacher in a pretense of seeking the truth. Yet, they stayed satisfied in the motion of seeking, never securing an immoveable grasp on their convictions. That task belonged to the soldier—to enter the battle and fight to the death. Longinus did not believe in the Roman cause, but his training made him stand firm in his duty, regardless of any threat.

Mocked by the poor as well as the religious rich, the assaults struck Jesus' ears, yet made no affect on his features. A spectator flung a scornful dare at the dying man. "If you are the son of God, save yourself and come down from the cross." Scoffing, the assailants turned to each other with smug sneers. "He cannot even save himself!"

Jesus' eyes held terrible sadness as he gazed steadily at the individuals standing near. Some shrank back to the safety of the crowd. Some stepped forward, spitting at the ground below his feet.

Longinus jerked his attention upward when Jesus' calm voice spoke from the cross, "Woman, behold your son." He directed his words to his weeping mother, huddled in a small group in front of him. She turned to the man standing near her. As Jesus called out again, his eyes held those of a trusted friend, "Behold, your mother." The man sheltered the woman in his arms as she sobbed and fell against him.

An instant after Jesus' outcry, opaque blackness overcame the afternoon sky. A dagger of fear pierced Longinus' chest. He gripped his spear and crouched in readiness. Fearful cries blasted the air from those who blindly tramped about Golgotha. And from within the city walls. Longinus ordered torches so he could keep watch over his prisoners and the crowd. People scurried to light lamps. Gradually the volume of the uproar decreased.

The sunless day took on the quietude of night. The boisterous mob lost their brashness. In some ways, the silence was more unnerving than the threats and harassment. It served to amplify the sudden anguished cry that erupted from Jesus. Longinus stumbled backward at the thunderous wail.

"*Eli, Eli, lama sabachthani?* My God, my God, why have you forsaken me?"

Unsettled, Longinus looked up, waiting for the certain answer from the heavens. Only dark silence met Jesus' tormented face.

After Jesus was offered a sponge to quench his thirst, the quiet was once more interrupted. He lifted humble eyes to heaven. In a moving decree, he acknowledged, "It is finished. Father, into your hands I commit my spirit."

In the ominous firelight of the torches, Longinus watched. Before Jesus' chin fell against his chest, a mighty earthquake shook the soldiers to their knees. Screams rang out as men grappled for solid earth to steady them. The rumble of stones, loosed from buildings and walls, added to the chaos of pain and fear that filled the darkness.

Eyes wide, Longinus turned back to the cross. He cried out, "Surely, this was the son of God."

As quickly as it had left, sunlight returned to the earth, revealing in full splendor the grisly day's work. Great dread filled Longinus and his men. "Let us be done with this."

The Pharisees had demanded that the bodies be taken down off the cross early, so as not to sully their Passover celebrations. The soldiers reached to break the legs of the victims, thus, allowing them to suffocate from their own weight. As one soldier approached Jesus, he reported, "He is dead already." Longinus raised his spear and plunged it into Jesus' side. Water and blood poured out, confirming their assumption.

His men hauled the bodies of the two thieves down from their crosses and dragged them toward the cemetery. Two other soldiers carried Jesus' body. While Longinus walked alongside, his mind and heart raged in conflict. *If this was the son of God, what have I done?* Great dread grew inside of him. He glanced at the face of Jesus and his spirit cried out for forgiveness.

"Follow me," he ordered. His men, anxious to be away from the dark happenings of this day, rushed after him. They made their way to the prison that had confined Jesus earlier. Longinus dismissed them and locked the door.

Little of the daylight penetrated the dismal cell. Two torches hung in their brackets on the walls at the feet and head of Jesus. The centurion knelt on the pitiless stones to study the face without distraction.

Jesus' skin glowed nearly translucent in the light. His grey, unseeing eyes, stared out with a gentle peace from a face contorted by the excruciating pain from the crucifixion. His mouth recorded sadness beyond bearing. Yet, he did bear it.

Longinus reached an unsteady finger to touch the slashes where the thorns had punctured his forehead. The skin, swollen and dark with dried blood, gave no resistance to the pressure, but flattened, allowing fresh fluids to escape. His cheek, swollen from the fists that smashed it, caused his face to appear distorted.

At once, a presence entered the cell. Longinus jumped to his feet and spun around, readying his lance. He saw no one, yet when he turned back to Jesus, the presence grew stronger. Heart racing, Longinus' throat swelled with a whispered utterance as he discerned the presence, "My God." He dropped to the floor, covering his face with trembling hands, astounded and overwhelmed.

Upon opening his eyes, he received his first instruction and stepped toward the alcove where the wax was kept. He must hurry. Joseph of Arimathea had received Pilate's permission to take the body of Jesus and would arrive soon.

Longinus placed the wax with great care to capture every detail. When he finished, he hid the death mask under his robe. Fighting a tremendous desire to stay with Jesus, Longinus had to force himself to leave. Glancing back one last time, he prayed this noble man would never be forgotten.

# EPILOGUE

While the American Religious Cultural Center was built, it did not become the powerhouse of religious and political authority the *Soci* had planned. The leaders discovered that unbelievers had little interest in stale artifacts. Neither did the broad mainstream of Christianity, which had turned its attention to the growing rumors of a precious object that brought great devotion and renewed faith to all who beheld it.

Known only as *The Proof*, it was shared by the faithful—from house to house, town to town, and continent to continent—as they waited for the return of Jesus Christ, the Alpha and the Omega, the Beginning and the End.

# A Note From The Author:

Jesus said, "Come to me, all of you who are weary and laden with burdens, and I will give you rest."

It doesn't matter if those burdens are physical, financial, relational, or mental; whether you carry the pain of betrayal, or a load of bitterness and unforgiveness, God never meant for you to carry that load.

If you want to know how to begin a healthy, loving relationship with God, please visit my website at: cheryllynncolwell.com and go to the "Knowing God" tab. You can also send me a note. I would love to hear from you.

Blessings on you and yours,
Cheryl

# About The Author:

Passionate about all things creative, Cheryl finds inspiration in the countryside of Ashland, Oregon - her family's ancestral home and the perfect venue for her interests in writing, gardening, art, and relationships. True to her tagline, "Stunning Suspense," her characters visit stunning locations while they pursue adventurous quests peppered with mystery, suspense, and romance.

**Other Books by Cheryl Colwell:**
 *The Secrets of the Montebellis*, Inspired Fiction Books 2013

**Coming Soon:**
*Adriana's Secret*, the second in the *Secrets of the Montebellis* series
is scheduled for release in April, 2014

**Connect with Cheryl:**
Website: cherylcolwell.com. (See photos that inspired this story.)
GoodReads – Cheryl Colwell
Facebook: facebook/cherylcolwellauthor
Twitter: twitter.com/CherylColwell3
Blog: inspiredfictionbooks.com
Amazon author page: http://amzn.to/1eMuMlG

# Thank You For Your Support:

Authors need reviews, so please take a moment to leave a great one on Amazon, GoodReads, or your favorite social media sites where other readers can discover her novels.

14297923R00191

Made in the USA
San Bernardino, CA
22 August 2014